BEST GAY LOVE STORIES

20 06

BEST GAY LOVE 2006 STORIES

EDITED BY NICK STREET

alyson books
new york

© 2006 by Alyson Books. Authors retain the rights to their individual pieces of work. All rights reserved.

Manufactured in the United States of America.

This trade paperback original is published by Alyson Books,
P.O. Box 1253, Old Chelsea Station, New York, New York 10113-1251.
Distribution in the United Kingdom by Turnaround Publisher Services Ltd.,
Unit 3, Olympia Trading Estate, Coburg Road, Wood Green,
London N22 6TZ England.

First edition: January 2006

Library of Congress Cataloging-in-Publication Data has been applied for.

06 07 08 09 10 **a** 10 9 8 7 6 5 4 3 2 1

ISBN 1-55583-921-5
ISBN-13 978-1-55583-921-5

Cover photography by David De Lossy/Getty Images.
Cover design by Matt Sams.

CONTENTS

INTRODUCTION
(OR, "AS IT HAPPENED")

When I was in high school, I usually spent a couple of weeks each summer with my big brother, who lived in New York City. For a gay boy growing up in a small town in Alabama, New York was like a trip back to the home world from which I'd been exiled. There were freaks in Tompkins Square and hustlers in Times Square and theater geeks on 42nd Street. And there were queer folks like me everywhere!

One brilliantly sunny day during the summer between my junior and senior years, I walked from my brother's place on the Upper West Side to the West Village. I knocked around Lincoln Center, browsed the shelves in Coliseum Books (the old location), bought cheap tickets for a matinee at TKTS, and had a couple of Long Island iced teas (nobody carded me!) at a café near NYU. When dinnertime rolled around, I found myself at one of those cartographically improbable intersections—like West Fourth and West 12th—in the leafy brownstone blocks between Seventh Avenue and Hudson.

I was supposed to meet my brother for dinner at his favorite sushi place, which was on the Upper East Side. At that point, walking was out of the question and taking the subway would have involved two or three time-consuming connections. The only way not to be insanely late was to take a cab—which was going to seriously deplete my drinking fund for the next day!

With faux urban panache I stepped to the curb and raised my arm to hail the next cab that passed by. After I hopped in and told the driver where I wanted to go, I settled into the backseat, glanced out the open window, and saw *him*. He couldn't have been more than 10 feet away. If the cab had arrived 30 seconds later or if I'd deliberated about whether to take the subway for another minute and a half, I would have *encountered* him and he would've *encountered* me and he would've stopped walking and I would've stopped deliberating and we would've stood in the golden late-afternoon light in front of some wise old queen's stoop and we would've...*what?*

As it happened, the cab pulled away just as our eyes locked. I've long since come to recognize the sensation I felt as a *connection*—the mysterious and mystical energy that passes between two people who should drop everything at once and find a good place to have a really gratifying conversation and/or some really nice sex.

But, as it happened, the cab kept moving east and I pivoted in my seat to face west so I wouldn't break the spell that had enchanted me and the beautiful man who was looking at me with the same wonderment I was feeling for him.

Why didn't I say "Stop!" to the cabby without taking my eyes off *him,* reach into my pocket and pay the fare for my one fiftieth of a mile trip with a wadded-up twenty without taking my eyes off *him* and step out of the cab and onto the sidewalk and take a deep breath without ever taking my eyes off *him*?

Because I was 17—a kid from Planet Deuteronomy—and I didn't know any better.

The cab kept moving, and in a flash the moment was gone. I felt thrilled, horny, and bereft. And, not long after, wiser for the experience.

A thread of nostalgia (sometimes bitter, sometimes sweet) weaves through many of the stories in this collection. There are the recollections of longtime lovers, tales of lost romance rekindled, period pieces—including a beautiful and unconventional evocation of New York in the '70s—and a fair amount of crashing and burning. Because, you know, shit happens.

I hope you'll enjoy the trip (and the trip-ups) as much as I have. Some folks, I know, have no use for nostalgia and believe they must keep moving forward, shark-like, to get what they want. Maybe. Me, I like to think each connection I make makes the next one deeper and better (or at least that much more fun). Since I was 17, I've had quite a few moments like the one with the guy near the intersection of West Fourth and West 12th. The bittersweet memory serves me well; these days, I seldom pass up the chance to make that kind of connection.

—Nick Street

Never Judge a Book

R. D. Cochrane

It was the eyes that got to Pace as he was hurrying from Food World to his truck. His only urge was to get home as quickly as possible because he was cold, hungry, and tired. Just two weeks into the semester, he already had more than 40 papers to grade, and he couldn't do that until he'd taken care of his other needs. But as he pulled his keys from his jeans pocket, he saw a man approaching the truck from the other side. He noted the layers of Army surplus clothes, the tangle of blond dreads, and the grime that had settled into the lines of the man's face. He had an urge to say, *I live off a graduate teaching assistantship; you probably make more from panhandling.* But as the man moved into the glare of the streetlight, Pace saw his eyes. Old. Weary. Beaten. Masking a sigh, he reached under his coat for the wallet in his back pocket even before the man had a chance to ask.

"Do you have a spare blanket in your truck?"

Pace's hand froze on his wallet, and he said, "No. Sorry." The man kept moving. Pace saw his own breath cloud the cold air between them. "Wait." The man stopped and turned around. "I can give you enough money for a motel room." He nodded toward the lights of the Motel 6.

He couldn't read the expression on the man's face. It seemed like a mixture of disbelief and pity. Even so, the eyes were unchanged; Pace thought maybe he was imagining it. He wasn't knowledgeable about the lifestyle of vagrants. Maybe motels didn't let the homeless check in even if they had cash. Or maybe it was ridiculous to offer a man a single night of warmth considering all the cold nights that would follow.

"No, thanks," the man said and kept walking.

Pace shrugged and got into his truck, reassuring himself that he'd tried. When he started the engine, the blast of air was still warm; he'd been inside Food World only a few minutes. He pulled onto the road from the parking lot. When he got to the traffic light, he doubled back. The man was standing under the lights near the doors to the grocery store. Pace pulled up and rolled down his window.

"Listen, I can't leave you out here on a night like this. Please get in the truck."

The weary eyes regarded him then, as if realizing he had nothing to lose, the man walked around the truck, threw his duffel bag in the bed, and climbed into the passenger side, putting Pace's bag of groceries on the floor.

They rode in silence for a few minutes before Pace gave the man his name. The man said simply, "Baker." Pace didn't know if that was his first or last name, but he guessed it didn't matter.

He concentrated on the road while he drove deep into the countryside outside Tuscaloosa. He could have driven to his grandfather's place in his sleep, but he was assessing the possibility that the rural roads and bridges might have ice by morning. He didn't have to be in class until after noon, but the county was ill-prepared for icy weather and would have to take care of more heavily trafficked roads first.

The house was dark when Pace pulled up; the porch light had burned out again. Something was always breaking or just submitting to age, but his parents had given him the house free and clear when his grandfather died. They'd moved to Florida by then, to be near his sister and her three children in Tampa, and they seemed relieved to get it off their hands—especially since their son was apparently never going to get out of college and find a real job with a decent salary.

"Mind that first step," Pace said as they got out of the truck. "The wood is rotting." He turned on lights as they went inside.

"Can you build a fire?" Baker nodded. "Why don't you do that while I get supper started."

Pace kept his coat on as he moved around the cold kitchen, unloading his few groceries, turning on the oven, doing a dozen familiar things as if a stranger wasn't in the next room. News stories about criminally insane drifters played through his head, but it was too late for caution now.

He'd always hated eating with anyone else in silence, so when he finally put the food on the table in the room warmed by Baker's fire, he turned on the TV. He noticed that Baker had visited the bathroom. His hands and face were clean. Pace surreptitiously studied him while they ate. The dreads had been pulled back into a single clump, and he'd taken off his jacket and thick gray sweater, leaving him in a thinner sweater over a thermal shirt and his fatigue pants. Baker wasn't as old as Pace had first thought— probably less than 10 years older than Pace. It was just the eyes that made him look old.

Baker ate slowly, carefully, as if he was straining to remember table manners, and his eyes traveled around the room. "You have a lot of books," he said.

Pace smiled and said, "I'm a graduate student in English. All I do is read."

Baker nodded. That was the extent of their dinner conversation. When Pace took his plate to the kitchen, Baker said, "I'll do those."

"Sure," Pace said. "I've got papers to grade."

He set up everything at the table: dictionary, pens, and a large mug of hot coffee. He was shaking his head over a student's lack of writing skills when Baker came out of the kitchen.

"Would you mind if I took a bath?"

"Go ahead," Pace said.

Baker dragged his duffel bag with him to the bathroom. Pace found it hard to concentrate on the papers, but he didn't think that was Baker's fault. There were so few freshman who were at ease with the written word that it was difficult to get enthusiastic. He doggedly kept at it until his Tuesday-Thursday 1 o'clocks were done. He could do the 3 o'clocks in the morning before he had to leave for his Early American seminar.

Baker had settled on the couch in a pair of sweat pants and a different sweater. The dreads were still pulled back in their clump, but Pace could see little stars of water scattered over them. Pace yawned and said, "In the morning, if the pipes aren't frozen, you're welcome to do laundry. Let me show you which room you're sleeping in."

Once again, Baker dragged the duffel bag with him. Pace turned on the light and pointed to the wall heater, told Baker to help himself to anything he wanted if he woke up first, then left him alone.

He went into the bathroom to brush his teeth and undress. The room was redolent with the smells of soap and the Comet that Baker must have used to scrub out the tub after his bath. At least Pace had picked a considerate drifter. If he killed Pace in his sleep, he'd probably do it without shedding a lot of blood.

Pace really wasn't worried about it as he climbed into bed. He frowned at *The Last of the Mohicans* as it stared accusingly at him from the bedside table. He was already behind in his reading, but he could fake his way through the seminar discussion because he'd read the book years ago, probably when he was 12 or 13, in this very house. His grandfather had always had a decent library, if a little out of date.

He slept dreamlessly and woke up early, wondering why the house felt different. Then he remembered that a guest was breathing the same air, using the space that was usually his alone. He lay in bed a while, thinking of the last two or three girlfriends he'd had. They never minded staying overnight in his little ramshackle house. In fact, they often seemed too eager to stay too often, and Pace inevitably found a way to break things off before they got near the moving-in discussion. The girlfriends were a little like his students' papers: halfhearted and incapable of stirring much enthusiasm from him. Maybe if they'd cared a little more, it would have moved something inside him. He wasn't sure if he meant his students or his girlfriends.

He got up, peed, noted that the door to Baker's room was open, and looked in. The bed was neatly made. The duffel bag was lying next to it, flatter than it had been. So Baker wasn't gone. But he wasn't in the living room, although the fire was burning again, and he wasn't in the kitchen. The washer and dryer were humming from the little laundry room that had been tacked onto the house when his grandfather was already old. There was half a pot of coffee, still warm, and three strips of bacon were draining on a paper towel next to the stove.

Pace absently scratched himself, melted some butter in a skillet, and cracked an egg. He looked up as Baker came in from outside, nodded toward the bacon, and said, "You could have served me breakfast in bed."

Even though Baker's smile didn't get anywhere near his eyes, Pace was warmed by the sight of it. "I replaced the wood on that first step," Baker said.

"Really? Thanks. How'd you know what to do?"

"I've always been good with my hands," Baker said. "You have a decent set of tools in that shed. Somebody once used them well, took care of them."

"My grandfather. This was his house until he died. Unlike you, I'm not good with my hands. Grandpa always said I was book smart and not much use otherwise."

"You're a teacher," Baker said. "That seems useful."

Pace grinned and said, "I'm not sure if my freshmen would agree with you. Nobody likes English class except people like me, who aren't good at anything else. Did you already eat?"

Baker nodded and went into the laundry room. Pace went to the television and checked the weather. Ice on overpasses and bridges, but no school closings. Apparently he was going to have to bluff his way through his seminar after all. He started grading his 3 o'clocks while he ate. After he finished the last paper and showered, he found Baker in the kitchen studying one of the burners on the stove.

"It's been broken as far back as I can remember," Pace said. "I have to get to class. You stay as long as you want. If you leave, don't worry about locking up. Nobody ever comes out here, and if they did, I've got nothing to steal."

Baker stared at him as if he was trying to find meaning in

Pace's words, and Pace blushed. He hoped he hadn't sounded as if he expected Baker to rob him.

He made it to campus without a problem, but by the time he got out of his seminar, the temperature had dropped another 10 degrees. He turned on the radio while he drove, listening to dire predictions of an ice storm and hoping Baker hadn't left. He didn't want to think of him at the mercy of the weather.

It was dark and even colder when he got to the house, but the porch light was working, and the fire was warming the living room. Lamps cast a soft glow, and as he stood looking around, Baker stepped out of the kitchen. "I hope you don't mind that I cooked supper tonight. I figured I owed you."

"Mind?" Pace asked and laughed. "I'm thrilled."

"You might should eat it first," Baker said.

"Where are you from?" Pace asked curiously. Baker didn't have a recognizable accent, but his choice of words was Southern.

"Tennessee originally. I haven't lived there in a long time."

Pace shrugged out of his coat and followed Baker into the kitchen to help him get their food. He noticed the pan of peas on the broken burner and said, "You fixed it?"

"The jets were clogged up; the spark couldn't catch. It wasn't a big deal."

This time, Pace didn't turn on the TV while they ate. He let the silence stretch a few minutes before he said, "What's your story, Baker?" When a mask of wariness settled over Baker's face, he said, "None of my business. I'm 26. I graduated from Alabama when I was 22, then got my masters at Ole Miss. I came back home to do my doctoral work, because my parents offered the house. I've never been married. I've never had a real job."

"Teaching's not a real job?"

"I'm a teaching assistant. It's basically slave labor to keep the faculty from having to endure freshmen, but it does pay my way."

"What are you going to do with that doctorate?" Baker asked.

"Teach, I guess," Pace said, laughing at his admission.

"Do you like it?"

"Strangely enough, I do," Pace said. "Even my freshmen aren't bad. I'm just trying to teach them the value of writing a decent paragraph. It's hard to make them believe good writing will help them, no matter what job launches them into conspicuous consumption."

This time when Baker smiled, his eyes were a little warmer.

They did the dishes together, Baker washing and Pace drying and putting away. They moved easily around each other in the kitchen, and Pace was prompted to say, "We're supposed to get an ice storm. It would really settle my mind if you told me you planned to stick around at least until this cold snap ends."

"I don't have anywhere to be," Baker said agreeably. "But as long as you're putting a roof over my head, is it OK if I fix a few more things around here? To pay for my room and board?"

"Knock yourself out," Pace said. "I'm getting the better end of the deal."

When Pace went to bed, Baker was studying the bookshelves. Pace tried to read, but he was more engaged by the stories he was coming up with about Baker. Desert Storm vet maybe. Or someone for whom things had just gone wrong. A lost job. An unfaithful wife. A run of bad luck. There were all kinds of reasons people fell through the cracks. Or maybe Baker had just been on his way to something better when the weather stopped him.

When Pace woke up the next morning, he realized that his freshmen would have to live without him on this Thursday. The landscape had a deadly beauty with its ice-encased trees and sheeted earth. He turned on the TV to find out that the schools were closed anyway.

Once again, Baker had been up before him and was cooking breakfast. They ate in silence. Pace brushed his teeth but didn't bother with a shower. He took *The Last of the Mohicans* to the living room and stretched out in front of the fireplace. Baker had just finished repairing the rung of an upturned rocking chair, and Pace thanked him.

"How long was it broken?" Baker asked.

"I don't know. A few months."

Baker shook his head and said, "A little wood glue and sawdust. Maybe I should stay around until I can teach *you* a few things."

"Maybe," Pace said without taking offense. "I guess broken things don't bother me."

"Leave it alone for 24 hours and it'll be good as new," Baker said.

Pace nodded and opened the book, breathing in the aroma of the old pages and wondering how many people had read it. Like his grandfather, Pace was rough on books. A worn book was a loved book, so he'd always taken his to the table, turned down page corners instead of using bookmarks, and often left books open, face down, without regard for their spines.

Baker moved the upturned rocker to a corner of the room and went to put away the repair supplies. Pace listened to him move around the kitchen. He realized that he'd read the first sentence of the first paragraph several times and still didn't know what it said. He remembered why he lived alone.

Baker came back, looked at the book, and said, "Can I read that with you?"

Pace didn't know what to say. He didn't see how two people could read a book at the same time, but he wasn't inclined to discourage anyone from reading. "All right," he finally said. They sat cross-legged next to each other in front of the fire, the corners of the book touching the knee of each one.

As he'd anticipated, they didn't read at the same speed. Baker was slower, and Pace found his eyes rescanning paragraphs before Baker would say, "OK," and he could turn the page. Pace was acutely aware of Baker's warm presence and his scent, mostly soap and cold air. He had expected the dreads to smell funky, but all he smelled was the fragrance of his own shampoo, which Baker must be using when he took his baths.

Pace's mind was sluggish. The words in the book had no meaning, and he finally said, "This isn't working. Lie down."

Baker did, and Pace began reading aloud. He occasionally looked up from the book, sure that Baker would fall asleep, but Baker's eyes stayed fixed on the ceiling and his body was completely still. It was Pace who started punctuating Cooper's story with yawns.

"My turn," Baker said, sitting up. Pace gave him the book and pulled a pillow from the couch to rest his head.

While Baker read, Pace closed his eyes. The soft voice soothed him, made him lose track of the words, and finally caused him to doze. When he opened his eyes, the fire was low but Baker hadn't moved.

"Did I fall asleep?" Pace asked.

"About an hour ago," Baker said. "I should have put more wood on the fire, but I didn't want to wake you."

When Baker moved to get up, Pace surprised himself by reaching for him and saying, "Don't. Not yet."

He hadn't done this since he was a sophomore, had almost forgotten doing it then, but as Baker opened up to him, he realized that it was what he'd been missing all along. Another man's skin, and Baker's was smooth and warm. Another man's mouth: Baker's tasted of coffee with a faint trace of toothpaste, and his lips were soft, his tongue eager. Another man's cock, hard in his hands, then next to his own, and they came together, staring into each other's eyes. Baker's eyes no longer looked tired, and Pace pulled him close, holding him, rocking him a little, wanting to give comfort and gratitude.

Neither of them spoke for a long time, then Baker slowly said, "You are good with your hands after all. I don't have anything else to give."

"You already gave me more than I've given you," Pace said. They were quiet again. "You don't have to tell me how you got here. It doesn't matter. You and I, we speak the same language. You might could tell me you'll stay?"

Baker rested his head on Pace's shoulder, and Pace felt him nod.

In Transit

Lou Dellaguzzo

"Ah, come on. Cut me a break, lady." Scott smiles at the bossy middle-aged receptionist. "Do I look like a homicidal maniac?"

A few weeks ago—in another midtown office building—a bike messenger had murdered two men in a hallway bathroom by using a switchblade. It was an attempted robbery. The double homicide made the news big-time.

Now some offices won't let bike messengers use their johns. And Scott *really* needs to use this one.

The receptionist studies Scott's face. She makes a performance of it for his benefit, squinting at his curly black hair and long, square face. A handsome, horsey face with a narrow, aquiline nose. She'd like to have his dark-blue eyes and long lashes for herself. *And so thin!* she thinks, following the line of Scott's lean muscles as they branch from his orange sweater and rolled-up pant leg.

From a side drawer, she takes the passkey. It has a little plastic man attached to it with a rubber band. "Don't forget to bring this back," she says.

"Thanks. I won't forget." Scott takes the key. His fair skin flushes from having to beg for bathroom privileges, from being scrutinized like a suspect in a police lineup. *Gotta get into something else,* Scott thinks, jogging down the hallway. *But not yet.* He likes the freedom of the streets. No boss to ass-kiss. No papers and files to bother with—or fuck up. Just racing through the streets, his life in his own hands.

Through groggy, hungover eyes, Toby stares at the lavish ceiling painting. The Rococo-style scene features a woman on a tree swing. She's getting pushed by her handsome suitor in an Arcadian setting. *Sure ain't my ceiling,* Toby thinks. He can't remember where he is this—
Monday morning!
He sits up like a released spring, looks around for a clock. With the transit strike still on, he needs more time than usual to reach work by 9, or thereabouts.
"Seven forty-three," Toby says, having spied a clock peering down at him from a heavy armoire that looks like it might crash through the floor. And then he remembers: "Shoot. I'm on 92nd Street." He needs to get to midtown.
"Ninety-sixth," says a deep voice from beneath the burgundy sheet. "*And* Park." A man wrestles out of the bedding. He has thick gray hair and a stocky build. "Good morning, kiddo," the guy says. His brown eyes squint until he puts his glasses on. The charcoal-colored frame matches his brush mustache.
Toby remembers something. The guy said he trades in *precious emeralds*—or is it *precious metals?* "Hey," Toby says, smiling affectionately at the man because he was patient with Toby last night—both times—and because Toby hasn't gotten paid yet.
"Late for work," he says when the guy strokes Toby's smooth, pale body for another go. "Really gotta hurry. The transit strike and all."
"You can make more money spending the day here," the guy says, half joking, half serious. But he likes that Toby has a job to go to.
Toby smiles, shakes his head. Long black hair falls in his sleepy brown eyes. His lean, straight nose glistens round the nostrils—morning drainage from his allergies. He strokes his long jaw. One finger rests against an upper molar. Toby doesn't feel anything. He hopes the dentist didn't bullshit him about needing two root canals—and crowns—or the molars would have to go.

"Toothache?" the guy asks, getting into his robe. He reaches for the wallet left wide open on his side table all night. Toby appreciates the gesture of trust. But he finds it scary. What if the guy picked up the wrong person?

"I'm fine," Toby says, taking the bills placed on the bed—after the guy turns away.

"Well, then. Let's get you off to work on time. What was it you said you do?"

"I'm a clerk," Toby mumbles. "Customer service—for a small manufacturing association."

"Oh, right," the guy says, unable to say anything complimentary. *How boring it must be,* he thinks, *and apparently unremunerative.*

As Toby collects his clothes, the guy calls a car service to pick up his young guest. The courtesy makes Toby feel bad. His having to forego breakfast will be a kind of penance, he thinks— for the nice guy, but much more for Scott. Toby can't wait to see his friend this evening, make amends for another lost weekend. If he can.

"So tell me, sweetie, where's the nutrition in that?" Jack asks.

At the stoplight, he glances at Sarah, who sits in the passenger seat. She munches on a cream-filled pastry and washes it down with strong black coffee she drinks from a slit in the plastic top. Some yellow pastry filling clings to her mouth.

"You promised me you were gonna eat better," Jack continues. "Now, I don't want to say anything." He pauses for effect. "But for someone who hates chicken wings and ice cream, you definitely like your junk food."

Sarah wishes she never mentioned the food she had to eat nearly every night back at the adult home: chicken wings and ice cream—or nothing. That was before she met Jack by chance during a cab ride to see her therapist. Before he eventually saved her from that cold attic room—the unlicensed hovel that passed for a *supervised residence.*

"I keep telling you, honey, it's the Thorazine," Sarah says. "Makes it hard for me to swallow sometimes."

Raising his eyebrows, Jack hits the gas pedal.

"What?" Sarah says. "You want me to choke?"

"Sorry I spoke," Jack says. "Sorry I'm concerned."

"Jack, watch the street!" Sarah yells. A bike messenger weaves in front of Jack's taxicab, inches from his fender.

"All right already. I see the little prick." Jack hits the brakes lightly and lets the guy pass. If Jack were alone, he'd give the cyclist a good scare. But not with Sarah in the car. She'd only think of her son, Scott, and worry all day that some *meshuggener* cabbie might run him over just for spite.

Why's a nice boy from Brooklyn working as a bike messenger anyway? Jack wonders—for who knows how many times. He likes Scott. *A good kid,* he thinks. *Not his fault he still lives with his father.* Jack grits his teeth until his bridgework hurts.

At another stoplight, he examines his jowly, hawkish face in the rearview mirror. His blue eyes are bloodshot from too many driving hours. The transit strike's been good to him. He's raking in the fares, generous tips too. But he's so ready for normal.

"And here we are," he says. The cab idles in front of Sarah's office building where she works as an administrative assistant. He ignores the car horns blasting from behind. "Door-to-door service for my sweetie."

Her mouth sticky with pastry filling, Sarah leans into Jack, plants a sugary kiss on his gray bristled cheek. He wants to tell her to clean her face. But Sarah bolts from the car before Jack can speak.

"What's the hurry?" he shouts after rolling down the window.

Sarah nearly didn't make it. Her shaky hand kept missing the keyhole. "Is this the summer I fall apart?" she asks the bathroom mirror. "Again?"

The yellow pastry filling still frosts her mouth. With pink dispenser soap, Sarah washes her face. She reapplies her makeup. Sometimes she thinks her cosmetics are the glue that holds her together—at least the image she presents to the world: *a sane-enough person.* With lipstick poised midair, she examines the lines around her gray-blue eyes, the deeper crevices that hug her small nose and mouth.

Below the thin hair—dyed chestnut and teased high—she can still see a beautiful, shapely girl. The girl who used to ride subways with a copy of *Ulysses* held against her chest—the book's cover displayed to impress discerning riders. Young men more so. Handsome ones especially.

"I probably should've read the damn book," she says to the empty room. Her tired smile Sarah paints dark red. The rich color lifts her spirits.

"Boy, I gotta get in shape—work out," Toby says, breathing heavily as he greets Sarah in the small office break room. He took the stairs this morning, only five flights. "Guess my quitting smoking isn't enough." Toby stares with longing at Sarah's cigarette. As he pours them both some coffee, he watches her take a deep drag. Her hand's shaky as usual, he notices. Her squat body appears more bloated, shorter even. Maybe it's the bright-yellow outfit.

"Come on," Toby jokes, leaning toward her. "Blow some in my face."

"I'm putting it out," Sarah says, tousling his black bangs, letting her small hand linger on Toby's smooth, hot forehead. "Before someone complains." They watch as the fiery tip turns black under the dripping faucet.

"Certain people should get over their no-smoking-in-the-office campaign," Toby says. "I mean, this is New York City. You want fresh air—move to Montana."

Sarah has a silent laugh. All the air exhales at once in a whisper. It leaves her winded, and then she coughs.

"Do some push-ups for me," she says between hacking.

"What?" Toby asks.

"When you work out—like you said."

"Oh, yeah. Maybe I'll take up cycling. Then Scott and me can go riding together."

At the mention of her son's name, Sarah's eyes shine. *Happy and sad,* Toby thinks. He hopes Sarah doesn't have second thoughts, has come to regret introducing him to Scott—who really deserves better. Toby wouldn't argue with that conclusion.

"We still on for this evening?" he asks. "For dinner?"

I should be asking her son first, Toby thinks. After their big argument last night, he's worried Scott will cancel their dinner date. Perhaps even their friendship.

Sarah's broad smile devours her eyes in puffs of crinkled skin. "Jack grumbled about being tired. But he'll be there." With both hands, she pats Toby's face. "We'll both be there."

Black sneakers—size 10—slap concrete. The sound of Scott's heavy tread echoes through the tenement hallway. *Six o'clock,* Toby thinks. He stares at the grumbling clock he bought from a vendor off St. Mark's Place. *Not much time.*

"Hiya," Scott says. His smile seems forced as he rolls his bike to a corner in the small kitchen. The front wheel he slips onto a giant wall hook. Like a glistening, red metal carcass, the bike hangs vertically. Its back tire barely touches the floor. As a surprise, Toby installed the bike hook a month ago—after Scott began staying regularly at the apartment. A few times Toby has asked Scott to move in. He keeps waiting for an answer.

"How was work?" Toby says from the cramped, disordered living room, which also serves as his bedroom. He sits on a permanently opened trundle bed. Its twin mattresses rest tightly together, the way Toby and Scott often fall asleep, their pale, tangled bodies lit by a whispering television.

"Work's OK," Scott shrugs. "Monster traffic with the strike—I used the sidewalks a lot. Some dick civilian gave me grief." (Scott calls pedestrians *civilians* when they behave badly.) "Guess he thought I passed him too close. The fuckin' creep tried to push me over; told me sidewalks are for walkers *only.*"

"You all right?" Toby stands up, eager to comfort Scott, who turns away. Toby stops near the blue wooden dining table left by a former tenant. Scott writes angry—sometimes incoherent—poetry at that table, while Toby works on spec ads for his portfolio. Toby hopes to break into advertising soon. He wants to start making a livable salary for himself and for Scott, if things work out between them. After all, it's a good bet a poet won't make much money, especially a poet who won't get his GED or take some college-level courses.

"I'm fine and dandy," Scott says, tight-voiced. He grabs a large water bottle from his brown backpack. "And how was work for you?" In his firm grip, the plastic bottle crackles as he pours water into his waiting mouth.

"Fine," Toby answers. He leans against the table, engrossed by the way Scott's rough beauty makes the simple gesture a marvel.

"And your part-time job?" Scott asks after he's quenched his thirst, wiped his mouth with his sleeve. "How'd that go?" His large blue eyes narrow, turn cold. "Was the guy generous—or should I say guys? Did you get tipped well for your trouble?"

Toby blushes. "Come on Scott. Quit it."

Scott runs his large hands through his curly black hair, slightly matted from a day's worth of sweat. Thick veins branch from his armpits to his fingers. A few white scars along his biceps cross blue veins like ghostly bridges.

"Hey, I'm concerned," Scott says. But even more, he's sore. He feels diminished—rendered supplemental—by strangers with the money Scott doesn't have to help his friend. He wants so much to have a purpose in life, even if it exists only in this small apartment. With Toby. *Either this thing between us is gonna mean something or not,* Scott thinks, looking at Toby, split between wanting to kiss him and wanting to shake him.

But Scott wouldn't hurt his friend. Or anyone. Not even a little. He's terrified where that can lead. *Like father like son?* His mom thinks he doesn't know—or doesn't remember. But Toby's right. Scott really is a smart a guy—he's figured things out. And yet he still loves his father. Doesn't know what to do with that love.

"It was my last time," Toby announces, surprising himself. He still needs another $500 to pay off his pricey dentist for the upper molars he's come to hate. "I mean it," he assures. Toby wonders if maybe he can ask his mother—or one of his former stepfathers back in Tallahassee to lend him the money, at least some of it. Toby can't remember to which of the three he owes more. Life in

Manhattan's too expensive on a clerk's salary, even on the Lower East Side. One emergency and you're screwed. Toby's had several in the two years since he moved up north.

The burglary. That was the worst.

"Come on, Speedo," Toby says. "Let's not fight about it anymore. It's over." Up close, Scott's warm body scents the air like fragrant burning wood. Toby's eager to get warm.

"I missed you," he says. "All day. Couldn't think about anything but you." Toby grabs his friend's slender waist. "I made a lot of dumb mistakes at work. Kept thinking you'd—" Superstitious Toby doesn't voice his fear. "So you're gonna have to forgive me," he says. "Otherwise you'll get my sorry ass fired."

"Sounds like blackmail to me," Scott says. "Moral blackmail." He runs his hand along Toby's long nape and down his back. "Even a high school dropout can see that."

"Shut up," Toby orders, swatting his friend's butt. He hates when Scott bad-mouths himself. "You're plenty smart. Take it from a community college graduate. And besides—moral blackmail's good for the soul."

"Oh, yeah?" Scott works his lips across Toby's neck. His tongue drifts down to the V of Toby's opened collar and back again. He loves the malted smell of Toby's skin. The pale softness grounded by firm muscles, pulsing blood. "How do you figure?" Scott asks.

"'Cause moral blackmail proves how good the victim is when he pays up. Does the right thing despite the circumstances—and the unworthy blackmailer, which in this case would be me."

"That's one convenient explanation." Scott draws Toby close. "Bullshit artist." They softly kiss. "Tell me," Scott says. "What's the *morally responsible* thing I should do to keep you from messing up at work? Should I stop seeing you?"

"No," Toby growls, holding Scott tight, burying his head in redolent black hair. "Fucking tease," he says. "Move in with me is what you should do. Save me from myself."

"And your horny customers," Scott can't help saying.

Toby pulls back. His pouting face makes him look 14 instead of 24. "Gimme me a break. I wasn't gonna walk around in pain—

risk an abscess—until I could afford to pay some pricey dentist. Should I have written the guy a bum check? My credit cards were all maxed. They still are."

"OK, OK. I'm sorry," Scott says. The thought of Toby in pain upsets him. But Scott's a little annoyed too. He wonders how the whole issue got turned around so that *he* winds up apologizing, feeling in the wrong. *I'm not the guy who sells his ass in some hustler bar*, Scott thinks, dragging himself close to another funk.

Taking Scott's hand, Toby backs up toward the main room. "Show me," he says, his face set in a mischievous dare.

"Show you what?"

"How sorry you are."

"I don't know. What if I'm not *that* sorry?" Scott says, resisting Toby's pull—but not enough to stop their slow progress toward the trundle bed. He tries to keep a serious demeanor. It doesn't last. Scott breaks out laughing. "I'm *mucho* ripe. Think I'll take a shower first."

"The hell you are." Standing near the bed, Toby jerks his friend hard. Scott falls across the twin mattresses.

"You know I like the way you smell," Toby says as he undresses hastily, nearly tripping. His pants won't release his feet without a struggle. "My hard-working man." Reaching down, Toby grabs his friend's baggy orange sweater. He lifts the garment over Scott's face and arms, leaving them hooded.

"Gotcha now, boy" Toby says. Climbing onto Scott, he fondles the nest of black hair growing on his friend's chest. He rubs his hands along the prone man's armpits. Bringing the moist, scented fingers to his face, Toby smells—and tastes—the salty essence of well-worked flesh.

Scott remains completely still—deeply excited. He likes firm treatment. But it's a thin line between *getting* him off and *turning* him off. Toby's learned the hard way. So he gives the impression of playing rough—while taking extra care. For every tender cuff, he gives passionate reassurances, soft kisses at the sight of each assault.

In rhythmic movements Toby removes the sweatshirt—like a coarse cotton mask—from his friend's pale face. Scott's pink with anticipation. His day-old beard ranges his square jaw like black moss. The stubble amplifies every angle of his face.

"Well, now, who've we here?" Toby says to the deep, impenetrable blue eyes. "Mm, boy. Am I gonna—" Toby stops his playful threat. Scott has this look on his face as if he's brand-new, as if he'd just fallen to earth or something. That look charges Toby more than anything, makes him feel his kisses—his *love taps*—driving air into his friend's lungs, sustaining Scott. Giving him life.

Although he's only three years older, Toby thinks he's much more adult, more responsible. The thought scares him—and excites him *because* it's scary.

"You're my—responsibility," Toby says, enthralled by the words, moving his body hard against Scott. With a blind man's touch, Toby explores his friend's lithe body. Lips follow hands as he undresses Scott, leaving the gray sweatpants and the boxer shorts bunched below Scott's knees. Feeling responsible for someone is the closest Toby can come to the idea of *ownership*. A wrong and crazy thing, he knows, between people. Yet he imagines possessing Scott anyway as he whispers, "You're my guy, Scottie. Mine."

"You can't even take care of yourself," Scott says. His lush baritone resonates beneath Toby. The words bear no criticism. Scott says them innocently, like a too-observant child.

"Kiss me here," Scott orders when he sees his friend's disappointment.

Toby complies, kisses the full lips.

"Now do—the *opposite*."

Toby obeys. He gently smacks Scott across his face—the strike precisely calibrated not to hurt. Scott kisses the hand used on him. Palm side first. He favors each fingertip with his lips. Welcoming more.

"I wanna understand," Toby says, although part of him doesn't.

Scott smiles, waiting.

"Where's Jack?" Toby asks Sarah as he and Scott tumble into their chairs. The two guys jostle each other like kids. Darting through the cool, light rain on their way to the Indian restaurant has made them frisky. So has lovemaking.

Toby likes Jack a lot. The young Southerner thinks the old cabbie is a quintessential New Yorker: tough only on the outside. And besides, Scott seems to love the guy although he won't admit it.

"Jack's hunting for a space," Sarah says, "for the cab." Then she chuckles, "What else?" Smoke from her newly lit cigarette hugs the wall. It drifts steadily in Toby's direction. He enjoys the secondhand smoke as a kind of long-deferred, postcoital cigarette. Scott notices two red-tipped stubs in Sarah's ashtray. (She's also on her second Thorazine of the day, but only Sarah knows that.)

"Sorry we're late, Mom," he apologizes. Even after a few years, having someone to call "Mom" still seems new to Scott at times. Like this evening. He has a special announcement to make—a surprise. For Toby as well.

"We got caught in the rain," Scott fibs, winking at Toby as he thumbs toward the restaurant window. The meager sprinkle hardly requires an umbrella.

"No problem," Sarah says to her son—a shy greeting. Scott dazzles Sarah every time she sees him. She's careful not to stare. But his big smile invites her to linger on his long, sharply angled face nestled in ribbons of glossy black curls. His cobalt eyes— *I made those*, she thinks, still amazed. *My son's eyes.*

But also his father's.

And then Sarah turns away quickly, looks at Toby—whom she thinks of as her second son. Toby's brown eyes are like Scott's, at least to Sarah. She sees the same affection for her in them, hopes she returns it fully. It's been years—more than a dozen—since she's had so many people who cared about her. First Jack, then Scott—after Sarah got the nerve to call him—after Scott stopped blaming her for not being in his life, for not having been a mother since he was 7.

And now she has Toby as well.

"Please confirm something for me," Toby asks her. "Tell your sonny Boy I do *not* smoke in the office. Tell him my clothes only smell like I cheat 'cause I work with two chimney stacks on legs."

And thank goodness, Toby thinks.

"It's the truth," she answers. "And when I visit Toby's department—that makes *three* chimney stacks." Sarah gives a demonstration. She takes a long drag on her cigarette, directs the smoke straight up, where it mixes with the aromatic scent of curry spices and roasting meats. If she couldn't have smoked all those years at Pilgrim Psychiatric—and then at that miserable adult home—Sarah's sure she never would've survived—medication or not.

"I smell a conspiracy." Scott says, shaking his head unconvinced. Sarah and Toby smile at each other.

"That's the tandoori chicken," Toby jokes.

"Hey, does anyone still remember me?" Jack shouts from the entrance, puffing his way toward the trio waiting for him. Outfitted with his left shoe partially cut off, he limps from a receding attack of gout on his big toe. Luckily, for Jack, it's the toe on his left foot. Otherwise, he couldn't drive.

"Where'd you park it, honey?" Sarah asks.

"New Jersey," Jack says, causing his *gang*—as he likes to think of them—to make the tunnel-shaped restaurant echo with laughter. Some other diners join in as well to Jack's delight. He loves an audience. The attention reminds him of his nightclub days tending bar—and telling bad jokes—before his gambling took over and his family gave up on him. Jack tries not to think about the distant past. He's convinced sad thoughts provoke his gout.

"Thank you, transit strike," he says, hobbling to the table. "Thank you, Jimmy Carter. You know, he promised 1980 would be better."

"Don't start with Carter again," Sarah says. "No politics during dinner."

"So what? It's not polite?" Jack asks.

"No, just boring." Sarah pecks Jack on the cheek. He turns toward her and kisses her properly on the lips. A silent message passes between them: *We're both all right. We've made it through another day.*

"She thinks the hostage crisis in Iran is boring," Jack says to Toby and Scott. "Go figure. Hey—this ain't gonna work." He presses his hefty stomach against the table's edge. "You skinny guys got all the room," he complains. "Give an old man a break, here—take up the slack." The two young men draw the table toward them. Some water from a glass spills onto the white plastic tablecloth.

After they order, Jack wags a cautionary finger at Sarah's son. *I almost ran over three of you today*, he thinks. Scott's youthfulness makes the old man fatherly—and envious—all at once. *Why are you wasting it?* he wants to say.

"What'd I do?" Scott asks.

"You bike messengers," Jack shakes his head. "Got balls the size of avocados." He can't resist talking shop.

"That's why we ride bikes instead of cabs, Jack. We need the space." Scott spreads his large hands wide.

"Please, fellas," Sarah complains. But she's not serious. The quartet has shared far racier jokes. It's just that Sarah doesn't know how to talk with Scott about his work. She hates it. So what can she ask her only son—*Did you almost get killed today?* Only once did Sarah ask him to change jobs for something—anything—safer. Scott looked hurt, then angry. "We all make our own choices," he answered. The accusation, barely perceptible, was clear.

I didn't leave by choice, Sarah wants to say. But she can't. Not without describing the beatings—always discreet—that slowly pulverized her mind. The beatings that had started before she got pregnant and only stopped when she was safely tucked away. Courtesy of the State of New York.

"Like I keep telling you, Jack," Scott says, digging into his crunchy raita salad. "Us messengers get paid by the piece. If we don't move fast, we don't make money. Now, you cabbies got a much better deal," he teases and winks at his mom. "You can sit in traffic on your lazy butts all day, and that fare meter—it just keeps on ticking."

"Wisenheimer," Jack scolds, a big grin on his face. "You're a real kibitzer, you are—but you wouldn't last a week driving a cab."

"And what about air pollution?" Scott says, ready to list the environmental hazards of the combustion engine.

Toby rolls his eyes at Sarah. "Oh, boy. Here we go again."

"Come on, you two," Sarah interrupts. "I'd rather talk about the hostages."

"OK," Scott says to his mother, his eyes bright, nervous. "You want a change of subject? I got a change of subject."

"Let's hear it," Jack says between spooning yellow mulligatawny soup into his mouth. He's a noisy eater.

Avoiding his friend's gaze, Scott says, "I'm gonna be moving in with Toby—if he still wants me too."

Jack and Sarah can see Toby's as surprised as they are. The older couple wait to see how he responds. "Yeah, it's great news—isn't it?" Toby says, like someone woke him up. He beams at Scott, wanting to grab him in front of everyone, kiss his face all over. "We've been talking about it for a long time."

Sarah's low sob—surprising her—turns into a whoop. *Don't cry,* she warns herself. *Don't start.* For so long she's hoped that Scott would move out, leave his father's home. But he kept losing jobs, wasting his money on God only knows what. *And he won't be alone,* Sarah thinks, looking at Toby, wanting to thank him, but only smiling instead. "Wonderful," she croaks, her throat tight, barely usable. But she manages another word: "When?"

Scott looks at his friend. "It's your call."

"I'm OK whenever—how about tonight?" Toby says, not kidding at all.

"Maybe this weekend's better?" Scott asks.

"That'd be great," Toby says. "In my head, I'm making closet space already—I mean for the apartment." He can't wait having Scott to come home to every night.

"So, Scottie-boy," Jack says. "You want a little help with my gas-guzzling cab? It's a station wagon, you'll recall: a *very* convenient invention. Or maybe you'd rather hitch a cart to your bike and not pollute?"

Scott grins. "You're a broken record, man."

"Thanks, Jack," Toby says for them both. "We could use the help." *And avoid paying for a van,* he thinks.

Scott and Toby walk the older couple to Jack's cab. The rain has stopped. Streets on the Lower East Side are crammed with pedestrians. From necessity, the quartet divides into pairs. Scott and Toby walk behind. They're fixated on Jack's stooped hobble and Sarah's occasional veering until Jack's hand—holding hers—draws her back. In his own way, each young man contemplates how nothing lasts, how life keeps on moving no matter what. And then they hold hands as well, gazing at each other, surprised by their own display of affection. Resistance.

"By the way, you two," Jack says, glancing backward. "About Scott's move. Not that I'd let you, of course. My insurance wouldn't allow it."

"Let us what?" Scott asks.

"Do either of you guys know how to drive?" Jack says, sounding a little testy, as if he already asked the question a couple times. His gouty toe's acting up.

"We both do," Toby answers for Scott. But tonight, holding his friend's hand, he feels they're still learning to walk.

Down the River

David R. Gillespie

I'd slept soundly that night. The sand beneath my sleeping bag had assumed the curves of my body. So when I woke, I felt good, better than I had in months. It was still dark, but the near-by splashes of some feeding fish and the chirping of birds in the trees served as nature's clock, telling me sunrise was on its way. I heard the whistle of wood ducks overhead as they were making their way up river in search of some cornfield in which to feed. It was a sound I hadn't heard in years, not since my high school days when I'd slosh through the swamps that punctuated the land-scape where I was raised.

Though only early fall, the predawn air was cold, more so than usual for the South Carolina low country, so I started to scrunch deeper into my sleeping bag. That's when I noticed the weight on my chest. I pulled my arm out of the warm sleeping bag and reached for whatever it was. Soft skin with a dusting of hair—it was Nathan's arm.

I touched the arm again, every so gently, near the wrist, then let my fingers glide down the arm's length to the elbow. I reversed course and found his hand. I traced each long, narrow finger as if to draw its outline on the exterior of my sleeping bag. They were the fingers of a pianist.

It was the first time I'd ever really touched those fingers, though I'd watched them a dozen times or more as they moved up and down the keyboard of the old upright piano in the church sanctuary. I eased onto my side to face him.

Nathan stirred. I thought it might be in response to my touch. He mumbled something as he repositioned his arm. Though the weight was gone, I could still feel the soft skin, at least in my mind.

The sky started turning from the black of night to a predawn gray. I could now make out his features. It was the first time I'd ever noticed his face completely at peace. That realization made me smile. The conflict and struggle and sadness I'd so often seen in it seemed to have vanished there on that sandbar where we'd chosen to camp the night before.

I lifted my hand and touched the skin where his upper and lower lip met. They were lips I had longed to touch for several months now, ever since Nathan had come home following his graduation from college. I felt my penis start to swell and withdrew my hand. I rolled over on my back, put my hands behind my head, and took a deep breath.

In a moment, Nathan stirred again, this time sliding over closer to me, like an animal seeking body heat. His head nestled into my side, and once more his arm draped across my chest. I guess it was instinct; I lowered my arm to cradle him.

Then, for a moment, I panicked. What if Rembert Frierson or some other member of the church came floating by? Or worse, Merle Duke, Nathan's father? The moment of panic passed quickly, however, as I realized that wouldn't happen. We were way too far downstream, far from the favored fishing holes and hunting grounds of those men. So I relaxed, closed my eyes, and relished the closeness of Nathan's body and the sound of his breathing.

In about 15 minutes he stirred again, and I turned my head to face him. His deep Gulf of Mexico–blue eyes opened slowly. I smiled, and he returned the smile, making no effort to move his arm or slide away from me. He said something that sounded like good morning.

"Good morning to you," I replied.

"You were watching me sleep, weren't you?" he asked.

I quickly removed my arm from around him and scooted a few inches away.

"No need to do that," he said. "Kinda normal to want to cuddle up with someone on a cold morning, don't you think?"

"Yeah," I said, "I guess so."

He pulled himself closer to me and said, "Besides, I kinda like waking up next to you."

"What?" I laughed.

I sat up and gathered the sleeping bag around my waist. "Come on," I said, "we'd better get moving. Got a long way to go today."

He rolled over and buried his head under his sleeping bag. "Aw, can't I sleep a little longer?" he asked.

I laughed again. "Who do you think I am? Your momma?"

"Not hardly," came a muffled reply.

"Guess I'll make breakfast by myself then," I said.

He stuck his head out, his blond hair going in every possible direction. "You're damn right you will!" He smiled.

"My, my," I said sarcastically, "such language. And in front of a preacher."

The camping trip had been Nathan's idea. He'd asked me two weeks earlier as we were cleaning the church sanctuary. It would be the "most awesome way," he'd said, to celebrate his 23rd birthday.

My erection now gone, I unzipped and threw off the sleeping bag. I stood, stretched and walked toward the river.

"Jesus, that's cold!" I shouted as I walked into the dark water. Nathan stuck his head out of his bag again and laughed loudly. "Such language for a preacher! I just might have to tell the deacons. Where did you get those god-awful boxers, by the way?"

I ignored the question. By then I was standing with the water above my knees. I watched as Nathan crawled out of his sleeping bag and stood up.

"Cold or not," he said, "I'm bathing." He slid his underwear down and stepped out of it.

I gasped involuntarily and quickly turned my head. I bent down and cupped some of the cold water and brought it to my face. Turning back to face him I said, "You're crazy," all the time thinking, *You're beautiful.*

I'd known Nathan for two years, ever since I'd come to preach at the McElveen Presbyterian Church. I'd seem him at community picnics, and on those Sundays during summer breaks and at Christmas when he'd play the piano, but I'd never seen him with his shirt off, much less as he stood there on that sandbar. He was thin, almost skinny. Everything about him seemed to be perfectly proportioned and what musculature he did have was nicely toned. His blond hair was shoulder length and its ruffled state added to his attractiveness. I watched him stretch. There were patches of hair under each arm, slightly darker than that on his head and wisps of ever so slightly darker hair around each of his nipples. Just below his navel, the hair started again, leading down to the nest of darkness above his dick. I forced myself to turn away.

I heard him splash as he entered the water. I turned to see him standing now waist deep. He started throwing water on his face, arms, chest and back. As he did, I waded past him, hoping he wouldn't notice how hard my dick was. I even squeezed it, trying to force the blood out of it.

"You're not going to bathe?" he asked.

"I'll do it later," I said. "Someone's got to get the fire going."

I hurriedly put a pair of shorts on over my wet boxers and slid the previous day's T-shirt over my head.

I turned toward the river and Nathan swung his arm hard, trying to splash me. "Two eggs fried," he yelled, "and crisp bacon!"

"What?" I replied. "No freshly squeezed orange juice, sir?"

"Not unless you have some champagne to go in it."

As I gathered sticks of driftwood for the fire, I occasionally glanced at the river, watching the naked, half-bathing, half-playing young man. It took me three kitchen matches and some wadded up brown paper bags from our lunch the day before to get the fire going. I found three good-size rocks at the river's edge and placed them in a triangle around the burning wood. I then walked to the boat, opened the ice chest, and took out the carton of eggs. With my other hand, I grabbed the Baggie full of bacon and the one containing instant coffee, took them to the fire, then returned to the boat for the cast iron skillet, metal spatula, and coffee pot. Nathan was standing by the boat, deep enough to cover his dick, but not the trail of hair above it.

"Get the birthday boy a towel," he said, with a broad smile on his face. Goose bumps covered his naked body.

I put down the skillet, grabbed a towel, and threw it to him. "There," I said. "Cover up that skinny body of yours." I picked up the skillet again and walked to the fire.

Nathan followed me, the towel wrapped around his waist. I glanced back as he was slicking his hair back with both hands, his toned but not overly developed biceps rising and falling as he did.

"Calvin?" he asked.

"Yes, my lord?" I replied jokingly.

"No, serious." He moved closer. "I just wanted to thank you for this."

We stood, inches apart, silent. I wanted to drop everything and put my arms around him, to press our mouths together, to remove the towel and taste him. Instead, I smiled and said, "You're welcome." I wondered if he could somehow sense the desire he was creating in me, if he somehow intuitively knew I wanted him.

An hour later, we were lazily floating down the river. I sat in the rear, steering with a paddle as Nathan sprawled in the bow, resting back on his elbows. He was staring straight at me.

"You know, I never did like coming on this river with my dad," he said.

"Oh, really?" I asked. "Why not?"

"I don't know. I mean I did it, like when I was a kid and all, but not when I got into high school. Had more important things on my mind, I guess."

"Like girls?" I asked, not sure if I wanted a negative or affirmative answer.

"Lord, no," he said, "I mean music. And trying to figure out a way to get out of this place for good."

"Didn't your folks encourage your music?"

"Mom did. She's always been great about that. Dad? I guess he liked me playing at the church and all. He didn't think much of me wanting to study music in college, though. You should have heard him, Calvin, the night when I told them I wanted to. Did it during supper. 'Now why the hell you wanna do that?' he said. 'Can't make no money playing the piano.' He told me I needed to get my ass in Clemson and become some sort of engineer. Said he didn't want a faggot for a son pissing his money away studying with a bunch of fairy musicians. Those were his exact words."

Nathan stopped talking and let his hand trail in the water beside the boat. After a few minutes of silence, he sat up and peeled off his shirt.

"Guess he was right," he said. "Look at me. I got my bachelor's degree and now I'm right back here in Bumfuck, South Carolina, with no sign of a job and playing stupid hymns for $50 a week."

"I know the feeling," I said.

"What do you mean?" he asked.

"Well, it was three months after I'd graduated from seminary that I got the offer to come here. I wasn't sure that I'd ever get a call to a church. I'm not that much older than you are, remember."

"Bet that made your day," said Nathan, "coming to this place. Not exactly a land of milk and honey, is it?"

I laughed. "I'm not sure your biblical reference is appropriate there," I said. "But hey, at least I met you."

I'd said it before I realized it. Nathan smiled broadly.

We drifted silently for a while then Nathan spoke hesitantly. "Calvin, may I ask you a question? A personal one?"

I told him to go ahead, thinking he'd ask about seminary or why I'd become a minister or something like that. His question threw me off a little. He asked me why I'd never married. I scrambled for an answer. All I could come up with was telling him that I supposed we were alike in that regard. When I said it, I noticed the muscles of his belly tense. He sat up quickly.

"Oh, really?" he asked.

I tried to escape the verbal trap I'd laid for myself by telling him that, like him, I had other things on my mind, like my studies. He didn't seem to buy it.

After a few more hours of drifting and talking about music— I carefully steered the conversation, just as carefully as I steered the boat—I guided us onto a sandbar.

"Ready for lunch?" I asked.

"That and a swim break," Nathan replied.

He hopped out of the boat and stripped off his cutoff jeans and his boxers. He walked out into the water and, cupping his hands, splashed me. I jumped out of the boat and ran into the water, still fully clothed. "You'll pay for that one," I said. I tackled him, my hands around his waist, my face buried in his chest, and we both fell into the water. Nathan wriggled loose as we broke the surface.

"Oh, it's on now, preacher," he said.

He lunged at me and back we went, under the water again. As we surfaced, he locked his hands behind my back. My arms went around his neck and we stood there, one naked, one dressed, both wet, saying nothing, our bodies pressed together.

Nathan slowly moved his face toward mine, those full lips of his parted slightly. As our lips met, my left hand went to the back of his head and I leaned forward, just enough to bend him a little to the left and down. Softly but passionately, our tongues moved in and out of each other's mouth. My right hand moved down his chest and around his back. I lowered it further, beneath the water and felt the rise of his ass. Soft, smooth, firm. My dick began to swell, and I felt his hardness as well, pressing against me.

He broke off the kiss and said, "Come on. Let's get out of this water and get you out of these wet clothes."

He took my hand, and we walked onto the sandbar. I watched his hard dick bounce as it led the way. We stopped and he turned to face me again. He started by unbuttoning my cargo shorts. While he worked those down, I pulled my soaked shirt over my head. He was on his knees now, his thumbs in the waistband of my underwear. Slowly, he pulled them down and, as he did, my dick snapped to attention. He took it in his hand.

My head was reeling, a thousand images flashing through my mind along with the light-headedness his touch caused. I saw myself on the podium of the church, surrounded by men laying their hands on my head as the ordination prayer was being said. I saw myself in seminary, listening to the ethics professor talk about "the sin not named among Christians." I saw myself in college, stretched out on my bed in the dark, listening to my roommate masturbate while wishing I could be doing it for him. I saw myself as an 11th grader, my parents gone for the weekend, my body pressed down on top of Josh, my best friend, as we humped each other to climax.

Those images disappeared as I felt Nathan's tongue slide along the underside of my dick. I shuddered. I looked down to see his head moving back and forth, to see my dick sliding in and out of his mouth. I groaned. It felt so good, so right—so normal.

I stroked Nathan's hair while his hands went behind me and caressed my ass. He pressed his middle finger against my hole. It slid in. I could feel my balls rise and my body tense. Nathan, too, must have sensed it. He stopped before I came.

"Not yet," he said as he stood up. "Not yet."

I kissed him again, more intensely than before, and with more longing.

"Don't move," he said, breaking off our kiss.

"OK."

He walked to the boat and pulled out his sleeping bag. He untied it and rolled it out on the sandbar. He then unzipped it and opened it up. He walked back to the boat and took something out of his backpack.

Clutching something in his right hand, he took my hand with his left and led me to the sleeping bag. He lay back on the soft interior of the bag and opened his hand. "You might need these in a little bit," he said, smiling. The condom and container of lube rolled out of his hand and onto the bag.

I knelt between his spread legs and simply looked at him for a minute. He began stroking his dick. I moved his hand away and replaced it with my own, my other hand rubbing his stomach and chest. He moaned, "You don't know how long I've wanted this."

"Me too," I said softly. "Me too."

I alternated between stroking his dick and then my own, all the while just drinking in the sight of the beautiful body stretched out before me. I lowered my head and slowly ran my tongue around the head of his dick, then, laying it against his stomach, ran my lips up and down the bottom ridge of it. I could taste the drops of precome that appeared at its tip. He half sat up, reached down, and rubbed the drops with his finger, then moved it toward my mouth. I opened my mouth and took his finger in. He pulled his finger out and put his hand behind my head. He drew me down, our lips together, our tongues again tasting each other, our hips grinding together. I lifted my head and looked down his body, so inviting. His nipples were small but hard, poking above the few hairs that surrounded them. I let my hand glide across them, then licked them.

"This is awesome," he breathed. "I want you to fuck me."

I sat back up on my knees and looked at him, maybe a little ashamed or nervous, maybe just in shock. Regardless of what it was, he noticed and asked me if everything was all right. I told him that I'd never done anything like that before.

"You've never been with a guy?" he asked, smiling.

I told him I had, that I'd done plenty of humping and grinding and sucking and being sucked, but not what he wanted, not what I felt an overpowering desire to do, to be inside him.

He sat up between my legs, put his hands around my neck and kissed me. "It's easy," he whispered.

He then stood me up straight on my knees, his face now just at my crotch. He took my dick in his hand and slowly slid his mouth over it. Blood was coursing through me—each nerve, it seemed, jumping, reacting, every part of me alive. He moved his mouth back and forth, and I watched as my dick appeared, then disappeared. He took it in all the way, and I felt his lips brush my pubic hair. I instinctively put my hands behind his head as soft moans escaped my throat.

In a few minutes he stopped, still holding my dick in his right hand. He reached down with the other hand and picked up the condom packet, tore it open with his teeth, and took out the condom. He looked up and smiled. I watched as he placed the condom on the tip of my dick. After he'd completely unrolled it, he released my dick and picked up the little black bottle of lube.

"OK," he said, "now some of this wonderful stuff."

He squirted some in his hand and rubbed it all over my sheathed cock. To be honest, I thought I was going to come right then and there.

"There," he said. He lay back, squirted some more lube into his hand. I watched, thinking I was in some vivid, secret dream, as he reached around his ass and smeared the lube up and down his crack and around his hole.

"I'm ready," he smiled. "Are you?"

I simply nodded. He raised his legs toward his chest and guided my dick toward his hole. He told me to push slowly.

The head of my cock popped inside him, and he groaned. For a moment I thought I was hurting him, but the smile on his face quickly removed any thought of that.

"Go deeper," he whispered. "Deeper. All the way in."

I leaned forward and closed my eyes as my dick slid farther into his ass, like a sword all the way to its hilt in a scabbard.

"God, that feels good," he groaned.

He was right. I'd never felt anything like it—the warmth, the desire. It was more than physical, though, and I know this sounds silly, but it was the whole experience of being inside him, being joined to him, that excited me most. I lowered myself, hands on either side of his head, and kissed him deeply while I moved in and out of his ass, sometimes slowly and gently, sometimes fast and hard. All of it felt totally natural, as if I'd been doing it all my life.

After a few minutes of this fucking and kissing, he whispered in my ear, "Get up on your knees. I want to look at you and jerk off while you fuck me."

I told him I didn't know how much longer I could keep from coming, but I did what he asked. I rested his legs against my chest and continued to plunge in and withdraw, feeling the cheeks of his ass against my hips with each drive. He grabbed his dick and started masturbating, all the time staring at my face. Watching him jerk off while I fucked him excited me even more, and I quickened my pace to match the movement of his hand. In, out, up, down; perfect synchronization, even in our breathing, a symphony.

"Oh, my." He eyes closed and he grunted. His body started to spasm. I touched his sack; it was taut. When he shot, the load landed on his stomach, chest, and the sleeping bag. I could feel the muscles of his hole tighten and couldn't stop myself. I came, squirting more with each thrust, filling the condom's reservoir. After one last thrust and twitch of my dick, I collapsed on top of him, kissing his lips, his neck, and his closed eyes.

We lay there, naked and light-headed, my dick shrinking inside him, not speaking. We didn't need to talk.

Three months later, I helped Nathan pack most of his worldly possessions into his Accord. He was driving to Atlanta to become the organist at a midsize Episcopal church. For that, I was glad. He'd be doing what he loved, and he'd be doing it in a church and city that would welcome him. He hugged me goodbye, then, looking at his mother standing on the porch of their house, waved. He looked at me again and asked, "You'll come see me, won't you?"

"Nothing could stop me," I replied. I hated to lie, but I knew I would not be going to see him, not until I had acquired the courage to live my life as authentically as Nathan was then leading his. After our trip down the river, he'd told his parents he was gay. His mother had cried but not for herself. She knew; she had always known. She cried for the pain, the secrecy in which he'd had to live his life. She cried because finally he could be free. His father had stopped talking to him and would barely acknowledge his presence with a grunt.

Nathan sat in the driver's seat, winked at me, and said he'd see me soon.

As he pulled out onto the road that would lead to the highway that would take him to Columbia and I-20 West, I hung my head and thanked God for him.

"I Do…I Don't"

Richard S. Ferri

"The problem," she said to me in her raspy voice, "is that the Internet has killed my phone sex business." She slammed an unfiltered Camel cigarette into her mouth. "How the hell am I suppose to make a friggin' living? Turn tricks to keep me in smokes and vodka?"

Apparently this was very funny, because she began to laugh a sandpaper laugh. I couldn't really tell if she was just laughing or drowning in her own saliva. As she sucked in the flame from her Zippo lighter I smelled such a cloud of butane, I wondered if I should alert Homeland Security. I watched with awe and horror as she sucked down half a Camel in one breath. I fully expected smoke to ooze out her nipples.

But instead I was treated to plumes of smoke rapidly escaping her nose as she skillfully flicked loose tobacco off her tongue with her fingers.

"Who the hell is going to pay me for some hot phone sex when any slob will get you off online for free? How the hell do you type and play with yourself at the same time?" She frantically shook her hands in disgust.

"Yeah, yeah, I know. So I do my calls while I do my ironing. But they don't know that. So I spritz a little water on a blouse and talk dirty, but damn, I can make 'em come. So as they moan, I fold. Now, that is talent." She stood stock-still and pointed a finger at my face. "It does not involve typing, for crying out loud."

I continued on in my silence in hope of a stroke or death. I wasn't fussy at this point.

"Excuse me, but who the hell are you?" I managed to say. I could see the Pilgrim Monument looming ahead and was happy to see other early morning beach walkers appear. But wisely, they were keeping a safe distance.

She sucked in another pull off of her Camel and hacked up a lung. "Me, honey?" she wheezed. "Everyone knows me in Provincetown! I'm Madge. I'm the crazy artist that paints little fucking Cape Cod scenes onto seashells. Can't stand the crap myself, but people buy them like crazy. So I guess I'm the actual 'she who sells seashells by the seashore' girl."

Madge fished another Camel out of her pocket and lit it with her other cigarette.

"But in the winter when the tourists stay home I do phone sex for some extra bucks."

It was a bright sunny day in Provincetown in late May of 2004. I had just moved to town from New York and had married Jeff. I was walking along the beach on the bay side of town and thinking how crazy my life had become. However, I was cutting myself some slack since meeting Madge. There are just some things you never really get to think about until somebody brings them to your attention, such as phone sex. But now I could not get it out of my mind. I started to look for a sharp object to impale myself with.

Madge had to be close to 60 and nearly 300 pounds. Her blond hair had been dyed so many times the ends broke off like fragile straw at the slightest provocation. I wasn't sure where her boobs ended and her knees began. Everything just sort of morphed together.

OK, I said to myself. *This is what living in Provincetown is like.* Jeff and I discussed this several times. Provincetown was full of colorful characters. It was part of its charm and partly why most people just come for a visit and leave.

Amazingly, Madge took another cigarette out and jammed it into her mouth. I must have raised an eyebrow, because Madge said to me, "I know I smoke too much. What the fuck can I say?

I'm a cigarette addict." Madge looked lovingly at her cigarette. "I just suck these babies down all day."

She paused in front of St. Mary's Church and stuck both of her arms out like she was being held up. "My name is Madge, and I am a tobacco fiend." With that she stopped and abruptly turned to me and said, "And what the hell is your name?"

Not knowing what to say, I foolishly replied, "I'm Steven."

"What a lovely, lovely gay name! Not Steve or Stevie, but the proper homosexual name—*Steven*."

Madge took another pull and finished off her latest cigarette. "I have come to the astonishing conclusion that we should be great friends. I like gay men with such solid homosexual names."

"Swell," I replied. I really could not think of a reason not to start up a friendship. So far the only person I knew in town was Jeff, and that certainly wasn't going to last very long.

"So what brings you to our fair town? Romance? Danger? A little summer fling?"

"You're very direct," I said.

Madge batted her eyes like a proper southern drag queen. "Thank you for noticing, kind sir."

I stood still and decided to tell Madge the truth. It seems like the truth and I had become very distant cousins of late, and I needed to make a confession. Since we were in front of a church I could see no reason not to bear my soul. I looked at St Mary's and felt warmth I had not experienced in a long time. I took in a big gulp of air.

I leaned into Madge and widened my eyes. "Can you keep a secret?"

Madge leaned right back into me with her eyes twice a big as mine. "Only if what you are about to tell me is depraved and somewhat sick. Stupid secrets, like 'I slept with someone from the board of selectmen,' bore me. I simply embellish them and pass them along." Madge paused and I could see her eyes dance a little in her head. I thought maybe her nicotine level had dramatically fallen. It had been nearly three minutes since her last cigarette. "Look, Steven, this is Provincetown. Gossip becomes hard cold fact here before the people that are being talked about even hear the rumor. Reality does not rear its ugly head here often"—she paused—"and that is just fine with us."

I decided to go for broke. I needed a friend. I needed to get this off my chest. I needed a drink.

"By any chance do you have anything to drink on you?" I asked like it was as common as asking for a tissue.

Madge was taken aback. "Where are my manners? Of course, I have my flask of brandy. I should have offered you a swallow ages ago!" She reached into her beach bag and pulled out the largest silver flask I had ever seen in my life. It must have weighed at least four pounds. I could hear the liquor slosh around inside it. I took it from Madge's outstretched hand and unscrewed the cap. The crisp morning sea air was suddenly filled with the mist of late night cocktails. The clock at Town Hall chimed 8 in the morning.

I tipped the flask back into my mouth and drank. The brandy went down just fine, and I was able to screw up my courage.

I looked into Madge's eyes and announced, "I moved to town to marry my boyfriend." I paused for dramatic effect. "Then divorce him."

Madge grabbed the flask from my hand and poured the remainder of the brandy down her throat. Then she thumped out another cigarette and plucked it into her mouth. As she flipped open the Zippo the fumes from the brandy became overwhelming. I fully expected spontaneous combustion to occur.

"You already have the divorce planned?" she asked, somewhat astonished. Blowing smoke out of both nostrils, she said, "That is just so fucking progressive!"

I felt a brandy-induced grin come over me. "Actually, we only got married to get divorced."

Madge spun around and looked at me. Her hair followed about a minute later. "Let's see if I got this right. You move to town to marry your boyfriend so you can divorce him."

God, I was wishing for more brandy. "That is almost right," I stammered. "We were not exactly boyfriends. Hmm, just friends."

"Oh, hell, this does get interesting," said Madge. "Time to bring out the reinforcements." With that she dove back into her beach bag and produced a full bottle of Skyy. "I sure hope you don't mind sharing," she said as she cracked the cap open. "You go first," Madge said as she handed me the bottle.

Without hesitation I tipped it back into my mouth and drank. What could be better then vodka on the beach first thing in the morning?

I handed her back the hooch and looked at the clear blue Provincetown sky. I also noted that I was officially getting drunk with a total stranger. However, I also noted I had sex with men for the price of a gin and tonic, so I did not think I had strayed to far off the path of sanity here.

"We got married to get divorced," I finally confessed with the help of the booze and the bravery of talking to a stranger.

Madge took another pull off of the vodka as we headed up the beach toward town.

"Who the hell do you think you are? Norman Mailer?" she grunted. "That man has been married so many times he can't even recall his ex-wives' names."

"No, you are not getting it," I said. I looked up into the sky, which seemed a little fuzzy to me—but then again, brandy and vodka have a tendency to make that happen. "If there is the first gay marriage, then there has to be the first gay divorce."

Madge just looked at me and stuck yet another butt in her mouth.

"I'm a writer," I continued lamely. "I wanted to write the first book on gay divorce. Kind of my story, but also a how-to book. So the best way to research it was to get married, then get divorced."

I could see the lightbulb flick on over Madge's head. "Aren't you the clever gay scribe? You could make a small killing with that kind of book!"

We stopped and sat a seawall that looked over to Long Point. Seagulls were diving for fish. *I couldn't imagine eating fish first thing in the morning,* I mused as I drank more vodka.

"However, there is one small problem that I wasn't expecting."

Madge just raised an eyebrow to make me continue.

"Something bad has happened," I lowered my voice so no one could hear me. "I fell in love with Jeff, and now I don't want to divorce him."

Madge put her hand to her chest and blew out a pall of smoke. "God, how awful!"

I hung my head. "I know. I just don't know what to do. I, mean, what if Jeff doesn't share my feelings? We haven't even had sex."

"Of course you don't have sex," Madge wheezed. "You're married!"

"The only thing we do is talk about getting divorced," I said with misery in my voice.

Madge's eyes brightened. "You know what you need?"

I looked at her and saw a sparkle in her eyes, like she had found the answer to my situation.

Madge made another dive into her beach bag and frantically pulled out a cell phone.

"You need to have phone sex! Right here and right now." She jumped off the seawall. "It will clear your head faster then a line of crystal meth."

I was sure I was drunk. How could phone sex be the solution to my woes? Talking dirty to a stranger and pretending to get off did not seem like a viable alternative to divorcing the man I loved.

Then again, I was shit-faced at 9 o'clock in the morning with a woman I had known for a little over an hour. My judgment was more then just a little off at that point.

"How is phone sex going to make me feel better?" the drunken part of my mind wanted to know. There was also a space in the tiny sober space of my mind that was also demanding an explanation.

"Phone sex," Madge explained to me in a serious tone of voice, "is noting more then performance art. You get to vent your frustrations and make strangers do things by your command. It's a total power trip. You'll feel like a new man!"

We had somehow strolled down the beach toward the middle of town near the Lobster Pot restaurant. The staff was getting the place ready for the lunch rush.

Madge pulled a big orange ribbon from her beach bag and tied it in her hair. "Rule one: Always gotta keep your hair off your face when you are doing phone sex."

Who knew that phone sex had rules? I was learning a lot in such a short period of time.

"Rule two: Always make them come within the first 15 minutes," Madge intoned in the voice of unmistakable experience. "Unless they are paying extra."

"Makes sense," I mused.

"Rule three: Never play with yourself. This is business. It's all about getting the guy off on the other end of the phone. Plus, have you ever tried to get a load of come off of a keypad? I once nearly caused a minor power grid blackout in Bayonne, New Jersey, because I forgot this rule."

Madge punched a few buttons on her cell, and her face beamed.

"Georgie, it's Madge. I know I said I would call you later today, but I have a nice young man with me here on the beach, and I thought it would be hot to watch him get you off."

She covered the mouthpiece and whispered, "He likes to go both ways and be dominated."

Oh, hell, now what was I supposed to do?

Madge held open her bag and I dove into it. A bottle of Dewar's smiled back at me. I found it mildly disturbing for a woman to walk the Provincetown beach with nearly a full bar in her beach bag, along with a couple cartons of cigarettes.

I cracked open the scotch as Madge said into the phone. "His name is Steven and he's hot as hell. He's about 6 feet with light red hair and a fucking hot body. Very lean and tight. He's only wearing running shots and his chest is a little sweaty." Of course, I was in jeans and a T-shirt, but who was I to screw around with fantasy?

Madge listened a little and said: "Remember, this is that freebie I owe you from that nasty toaster oven and dildo incident." She covered the mouthpiece of the cell phone again and mouthed, "Don't ask."

I shuddered at the possibilities. Then Madge shoved the cell phone into my hands. I nearly dropped the scotch, which ticked me off.

"Damn it! That was close," I shouted as I set the bottle upright on some rocks.

"What was close?" a meek little voice asked at the other end of the phone.

"None of your damn business," I snapped back. Being drunk was very helpful at this point in my virginal phone sex career.

"Now listen to me, Georgie. My job is to get your sorry ass off. Your job is to do it. And you only have three minutes. Got it?" I had slipped into another personality. I actually liked being a drunken pig screaming sex talk at a total stranger. Madge was right. It was incredibly freeing.

"I don't have all day to play with you. I want you hard and stroking in 60 seconds. I want you to prove to me that you want me to get you off!"

Madge gave me the thumbs-up sign and did a little jig on the beach.

"Now take your dick out and make it hard, because I want it hard. This is all about me. I want you to come on command!"

"Yes, sir!"

Madge crammed another cigarette into her mouth and rasped, "Very impressive..."

"OK, buddy, you have two minutes left. I want you to blow a load just because I want you to. Got it?"

I could hear him panting. I took a slug of scotch. We were now down near the outside deck of the Lobster Pot, and a small group of onlookers had gathered and watched in amazement. I figured the police would be arriving in about five minutes.

With nothing left to lose I screamed into the phone, "Damn it, Georgie! Let it rip!" And he did. I could hear his breathing crescendo and hear him let go.

"Good boy! Just like I told you." I raised my arms up, signaling victory, and thunderous applause came from the people on the deck. I turned and faced my adoring fans and took a deep bow. When I turned around there was the biggest cop I had ever encountered. He had to be at least 300 pounds of solid muscle with a dyed blond crew cut. He had one hand on his nightstick, and I almost lost my balance looking at him.

"Sir," he said in a deep, steady voice. "I think we may have a problem."

"No problem here, officer." I could practically see the booze fumes rush out of my mouth.

"Sir, I believe you are intoxicated," the cop said firmly as I watched his biceps dance under his shirt. How the hell did he get dressed in the morning without ripping his clothes to shreds?

"No, officer. I passed intoxicated about an hour ago." I tried to rustle up some dignity. I failed miserably. "I believe I am now drunk." I snapped the cell phone shut and handed it back to Madge.

"Thank you, kind lady, for loaning me your phone."

"Hey, no problem. You need anything before Officer Hunky hauls you off to jail to sober up?" Madge launched into her bag one more time searching for something. I prayed none of her booze bottles would shatter. She pulled out a piece of paper and scribbled her phone number on it.

"Thank you, but no," I said. "I'm sure I will be dealt with justly." I waved my hands in front of my face to disperse the fumes from the alcohol.

"I think you better come with me, sir," said the cop as he led me away. I looked back at Madge and shouted, "How did I do?"

Madge shouted back: "You're a fucking pro!"

The officer leaned his massive body into me and said, "Do I need to know what you two are referring to?"

I shook my head no. "It would only confirm your impure thoughts about me."

"Well, we couldn't have that now, could we?"

"Heavens, no."

At the police station I was told I was in protective custody and not under arrest. I got to make one phone call. *Just like in the movies*, I thought. Well, who the hell was I going to call? Then I realize the only other person I really knew in town, outside of Madge, was my soon-to-be divorced husband. So I dialed Jeff's cell phone and got his voice mail.

"Jeff, this is Steven," I said with great effort. "I am drunk and in jail and I need you to bail me out." Simple and direct—I liked that. After me call I was escorted to a jail cell and told to take off my shoes so I wouldn't hang myself with my shoelaces. Considering I could barely untie my sneakers, the notion of my constructing a noose from a pair of shoelaces seemed pretty absurd.

After I was placed in my cell I feel fast asleep. I dreamed

about banging a tin cup against the bars and demanding to see my lawyer. As I slept I make a mental note to stop watching so many old prison movies.

A few hours later I was awakened by the sound of rattling outside my cell. I peeled my eyes open and saw Jeff staring down at me in horror with yet another cop by his side.

Jeff looked at me and said, "Do you have any idea how long it took me to find you? You could have told me you were in jail in Provincetown!"

I pushed myself up and replied, "You thought maybe I was in a lockup in Budapest?"

With great exasperation, Jeff said to the cop, "Writers!"

The cop went to open my jail cell. "Not yet!" Jeff hissed. The startled cop backed away. "I want to have a few words with him to make sure I want to bail him out."

The cop eyeballed the situation and shrugged. "OK by me. It's time for me to medicate myself anyway," he said as he ambled back out to his office.

Jeff leaned into the bars and lowered his voice. "Can you please explain to me what the hell you were doing drunk on the beach at 9 in the morning?"

"Oh, that part is easy. I met a woman named Madge who carried a fully stocked bar in her beach bag, and we got drunk and she made me have phone sex with some guy named Georgie."

Jeff just stared at me. "Well, as long as there's a logical explanation, then I guess it's OK."

I got up. "Good. Let's go home."

Jeff looked at me as if I was insane. "Steven, are you nuts?"

"Kind of." I sat back down.

Jeff squatted on his haunches and looked at me. His anger had dimmed. "Steven, what's wrong?"

Thanking the good Lord almighty that I still had enough alcohol in me for my tongue say things it would never say if I were sober, I muttered, "I'm not so sure we should get a divorce."

Jeff's eyes widened. "I thought this was what you wanted! I was just some friend helping a friend. I mean, for God's sake, we've never even kissed!"

"This is not about kissing! Or sex!" I said from the safety of my jailhouse bed. "I wasn't expecting anything to happen, but then we spent real time together. I got to like it, and I guess I fell in love in with you."

Jeff ran his hand through his hair. I loved the way he looked. He just stood there and didn't say a word. I waited patiently for about 15 seconds.

"Jeff, did you hear me? I fucking love you!"

Jeff put his hands on the bars of my cell and hung his head. Softly he said, "I think I love you too."

I jumped off my cot and screamed, "Don't fuck with my head because I'm drunk!"

Jeff shouted back. "I'm not fucking with you! I started to have feelings for you the day we met. But I never let them come to the surface. You were this big-time writer and I just sold real estate. You're wickedly handsome and smart." Jeff paused. "I get by," he said. "Why the hell do you think I agreed to this harebrained scheme of yours? It was just to be near you."

I could barely breathe. "I think you're the most beautiful man in the world."

Jeff sat on his butt and crossed his legs. He looked me right in the eyes and said, "But getting married *and* divorced was your idea. Great book, you said. It'll make you a nice bundle of money."

"The best-laid plans…"

"So now what do we do now?"

"Kiss me," I whispered.

I lowered myself to the floor of my cell and put my lips between the bars. Jeff leaned forward and gently kissed me. My body went weak, and I felt a happiness I had never known before.

Jeff looked at me and said, "Maybe someone else can be the first gay divorce and we could just be something else."

"Like what?"

"How about married?"

Kid Omnivore

Tom Mendicino

The waitstaff dashes in and out of the kitchen, nimbly side-stepping collisions and narrowly avoiding disaster as they haul mounds of whipped potatoes and ponds of thick brown gravy to the buffet tables. Harry tightens his abdominal muscles, bracing against another attack of stomach rumbles, and grinds a wad of chewing gum between his teeth. His mother seems distracted, miles away, crossing and uncrossing her legs and constantly touching her hair. She smiles, looking a little sad, when he asks if everything is all right. Of course, sweetie, she says, reaching across the table to pat the top of his hand. Harry opens the Penn Valley Tech baccalaureate program, nothing fancy, just a few pages designed by the candidates for Microsoft Office specialist certification. He flips to page 3, not trusting he'll find his name among those about to receive their associate degree in maintenance and construction electricity technology, despite having checked for the third time just two minutes ago.

There he is. Harry Aldorotti, first in his class, at least when they're listed alphabetically.

He scans the page for a name far more compelling to him than his own.

Jonathan Preston, graduating with highest honors.

He's worried. It's not like Jonathan to be late. After all, he's the dude who's going to win both the perfect attendance award and the citation for highest grade point average tonight. Harry's belly is growling now. He tries not to think about food, but if they

47

don't start calling the tables to the buffet line, dinner will be soggy and cold. What does it matter? He can't eat anything anyway. He feels weak in the knees and dizzy in the head. He's 60 pounds lighter than the day he started at Penn Valley. Even now, at 195, he's not exactly lean and mean. But he's getting there. He's got some definition in his arms and the beginning of a chest. Yesterday, in the shower after working out, Jonathan complimented him on his progress and called him "stud. " He wants to fix Harry up with his girlfriend's sister. No pressure, he promises—a foursome, just bowling and beer. *Don't worry, man, she's not a dog.*

Not that it matters. She could be as wide as a house, big as a barn, bucktoothed and bug-eyed with a head of frizzy Orphan Annie hair. Harry doesn't care if she's a pit bull that walks on four legs and wags her tail. She doesn't even have to show up. All that matters is Jonathan will be there. For the past two years, Harry and Jonathan have sat side by side or front and back, Monday through Friday, squeezed into those tiny desks, their long legs and big feet spilling into the aisle. Jonathan studied electricity and Harry studied Jonathan. Everything about Jonathan fascinated Harry: the ragged scar on his knee, the freckles on his forearms. Harry could spend 10 minutes describing the shape of Jonathan's ear. One particularly boring afternoon he tried counting the hairs on Jonathan's unshaven neck.

Jonathan couldn't wait to graduate. Harry never wanted to leave. They both applied to the International Brotherhood of Electrical Workers apprentice program, expecting the daily routines of Penn Valley to continue uninterrupted: Harry stopping for coffees, milk, and extra sugar for Jonathan; having their first smoke of the day and bitching about not getting enough sleep; eating lunch together (Harry having learned to make do with a turkey sandwich without the bread and even getting used to the taste of nonfat yogurt); hitting the gym in the evening, spotting each other, running laps and playing one-on-one on the basketball court. The day ends at the Road Toad where Jonathan's girlfriend, Allison, waits tables and the bartender doesn't ask to see ID, and then they wake up the next morning and do it all over again. Jonathan won an apprenticeship; Harry's only offer was from a general contractor building a subdivision of mock Tudors in central Bucks County.

At least they have tonight. They'd made plans, reserving a table for themselves and their parents—no Allison—at the graduation ceremony. Then they're heading to Atlantic City, just the two of them, to celebrate with a night of drinking and blackjack. They have a reservation at the Trump Taj Mahal. Jonathan's dad is paying for the trip and spotting them $500 in seed money because his kid has worked hard and he's proud of his son. Jonathan and his dad are more like buddies than father and son. They're always doing things together, then making plans to do even more things. Sometimes Jonathan calls his dad because he just thought of something he knows will make him laugh or because he has a question and is sure his dad will know the answer. He knows it's stupid, but Harry can't help being jealous of Jonathan's dad.

The servers are calling the tables to the buffet trays. Harry's starting to get worried. The smell of pan drippings sears his nostrils.

"Harry, have you eaten anything today?" his mother asks.

Christ, he must look like a starved animal, wild-eyed at the prospect of food. He wipes the back of his hand across his mouth, just in case he's salivating.

"Sure."

He expects 20 questions, but she accepts his answer without grilling him about what, how much, and when. His mother has tried to seem enthusiastic, but he knows she's suspicious of his dieting. He'd thought she would be supportive of his goals. After all, he's been fat his entire life, the blimp in a family of twigs. His mom says Harry has a movie star face, with beautiful blue eyes and thick black hair he'll never lose. You can't have everything, she says. *Why not?* he thinks. Look at Jonathan Preston.

Mr. Coleman, the dean of Penn Valley, steps up to the podium.

"Welcome, graduates and proud parents. Every one of us at Penn Valley Tech is thrilled to have this opportunity to recognize and celebrate the hard work of all the wonderful young men and women in this room tonight. This is your evening. Each and every one of you deserves a big round of applause."

The crowd claps and whistles and wolf calls. Mrs. Garritano, the registrar, says the blessing, and the stampede to the serving table begins.

Harry swallows a glass of water, and the gnawing in his stomach subsides a bit. He shoves another stick of chewing gum into his mouth. He could pop a few extra capsules of his appetite suppressant to help him resist the temptation of rigatoni smothered in tomato sauce and sticky cheese, golden chicken thighs with crackling, crisp skin, and slabs of roast beef swimming in its juices, but the stomach cramps and diarrhea would fuck up his plans for later.

"I'm going outside," he says to his mother, needing to escape the smell of food.

"I'll join you," she says.

Harry checks his cell phone. Maybe Jonathan called and he didn't hear the ring. No calls. It's still light out. The longest day of the year is only a week away. His mother squints into the sun. She seems to be searching for something in the distance. Maybe she's looking for his father, who's sleeping off another binge, hoping he's managed to crawl out of his stupor and is on his way to the ceremony. Harry's surprised to see how old she looks in the harsh sunlight. Her eyes are puffy from lack of sleep or crying or both. Her skin looks cracked and dry and patches of fiery scales creep across her scalp. He's always thought of his mother as pretty, and maybe she still is or will be again if she could crawl into bed and pull the sheet over her face and sleep for two days. Always thin, she's almost gaunt now. Her blouse hangs from her collarbones and her pants are threatening to slip off her narrow hips. Harry has a scary thought as he watches her take a long drag from her ultraslim 100 menthol cigarette. Does his mother have cancer?

Harry loves his Mom. They've always been close. He's her baby. He's going to miss her when he moves out. He starting a new job and, even though it's shitty nonunion work doing residential wiring a 10-year-old could learn by reading the instruction book, it means a steady paycheck. Harry's been reading the classifieds every day, and it won't be long until he's saved enough for a deposit, first and last months' rent, on a one-bedroom apartment in Bristol. He can't afford a two-bedroom. Jonathan says he won't pay any rent since he's happy living with his parents and putting his money in the bank, but he'll take a key. Harry's promised to crash on the couch when Allison stays over. Harry would do anything for Jonathan. That's a best friend's job. There's nothing your best friend won't do, especially when you're both shitfaced and it's 3 in the morning and you're crashing on the pullout sofa in the family room. Your best friend lets you put his hand on your crotch and slips his fingers inside your briefs when you pull down your zipper. He sucks your dick and swallows your load and doesn't expect you to do anything but lie back and smile. Harry knows he can never initiate anything. Jonathan can throw a headlock on Harry and wrestle him to the floor. He can pry Harry's mouth open with his tongue. He can flop on his back and pull Harry on top of him. He can unbuckle, unbutton, and unzip. Harry can only wait. He knows that talking about any of this means it will never happen again, that he'll be banished from Jonathan's life, his calls never answered, ignored when they see each other at a bar or the mall. Allison will probably be at the apartment more often than she isn't, especially on the weekends, but at least Harry and Jonathan will have the place all to themselves a couple nights a week.

Where the hell he is he? Harry dials his number.

Hey, man, it's Jonathan the Mighty. Can't talk right now. Leave a message and I'll get back to you.

Jonathan the Mighty. Christ, he cracks Harry up.

"Harry, let's go back inside. I want you to eat something."

How can he possibly eat? He's so skittish about Jonathan's being late—really, really late—he couldn't swallow. He's high as a kite and down in the dumps at the same time. The thought of food makes his stomach tighten like a fist. But he obediently follows his mother, turning to look back one last time, expecting Jonathan to burst through the door. She forces him to the serving table and he plops a single greasy chicken thigh on his plate and sits down to eat. His mother can hardly criticize him since she barely touches her salad except to poke the cherry tomatoes with the prongs of her fork.

"I wonder what's happened to your friend." she says.

She's made it clear in a thousand ways, without ever coming out and admitting it, that she doesn't like Jonathan. Harry can't believe she might be jealous of Jonathan. She's always wanted him to make friends, encouraged him to join in, to belong. She volunteered to be a den mother so he would agree to be a Cub Scout. She coached his T-ball team, ignoring the nasty comments from his teammates' fathers, to lure him onto the field. She chaperoned school bus trips, did more than her fair share of car pools, but he never made friends. Harry was just too weird, preferring to bury himself in his comic books, wanting to play superheroes and race around the yard wearing a bath towel as a cape, pretending to save the world from imminent destruction. The only kid who really liked Harry was his retarded cousin Billy.

Until Jonathan Preston.

"You know his name," he snaps. "Why don't you call him by his name?"

Harry jumps up from the table and makes a beeline to the serving trays. He spears another thigh, then a breast, and slops the crusty edge of what's left of the ziti on his plate. He might as well have potatoes too, and he drenches them with the cold, congealed gravy. There's only a small heel of beef left. No one else is going to eat it; they'll just throw it in the kitchen trash if he doesn't take it.

"Are you happy now?" he asks his mother as he slumps into his chair and begins shoveling the food into his mouth as he fights back tears.

Mr. Coleman taps his spoon against his water glass and introduces state representative Curcio, thanking him for graciously agreeing to take time from his very important duties in Harrisburg to address the graduates of Penn Valley Tech. State representative Curcio says it's an honor to be a part of this occasion and hopes that, come November, everyone remembers his support of the working men and women of the Commonwealth, reminding them that he has always been and will always be a true partner of the trade unions. He finishes with a stupid joke about Mr. Coleman's golf handicap and the presentations begin. Harry hunkers down over his plate, stripping the chicken to its naked bone, demolishing every scrap as the possibility of the inconceivable begins to seem inevitable. Maybe Jonathan isn't coming.

Melanie Gregurina, awkward in her new Lane Bryant business suit and tottering hesitantly in her wide pumps, lumbers to the podium to receive a hug and a kiss and recognition as the highest achiever in the business administration (accounting and finance) program. She blushes at the tribute to her proficiency as a Microsoft Office specialist. She's mortified when Mrs. Garritano brags that Melanie's landed the highest-paying entry-level position of any graduate in the history of Penn Valley. Melanie's classmates applaud halfheartedly, resigned to their low-paying futures in offices with cheap faux-wood paneling and Venetian blinds and workdays spent resisting the advances of the ambulance chasers and insurance agents who employ them. Not one of them envies the lumpy, hangdog girl with stringy hair slumping back to her table.

Mr. Coleman announces that Peter Wray is the winner of the award for excellence in architectural and mechanical computer-aided drafting and design. Peter, a skinny boy with frizzy hair who's wearing an orange shirt with a pointy collar, a dead ringer for a *Brady Bunch* son, fumbles with his napkin, drops his dessert spoon, and stumbles to the front of the room. Harry stares down at his plate, avoiding any eye contact, just like he has since the afternoon before last Thanksgiving when, bored and lonely because Jonathan had gone to Providence, R.I., with his family, he offered Peter a ride home. Peter's mother worked the 3-to-11 shift, and alone in the house they smoked a bowl and traded blow jobs as Metallica blasted through the speakers in the audio system in Peter's bedroom.

Peter thought it meant they were friends—he even called Harry during the Christmas break to ask if he wanted to hang out. Harry still feels bad about calling Peter a faggot and threatening to make trouble if Peter didn't leave him alone. He almost backed down when Peter started to cry and would have ended up apologizing if Peter hadn't spun on his heel and run away, keeping a safe distance from Harry ever since. Harry the Fat Boy should have acted better, even though he had to admit it felt good to be on the giving side of humiliation for once. Why couldn't he have been nicer to Peter? Why couldn't he have acted more like Jonathan?

He'd expected Jonathan to laugh his ass off when he grabbed the comic book out of Harry's hands their first day at Penn Valley. He was sure Jonathan was going to mock him in front of the entire lunchroom. Blushing and embarrassed, he shoved an entire Twinkie in his mouth, wishing he could slink away from his tormentor.

"Man, I love this story arc. So, dude, who do you think is the traitor in the Alliance?"

Harry could hardly believe it. Jonathan wasn't fat. He didn't have bad skin. He wore cool clothes. He didn't stutter or spray spit when he spoke. He looked you in the eye instead of dropping his head and mumbling into his collar, and he had a big, friendly smile. He didn't look like the geeks who posted their pictures on the Internet fan sites dedicated to the Alliance of Super-Heroes. They became best friends on the spot.

Harry got goose bumps as they raced through the plots of their all-time favorite issues, impressing each other with their encyclopedic knowledge of the members of the Alliance, the Defenders of Interplanetary Justice. They debated whose superpower was the most awesome. Harry's favorite member of the Alliance was Orsted (supermagnetism); Jonathan's was Amp (super electric force, and a babe to boot). They compromised on Orb (super telepathic abilities). They argued over whose superpower was lamest—a toss-up between Triathlon (who could only use his three superpowers, one at a time—"pointless, dude") , and Fanastasia ("she's a dog, and what the fuck does super illusion projector mean anyway?"). They agreed Black Belt should be kicked out of the Alliance since karate's not a real superpower. Harry started calling Jonathan Cerebro IV (the resident genius with a 12th-effector-computer-aided mind) because he was the smartest guy at Penn Valley. It didn't bother Harry, at least not too much, that Jonathan called him Helium Boy (the fat-ass Inflatable Kid with super bouncing ability) for the obvious reason.

Harry was used to being called a lot worse. Fatso. Lard Ass. Tubby. King Kong. Elephant Boy. Wide Load. Pig. Fat Pig. He'd heard every name ever used to mock the fattest kid in class, to taunt the boy who wheezed when he walked, who snorted through his nostrils, sweat dripping from his armpits. He tried to ignore the cruel remarks, retreating into food, half gallons of ice cream and a dozen doughnuts, not tasting what he ate, just taking comfort in the simple act of chewing. Harry the Fat Boy was resigned to his fate, not believing there was an alternative.

Until he met Jonathan Preston.

"Yeah, it's a shame. A fucking shame. I'm going to have to kick you out of the Alliance," Jonathan announced one drunken night. Harry was devastated. He'd thought he was making progress, starving himself, running, lifting, rowing, his muscles constantly sore, his joints always aching. "Looking good, man," Jonathan would say, sucker-punching Harry and challenging him to a sprint around the lap track. The weight was melting away—10, 15, 20 pounds. "Keep it up, dude," Jonathan would urge, daring him to add more plates to his bench press. Harry huddled in the sauna until his heart raced in his chest and he started deflating like a leaky balloon. Slowly but surely, he was losing the fat and adding muscle only to be shot down unexpectedly, abruptly banished and expelled from the Alliance: "Too bad, man, just like the real Helium Boy. Lost his superpowers and got tossed out on his ass." Harry protested, but Jonathan had the proof.

Quest Comics, number 231, "The Code of the Alliance."

"Unless…" Jonathan said.

"Unless what?" Harry whimpered, barely able to keep from crying.

"Unless you found a new superpower."

"Like what?"

"I can think of something."

"What?"

Jonathan drained his beer can and spread his legs. He unzipped his pants and pulled out his pecker, waving it back and forth like a joystick.

"Kid Omnivore," Jonathan said. "Super eating and digestive powers."

The refrigeration, heating, ventilation, and air conditioning program graduates are standing by the podium, certificates in hand and basking in the applause of their proud parents. Mr. Coleman smiles benignly as they return to their seats.

"Forty years ago, the young families of America were on the move," he starts.

The faculty gird themselves for the annual recitation of the history of Penn Valley Tech.

"The suburbs were growing. Developers were breaking ground for new office buildings and industrial parks, for beautiful and affordable homes, for shopping centers and parking garages. The demand for skilled electricians outstripped the supply. Contractors and the building trades snatched up our first class as they walked out the door, degrees in hand. Today, our fine maintenance and construction electricity technology faculty continues to turn out the most highly sought-after electrical trainees in the tri-state area. Graduates and parents, let's give these hardworking and dedicated gentlemen a big hand."

Harry can barely bring himself to slap two palms together for his balding, potbellied antagonists. If it hadn't been for Jonathan Preston, they would have succeeded in driving him out of Penn Valley two months into the first semester. But Harry was determined that a 2.05 grade point average wasn't going to break up the Alliance of Super-Heroes, and each time the bastards thought they had him at the brink of expulsion, he'd rebound with a miraculous B+—once even an A-!—that would drag his GPA just above the failing point.

"And now it's my pleasure to introduce one of the most distinguished students in the history of Penn Valley, the winner of three of tonight's awards: perfect attendance, highest honors in maintenance and construction electricity technology, highest GPA, and number 1 class ranking. Please join me in congratulating the top student in this year's graduating class, Jonathan Preston."

All present rise to their feet, cheering Jonathan's achievements. Mr. Coleman is left looking awkward at the podium. The applause fades away, and everyone sits down to finish dessert before it melts.

"Apparently Jonathan can't be with us tonight," Mr. Coleman says, unable to conceal his annoyance.

"Take back his perfect attendance award," some smart-ass shouts.

Mr. Coleman pretends to laugh good-naturedly, but he practically shoves Jonathan's awards into Mrs. Garritano's arms.

"Well, I'm sure Jonathan has a perfectly good reason for not being here tonight. We'll make sure that he receives these well-deserved prizes," he says, nearly choking on the word "well-deserved." "Let's move on to the presentation of the maintenance and construction electricity technology degrees."

Mr. Coleman invites the graduates to join him at the front of the room. Harry feels like he's lost in a dream—no, a nightmare. How can they pass out the degrees before Jonathan gets here? Harry's mother almost has to pull him out of his seat. Nothing seems real as he plods through the obstacle course of tables and chairs, his feet not seeming to touch the floor, his elbows colliding with the backs of the heads of his classmates and their parents. He doesn't hear his name when it's called, and Michael Bancroft, next in alphabetical order, pushes him toward the podium. Harry grabs his diploma and his transcript, leaving Mr. Coleman's extended hand unshaken, and thumps back to his table.

"Maybe something important came up," his mother says, doing her best to suppress any trace of "I knew there was something untrustworthy about him" that might creep into her voice.

"Like what?" he nearly shouts, at once angry at her and hoping she's right.

"I don't know. Maybe one of his parents got sick."

But Jonathan should have called if his father had a heart attack or his mother had a stroke. After all, they've been planning the trip to Atlantic City for weeks. Harry's been like a kid waiting for Santa Claus, tossing and turning when he should be asleep, barely able to concentrate. He's nervous about what is going to happen later tonight. He hopes it won't hurt too bad. He doesn't expect he's going to like it. But he's made up his mind and there's no turning back, not even if he feels like he's being split in two. Tonight he's going to let Jonathan do the one thing he's never allowed him to do before.

Tonight Harry is going to get fucked by Jonathan.

The last time they messed around Jonathan kept rubbing his finger on Harry's ass.

Dude, please, dude. My nuts are busting.

I'll suck you again.

It ain't the same. Please...

Harry felt himself getting loose, almost wanting Jonathan to do it, but not then, not yet. The first time ought to be special.

Fuck Jonathan.

Motherfucking Jonathan.

He's no fucking friend. He sure ain't a standup member of the Alliance. Harry tells his mother he'll be back in a minute and, finding the bathroom, locks himself in a stall. He dials Jonathan's number, intending to tell him he can kiss his ass.

Hey, man, it's Jonathan the Mighty. Can't talk right now. Leave a message and I'll get back to you.

Harry's resolve crumbles at the sound of Jonathan's voice.

"Cerebro, dude, where are you, man? Shit, Coleman is totally pissed."

Harry forces a laugh, like Jonathan and he are in on the joke.

"Man, where are you? What happened?"

Harry hangs up, then dials back immediately, wishing he had a superpower that would force Jonathan to answer his phone.

Hey, man, it's Jonathan the Mighty. Can't talk right now. Leave a message and I'll get back to you.

"Cerebro, pick up man. Come on. Pick up. I'm gonna do what you want tonight."

Harry can't believe his own stupidity. Now Jonathan will never call back. Harry's broken the sacred rule. Dinner flip-flops in his stomach, and he's on his knees, gagging and chucking solid pieces of ziti and greasy chicken and beef into the toilet bowl.

"Dude, you OK in there?" a voice asks.

"Yeah, man. I'm OK."

"Oh, Cerebro, I'm going to do what you want tonight!"

Harry recognizes Peter Wray's voice, mocking him.

He stands up straight, almost ripping the door off the stall. He's going to kill the little fuck, but Peter, laughing hysterically, bolts for the safety of his family. Harry finds the honors certificate Peter dropped in his rush to escape and uses it wipe his mouth, then rips it into shreds, flushing the pieces in the toilet. All he wants is to get the hell out of this place.

"I'm going to meet Jonathan," he tells his mother.

"What happened to him?" she asks, suspicious.

"Nothing. I just talked to him. I'm going to pick him up."

His mother slips his diploma in her handbag and Harry walks her to her car. She kisses him good night.

"Be careful, honey," she says. "No drinking and driving."

"I will. I mean, I won't," he says, running to his car.

Harry ignores the yield sign, and a pickup truck speeding north on Route 1 veers into the passing lane, narrowly missing him, the driver smashing his palm against his horn. Harry floors it, determined to beat the yellow light at the first intersection. *What's the fucking hurry?* he asks himself. *You don't even know where you're going.* He thinks of every possible place Jonathan might be. Gold's Gym. The Road Toad. It's too late for the gym, too early for the bar. Maybe the mall. Why would Jonathan miss graduation to hang out at the mall? The theme from *Star Wars* announces an incoming call. Thank fucking God! Jonathan is finally calling back.

"Oh, Cerebro, I'm going to do what you want tonight!"

"Motherfucker, I'm going to kill you!" he screams, almost rear-ending the car stopped a few feet in front of him.

"Promises, promises," Peter laughs and hangs up. Traffic is at a standstill. A few assholes blast their horns, but most of the drivers are slumped in their seats, resigned to forced imprisonment. Harry finds the news radio station. There's a four-mile backup on Route 1 northbound due to a collision at the State Road intersection. Travelers are advised to take an alternative route. Police and fire are clearing the accident scene. Southbound traffic is slow due to gaper delays.

Harry crawls toward the next intersection and turns right, not caring if he gets lost on the meandering back roads. He plays with the dial, looking for Y-100, the modern rock alternative. The DJ is playing a double shot of Green Day, first a classic track from Harry's freshman year in high school, then the single from the brand-new record. He cranks up the volume, singing along. Harry told Jonathan he looks like Billie Joe, the lead singer, but with a better chest and bigger biceps. They have the same cocky, friendly swagger. Jonathan acted pissed, saying Billie Joe looks like a fag, but Harry knew he was secretly pleased since Billie Joe's the coolest guy in rock. The music and a cigarette calm Harry's nerves. There's no way Jonathan has forgotten their plans tonight. Harry's mom must be right. One of his parents must be sick or maybe his grandma died and the family is packing to go to the funeral in Providence. Poor Jonathan, Harry thinks, ashamed of being a selfish bastard, thinking only of himself. Jonathan needs his best friend now. There's only one thing to do. Drive to Jonathan's parents and offer to help.

Harry has a brief panic attack, remembering the phone message. But, with a clearer mind, he realizes he's overreacting. There's no way Jonathan could know Harry's plans for tonight. It's not like he was explicit. *I'm gonna do what you want tonight.* He could have meant anything. Blackjack. Tequila shots. Titty dancers. Fill in the blank. Maybe Jonathan won't even ask. And, looking at the upside, the message may be a good thing so that Harry can act reluctant, hesitant, when Jonathan starts pleading for more than a blow job. *Come on, dude, you promised. Whatever I want tonight.* Then Jonathan can never accuse him of being a faggot who gave it up so easily.

The sun is dropping below the horizon as he drives by the familiar landmarks leading to Jonathan's house—the all-night Exxon station, the McDonald's with the 24-hour pickup window, the convenience store, the last pit stops for gas and greasy food, cigarettes, and rolling papers, after a long night of carousing. Up ahead on the right is Woodhaven Crest Lane, a street of Cape Codders, once identical before 30 years of custom additions. There's the Preston mailbox. Number 112. Harry pulls into the short narrow driveway. The Space Cruiser, Jonathan's Honda Civic, fully accessorized and ready for duty, Pennsylvania vanity license ALLIANCE, is parked, awaiting the next adventure of the Alliance of Super-Heroes.

Christ, Harry could kick himself for doubting Jonathan! He should have known there was no way Jonathan was going to take off without his best friend tonight of all nights. Why doesn't anyone answer the doorbell? Harry's slipping back into a state of agitation. He walks around the house, peering into the windows. The rooms are dark except for the kitchen, where a small appliance light in the range hood casts a soft glow and the only evidence of life is an open can of Pepsi on the table. Harry taps on the pane, certain someone must be home. He's at the end of the road, nowhere to go, nothing to do but wait. He tries knocking on the front door— maybe the bell is broken—and sits on the steps, burying his face in his hands. He doesn't want to cry, but there's no one here to see him and he couldn't stop the tears if he wanted.

An eerie red flash illuminates the black sky. Maybe aliens have abducted the Prestons. A squad car, its siren silent, pulls in the driveway. What the hell has Jonathan done? Why's he been arrested? The officers, a man and a woman, get out of the car. The neighbors open their doors and stare out their windows; kids come racing down the street, drawn by the commotion. Jonathan's mother asks the cops to help her with her husband. Mr. Preston is unsteady on his feet, his eyes glazed from large doses of tranquilizers. He looks right through Harry as if he doesn't recognize him.

"Where's Jonathan? Where's Jonathan?" Harry's voice is shrill and metallic.

"Please, son," the female cop says.

"Where is he? Where is he?"

"Are you family?" she asks.

"Yes. I'm his best friend."

The neighbors are circling the car, hollow-eyed zombies drawn by the light.

"Please, just give us a minute," the cop says, leading the Prestons into the house.

The curious men huddle with their agitated wives, murmuring among themselves, horrified by the proximity of tragedy and relieved and grateful that it chose to strike someone else's home.

"Go away. Go home. Get out of here!" Harry screams.

"Listen, kid," one of the neighbors says, stepping forward, intending to comfort Harry, but backing away when he sees the animal look in Harry's eyes.

The male cop comes to the door and asks Harry to step inside. He's young and handsome, with a square jaw and thick, cropped red hair, a dead ringer for Orsted.

"You don't know, do you? There's been an accident," he says, unintentionally gruff. Gentleness is not second nature to him.

"Where's Jonathan?" Harry shouts.

"You have to stay calm for them. They saw everything. They were following in the car behind."

Lies! Who is this fucking liar? Why is he making this shit up?

"Not true! Not true! Jonathan's car is in the driveway!" Harry screams.

"Kid, I told you to stay calm. The girlfriend was driving. It was her car. A drunk ran a red light at Route 1 and State Road. The boy's on life support."

"No. It's a lie. It's a fucking lie!"

"Settle down."

"It's a lie, a lie, a lie…" Harry says, knowing that it's true. The cop assumes Harry's in shock, devastated by the news about his friend, but all Harry feels is empty. Some day he may forgive Jonathan. But right now the emotion that's slowly filling the void is hatred so intense it blinds Harry to any reality but Jonathan's betrayal.

Jonathan deserves to die for being with her tonight.

So, dude, who do you think is the traitor in the Alliance?

You, motherfucker. You.

"Mrs. Preston wants us to take her back to the hospital. Can you stay with her husband until her daughter gets here? It would be a big help," the woman officer asks.

Harry bolts. He never wants to see a Preston, any Preston, again. The cop calls after him, asking if he's OK to drive. The squad car is blocking the driveway, so he pulls onto the lawn, eager to be far away from 112 Woodhaven Crest Lane. For the second time tonight, he drives without having any idea where he is going. The Golden Arches blaze just ahead. The cashier at the drive-through hands him two bags of Big Macs and fries, enough food for three, all for Harry. He parks the car in a far corner of the lot and methodically begins to chew, berating himself for being so stupid to think someone like Jonathan could be his friend. Nothing's changed since he was a kid. No one wants to play Super-Heroes with a fat boy. His cell phone's ringing. He has to be quick, ask the question before Peter has a chance to speak, throw him off guard, make him say yes.

"You wanna go to Atlantic City tonight?"

A Body in Motion

Sean Meriwether

Cute Man Who Reads stands on the subway platform in front
of you, an angelic vision in rumpled grad-school wear. He is wearing his tortoise-shell glasses that make him look bookish and
remind you of sex in the library. The cameras roll and you play out
that future pivotal moment when the two of you will be pressed
together over some wordy tome. He'd point out a poignant sentence with a long and perfect finger, then turn to you, full lips and
eyes. "I don't understand," you would lie. He'd answer by pulling
you to him and passionately kissing you. He wouldn't be able to
stop himself.

Your body tingles with nervous energy at the thought and you
shift your pants to accommodate your growing enthusiasm. The
first time you saw him you knew he was The One, not a quickie
back-room hand job but a Real Relationship. Your reverie lasted a
minute before that Wall Street Boy with the sexy snarl distracted
you and provided three mind-blowing hours of instantly gratifying
sex but left when it was over.

You rediscovered your destiny on campus while you were racing to make a class. His dark curly hair made your hand quiver to
touch it and you couldn't think about anything else for an hour.
Then you met that Hispanic Guy in the bathroom at school who
made you forget everything—at least for 15 minutes. When you
finally mustered up the courage to approach Cute Man Who
Reads, you lost your nerve at the last moment and ended up

sleeping with a boy who looked (vaguely) like your handsome graduate student. There are at least a dozen more examples to highlight your life of procrastination and wish unfulfillment, but none of that matters now. You can change everything.

It's now or never, boys. A cavalier thought as the train approaches; there is not a moment to waste. You set the plot in motion and move in behind Cute Man Who Reads, accidentally "trip," and fall against his arm with a light touch. He smells like knowledge: the rich scent of old books and his strikingly familiar aroma of patchouli. Your senses swim.

"Excuse me," you say in a deep voice—masculine with a dash of het.

"That's all right." He looks at you and smiles shyly. His eyes are the deepest shade of brown and you know you could lose yourself in them forever. "Don't worry about it," he tells you. His voice is mellow and singular, like a French horn in the fog. It is the first time you have actually heard him speak, and you aren't disappointed.

You have an urge to take his hand and lead him to the dance floor like Gene Kelly in a black-and-white musical. You would lean over and kiss him conspicuously on the lips as the unisex suit-people fanned out in a perfect circle, flailing their briefcases. The glistening silver train would slide into the station carrying a sign that read "And They Lived Happily Ever After" in sparkled typeface as he looked at you, love lighting his eyes.

To your consternation, the train screeches in and flattens the cinematic quality of your fantasy with its din. The metal wheels toss sparks into the damp abyss beneath your feet. "Don't I know you?" you say as the train shudders to a stop.

The doors open, people push past, and you follow him on, thankful that he did not hear a word you said. Your eyes are free to invade the pockets of his pants and cup his crotch as he maneuvers into an unoccupied seat. You stand against the door facing him and casually tilt your head to read the posters along the edge of the ceiling. "All you need is…" the ad claims. You dip your eyes so that you can view his sensuous lips. "All you need is…" You look down, his exquisite fingers rub the bridge of his nose. "A dollar and..." He parts the dog-eared pages of *Anna Karenina*. "A dream."

His marble-smooth face descends into the book and he is lost to you once more. You have developed a blind hatred of Tolstoy because of his distractive and lengthy novels; they have caused you nothing but postponement and misery. You stare hopefully at Cute Man Who Reads, observe the gracefully masculine architecture of his hands, like twin suspension bridges. They should be wrapped around you in slumberous postcoital embrace.

You feel self-conscious standing when there are open seats, so you sit down. Cute Man Who Reads is at the other end of your bench and you can see his reflection in the elongated window when the train returns to the tunnel. You imagine that split second when he would look up and lock onto your mirrored gaze. Then he'd drop his book and rise to find you. He would pull you out of your seat and sweep you up in his arms with a kiss, like Richard Gere in *An Officer and a Gentleman*. The other passengers would erupt into tears and frantic applause as he carried you off the subway and into his life.

Mrs. Karenin has stronger charms than you, for his attention never wavers.

You watch your stop come and go and wait nervously for him to look up. You start to doubt it will ever happen and glance around the car for other prospective costars. The pickings are lean, so you redouble your mental efforts to get Cute Man Who Reads to look at you once; that's all it will take.

Most of the other passengers get off at 125th Street, and the train goes express. You have never been this far north, and you take a deep breath before panic sets in. The train shuttles through the dark, and you move across the aisle from your future husband. Seeing his familiar face calms you down. You stare at his black shoes then ride your eyes along the inseam of his dark pants into the promised land of his crotch. You give yourself x-ray vision to view his gentle skin, his less-than hairy legs, his moderate- size penis. You are afraid that your torso is about to explode as the pressure builds beneath your navel. He has to make a move on you. Now.

At the end of the line you desperately plead for five more minutes so that he can fall in love with you. He closes his book and stands by the door without a glance in your direction. You stand directly behind him, so close that were he to take one baby step backward, his body would mold itself against your own. You are floating on the scent of patchouli that fills your mind and your pants simultaneously. The doors open, and he moves out beyond the cluster of people waiting to board the train. Then he stops dead. You don't. You slam into his backside, the telltale lump in your pants betraying your thoughts, and you pray he didn't notice. He turns around with a sharp grin and moves past the others. He looks back again, and your stomach does a nervous flip. You feebly attempt to blend in with the departing passengers as he hesitates at the bottom of the stairs.

He says "Hello" when you reach his side. You say the same. Then he says, "Don't I know you?" and you laugh because it is the same terrible line you gave him. "Don't you go to NYU?" he asks. You say you do, delirious in the knowledge that he recognizes you.

You float into nonexistent clouds as you exit the station, side by side. You are actually walking next to, *talking* to, the man you have wanted for the past four months. All the others fade into anecdotal trysts as you look at him. He is so confident and shy, smart and attractive, and most notably has an ass you would commit crime for. And, you think, in 10 minutes you will be in his apartment having sex with him, and that sends you dripping onto the sidewalk.

A charged silence zings across the sliver of air separating your bodies. His hand brushes yours "accidentally," and your arm tingles with a fluid charge.

"Would you like to come up and talk?" he asks when you reach his building. All you can do is nod your head. He leads you up the stoop, through the door and into his second-floor apartment. He says, "It's a little messy right now," but you don't care. It could be the Freshkills Landfill and you wouldn't even notice, not until after.

"Sit down," he says. You sit on the edge of a worn-down futon. It is the only major piece of furniture in a room littered with books. He sits down next to you and starts talking about *Anna Karenina*, which he holds up for reference. You find it endearing that his hands shake a little and are somewhat surprised that though he is a few years older, you appear to be more sexually linguistic. He is talking and talking and you hold your breath and count to 60. And then count to 60 again. He points out a passage in the book and you are in the middle of your fantasy. You smile at him, thinking you will have to make the first move. He says, "Do you like Tolstoy?" and you say, "No, but I like you." You kiss him. You can't stop yourself.

He edges away, then stands. He pulls you up from the futon so that you are standing next to each other as if you are about to dance. Then he kisses you lightly. Your head and body part ways as you think despondently that his kisses are not as passionate as you would like, nor his body quite as hard, especially a certain part of it. Your body, however, is being explored gingerly, and it frantically returns the favor. Your hands cup delicious wedges of butt and crank the man's body up against your own.

Still no hard-on.

Unbuttoning his oxford shirt reveals a tufted field of brown hair on his chest. You frown. An attempt to unzip his pants is waylaid when he takes your hand in his and whispers, "Not yet." And you think, *Yeah, 'cause you ain't even hard.* Then you worry that you are doing something wrong. You don't want to lose him so easily.

You kick off your shoes, shimmy out of your shirt, jeans, and underwear in just 20 seconds (a personal record) while kissing him. He is certain to fall in love with you, a lean 18-year-old with a decent-size prick and blue eyes that everyone compliments. Though you are completely available and ready to go, he looks disappointed.

He says, "Uh, what's your name?"

You look down at your penis. It practically pokes you in the eye. You look up at him pleadingly and tug on his pants.

He looks at you and asks, "Why do boys just want sex? Why can't we like each other first?" You shrug. You look at your watch.

He hugs and releases you. "I thought we could get to know

each other first, talk, kiss, you know. I'm...I would rather know you, I don't want to ruin the possibility of a relationship by jumping right into bed." He smiles shyly and brushes the downy hair of your arm. "I hate to ask again, but what is your name?" He looks at your eyes only, not even a glance at your dick, and you feel scrutinized.

"How old are you?" you ask instead of answering. He frowns. You sit down and cross your legs to cover your persistent erection. You blindly hope he will give you head, but he just stands there. There must be something wrong with you. Perhaps your breath? You smell your armpit, but it isn't that. You beg, "Fuck me," but not out loud.

"I thought you might be different," he says. "You looked, I don't know, *innocent*, and I was flattered you were interested in me, but I knew you were too young."

"Too young?" You are insulted but can't explain why.

"For a relationship," he says. "I want a boyfriend, someone I love and trust. You're very cute, but I'm not looking for a boy who just wants a fuck." He sighs. "I don't think this is going to work."

The fantasy collapses like an exhaled breath. You are yanked out of the scene and thrust into the audience. You see a cute naked boy sitting beneath an attractive man, and you realize that the boy in this story is not going to have sex. You lose your hard-on. This isn't the way it's supposed to go. Cute Man Who Reads is supposed to fall in love with that boy on the screen, want to be with him, want to make love to him. Wetness builds at the corners of your eyes and you curse your stupidity.

You squirm into your underwear and pants and hope he will tell you not to get dressed. He is talking about romance and intimacy as you put on your shoes. It hits you hard while you pull on your T-shirt. It not that he doesn't want you now, he doesn't want you at all. And if someone like him can't love you, then who would? Your throat closes up and you look at him through swollen eyes. "I can't stay," you say between pursed lips. Your stomach churns, leaden, and you are afraid of throwing up in front of him.

"Are you all right?" he asks. His fingers graze your arm and you stare at them in disbelief. "What are you doing?" His touch makes you melt, but your fist itches to meet his nose.

"Would you like to talk?" He leans forward, his beautiful brown eyes dragging you in and rejecting you simultaneously.

You are an idiot to fall for him. You don't want to talk to him; he doesn't love you and never will. You stand and dash for the door as if moving underwater. You imagine he must be in hot pursuit to catch you and apologize, tell you that he loves you and wants to make love to you, but when you reach the street and turn around no one is there.

You rub your damp eyes on the short sleeve of your shirt. It reeks of patchouli, and the smell sweeps you up and holds you until the world dissolves into that one singular aroma. His smell. You close your eyes and swallow the hard lump of phlegm that threatens to turn into tears. It hardens you. You passionately assure yourself, the tragic hero, that you shall walk through life alone with the sour taste of spit and the terrible hurt at the back of your throat.

You cross the street and look up into his window. There must be a way to undo whatever it was you did wrong, rewrite the ending. You scan every movie you have ever seen for an infallible plan. Could you scale the fire escape, rush in and make love to him, talk late into the night and watch the sun rise before doing it again? Could you press his buzzer repeatedly until he comes down, a dopey grin on your face that he couldn't say no to? Or could you proclaim your love for him from the street, hopefully blocking traffic, in a voice so loud and true that he would be yours once more? "Hey!" you yell to him. "I really am romantic. Let me show you how much!"

He comes to the window and you realize how hopeless you are. You turn away, certain that the camera will pan his tear-streaked face before it centers on you, the departing stranger. Yes, it is just a movie. You force the scene to fade by closing your eyes. The credits roll over your body and when you open your eyes it will all be over and you can leave, dissatisfied but unaffected. The sunlight burns through your eyelids and mires your hopes in murky orange. You squeeze out every patch of light until your head throbs with the effort. The silver screen remains empty, the audience gone, but you wait, certain there is another reel: a reconciliation, a happy ending. Nothing happens. Someone bumps you out of your trance and your eyes open. You are looking at the cutest Dominican Boy you have ever seen. He doesn't even know you exist—just that you are in the way. You follow in his wake. You picture what it might be like with him, grateful for the distraction. This is so much easier, you sigh, and you can't imagine what it was you saw in that nerdy grad student anyway.

From Kissing

Michael Graves

Marry Me

That afternoon premiered like some show.
I played a broken boy who was lonely and bored and blonde.
After 12 seasons, each day felt like another repeat. All my scenes
were the same.
But, once again, cameras began churning.
4...3...2...
ACTION!

Footballers crashed, pantry to porch. Launching blows, they
tackled and broke through the windowpane. A spritz of crystal
crumbs gouged their faces.

And we began scoffing.

"Steroids are wicked gross," I said. *"Nasty!"*

Bundles of thread were safety-pinned to my cutoffs. I was
twisting, tying, braiding, binding.

"Fuckin' A!" Sherrie grumbled. She thrust her two middle fingers at the School Break Special. "All these shows are fake. They
ain't real, Butch. They ain't like us."

Sherrie was my second cousin, and most days we'd watch
Sally Jessy or *Jem* or *Dance Party USA*.

"TV's *so* queer," she said.

Knotting the last rung of color, I smiled at perfect black-and-blue zigzags. "This bracelet's done," I told her.

"Who ya gonna give it to?"

"You."

"Where am *I* gonna put it? Already got 13," she said. "Just keep it."

"Can't give *myself* a friendship bracelet. That's *retarded*."

Sherrie poked at her new spiral permanent. Bunching the kinks, she locked them with an orange banana clip. "I gotta get home."

"*Kids Incorporated*'s on in 10 minutes. Don'tcha wanna stay and watch?"

"Can't. Homework. Fuckin' fractions."

"Eighth grade's hard, huh?"

"It rots. Two more years and then you'll see."

I snatched a dusty white Sweetheart from the candy dish. It read, "Marry Me." Slipping the Necco in, I nursed noisily.

"All right," Sherrie said, "Have fun with What's-His-Face tonight."

Soon the lights paled to death.
There was only darkness.
Chomping on my chalky heart, I waited for the next scene.

Monsters

Monsters were growling, grinning, snarling, spinning.

Predator ripped through black slush and mire. Bawling, the beast rumbled, rocketing near. As he shot toward heaven, fat dollops of sludge drizzled down over us.

And the crowd jolted.

Foxboro Stadium was thumping like an earthquake. (The booms, the T-shirts, the kids. The swearing and hooting. The gasoline, the pretzels. And high fives. The clapping, the howling. The mad dads too.)

But I watched Milo Morgan. I stared at the heart-shaped, violet bruise that shone on his bicep. The boy drooped, hunched. He was sucking up another Slush Puppie.

"Cool...huh?" Milo said, catching my gaze.

"Yeah!"

"Black Jack's the best! That one *rules!*"

Since summer, Milo had lived two floors above me, and we'd sometimes watch *Alf* or *Batman* or *The Dukes of Hazzard.*

"I think the Crusher's comin' up!" he told me.

Suddenly, one truck cartwheeled, toppling twice and soon sparks burst from beneath his jutting fangs.

And the flocks froze.

"Holy shit!" Milo cackled.

In an instant, plumes arose. Black swirls soared, choking the stars, crowding the crescent moon.

"Hey!" he yelped. "Let's go take a piss!"

"Um...I don't gotta go right now."

"*I* do! Don't be *gay.* Just come on!"

A Friendship Band

"That guy's fuckin' dead!" Milo whooped. "Wipeouts are the best!"

Wrenching down my Jockeys, I began to pee and a dim, murky drivel splashed over the seat.

"This is my third truck show, ya know," he called out.

"Awesome."

"Yeah. Just *wait* till the finale."

I could hear his voice swell, bouncing between cinder-block slabs.

"Hey...Butch?"

"Yeah?"

The cuss-covered door squeaked behind me. Instantly, I spun round, squirting my stonewashed leg.

And I saw him.

Milo was smirking at me.

For six long seconds, I couldn't budge. My eyes were locked on the curves of his smug smile.

"What are you doin'?" I finally asked.

"Nothin'. Just messin' around."

"Well...*get out.*"

"No," he sneered. "I ain't movin'."

Gushing with grins, Milo bent over and flicked my dark magenta head. It hurt.

"Yours is way fatter than mine," he told me.

I quickly tucked myself away, then kicked the silver knob. Toilet froth blasted as butts and cups bobbled about.

"We should get back," I said.

"Yeah. In a sec."

"We're missin' the show."

He scuffed closer. He pinched my best bracelet. "So...uh...what's *this* thing anyway?'

"A friendship band."

"Oh, yeah?"

"I make 'em all the time."

Slowly, Milo slid his pointer between my wrist and the purple strap. "Looks kinda...*girly*."

"*No, sir.* It's cool. It's the oldest one I got. The thickest too."

But the bathroom door whooshed open. Cackling crowds of men charged through.

"I'll go out first," Milo said. "Meet me by the Pepsi machine."

Nosebleeds

It was dark.

Milo hauled me beneath the booming bleachers. Hand in hand, we tripped through shadows and neon ribbons of light.

"These are the shitty nosebleeds," he told me.

"Where are we *going*?" I griped.

"This way."

Above us, work boots were beating, bumping, pounding, pumping.

"Look," he grinned. "I wanna show you somethin'."

With a crooked smirk, Milo reached down and shed the beat T. Every lump of his muscle bulged through caramel skin.

"Why...why'd ya do that for?" I asked.

He stroked the butterscotch bumps. "See. These new muscles started comin' out. It's 'cause of all my sit-ups. Ain't they cool?"

Inside me, jitters twitched, snapping like pistons.

"If ya want…ya can feel 'em," he smiled.

"Uh…"

"Go ahead. I don't care."

I was colored crimson. Fighting fidgets, I began to paw Milo's nubs. My shaky palms steered breast to belly button.

"Ain't I *hard*?"

"Yeah."

"Neat…huh?

"Wicked cool."

"Hey," he snickered, "got a triple dare for ya. Will ya do it?"

"We're gonna get in trouble."

"Don't be a *gaylord*."

I glanced away. I thought of *Dallas*. I thought about *Falcon Crest*. Milo said, "I triple dare you…to French me."

"But…"

And he began kissing.

Milo pecked and puckered and bit. With long laps, he licked my pimpled chin and two goopy streams of dribble stretched between us.

"Don't I feel good, Butch?"

"Yeah."

My penis grew. It curved against my thigh, swelling solid.

"Kissing's cool," he told me.

Our scene faded and I felt numb, washed in electric waves of thrill.

I could see new scripts. (The gazes, the rubs, the smiles. The laughing and hand-holding. The sleepovers, the walks. And twilight. The giggling and making out. The close-ups too.)

Pretty

Scooping through my toy chest, I dug out soldiers and Snorks and Smurfs. At the bottom, a heap of fliers lay pig-piled.

I had only saved my favorites. (The Jockeys, the French cuts, the red bikinis. The Caldor guys, the Kmart guys, the Lechmere guys. And bumpy muscles. The thongs and the Hanes. Polka-dotted silk ones too.)

Thumbing to each dog-eared page, I fanned them across my bed so I could see all the pretty men. They smiled. They gawked at me.

And I spat a bubbly phlegm gob in my hand.

I began pulling, gasping, tweaking, rasping.

"Milo…"

After 12 quick strokes, it began to leak over my leg.

"Put it *i-i-in*."

Faggots

Once Ma mixed her second Bay Breeze, I edged down the hall. In silence, I hid and watched.

Faggots began flashing on our fingerprinted screen. It was a news show called "AIDS in the USA."

I could see everything. (The vials, the doctors, the swim trunks. The towels and dancing. The hand-flicking and the sneezing. The mothers and bodies. The shorts, the lights, the powder.)

One fruit cried, "Thought I had the flu…but it never went away. This is *terrible*. This is *awful*."

Red-faced, I sank backward.

"Serves ya right," Ma snapped. "Fuckin' fudge-packers."

Play

That next morning began like an episode.
But I just couldn't act as my character.
I couldn't lie or pretend or fake-laugh.
Still, we plodded through another scene.

Star beams bounced off his links. Hurdling, B.A. cut through Malibu's sparkling midnight surf. As machine guns sputtered, he dove behind a range of rock.

And I began hacking.

Bed-headed, I watched an old episode of *The A-Team*.

I could feel the scorching fevers that flared beneath my skin.

Flames burned and blazed (like bonfires, like hot pins).

"Poor little guy," Ma said. "Ya look like death. Better rest and take it easy."

"Ya think...maybe...I could get a Happy Meal for lunch?"

"Butch...*no*," she hissed. "Have some crackers or bologna or something."

"OK."

She placed three grape Chewables by the set. "Take these. And drink some Coke too. Least ya had a good time at the truck show last night. I told ya it would be fun. See...ya need to be friends with boys too. Boys gotta play with boys. So...call that nice kid from upstairs. Tell him thank you."

My face sloped into a jumbo smile.

Dick Disease

"You twerp! Got a couple days off! Lucky duck!"

Sherrie sat, legs like a pretzel. She had just begun making another band. Her ponytails of pink and orange thread were taped to the TV tray.

"I'm sick," I whined. "For real!"

Her eyeballs plunked back. "Yah, right. *Faker!*"

I tiptoed over to the medicine drawer. It was packed with bottles and Band-Aids and Kotex. Sifting, I snatched out a fistful of Cherry Luden's.

"Hey...ya wanna snack?" I called out. "We got Fruit Roll-Ups."

"Can't! Remember? My diet?" Sherrie poked a pouch of blubber hanging from her hip. "Mom wants me to lose 10 more pounds. If I don't, she said she'd put me on those Deal-a-Meal cards."

I fake-frowned, stripped a drop, and tossed it in. The candied sweetness bled over my tongue.

Sherrie asked, "So...did ya have fun with What's-His-Name?"

Since that special Sunday, I'd wanted to talk about Milo. I had wanted to tell her everything.

"Know what?" I said. "Somethin' happened."

"Like what?"

"Um…I had my first kiss."

"Thought you already did! What about Shannon B.?"

"Don't count."

"Well…then…who?"

And I began to wish and wish.

"OK…see…a couple nights ago…at the Monster Truck Show…"

"Yeah?"

"Well…like…*Milo kissed me.*"

Sherrie squinted, blinkless. her lips curled. "You kissed *a boy?*"

"Well…*he* kissed me. It was a dare."

"That's nasty, Butch! Gross!"

"But…"

Sherrie kicked on her crimson Reeboks. "That's why you're so sick."

"Whattaya mean?"

"You kissed him and now…*you* got the dick disease. *You* got AIDS."

"No, sir!"

"That's what happens to boys that mess with other boys. They end up being big fairies and fudge-packers. And they all die."

Right then, I thought I might burst (like a bomb, like a firecracker.)

"That ain't true!" I squealed.

By Heart

I had memorized every single word.
Patting cowlicks, I reached for one last pocket of air.
Cameras rushed in.
4…3…2…
ACTION!

I knew his number by heart.

Curling up like a capital G, I sucked back the goo. It filled my throat and packed my mouth. With a gulp, sweet snot slowly crept down.

And his line ticked.

"*Who's this?*" Milo huffed.

"It's Butch. From downstairs?"

"Oh. Hey. What's up?"

"Nothin'. Whatcha doin'?"

"Dumbbells. Push-ups. I'm just workin' out," he groaned.

I swabbed my drippy nose with the electric blanket. I told him, "Stayed home from school today. I'm *wicked* sick."

"That sucks ass."

"Yeah. Just got into a fight with my dumb cousin too."

"Girls blow," he said.

Twice, I glanced at the girls on *Facts of Life* giggling on mute.

"Hey...um...Butch?"

"Yeah?"

"Can I ask ya somethin'?"

"Yeah."

"And promise ya won't laugh?"

"I swear."

"Well...ya think...ya think *I* could be famous? Someday? Like Ricky Schroeder, maybe?"

"Sure. You could be a star too."

"Cause...ya know...life seems kinda like some sort of TV show anyway. Feels like I'm actin' all the time. Does that sound queer?"

I grinned at the joke he hadn't meant to make. "Nope," I said. "That don't sound queer."

"Hey...um...Butch?"

"What?"

He began whispering, "Ya think I'm...good-lookin'? Good-lookin' enough to be on the tube?"

"Yeah. Yeah."

"Ya think...I'm...*sexy*?"

"Sure."

"Ya think I'm *hot*?" he asked.

Again, my penis began to bloat. It peeked out. It pushed through my front flap.

"Totally," I said.

No Gerbils

I was the only one being taped.
Sherrie hadn't come to the set in four days. Like everyone else, she
hated queers and faggots and gaylords.
No one wanted to see a fairy on TV.
But I felt different from all the others. (No dresses, no gerbils, no
rainbows. And no glitter. No flags or chaps. No triangles. And no
high heels. No make up. No confetti. And no mustache.)
I knew I was a fag too.
But I knew I was still me.

One Day

I waited outside Honey Farms, cradling a new *Teen Machine*, and I flipped past pinups and glossy centerfold pullouts. Each star was batting, beaming, laughing, leaning.

Then I saw her.

Sherrie bopped toward me with long, sassy strides. She clutched her Walkman. She grooved. She lip-synched.

"Hey! Hey!"

"Oh...*hi*," my cousin said. She panted and pried the phones from her head.

"Whatcha doin'?" I asked.

"Nothin'. Fuckin' exercisin'."

For 32 seconds, we shifted around, blowing sighs.

I could only watch the bare traffic that crawled by us. I prayed and I prayed.

"So...um...ya think you're gonna come by soon?" I finally asked.

"Don't count on it."

"Sherrie...this ain't no big deal. *I'm still me*."

She tapped her speckled jelly shoes. "Butch...now..."

"Now, I'm a faggot. But *really*, I'm the same old me. And ya know what? Milo's *wicked* cool. He's awesome..."

"What? You think you're gonna *marry* him or something?"

Twirling my blond ducktail, I smiled. "Maybe we *will* get married. One day."

"You can't! Gaylords *can't* get married. And gaylords *can't* have no kids."

"I can if I want!"

"Look," she said, snaking her hips, "We ain't friends no more. 'Cause *I* don't wanna die. And you got it. You do, Butch. That's why you're still sick. *Du-u-uh*. If you don't believe me, ask your doctor."

But I did believe her.

Tiny puddles of pain flushed in my eyes. Right then, I hated Sherrie (more than Dad, more than the devil).

She shrugged. "I'm sorry."

"Look! Just please don't tell anyone I got it!"

So Much More

Bulbs blared, cooking my skin.
And I was frightened of being canceled.
I wanted other things. (The face, the clothes, the premieres. New stories. The earrings and longer hair. The money, the fans, the limo rides. The mansion. And parties too.)
I wanted so much more. (The Emmy, the cool friends. The interviews. The diamond ring, the big wedding, and the husband. Puppies. The straight teeth and baby boys. The dinners, the pictures. The valentines. And the Oscar too.)

A Little Bit Funny

With a wet face, she jerked up the dial and beats began surging from her peach plastic box. As the DJ scissored, she thrust about.

And I bit down.

A raspberry Ring Pop was locked between my molars. Cracking its sugary diamond, I watched another half hour of *Full House*.

"Butch! Butch! Turn off the fuckin' set!"

Ma boomed in, ruby with rage. Her arms gripped around a stack of my weekend fliers. "What ya got all these Sunday ads for? Found 'em in your old toy box."

Quickly, I tried to think of good lies.

"Its just…junk."

"Ya must've saved 'em for *some* reason," she said.

"Um…no."

Ma shook her peppery bob. "Just *tell* me. Why ya got 'em'?"

"I…I dunno."

"Throw 'em away, Butch. *All* of 'em. Ya keep stuff like this…somebody'll think you're a little bit funny."

Fucking Bitch

Another scene was set to begin.
But I hadn't rehearsed. I wasn't sure how to play.
Quaking, I hid from the lens.
4…3…2…
ACTION!

Milo's first friendship bracelet curled around my fourth finger (like an emerald band, like a diamond ring.) I tugged it tight, squeezing the skin scarlet.

Behind his door, Max Headroom droned. The tube buzzed and beeped.

And I knocked hard.

"Milo?"

For 16 seconds I listened.

"Milo? *Milo*? I can hear ya. I *know* you're there. I need to talk to ya…about some stuff."

There was no answer.

I began to grow dizzy from my dick disease and I could feel it driving, sweeping through me.

"Ya don't have to come out if ya don't want to, but I gotta tell ya somethin'. I think…I *know* that we're sick. We're *very* sick. With AIDS. We…have it. But it's gonna be OK. It *will*. 'Cause we can do it together. We can do it. I'll take care of you…you'll take care of me. Like…we don't have to *be* like everyone else. We can be…together. And maybe one day…"

But his door swung open.

Milo was sneering. He stood, bareback, in only briefs.

"Hi."

"I ain't sick!" he shouted. "I ain't got *that!*"

"No. Ya do. And I do too. *We're fags.*"

"I ain't no queer!"

"Listen..." I said, holding out his bracelet. "I made this for you."

Milo pinched my left ear. He twisted twice. "Shut up!"

Sobbing, I caved to the damp hallway carpet.

"You're a fucking bitch!" he screamed. "Be quiet. Go home!"

He slammed the door, cussed five times and, in seconds, his TV shot up all the way.

"Milo?"

I could feel my innards split. They began to bust (like a grenade, like an M-80).

"But I got it from you!"

I Got the Cure

I knew that there would be a big finale. (No Christmas, no high school, no wardrobe. No vacations and no friends. No summer, no stories. No birthdays, no sundaes. And no Sherrie.)

I knew that soon, my life would be over. (No Ma, no laughter. No graduation, no semi-formals, no happiness, no yearbooks. And no pictures, no dreams. No debuts. No cliff-hangers. And no Milo.)

ACTION!

"Hello there, Butch," Dr. Magnum said with a sideways smile.

"Hi."

I sat in red Fruit of the Looms. My legs were crossed.

"Jeez. Can't believe how much you've grown. Looks like ya started to get some big-boy muscles."

"I guess."

As always, tufts of silver hair poked from beneath his collar and cuffs.

"How's school?" he asked.

"OK."

I didn't smile. I couldn't.

Dr. Magnum slid a drawer open. Scratching his crinkled brow, he pulled out an instant Polaroid camera.

"Listen," I said. "I know what's wrong with me. And I have to tell ya."

"Well...go ahead."

"I'm sick...with the flu. But it ain't *really* the flu."

He sat on the spinning, squealing chair.

"See...I kissed a boy...and now...I got AIDS. "

My doctor looked at me blankly for a second, then cackled and clapped once.

"It's true. It's true!" I said.

"Well, I betcha didn't know...but *I'm* a lot like you." Dr. Magnum said. "See...*I've* kissed boys too. Lotsa boys. Really, all kinds of boys kiss boys. Nothin' to be ashamed of. Just gotta keep quiet about it."

As fat tears ballooned in my eyes, I pushed down the moaning. I tried to hold back.

"But...see...I just wanna be...all these things."

"Oh, yeah?" he said, gliding closer.

"I don't *wanna* be like all those other faggots," I blubbered. "I wanna be more famous. And I wanna be rich. I wanna be cool. And I wanna be married. I wanna be skinny. I wanna baby too."

He cupped his smirking mouth. "Well...you have to be what you are. You can't change things."

My face gleamed with grief while whimpers began to squeak free. "Plus I'm dying!"

"Look, Butchie, I'm your doctor, and I'm gonna make sure you're OK."

"Really?"

"Really. I got the cure."

"And I'll live?"

"Yep. I promise. And we don't even have to tell your Mother about it." Dr. Magnum aimed his camera. "So...take off those shorts and let me have a good look."

Dum Dum

Everything was hushed.

I slid up my briefs and rubbed away leftover tears.

Still clad in latex mitts, Dr. Magnum tightened his holiday necktie. He said, "Don't forget to give the nurse a sample."

"What do you mean?" I whispered.

"A sample. Of your urine."

"Oh. My pee?"

"Yes, Butch."

My oily bottom still burned. It still ached.

Suddenly, Dr. Magnum began to grin. "Hey…you wanna Dum Dum?" he asked, pulling out one pink pop.

"No, thanks."

"Aw…come on, Butchie."

"I don't want one."

"Just because you suck on it…doesn't mean you're *really* a Dum Dum."

CUT!

WINTER

Curtis C. Comer

The sound of Gabe's voice made me jump; I thought that he had fallen asleep in his armchair by the fireplace.

"What, sweetheart?" I asked, peering over the book I was reading.

"I said that I think it's going to be cold tonight," he replied, his eyes sleepy.

"The Weather Channel says 27 degrees," I said. "I'll turn up the heat before we go to bed.

"Looks like an early winter," I added, looking out the bay window at the gray sky.

Gabe nodded and directed his gaze to the crackling fire.

"I hate the winter," he mumbled.

"Where have I heard *that* before?" I chuckled.

Every winter, for the last 52 years, Gabe had found it necessary to remind me how much he hated the cold, and while I was inclined to point out the beauty of having four seasons, I couldn't help but agree with him. In the winter it's harder to get around. In the winter you're stuck inside for long periods of time. In the winter you're more likely to become sick, and, my least favorite, you're less likely to run around the house naked. I suppose a saner couple would have moved to a warmer climate, but we had decided to stay put in our cozy little house on Connecticut Street.

"I should just enjoy it," he continued, almost to himself.

"Since I probably won't be here for another winter."

"*Going* somewhere?" I asked, arching an eyebrow. Though it was a conversation that I didn't particularly care to get into, I wasn't about to let Gabe talk this way.

"You know what I mean, David," he replied matter-of-factly.

"You're not going anywhere," I said, returning to my book. "Not for a while."

Gabe wasn't normally this fatalistic; even though he was in his late 70s, with all of the associated aches and pains, his sense of humor and upbeat personality still reminded me of the 26-year-old guy I had met so long ago. We had never bothered to have a marriage ceremony; even after our state had legalized gay marriage, we decided that we had been together long enough that a stupid piece of paper wasn't going to change anything between us. "If it ain't broke, don't fix it" was our joke.

I knew what the problem was that night, though. It was the recent news of the death of one of our dearest friends, Karen, that had him down.

"You're thinking about Karen, aren't you?" I asked, searching his face.

"I suppose," he muttered.

I rose from my seat and crossed to the fireplace, taking his hand. He looked up at me, his eyes moist.

"I'm tired of burying friends," he said, his voice catching on the words.

"I know," I replied tenderly. "But we *are* at that age, sweetheart."

"I know," he sighed, squeezing my hand. "It still sucks."

Though I knew I would regret it, I lowered myself to my knees in front of his chair, hoping that the arthritis would ignore my folly.

"You're still the best-looking guy I know," I said, reaching up and mussing his white mane. Unlike my traitorous hair, which had deserted my scalp long ago, Gabe's curly hair had remained, and what was once blond was now a brilliant white.

"Liar," he said, swatting my hand. "You'd leave me for the first hot, young thing that comes along."

"Probably," I teased. "Do you *know* any?"

"If I did, would I still be with an old grouch like you?" he replied, grinning.

Seeing the familiar smile on his face made me feel better. Slowly, using the arms of his chair for support, I rose from my kneeling position and offered Gabe my hand again.

"What should we have for dinner?" I asked.

"There's still turkey," he suggested, slowly rising from his seat.

"I don't feel like turkey again," I replied, a grimace on my face.

"Don't you like my cooking anymore?" Gabe asked, wrapping me in an embrace.

"I've always loved your cooking," I said, my face buried in his messy hair. "I'm just tired of that turkey." I squeezed him tightly.

"Maybe I can make something else," he said, releasing me from his grasp. "I think that I've had enough turkey too."

"Feeling better?" I asked, kissing his forehead.

He merely nodded and took my hand, leading me toward the kitchen.

As we traversed the house, winding through the crazily laid-out hallway that stretched from front to back, I marveled at the things we had acquired over the years. It's funny how cluttered a house can get in one short lifetime and how the smallest memento can bring back a flood of emotions. I paused at a section of wall that was covered in photographs.

"What's the matter?" he asked, turning to face me.

"Nothing's the matter," I replied, smiling up at all of the framed faces looking down on us. "I was just thinking of how much fun we've had over the past 50 years."

"Fun," mused Gabe, smiling up at the wall. "It hasn't *all* been a picnic."

"I think it's been pretty fun," I said, placing an arm around his shoulders.

"Your triple bypass wasn't fun," he replied, casting a sideways glance at me.

"That was nearly 20 years ago…"

"Or," he continued, "burying our parents."

"Who's the old grouch *now*?" I said, turning to face him. "You *are* in a mood today."

I turned back to the wall and its scores of memories: graduations, vacations, weddings, holidays, births, parties.

"Recognize those two?" I asked, pointing to a faded picture of us in Italy.

"Hard to believe I had all of that hair," he replied, smiling.

"Let's not get into *that*," I said, rubbing my smooth scalp. "You have nothing to complain about in *that* department."

"Remember this?" asked Gabe, laughing and pointing to a photo of us in Ireland. It was a photo of a much younger me, soaked from head to toe.

"Didn't realize how close I was to the edge," I replied, adjusting my glasses to get a better look at the photo.

"I told you to be careful," admonished Gabe.

"Yes," I replied, playfully swatting his arm, "and you've reminded me of that fact for the past 40 years!"

"Don't ever die," Gabe said suddenly, throwing his arms around me. "I don't know what I'd do without you."

"Cash the insurance check and go to Europe," I said, hugging him.

"I'm serious," he replied, squeezing me tighter.

"Listen," I said, cupping his chin so that I could look into his eyes. "Have we ever taken separate trips anywhere?"

"No," he replied, his eyes misty again. "Not for a long time."

"No," I agreed. "And when the time comes, I'll be there holding your hand and you'll be holding mine. Nothing can keep me from my boy. Trust me, sweetheart; whatever happens, I'll be right behind you."

"I love you," whispered Gabe.

"I love you, too," I replied, kissing him on the mouth.

Though sex was something that happened with less frequency in our old age, Gabe still tasted the same to me, still had that same masculine, earthy scent, and it caused a stirring in me that night. I squeezed his ass.

"Maybe after dinner, we can go to bed early." I winked at Gabe conspiratorially.

"Really?" he asked, pulling away and searching my face.

"Really," I said, kissing him again.

"I'd like that," he replied, smiling. "So long as you don't fall asleep after dinner."

"I promise," I said.

"Now, why don't you put on some music while I go see what I can make for dinner."

"OK," I replied. I was all too happy to leave Gabe to his realm, the kitchen.

As he turned and continued down the hall, I glanced back at the photos on the wall. It occurred to me that, just as winter was coming early this year, it stood to reason that so might the spring.

"Why don't we go to Ireland next spring?" I called after him.

Gabe peered around the door, a frown on his face.

"I don't know," he said. "What about someplace warmer, like Spain?"

"Spain might be nice," I said. "Anyway, there's plenty of time to think about it."

"*Plenty* of time," agreed Gabe, his head disappearing back into the kitchen.

And so, with the familiar sound of Gabe in the kitchen, I headed back to the living room to find some appropriate music. As I pulled out Billie Holiday, one of Gabe's favorites, I had to smile. Sure, we may have already had our spring, summer, and fall—and this might be the winter of our lifetime—but it was still *early* in the winter, with plenty of love to see us through the cold.

THE SUN AND THE MOON

Mark Wildyr

Michael Lanier had been my best friend and next door neighbor since forever. At the El Rey Community College, M&M wasn't chocolate candy but Mitchell George and Michael Lanier. Yet we were so different it was hard to imagine us as buddies. I was physical; Mike was cerebral. He nurtured me through the classroom; I protected him on the playing fields. I was a healthy, popular, golden-haired blend of many cultures and bloods; he was a dark-haired, pale, mystic Celt. We got along like the north and south poles of magnets. He was a great guy if I could keep him out of his notebooks. He had volumes of them filled with his constant scribbling, part diary, part observations, and part poetry.

How close we were was brought home hard when his cancer showed up last year. I hadn't understood how much of a hole he would leave in my heart—my life, my very soul—until he died three months ago. The last time I saw him alive is etched into my brain for eternity.

"Sunshine," he wheezed weakly. God! "Hello, Sunshine" was his way of greeting me each morning. Thereafter it was Mitch or Mitchell, but always the first time of the day was "Sunshine."

"Hi, Tiger. How you feeling? I saved you a place on the soccer team."

He gave a shadow-smile. "Gimme a week, OK?" Damn, I hoped I could get through this without bawling. I didn't mind him seeing me cry; I just didn't want him to know how scared I was.

"Mitch, I want to give you some things, OK?" he continued, nodding to the table beside the hospital bed. That sentence wore him out and tore me up inside.

I damn near lost it when I saw what was there, going blind in spite of my resolution not to weep. The silver Celtic cross he'd worn around his neck as long as I could remember lay waiting for me. Beneath it was a thick blue binder, one of his famous notebooks.

"The cross is to remember me by." He clutched my hand, surprising me with his strength. "The notebook is to know me by."

"I know you, Mike. Better'n anybody." I swiped at the tears so I could see him.

"Maybe," he acknowledged. "But promise me you'll read it. Might take more than…once," he faltered.

"I'll read it until I can recite it," I swore.

"Don't go nuts on me, Mitchell," he chided.

Michael Roger Lanier died that night. I didn't know a jock could blubber so much, but that's what I did in the privacy of my room.

Afterward, the cross hung around my neck always and forever; the notebook I read through twice simply because I'd promised, sobbing over some parts and laughing over others. Someday he would have been an author or a poet or a journalist or all three. His writing reflected him so perfectly that I felt we were reading it together. But I was puzzled by his last words in the hospital; there was nothing in the book I did not already know except for one poem or poetic essay I did not understand. He'd gone mystic like he sometimes did in real life. Determined to figure it out, I sat down in my bedroom and reread the piece he'd written about nine months ago, just before they discovered the cancer.

"Naught but a distant Star, I am Venus glittering low in a sun-starved, moonless hemisphere, one of a myriad of icy astral motes slung carelessly across the distant cosmos."

The hair on the back of my neck rose, unbidden, unexplained. I glanced around my room, freaked out by my own skittishness.

"The Helios of my universe cuts bright and blinding across my path, nourishing even as he eclipses my luminance with his green Phoeban fire. Oh, how I long for this enervating, nurturing Apollo, this Greek Charioteer, this beautiful Egyptian Ra, would not his glowing incandescence sear my caress, shrivel my kiss, turn fevered passion to pale ash. Thus is Venus fated to orbit second in his precious galaxy."

I whirled about in my chair, convinced I was not alone. But I was. Hackles raised, I rubbed my puckered forearms as if cold. I swallowed audibly and resumed reading.

"Then came Luna to my sky, whose shimmering beauty merely bedims my glow with his shaded shine. This Artemis, this brother of Helios, this sibling of Eros, accepts my timid suit, my kiss, my shy caress, enriching my aura with a molten, milk-white nimbus.

"Selene's time is tender, but fleeting. Then again Hyperion's son ascends, obscuring my silver-footed king whose taste is oh, so sweet, except…he is not my Roman Sol."

I finished reading, uncertain why my lip was touched with sweat. Whatever the cause of my unease, it receded as I closed the notebook. I was alone again. Of course I was; I had been all along.

No doubt this was the piece Mike intended me to "know him by." I'm a jock, not a brain, but this was something he'd asked me to do, so by damn, I would understand this piece if it blew out all my cerebral circuits. So I dragged my fanny down to the library and took a stool before the biggest, fattest dictionary in the place. An hour later I moved to a table and chair to assimilate what I had found.

Venus, of course, is the second planet from the sun, moonless and the brightest star in the solar system. And Mike equates himself with Venus in this poem. Helios is the ancient Greek god of the sun, sometimes known as Apollo. The Egyptians called him Ra; the Romans, Sol. OK, so he had a sun in his heavens. So far, so good.

And the sun turns off the stars. Shit, he'd have my ass for thinking like that. The sun obscures the stars, or *eclipses,* as he puts it. And it's both enervating and nourishing, like the real sun, I guess. So this sun makes the planet feel inferior. OK!

"Then came Luna to my sky." Luna was the Roman goddess of the Moon, sometimes known as Diana or Phoebe or Selene or the silver-footed queen. And Artemis was another name for the moon goddess. Hey! The guy found himself a girl. He'd fallen in love with a girl! The devil! I was his best friend, and he never told me.

But wait! Something was wrong. "Luna bedims my glow with his shaded shine." *His* shine? The goofball mixed up his genders. He meant *her* shine. I frowned as I reread something else. Artemis the *brother* of Helios? Silver-footed *king*? Uh-uh. Mike wouldn't have made *one* mistake like that, much less three! He'd turned the moon goddess into the moon god.

I dropped the papers on the floor as the truth struck me. Jesus! *Sunshine!* Every morning he called me "Sunshine." Helios, the sun! He'd used sun in the Greek and Roman and Egyptian personifications. Among all the other nationalities flowing in my veins, those were the three we had talked about most! And that "green Phoeban fire"—*bright* green fire. I had green eyes. And I would singe his touch, shrivel his kiss, turn his passion to ash!

Oh, my Lord! Mike loved me! Loved me in a different way! I always missed the hell out of him when the Laniers went to their cabin on the lake each summer, but his yearning went beyond what I'd understood. Eros! He mentioned Eros. That was the god of love. And Apollo, he wasn't only the sun god; he was also handsome, desirable. Mike always told me how handsome I was, but he did it in a way that I never suspected. "Gee, Mitch, you look like a million dollars today" was one of his favorites.

"Thus is Venus fated to orbit second in his precious galaxy." Venus, the second planet from the sun. He knew that someday I'd get married, and he'd be second forever in my life. Shit! Venus? Wasn't she also the goddess of something? Love? He cast himself in the female role.

Had I really known Mike Lanier so little? Was he a total stranger to me? No! I knew him better than anyone in the world, his family included. We shared secrets they'd never know. How could I have been so dense?

I retrieved my spilled articles and sat back in my chair. How would I have reacted? Right at the moment, I'd give him anything he wanted! Come back, Mike, and I'll surrender it all: my ass, my cock, my lips! Anything! That was easy to say, even easy to *mean*.

He was in the grave. Back then I'd probably have exploded and told him to grow up.

Halfway down the library steps, I almost dropped everything again. The second part of the poem! Luna…the moon. Had there really been a male Luna in his life? I plopped my butt down in the grass beneath a tree and opened to the poem again. "This sibling of Eros accepts my touch, my kiss, my timid caress."

Yes, there was a moon in his sky. And they got together. They…they made love. "Enriching my aura with a molten, milk-white nimbus." Shit! The guy *came* in him!

I fought with my stomach, amazed it was a fierce jealousy that gripped me, not revulsion. "Oh, Mike! Why didn't you let me know?" I whispered. The answer was crystal clear and unerringly on the mark. Because he knew me too well. He knew me better than I knew him. Sadly, I went back to the poem.

"Selene's time is tender, but fleeting. Then again Hyperion's son ascends." Hyperion was a Titan and the father of Helios and Selene and Eros. "Obscuring my silver-footed king whose taste is oh so sweet, except…he is not my Roman Sol."

Overcome by unidentifiable emotions, I closed my eyes and wept silent tears, not caring who observed them. I almost sobbed aloud recalling the time back in high school when we jacked off together after a double date. I wish I'd known he wanted something more; it would have been easy to accept his touch at that moment. Maybe that would have banked the fire.

For the rest of the school term, I examined every male on campus through new eyes to identify the moon to Mike's Venus. So help me, I couldn't find a fit. Finally, I questioned Mr. and Mrs. Lanier about the cabin, wondering if maybe Luna was from there. After all, "Selene's time is tender but fleeting." Still broken up over the loss of their eldest son, they weren't ready to return to the place where he'd spent his last decent summer, but they generously offered me the use of the place. After thinking it over for a week, I accepted. So instead of working as planned after my freshman year, I headed to a mountain lake, or "tarn," as my poetic friend would have termed it, on a sojourn for the truth.

The trip was a mistake. Mike was everywhere in the cabin. There were pictures of us in his room. His .22 rifle hung over the fireplace, then I came across his fishing rod and reel, his floppy hat—his very spirit inhabited the place. I masturbated that first night with a photo of a laughing, handsome Michael Lanier before me. What would it have been like with him in person? Then I cried myself to sleep, waking once in the night to the eerie feeling of a presence in the room. Unafraid, I grinned lazily into the inky darkness and went back to sleep.

I used the Laniers' canoe to visit everyone on the beautiful mountain lake, finding lots of handsome people, but none I could picture as the "silver-footed king." Gradually, I wormed my way into the heartbeat of the small summer community to pursue my quest. I met a girl whose folks probably saved me from starvation since I'm not much of a cook. Julie was fun and knew all the summer folks. On the second Monday of my stay, I gnawed barbecued ribs in a lawn swing.

"You've met everyone," she said, a little exasperated that I seemed more interested in others. "Except Sam, of course."

"Sam?" I asked, my ears pricking up.

"Sam Pritchard. He lives here year-round and takes care of a lot of the cabins over the winter. He always goes to visit his dad for a week or so after most of the summer folks arrive. He's everybody's handyman. Most of us can't even turn on our own water pumps, much less repair them."

"Doesn't sound like my guy." I settled back in the swing.

"Your guy? You're looking for someone in particular?"

"Just someone who was friends with Mike."

"Mike was friends with everyone," she said dismissively.

I smiled and changed the subject. It was easy—we just talked about Julie.

Meeting this errant caretaker proved no problem at all. The next morning, as I was trying to fry my third egg over easy without turning the yolk into something like dried plaster, a noise drew me to the front of the cabin. Who in the hell could that be? I opened the door and stood face to face with Mike's Artemis. An easy six feet of handsome young man in his mid 20s stood with an expectant smile on his slender face. Slate-gray eyes crinkled with his grin; hair the color of pale smoke floated about his crown. His greeting faltered as he faced a stranger on the threshold. I rescued him.

"The Laniers loaned me the cabin for a couple of weeks."

"You must be Mike's friend Mitchell," he said, rubbing a broad hand on his pant leg before offering it to me. "I'm Sam Pritchard."

I accepted the hand. It was strong but ordinary until I remembered it had touched Mike in private ways, and then it vibrated with secret life.

"Yeah, I'm Mitch George. Nice to meet you. Come on in. I'm trying to cook an egg without turning it into a piece of vulcanized rubber."

He laughed, a sound like the ring of good sterling. Mike's "silver-footed king." "I'm not a bad cook if you want me to try," he volunteered.

What was it about this young man that drew my boyhood friend in a way he could not share with me? I saw a handsome man full of grace and masculine mannerisms, certainly nothing that would betray him as...deviant. Then, as he turned and handed me my plate with a flourish, I saw it. He brimmed with a sultry sexiness uncommon in a male, at least to another male. He was so physical that the eye was drawn to the firm flesh beneath his T-shirt, to his thighs, his flat belly. That fine framework of chest and shoulders would have sent Mike flying to his notebooks to record its magnificence.

"You still miss him?" Sam's baritone broke the spell.

"More than I can express."

"Yeah, me too. Mike was something else."

I swallowed hard. "Apparently." Shit! Couldn't I say anything right? Mike would have laughed and said I'd lost my ability to communicate. He'd have been right.

"You're just like I thought you would be, Sunshine," he observed, pulling me halfway out of my chair. "Sorry," he apologized immediately, "but that's what he called you. It used to be Sunshine this and Sunshine that. I envied you sometimes."

"We were friends forever," I said with a little hostility.

"I know. He loved you, Mitch. Can I call you Mitch?"

I shrugged. "I thought he was my closest friend too. Until he gave me this." Watching him closely, I opened the binder to Mike's poem and handed it over. Sam read it twice without comment.

"You know what it means?" he asked at last.

"Of course I know!" I snapped. "It means my best friend got with another guy. *Got* with another guy."

He looked at me sadly. "He would rather it had been you." Sam paused. "You came here to find me, didn't you? To find Luna. Well, that's me, and I'm not ashamed to admit it. He was a beautiful person, and I'm honored he accepted me as your substitute."

My anger fell away as I realized the utter truth of those words. "How...how did it happen? How come...how come..."

"How come he didn't approach you?" Sam sat opposite me at the table and glanced at the forgotten eggs. "Maybe he did, but you just didn't know it. Maybe because he was afraid you'd reject him. He told me how he felt about you, Mitch. Right from the start, he warned me that if you ever lifted a finger, he'd be gone in a flash. I worried about it; isn't that a laugh? I worried you'd take him. I never thought of something else snatching him from both of us."

"Tell me how it happened, Sam. I need to know." He gave me an unconsciously smoldering gaze from beneath his brows. I could understand how he'd fired Mike to fever pitch.

He smoothed the light sprinkling of fine hair on the back of his hand as he considered my request. "We went boating up at the headwaters of the lake. Spent the night. I was cleaning up after a long day of rowing. He'd already taken a bath in the lake while I cleaned our mess gear. I caught him staring at me. I could see what he was thinking, read it right on his face."

Sam studied me again with those strange eyes before continuing. "I don't know how to say this right, but it was like a beautiful girl was sitting there inviting me to come over. I know, I know! Mike wasn't girlish or effeminate. But there was a quality about him that let me forget he was a boy. And after the first time, it didn't matter."

"We jacked off together," I blurted, not quite sure what that had to do with anything.

"I know. He told me. He always hoped you'd do it again. He claimed that would have been enough for him." Sam paused a long moment. "But it wouldn't. He'd have wanted more from you. And he didn't think you could give it."

"But you could."

"I did," he answered simply.

"He accepted your 'molten, milk-white nimbus,' and even a jerk like me knows that means your semen." A pain shot through me. "Where did you give it to him?" I demanded.

"Do you really want to know?" I sat frozen, so he proceeded. "All right. I went over to him and pulled him to his feet. The blanket he was wearing fell away, and we were both naked. I kissed him."

"Jeez," I started to protest.

"Then he went down on his knees and did something beautiful. He took me in his mouth until I came. And it was the greatest, grandest orgasm I'd ever had. And that night I gave it to him another way. It was even more magnificent. I've heard of ecstasy all my life; I never knew what it was until then. And I've screwed my share of girls, Mitchell George."

I sat mute, eyes closed, seeking a mental image of my handsome, dead friend. "I'm jealous," I admitted slowly. "Jealous that he couldn't look at me like that. No, that's not right. Pissed off because he did, and I was so fucking dumb I didn't know it. I wish he was here so I could apologize for being so blind."

"You were his sun, Mitch. And I'm damn proud to have been his moon. Talk about jealous? Man, I envy you all those years with him. I only had him as a friend for three and as a lover for one short summer." He paused again, studying me beneath those fine, arched brows. "Do you think any less of him?"

"God, no!"

"Good!" he said emphatically. Rising, he glanced at my untouched plate and was gone.

I had what I came for and should have left, but I didn't. Mike wasn't finished with me yet. I beat my meat again that afternoon, picturing my Mike kneeling before Sam and prostrating himself beneath the handsome young man. In the throes of my orgasm, I achieved a modicum of understanding. I whispered my friend's name until it was over.

The next day I started early, striking out across the lake in the canoe. Near the headwaters of the lake I found an obvious camping spot. Beaching the boat, I sat in the sand and imagined this as the place where they consummated their love. And it *was* love, because Mike wouldn't go down or bend over for just anybody, even if he was looking for a substitute for me. I suspected Sam Pritchard wasn't a guy who stuck his cock in strange places indiscriminately either. I grew hard at the thought of the two of them together.

On my return trip, a boat with a small Mercury motor mounted on the rear intercepted me half a mile from the Lanier dock. Sam Pritchard killed his motor and glided to my side, grasping the canoe as he drifted past.

"I need an answer, Sam," I said by way of greeting. A quick frown marred the features of an Adonis. How about that? Apollo and Adonis facing one another in the middle of a lake. "Why did he come to you instead of me?"

"I already told you—"

"He knew me, Sam. We talked about everything under the sun. We talked about sex and doing it to girls, and hell, we even jacked off together. He wasn't afraid of me. He could have said anything he wanted to me. He knew that."

Sam adjusted his Bronco cap over the smoke that he called hair to shade his eyes better. "Yes, he did. He knew he could approach you, but he was afraid to risk your special friendship."

"Then why did he give me the poem?"

"Because he knew he was going and needed you to understand him...his true feelings. If you didn't know how he felt, then you didn't really know him, and he couldn't abide that."

"I wish he'd told me himself," I said fiercely, my voice ringing across the quiet lake.

"What would you have done?"

I looked into those slate eyes. "Anything he wanted!"

"It's easy to see why he thought about you the way he did," Sam said in a strange voice.

"Man, don't go weird on me. I'm getting kinda squirrelly myself."

Sam chuckled, and we sat there, boats rocking while birds wheeled overhead and the fishes swam beneath us and wildlife grazed along the shore. Finally, I spoke.

"Help me, Sam. Help me understand."

He shook his head. "You don't know what you're asking."

"No, but I'm asking anyway. Help me, Sam."

He removed his cap and rubbed a hand over his eyes. Then he seated the cap firmly. "I wouldn't know how. Mike was different, receptive, I guess you'd say. But you're everything society ever preached about being a man. If I showed you a hard cock, you'd haul off and slug me, but you're not about to lie down for me." He pulled on the cord three times before the outboard kicked over. "Sorry, man, wish I could help."

I had trouble sleeping that night, so I took a blanket out on the porch and claimed a rocker. It was pleasant, peaceful. I'm not sure when I realized someone or something was there, but the hair rose on my neck just before he spoke.

"Couldn't sleep either, huh?" Sam Pritchard stood at the end of the steps.

"Nah. Too much going on in my head. You?"

"I got to thinking over what we talked about. Maybe there is a way to help you. Like you and Mike did it that time, except I can do it for you."

"You'd do that?"

He seemed to need to explain himself. "When I was younger, my best friend and I went hunting. Somehow we ended up fooling around. We did it a few times after that. Then we grew out of it, or at least he did. I guess I never really stopped looking for somebody else to do it with, and when I saw Mike I knew he was the one. Now you know about me."

"How about Mike? Had he done it with a guy before?"

"No. He just *dreamed* about doing it with a guy."

I think I flushed; it was an indictment of sorts. "I didn't know, Sam. I swear I didn't."

"I believe you. Otherwise you wouldn't be out here floundering around like you are."

"Was it good? With Mike, I mean?"

"Yeah. The best. For him too, even if I wasn't the one he wanted."

Going inside the cabin with Sam was one of the hardest things I've ever done. It went against everything I was brought up to believe. This was sin, perversion. It wasn't spontaneous like that one time with Mike; this was cold-blooded and deliberate. But that didn't matter; I was going to find out something tonight regardless of the consequences. I snapped off the light in the bedroom as we undressed. I slipped onto the bed and lay on my back, flinching when his hand touched my chest.

"Didn't mean to startle you," he said easily as he lay down. The room was dark, but I could faintly make him out beside me. "Are you sure about this, Mitch?"

"Yeah," I replied with feigned confidence. Did Sam sense another presence in the room as I did?

His hand gently caressed my chest, fingering the light hair. "Good muscles. I can tell you're a jock." A finger caught a nipple, causing me to jump again. He took it between two fingers and kneaded it lightly. "Well, that stood up, OK," he laughed. I felt the silent chuckle of another in the room. Sam continued his gentle stroking, moving to my belly. "You're a good-looking, sexy guy," he whispered.

"So are you," I responded without thinking. Then he almost spooked me. He threw one leg over mine, his groin unnaturally hot against me.

"It's all right. Just getting comfortable. Not making a move on you."

"Better not," I warned. Suddenly, we laughed aloud. Here we were buck-naked with the guy working his way down to my cock, and I'm telling him not to try anything.

Then he stroked me a few times before abandoning my cock to hold my sac in his hand, sort of kneading the balls like marbles. I'll have to admit that I felt that a little. My cock moved. Slowly, patiently, Sam coaxed me to life. His cock throbbed urgently against my thigh. He'd gotten hard just playing with me, like I would fooling around with a girl. Then I was there. Hard as a rock. He murmured approval and slowly began stroking the length of it.

"Close your eyes, Mitch. Pretend this is Mike. I'm doing it for him. This is *his* hand making you feel things. Remember jerking off with him and imagine he reached over and took hold of you. This is his hand, Mitch. He's masturbating you."

My cock grew as he talked. His hips moved gently, his hot, pulsating cock rode my leg. I didn't care. I just wanted him to keep pumping me. His chest was against my arm; his flesh seared me. Nerve ends sparked; my legs twitched.

"Oh, man!" I groaned and pulled him on top of me. His cock rested on my belly, mine thrust against his. I wrapped my legs around his butt and humped, fucking his flat, hard abdomen. He thrust back at me. His balls rubbed against my own, adding to the sensory excitement. I experienced his strength, his manliness, his beauty.

His lips found mine; his tongue invaded my mouth. I groaned again and erupted. My energy should have electrocuted him. Nerves discharged, wracking my body and sending my muscles into spasms. I groaned into his mouth. My come spewed all over us and dribbled down onto the mattress. "Oh, Artemis!" I mumbled through my exquisite torment.

His own explosion came. His muscles trembled, contracted, danced as his release flooded us with semen. "Helios!" he replied softly.

I expected embarrassment and shame in the aftermath, but they never showed their faces. I was comfortable with his weight on me, and I sensed he was in no hurry to disengage. Finally, he lifted his head and peered through the darkness.

"Awesome, huh?"

"More than I expected," I admitted.

"Next time will be better."

"Is there going to be a next time?"

"There will be if you let me stay the night. Will you take a shower with me? I want to see you in the flesh."

We showered, and he stayed. I don't know how to describe

what happened afterward because I don't understand *why* it happened. But it did. He took my cock in his mouth and accepted my seed. And then I shed my prejudices and took his. He was a man, and I was a man, and we did man things to one another. I learned to like his "molten, milk-white nimbus" and he declared mine to be absolute ambrosia.

The presence was still with us, and I could picture Mike's shy, engaging grin of approval. The sun had found the moon by the dying light of a Venus extinguished forever. And each would be eternally grateful to that beautiful young man we both so deeply loved.

KISSING FISTS

Scott D. Pomfret

A surveying stake marked the border between the back yard and the sea wall. A white chum bucket hung from the railing of a bleached staircase that dropped down to a narrow strip of beach below.

"You like?" Suzanne asked. She was lying swaddled in white beach towels in a deck chair pulled close to the sea wall. A straw sun hat and large sunglasses shaded her face.

"I expected something different," Alan said. He glanced back at the cottage she had rented. "Something more Yankee and austere. You know what I mean?"

"You're disappointed."

"No, no, not at all. I'm just saying, check out the neighbors' mailboxes—it's like a passenger list from the Mayflower: Cabot, Lodge, Moor. I'm surprised they even let an Irish girl like yourself in here."

He lifted her sun hat and removed her sunglasses and kissed her forehead. She was thinner than she had been, and ghostly pale. The still, fixed look of resignation that came over her features made her look older than she was.

"They know I'm not here long," she said.

"How're you doing?"

"Don't sit there!"

Alan jumped up. "Why not?"

"Allison goes there. You're on my right."

"We have assigned seats?"

"I've got it all arranged," she said. "Wayne's going to take that one, next to you. He's still sleeping."

Alan sat in the deck chair she had assigned to him, and Suzy looked relieved.

"Are you sure you're OK?"

"I'm perfect," she said. "Just perfect! And you've now official-ly used up your allotted expressions of sympathy. Not one more goddamn word about my health, got it?"

"Deal."

"Don't look so relieved."

"I'm not…"

"Bullshit. But I'm glad you're here." She smiled affectionate-ly, leaned closer, and dropped her voice. She said, "Enough about that. Let me tell you about Allison. Her husband just dumped her. No warning at all. He said he didn't want their life any more."

"Affair?"

"Yeah, but he said that wasn't why he left. Anyhow, I just thought you should know, because she's in about the same place as you. She needs to decide what to do with the rest of her life."

"Same place as me? Yeah, except that I'm a gale, average-look-ing, 39-year-old copy writer with a steady boyfriend, who's strug-gling to make ends meet, and Allison's one of those beautiful, improbably flat stomached, newly single Manhattanites with two children, a nanny, a four-bedroom apartment on the upper east side, and no visible consequences of childbirth on her whole body."

"Gale?"

"I meant gay male."

"And *I* meant that you've got to decide…"

"I know what *you* meant."

"Did I tell you I'm glad you're here?"

"You must be getting soft in your old age."

Allison arrived just after noon. She emerged from the cottage lugging a giant plastic beach bag and surrounded her assigned seat with supermarket checkout magazines, a pair of sunglasses, a tennis visor, an absurdly small cell phone, three colors of nail polish, a bottle of bright green aloe that looked too cheap, and a slender tube of sunscreen with gilt lettering that looked too expensive. Straddling her deck chair, she stared at her belongings as if she had forgotten something immensely important. She turned to Alan. She asked bluntly whether he would mind if she sunbathed in the nude.

Alan swallowed hard. In his view, there were certain things in this world a gay man should really not have to be exposed to. The prospect of seeing Allison's breasts completely skeeved him out.

"What about Wayne?" Alan asked.

"Wayne's asleep."

Alan glanced suspiciously at the cottage. "I don't trust him. Wayne's the kind of guy who watches women solely to demonstrate to other men that he watches women. Even with me, Wayne wants to be mistaken for what he's not: a man who appreciates a lovely set of ta-tas."

"You're don't appreciate ta-tas?" Allison asked.

"You have lovely ta-tas, I'm sure, Allison."

"Thank you," she said. She shed her top, which gave Alan a strange feeling of vulnerability, as if he ought to throw a wet blanket over her breasts the way you'd douse a fire.

"I worship them," he said. "From a respectful distance, of course."

They laughed.

"In any case, I certainly appreciate my *boyfriend's* ta-tas."

"Those aren't *real* ta-tas," Suzy grumbled.

"What's your boyfriend's name?" Allison asked.

"Gar."

"Gar? That's…kind of ugly."

"It's short for Garfield."

"Like the cat!"

"Uh…no. He's a distant relative of the president."

"Bush?" interjected Suzy.

"Not *that* president. President Garfield. Gar's parents were confirmed Yankees."

This explanation drew a blank stare.

"Why's he not spending the week with us on the Cape?" Allison asked.

Alan shrugged. He was uncomfortable talking about Gar in his absence. To Alan, that was the definition of cheating. His motto was "Fuck anyone you want, Gar—just don't get personal behind my back." On account of this attitude, Gar regularly accused Alan of intellectualizing infidelity, which, in Gar's view, was an obvious strategy for making cheating easier to countenance and therefore more likely. Arguing over infidelities they were not having, Alan reflected, had become a regular parlor game.

"No, really," Allison persisted. "Why's Gar not here? I mean, the rest of us…"

"We have an arrangement," Alan explained. "I've got 10 years on him, so I've built up more vacation time. That means I get to go off on my own sometimes."

Allison's skeptical response to the arrangement was drowned out by a handsome, shirtless boy on a riding mower, who cut circles in the lawn about 10 feet away.

"Unlike Wayne," Alan shouted, "*he* actually likes ta-tas."

"Would you say he's cute?" Allison shouted back.

"He's, like, 14!" Suzy objected.

"Oh. You think? I guess I can't trust my own judgment anymore."

Allison rolled over on to her stomach. The boy immediately drove off toward the side lawn.

"I think I scared the kid off," Wayne announced, lumbering down from the house. Alan wondered if Wayne had heard what he said about him, but Wayne was intent on the lawn boy. He was tabulating every inch of the kid's skin, every limb. The expression on his face said: *So this is what cute is. This is what gay guys and women think is cute.* When Wayne turned back to the rest of the group, there was a certain pride in his features, as if he had mastered advanced calculus.

"Look at the cormorants!" Suzy cried. A pair had perched on pilings at the end of the jetty that stuck out from the seawall. "God, they're ugly. Swim out there, Alan, and see if they're ugly."

"I can see they're ugly from here."

"Swim out there. For me. Please."

Alan did as he was told. Up close, the cormorants' faces were drawn, their eyes suspicious. Their black feet looked like thin arms in leather driving gloves drawn up to the elbow.

"They're ugly," Alan confirmed, "in an elegant sort of way."

Suzy was pleased. She said, "I may be dying, but *my* judgment is just fine."

"You're not dying, Suzanne," they all said at once.

"Shut up."

"So, Alan," Allison said. "Back to business. How do you know Gar's the right one for you?"

"He makes me laugh."

"*I* make you laugh," Suzy volunteered.

"Yes, but unfortunately, Suz, you have boobs and no penis."

"What's wrong with boobs?" Allison asked. "You just said mine were lovely."

"More important," Suzy added, "what's wrong with *my* boobs?"

"And is that enough to sustain a relationship?" Allison persisted.

"What? Boobs?"

"That he makes you laugh?"

"What is this?" Alan asked. "All the people with wombs are going to gang up on me? Wayne, help me out here."

Wayne looked up from the sheaf of legal briefs he had bought with him. "I'm the last person to ask about what sustains a relationship," he said. "I thought it was hot sex."

The women groaned.

"Are you sure?" Allison asked. She sat up, kneeling in the deck chair and covering her chest with a white towel. "Are you sure it hasn't already slipped away between you and…what's his name again?"

"Gar."

"Gar-bage," said Suzy.

"Easy," Alan warned.

"What?"

"At least I've *got* a boyfriend."

Suzy let loose a four-minute, steady stream of withering invective. She tore down Gar and exposed all his worst qualities and belittled any surviving attributes until there was no other possible conclusion except that, although Suzy might be fucked and alone and dying, she was still better off than Alan ever would be.

Allison looked out at Nantucket Sound. Wayne cleared his throat. Alan tried to decide if this was when he should draw a line in the sand. He had learned over the years to pick his fights and steer clear of gratuitous conflict.

Allison asked quietly, "How can you be sure it's working out?"

"Hot sex," Alan snapped.

"No, seriously," Allison complained.

"Don't mind him," Suzy explained. "He's just pissed at me, that's why he won't give you a straight answer. He's just too much of a pussy to say anything."

"Do you mean it?" Allison asked shyly. "Do you really have hot sex? What do you do?" She seemed to think that if she were given the right sort of instruction, her husband might come back.

"Use your hands," Alan counseled. "No blow job can be all mouth. Cup the balls."

She nodded earnestly, one hand curled around a large imaginary penis, and the other cupped under a generous imaginary scrotum that would easily have contained a pair of grapefruits.

"My God, Allison," Wayne said. "I think you're setting yourself up for disappointment."

Back in 2000, Gar had been just another impossibly gorgeous, smooth-chested, pouting pretty boy a decade younger than Alan, who had initiated their encounter by dropping a five-pound collector's edition of *Leaves of Grass* on Alan's left foot in the gay literature section of the local Borders Books.

"Oh! I didn't see you," Gar had sniffed, his hands all aflutter. His body had struck impossible feline poses suggesting a paucity of bones. He bent over from the waist, thrust his butt in the air, and retrieved the volume with a practiced air. He handed it to Alan like it was his own head on a platter.

"Come home with me, boy," Alan had grunted, "and I'll make all your wildest dreams come true. I am your love slave and you will be my pig bottom."

Except Alan didn't actually utter those words aloud. Instead, some scheming spineless lowlife utterly untrustworthy portion of his brain hijacked his lips and tongue and proposed a much less ambitious, less guttural course of action: "Coffee?"

"Coffee! How about a drink instead?"

"I like to drink!"

"So do I. Maybe we should get married." Gar had flashed Alan a fetching, absurd glance as if at that moment they both knew life was going to turn out exactly the way they planned.

Over the next four years, Alan and Gar discovered other similarities in taste besides drinking. These interludes when they agreed on momentary pleasures were equivalent to little sunsets, except they could happen at any time of day. Their broader philosophies, on the other hand, remained far apart. To Alan, Gar seemed to be resisting any kind of stable, comfortable place in their relationship. There was some inscrutable point Gar was trying to convey by blurring the fixed boundaries and challenging Alan's pieties. They had therefore reached a point of pull-and-tug, where every negotiation (except the hot sex!) felt like a pitched battle over contested space.

"You don't want a boyfriend," Gar often said. "You want a marionette."

Most recently, just before Alan left for the Cape, Gar had launched an all-out campaign against Alan's Catholicism. To counter it, Alan had conceived the idiot notion that it might do Gar some good to meet a real live priest. He had wanted to demonstrate that not all priests were perverts and child molesters, and that Alan's persistent Catholicism—which Gar believed was nothing more than self-hatred and a not-so-secret desire to be punished like a naughty altar boy—was actually a good thing.

Unfortunately, the only priest Alan knew was Father John, and Father John was without question the gayest man Alan had ever met. Still, Alan decided to take the chance, because there was at least something refreshing about Father John's attitude. He always seemed blissfully unaware of his homosexuality, like a little boy who has to be dissuaded from wearing his sister's tutu to school because he does not yet know that it is wrong.

The night of the dinner party, Father John showed up without his Roman collar. It made him look as sleazy as a businessman who removes his wedding ring when he travels.

"Alain!" Father John scolded in French, "I didn't see you at Mass last Sunday." He kissed Alan on the lips.

"Father John, you're amazing. 500 people at Mass, and you can tell with a glance who's been naughty or nice."

"Maybe he's just autistic," Gar suggested. "Maybe it's one of those idiot savant things."

"Father John, this is Gar."

John minced and grinned. He picked cherry tomatoes from the radicchio salad and whispered in Alan's ear, "Where did you meet *him*? He's *gorgeous*."

"What're you two whispering about? You guys plotting to sneak off to the back room to fuck?"

"Sorry, Father. Gar gets off on dropping conversational bombshells."

Father John threw back his head and laughed. Gar looked at the priest with sudden interest. Alan could tell exactly what Gar was thinking: that the priest would be the kind of person who laughed at many of the things Gar said. He would therefore be a welcome guest.

"Do we like priests now?" Alan asked after the dinner party was over.

"I'm sure you like priests," Gar said. "But you're a tortured, delusional Catholic boy who probably played secret hide-the-sausage games in the sacristy. Of *course* you like priests." He squeezed Alan's ass playfully.

"Father John liked *you*."

"Yes. But he's gay. They're *all* gay."

"Gar."

"What?"

"That's exactly what I've been talking about."

"What have you been talking about?"

"You making these grand sweeping pronouncements about the way things are without a care in the world for nuance. And then look smug as if you won the argument."

Gar shrugged defiantly and took a large swallow from the wine at his side. He always drank too much just before Alan went on vacation alone. Alan had not yet determined whether it was envy or fear of infidelity or just a plain old garden-variety feeling that distance would put Alan out of Gar's control.

The week on the Cape went by in a regular, mindless rhythm. They steered the conversation away from unfortunate topics like Wayne's Republicanism and Suzy's feelings about Gar and the relative merits of any particular set of ta-tas. They lounged in their assigned deck chairs. They followed the flight of cormorants. They sipped slow summer drinks with crushed ice. Between dozing and reading, they held random conversations about all sorts of safe topics, from Suzy's recent Brazilian to a studied comparison between attractive teenage lawn boys and ugly cormorants. They discussed lunch immediately after breakfast, and cocktails immediately after lunch, and dinner during and immediately after cocktails. Whenever the house phone rang, they looked at one another and laughed and said "Not it."

Then, on Thursday evening, when the four of them were out by the sea wall huddled around a citronella candle, the phone would not stop ringing, and Alan's Catholicism made him feel obliged to answer.

"Hello," he said. "Betty Ford Clinic."

"I'm fine," Gar said. "Absolutely fine. Nobody got hurt."

"What?" He felt as if the middle of his body was being gripped in a fist and squeezed out at either end.

"We like to be fine, don't we?" Gar joked. "We like it when no one gets hurt."

"Gar, what happened?"

Gar and two of their mutual friends had been walking in the South End, near midnight, in the shadow of Boston's old Precinct D police station. Seven young men had been gathered around a parked Boxster in various states of repose. They wore pressed shirts and shoes that gleamed under the streetlight and looked as if they were involved in the mutual fund business.

One of them said, "Hey, faggots. Why don't you go suck each other's cocks?" Others said, "Keep walking, faggots" and "Cocksuckers."

One of Gar's friends was an art director for TJ Maxx named

Tim. Tim was about 5 foot 4 in heels. Drawing out each word like toffee, Tim said: "I…am…going…to…fuck…you…up the ass."

The young men surrounded him greedily, but Tim didn't flinch. He repeated: "I…am…going…to…fuck…you…up the ass." He repeated this crazy incantation a third time, and in the end it must have crossed each of the young men's well-bred suburban minds that this diminutive motherfucker might be as crazy as he seemed.

"Go ahead," Tim said. "Go ahead and commit a hate crime. Go ahead and get arrested and taken to jail where *my* fucking you up the ass will be nothing compared to the ass-fucking you pretty little fucks will get in there. Go ahead and commit a hate crime. Lose your jobs. Get your names in the paper. Have your mother come down to the trial each day, weeping when the judge puts you fucks away."

One of the young men swore viciously, climbed into the Boxster, and gunned the engine. The rest muttered curses and stalked off.

Alan said, "Gar, that's crazy. You guys could have been killed." A thousand questions raced through Alan's head. What if Tim had been less persuasive, or these young men had had less to lose? And why was it that seven bored young professional men in the most sophisticated city in the United States would feel license to lash out?

Alan had a sense of a world disintegrating that he could not face. Planets whirling in a dark universe. He had control over nothing. Not his looks. Not his mouth. Not his lover. Not Suzy's disease. Not her choice of friends. He had cultivated this idea that Boston, at least, was safe from the worst of things that could happen to a gay man. And now that too was casually snatched away.

"Don't worry about me. I'll be down tomorrow," Gar promised. There was a persistent innocence in his tone, as if the impossibility of his having escaped unhurt outweighed only slightly the improbability of their having been confronted in the first instance in their own neighborhood. "Just like we planned. Go have fun. I love you."

"I love you too," Gar murmured. He put down the phone. He was exhausted. It was not a day-end exhaustion or the exhaustion of a couple hours' run. It was a lifetime's exhaustion, the sum of every injury or slight or humiliation he had ever endured that related to being gay.

"Who was it?" Suzy asked when Gar rejoined them in the dark out by the seawall.

"Gar."

"Oh."

"What's up, guy?" Wayne asked.

Alan repeated Gar's story.

"What difference does it make that some jerk called him a faggot?" Allison snapped. "Why do you guys care?"

"I guess I don't care," Alan said. "But I know *he* cares. That's what counts."

Wayne murmured, "You can't let that shit go."

He stretched out a fist and Alan too made a fist. They knocked fists, knuckle to knuckle. *Kissing fists,* Alan thought. And was instinctively dismayed: *What a faggot thing to have thought. "Kissing fists"—no wonder we end up getting the shit kicked out of us.* He laughed and didn't know why.

He said, "This is how a gay man goes through every second of his life: constantly walking this gauntlet. Outmanned. Humiliated. Every fucking day. On the defensive."

The light of the candle briefly lit Suzy's face.

"Being gay…" He trailed off, for a moment forgetting what it was he had meant to say. He shook his head. "You can't win."

Wayne opened his mouth to speak, but Alan turned on him.

"Fuck you, Wayne," he said. He was furious that he had not defended Gar on that first day when Suzy insulted him. He was furious that Wayne and Allison had witnessed it. He hated himself for not having Tim's courage. "I should be able to go through life without having to deal with this bullshit. Without fearing that at any moment the person I love is in constant danger and there's not jack-shit I can do about it."

"Don't be such a child," Suzanne said sternly. "Everyone lives that way."

"You don't know how we live, Suzanne. You can't even *conceive* of it."

The three of them stared back at him. The wild blueberry bush shivered. Beach grass danced at the fringe of the yard, and the ocean rushed in and out like the breaths of a ventilator. Alan savored the ugly little triumph of their silence, and then he stalked off and lay in bed, scalded. He tried to picture what the bullies had said to one another as they walked away from Gar and Tim. He wanted to speak to the young men and understand their motivations. Father John would want him to do this, to be generous. Maybe they would be converted and go home and kiss their mothers and marry the girl next door and no longer oppose same-sex marriage. Alan prayed that would happen, but for the first time he felt that Gar was right—prayer was just a way to create the illusion of control.

After the last footstep had sounded in the hall and the house lights were out, Alan packed his bags and stole through the darkened house, intending to drive back to Boston. He tripped a power cord to a lamp, which flashed blue. Wayne was sitting alone in the dark, facing the sea. He said, "Makes you feel puny, doesn't it?"

By the time Alan woke, Wayne and Allison had set off on a field trip to the Lower Cape. Suzanne was out in her deck chair, groping herself beneath her shirt.

"What in God's name are you doing?"

"I think I've got a lump. Feel this, is that a lump?"

Alan gingerly poked at her breast with his index finger.

"Don't just *poke* it," she snapped. "*Feel* it. It's not going to kill you to feel a tit." She forced his palm around her breast. "What do you think?"

"I think the whole thing feels like one great big lump."

Suzy frowned.

"I wish Gar would get here," Alan said, glancing at his watch.

"Is my breast cancer boring you?"

Alan smiled grimly. "Come on," he suggested. "Let's go for a swim. You haven't been in once."

"I don't think so."

"C'mon! I'll hold you up."

An emotion Alan could not read crossed Suzy's face and then she gave in. She removed her robe and her sunglasses and the towel that turbaned her head. She removed the socks she was wearing and the flannel pants and the T-shirt. Under all the layers, Suzanne was wearing La Perla lingerie, as if despite the illness she was determined to feel sexy. Alan led her down the bleached wooden steps to the beach. Cape Cod Sound was calm as a lake. They waded in.

"They *are* ugly!" Suzanne exclaimed, pointing. The cormorants were unsettled by her voice, and opened their black wings.

"I told you they were ugly."

"Hold on to me," she demanded.

He held her. He had forgotten how small women's bodies were. He yearned for Gar's body, its solidity and weight and beauty.

"Hold on to me," she said again.

"It's salt water. It'll hold you up, if you let it. Unlike fresh water, you know?"

"I guess it's not salty enough. The Dead Sea, now maybe *that* would do it."

"You're not dying."

Suzanne gave him a short, pinched, reproachful look. She said, "I think that's enough for today."

Dripping, they climbed the bleached ladder to the top of the sea wall. Suzy put a hand out to the railing to steady herself and knocked the chum bucket from its place. Rainwater, sand, and something unspeakable spilled out into the grass.

Gar swept into the house precisely at seven o'clock. He had been sitting in traffic and listening to NPR and boiling over at the coverage of the Vatican.

"Did you hear the latest about your precious church?" he fumed. "They're saying that the Vatican's going to issue a rule barring gays from the priesthood? Can you imagine? There goes your calling, sweetheart. How's that for a kick in the pants? Those guys don't know what side they're—"

He interrupted himself for a kiss, and then seemed to think

that was not enough. He leaped into Alan's arms. Alan caught him and pressed him back against the door frame. He ran a feverish hand over Gar's body as if he was searching for wounds. Alan was unreasonably, disproportionately, embarrassingly thrilled to see Gar. He felt vulnerable and shy and indulgent and acutely conscious that this overpowering gratitude might be a direct route to further humiliation.

"I missed you," Gar said. "Did I dream it, or did some handsome devil come and ravish me one of those nights you were away?"

Alan grinned sheepishly. On the first night in Truro, spooked by Allison's hounding, Alan had driven all the way back to Boston well after midnight. Gar had been asleep, his bare shoulder exposed, his hair matted. He had been too sleepy for some smart comeback or a joke. He had tested a smile, and when Alan responded, it had spread over Gar's face.

"Stealth love," Alan quipped.

Gar grinned from ear to ear. "We like stealth love."

They stared at one another stupidly. Their affection was as thick as chrism.

Suzy said, "Stealth love sure beats no love at all. Believe me, I know."

"Suzanne," Gar said guardedly, stiffening visibly.

"Gar."

"Ketel One dirty martini up olives?" Alan suggested.

"Ketel One dirty martini up olives," Gar confirmed. "We like that."

Gar's momentary stiffness ebbed with administration of the drink. Gar sipped. Feeling Alan watching, he looked up, smiling, his lips still pressed to the glass.

"How about dinner in P-town tonight?" Alan proposed. "I'm having a craving to be in the majority."

"Done."

Provincetown didn't prove to be the sanctuary Alan had hoped for. In fact, predatory men unabashedly cruised Gar even though Alan was standing right by his side. On Commercial Street, a very young, very handsome boy sauntered toward them with a Mona Lisa smile trailing across his lips, as if he still had not decided which of the Provincetown men he was going to please that night.

"You like that?" Alan sneered, when he caught Gar taking a second look.

"Jeez, I was just *looking*."

"You know, Gar, from far away everyone looks pretty. It's only up close you can see how ugly they are."

"Sorry," Gar mumbled, but Alan's mood had soured. He was annoyed to find Commercial Street jammed. Club music flared from a storefront. Someone overturned a trash can for a drum. Another boy rattled a plastic cylinder of dried beans, and somebody knotted a pair of spoons with a rubber band to make castanets. There was a group playing matador using a colored beach towel.

"Oh, fuck," Alan muttered.

"What?"

"Nothing."

Alan felt betrayed: One of the bulls in the matador game was Father John. He was awkward, cherubic, tottering, and having a blast. If Gar set eyes on him, Alan would never hear the end of it.

John and his companion were lost in the melee. A moment later they became visible again, as if they were bobbing in water. John was laughing. He looked at his friend (who was also a priest) and laughed. Then he looked at Alan and laughed, and then at Gar, and then at all the people in the street, laughing all the while.

Directly in front of Alan and Gar, the Mona Lisa boy found a friend—his boyfriend, apparently—a young, equally beautiful boy just his size. They shared a long, drawn-out kiss, which made Alan feel both old and benevolent and preternaturally calm.

"We like to see that," Alan murmured buoyantly. Gar reached for Alan's hand, as Alan had known he would. Gar pulled him close, raised his hand to his lips, and kissed it.

"We like to see that," Gar confirmed, looking into Alan's eyes. They smiled, and their next kiss felt stolen and illicit, like a conspiracy. Before the spell broke, Gar steered Alan off Commercial Street, down toward Bradford where it was quieter and less well lit, hustling Alan safely from the crowd as you might hide a child

from things he really should not have to see.

Queen Beats a Jack

Rob Rosen

Another Friday night and George was alone at home. The thought of putting on his sweats and plopping down on the couch for the third weekend in a row depressed him to no end. He could, of course, call a buddy and go out for a drink somewhere, but he was tired of that option as well. He never tended to meet anybody when he went out with his friends. They usually got laid; he usually ended up by himself and hungover. No, he figured, if he was going to spend the money on a cab and some drinks, he might as well wake up with someone by his side. Slutty, but honest, he felt.

But where to go? He was sure to run into any number of his friends at one of his usual haunts, and then he'd be back to square one. There were, of course, the bars along the river, but he never dared step foot in one of those before. He figured it was generally best to keep with his own kind, namely, yuppie preppy queens. The bars on the other side of town were largely run-down and frequented by quite a different echelon of people, or so he'd always been told.

Still, he figured, gay is gay. Outside of their clothes they all looked about the same. Maybe a bit burlier, but that wasn't such a bad thing. So he called a cab before he could back out of his decision and quickly changed into a pair of Levi's and a white cotton T-shirt. The clone look seemed a safe bet.

Minutes later, he was on his way. He was excited, nervous,

and horny—in no particular order. George rarely did the unconventional thing. It was completely out of character, and his inner circle would have been shocked at his impetuousness. That, however, was what George was going for. He needed a little shock value in his life. A little unpredictability.

And yet, when the cab pulled up to the area where the bars were located, he almost chickened out. After all, what did he know about those sorts of places besides what he saw in the occasional porn movie? He paid the driver and hopped out before he could convince himself otherwise. And then he was standing on a street corner surrounded by vacant warehouses and the dreary gray landscape. The smell of stale urine and the nearby waterfront wafted over him. He breathed in deeply and promptly coughed.

Dorothy, you're not in Kansas anymore, he thought. He whistled a happy tune and tried not to look like a victim, though he didn't actually know what that might look like. He tried scowling instead and kept his head down. He tripped twice but was relieved that the only people who could see him were two guys hustling on the corner.

The first bar he passed was called Stirrups. He had only to hear the twangy country-and-western singing voice resonating from the entrance to know better than to try that one out. A few doors down was Lolita's. He popped his head in, spotted the hodgepodge of trannies and drag divas, and quickly turned right back around. If the point was to get laid, he preferred his date to at least have pants on. Number three was Spikes. Fine, it was a bit run-down and seedy-looking, but at least all the men were dressed similarly to him and they were playing a nice selection of '70s rock and roll. One drink won't hurt. So he steeped all the way in, squinted through the darkness, and found a stool in the back. A minute later a shirtless waiter with tattoos from neck to toe took his drink order.

"Gin and tonic," he asked. Not too butch, but not too nelly either. He figured a daiquiri might be pushing his luck.

The drink arrived, and he felt more secure. He sipped at it and nearly choked. The bartender was stingier with the tonic than what he was used to. Still, he was glad he wasn't sitting at home watching A&E and waiting to fall sleep. He wiped off the spillage from chin and hummed to the music.

Once he grew accustomed to the dim lighting, he scanned the crowd around him. There were perhaps 50 or so other patrons in the bar. All were about his age or older; that is to say, 30 to 50, give or take a few years: a considerably older crowd than at the bars he usually hung out in. There were also many more beards, goatees, and sideburns than he was used to seeing, plus the occasional potbelly. Still, not an awful looking group. *It could be worse,* he imagined.

Actually, he kind of liked the place. The oak paneling, the old lithographs of long-forgotten bars, the casual atmosphere, and the music, which was definitely not the Madonna, Janet, and Beyoncé he usually heard when he went out, all lulled him into a state of bliss, though it might have been because of the strong drink he had already guzzled down.

With round two ordered he started his search for a potential date. He preferred the word "date" to "trick", which painted a cheaper image of himself than he liked. He remembered that scene in *History of the World Part 1* when Madeline Kahn went down the row of naked Roman soldiers, sing-songing, "Yes, yes, no…" Only for George it was, unfortunately, "No, no, no." It wasn't that he was too picky or anything. It was more like he wanted a type and he was sticking to that—not that it had got him very far up to that point, but why rock an already-shaky boat?

Now, George's type was fairly standard: younger than 30, shorter than 5 foot 9, lean, blond, fair, and clean-cut—squeaky clean, for that matter. And no, there was no one at the Spike that even almost resembled that description. George wasn't surprised, but he was a trifle depressed. *OK, maybe I need to expand my horizons a bit.* So again he scanned the crowd, which had grown considerably since he arrived. The Spike, it appeared, was a very popular place.

It was also getting harder to cruise. There was now very little floor space and the crowd was packed in. All George could see were the 20 or so people that surrounded him as he sat on his stool and drank his powerful gin and tonic. That's when he spotted the guy sitting about 10 feet over.

The guy was about George's age, somewhere in his early 30s and clearly taller than George. He had short jet-black hair with sideburns running completely down his jawline, and on his chin was an inch-long goatee. Both his ears were pierced with silver hoops. And his eyes were a piercing crystal blue. He had on jeans and a white tank top and black combat boots. Obviously, nothing about this guy even remotely appeared to be what George would have normally gone for. But then again, nothing was normal about that night. Anyway, there was just something about the stranger that George found instantly attractive.

Sadly, George was not the only one who felt that way. Just as he was about to sidle over and introduce himself, another patron beat him to the punch and started chatting with the guy. *No more prospects on the horizon. I should have stayed home and watched a repeat of* Queer Eye. *Fuck.* But that's when George noticed something that boded well for him. His object of affection definitely wasn't interested in the new pursuer. In fact, it was obvious he was trying to ignore him. Too bad the guy wasn't easily ignored.

The intruder was way over six feet tall and easily weighed in at a good 200 pounds. He wasn't ugly, necessarily, but he was scary-looking as hell. *Intimidating*, George thought. And clearly, he was after the same hottie as George. He kept putting his hand on the guy's shoulder, only to have it repeatedly brushed aside. With each passing minute, it was obvious that the hunter was becoming more insistent and the prey more elusive.

Emboldened by the alcohol, George decided to help out his object of desire. He stood up and casually walked over to where the two men were. "I'm ready to go now," he said to the harassed cutie as he slid between the two men. Both men looked up at George with a confused look on their face, but the man he was after quickly got where George was coming from and played along.

"Oh, OK, sweetie. I'm ready," he said to George, getting up off his stool.

"Wait a minute," said the giant interloper. "Who's this guy?"

George and his new friend looked at each other before the latter answered, "He's my boyfriend."

George nodded and pulled the stranger forward, but the bigger man blocked their way. "How come you didn't say nothing about him before?" he growled.

"Because you didn't ask and because it's none of your business." And George's new partner kept walking forward, pushing the other guy out of the way. He and George walked arm in arm, quickly exiting the bar out into the cool night air.

"Thanks," the stranger said. "That guy was an asshole and a drunk one at that. Sorry you had to leave, though."

"Oh, no sweat," said George. "I was just on my way out anyway. Glad to be of service. Name's George." He offered his hand to the guy.

"Steve," came the response, along with a big, strong hand in return.

The two shook hands, and then Steve turned around and started to head up the sidewalk. "Bye," he said, "and thanks again."

"Sure. Bye," George yelled to him, before he could think of anything else to say—like, *Come home with me. Please.* Or something equally as smooth. But the guy just kept walking and raised his hand over his head to wave a final goodbye. *Damn. Damn. Damn.* George stood there and waited for a cab to pass by. *Fucking waste of my night and my money.*

Two minutes later a car pulled up in front of him and the window rolled down. "Thought you were headed home," Steve said.

"Waiting for a cab," George replied glumly.

"Hop in. I'll take you home."

Oh, joy! George ran around to the passenger door and hopped in. "Thanks, I appreciate it," he said, slamming the door. "Don't think cabs circle this block too often."

"Not unless they have a death wish. So where are we headed?" Steve asked, as he turned to look at George. Those searing blue eyes nearly burned a hole right through him, but George kept his cool and told him where he lived. Too bad that's when fate stepped its ugly head in, fate being the unwanted pursuer from mere minutes before, who quite literally stuck his menacing head into Steve's window and grabbed him by his tank top.

"Hey, I'm not through with you yet," he shouted and slurred, as he yanked Steve's head up toward the open window.

Both Steve and George were caught off-guard, thinking they were done with the guy for good. And with Steve pressed hard up against the door, only George could intervene. He looked around the car for something—anything—that would detach the guy's hand from Steve's shirt. But all Steve had lying around was some CDs. *Hey, that might work.* Quickly, George popped open one of the jewel cases, removed the CD, and slashed across the intruder's wrist. The guy looked pissed, but otherwise whole.

Steve started pounding on the guy's arms, but the guy still wouldn't let go. He just kept pulling on the shirt as if he meant to pull Steve right through the window. Luckily, they don't make tank tops like they used to. A couple more seconds of yanking and the thing finally gave way and ripped right off Steve's body, sending the maniac toppling backward. He landed hard on the sidewalk with the ripped shirt still in his hand. Steve took advantage of his newly found freedom and put the car in gear. They sped away, leaving the asshole in a cloud of dust.

"You OK?" George asked.

"Um…I think so," Steve responded, but he clearly sounded shaken. "By the way, I think they purposely make those CDs kinda blunt so you can't cut yourself with them. But nice try."

George blushed and giggled a bit.

"Yeah, real funny," Steve said.

"No, not that. It's just that I looked at the CD I tried to cut him with…"

"And?"

"And it's Britney Spears." George giggled again and popped the CD in.

Steve relaxed at the wheel and started to laugh a bit as well. "Yeah, well, it's a good CD, just not for slitting people's wrists with."

"Apparently not." And George broke out into hearty laughter, which was promptly cut short when he spotted something in the passenger mirror, or rather, someone. "Um, don't look now, Steve, but I think we're being followed."

Steve glanced up at the rearview mirror and said, "Uh-oh. Fucker's right on our ass. Some people just can't take a hint."

"Maybe he wants to return your shirt," George said, glancing over at Steve, whom he hadn't looked at until that moment. *Man, he looks yummy. Just look at that hard, hairy chest.* "What are you gonna do?"

"Dunno. We could pull over and reason with him, or we could try to outrun him."

"I say we crank up the Britney and opt for plan B." George even surprised himself with that one.

Steve turned to face George and cracked a grin. "Plan B it is then." And they were off, with Britney blaring from the speakers.

Too bad an '87 Impala can't even begin to outrun a '99 BMW. Their pursuer was clearly an asshole with a nice taste in cars. Within seconds, George and Steve felt him ramming their rear bumper. "Goddamn it!" Steve shouted. George held on tight to the passenger door and silently said a prayer. Apparently, no one was listening. The final ram bumped them clean off the road.

"Run and get help, George!" Steve shouted.

"No. I'm staying here and helping you."

"Look, I can handle this guy. But just in case, you should run back to one of the bars and get some help."

George thought about what Steve was saying. *Perhaps he's right. But what if I don't make it back in time? I suppose I should at least try.* "OK. I'll run. Good luck." Impulsively, he reached over and gave Steve a kiss on the lips. *Man, he tastes as good as he looks.* "I'll run real fast!" And he opened the door, ran across the street, and sped around the fucker and back the way they had just come.

He stopped when he had run about 100 yards and turned around to see what was happening back at the car. Mr. Nasty was pounding his fists on Steve's window and shouting for him to get out of the car. Wisely, Steve appeared to be staying put. Still, George thought, *What if the glass held like the shirt?* Within minutes, Steve could be at the mercy of the lunatic. George couldn't let that happen. And it wasn't just about getting laid anymore. *Well, maybe a little.*

George turned around and headed back toward the two cars. The asshole had his door flung open, so on impulse George snuck over to that car. He crouched down and slid inside. Neither Steve nor his attacker noticed. George checked the ignition for the keys, but apparently the jerk had left something even more valuable behind.

"Bingo," George said, after flipping through his find. Then he smirked and honked the horn three times. The drunken marauder stopped his pounding and looked back toward his car. He wasn't the least bit happy seeing George sitting in his driver's seat.

"Get the fuck out of my car!" he shouted.

George responded by honking the horn again. That further enraged the man. He kicked Steve's car and started to lumber over to George. He stopped dead in his tracks when he spotted what George was waving out the window. A look of absolute terror spread across his nasty face. He raised his hands in the air, as if to say stop, and backed up a couple of feet.

"Move over to the other side of the road," George commanded from the car as he got out.

"Sure, sure," the man said, obeying the order.

"Now, get down on the ground," George shouted as he moved toward Steve's car. The man quickly fell to the ground. George ran over to Steve's car and shouted one final thing to the man on the ground. "We'll mail this back to you. If you follow us, you'll be sorry." And with that he hopped into Steve's car, slammed the door behind him, and hollered, "Go!"

"Yes, sir," Steve said, with a new sense of awe in his voice. When he had driven about a mile he asked, "So, what've you got there?"

"The wallet of one Mr. Jack Savoy: age, 42; from Minneapolis, Minnesota; 6 feet 4 inches,180 pounds. He must have put on some weight since he got his driver's license."

"Apparently. Guess he was ashamed of it, judging from what just happened back there. Here, let me see that." Steve took the wallet from George's hands. "Not very photogenic."

"Nope. Look through those other photos," George giggled and once again turned up the music.

"Ah, nice. Don't suppose his wife and kids would have been to happy to see old Jack at the Spike tonight."

"That makes five of us," George said, though he was sure thrilled that he had made it to the Spike that night despite the unusual turn of events. Now he just had one more thing to accomplish to make his evening complete. "Um, Steve, would you like to go back to my place and borrow a shirt."

"Hmm, I was thinking of going back to your place and taking off the rest of my clothes—that is, if you don't mind."

"Can we bring the Britney CD up with us?"

"Hey, why break up the team, right?" Steve reached over and put his hand in George's.

"Good point." George squeezed Steve's hand and started to giggle again.

"Now what's so funny?" Steve asked.

"Oh, nothing. I was just thinking about poor Jack back there."

"Poor Jack? Why's he poor? Because you have his wallet?"

"Well, yes. That and…these."

Steve looked over and echoed George's laughter with his own. "You're one sick motherfucker, George. Where have you been all my life?"

"Guess I've been hanging out in the wrong bars, Steve," George said and cranked up the stereo just before he threw Jack's car keys out the window. "But not anymore. Not anymore."

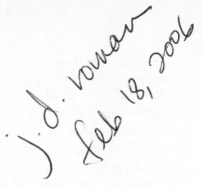

FRIGID

J.D. Roman

The door creaked opened. A waterlogged gust of wind stirred napkins, cigarette ashes, and the out-of-date opera posters sagging off the walls—*Faust* buckled at the knees. The breeze crept across the room, whispering behind the bar to flutter Simon's soiled apron. Like a wave rippling calm seas when a magnificent creature breaks the surface, Simon thought, working the beer tap. Or, long ago, like Simon's hands through Wray's scythed wheat- field hair, tremors trailing his squat fingers through the stiff yellow shocks.

The sound of rain slapping the pavement fought with the jukebox, which was heaving out an aria from the opera *Rusalka*. Simon played the mermaid's aria whenever he was in his most melancholy moods. Surf pounded the nearby seashore, booming thunder.

A man stepped across the threshold, tossing wet hair out of his face. Topher dropped his busboy's tray. Shattered glass slashed an eerie silence into the night. The closing door choked off the hammering rain and fisted ocean waves. *Rusalka* fell mute.

"We're closed!" Simon scowled at Topher. Laugh lines furrowed around his eyes told a different tale from his now rare smile. "I told you to lock the door."

"I did! I swear! Maybe the lock's busted, like everything else around here."

130

The stranger doffed his sunglasses and swept his gaze across the room, a lighthouse beacon that settled on Simon.

Topher reached behind Simon for the broom. "Do you have any idea who that is?" he hissed. "Sell one photo of him in a gay bar to the tabloids and you'd pay off what you owe on this place. Maybe then my next paycheck wouldn't bounce."

Simon could believe the stranger was no ordinary nine-to-fiver. He possessed the fuck-you beauty that lurked behind Holocaust-gaunt fashion models dressed in savage clothing. Tonight's few customers had scampered in like drowning rodents, but this one didn't scurry. It would take more than acid rain to corrode the chiseled alabaster of this face. A little assault of nature beckoned lesser mortals to hand him a towel and park him before a fire, knowing he'd give you nothing but muddy boots to clean.

Beguiling. Bewitching. But not gay. And yet...something pulsed across the room between them, a careening butterfly of current. "Sorry, closed!" Simon repeated, dousing the electric snap the stranger flicked at him. He sopped up the beer he'd let overflow its glass, a well-earned drink for himself after enduring yet another day. "Time for bed."

The stranger perched his sunglasses on his head.

"Don't blow this, Simon." Glass tinkled as Topher swept and whispered, "Either be nice and make friends with his deep pockets, or..." He nodded at the security surveillance camera. "The more compromising the pose, the more it'll fetch."

Sunglasses in the rain past 3 A.M.—Simon had little patience for such displays of self-importance. "Don't stand there dripping unless you want to mop it up."

Topher threw down the broom. "For once why can't you listen? Give me a call when you can pay me in cash." To the stranger, he called out, "Come right on in and dry yourself off. Simon's got nowhere to be, except nowhere fast. Me, I've got someone waiting. Like Simon said, time for beddie-bye." Topher sashayed to the door. Behind the stranger's back, he threw one last glare at Simon and pointed at the camera. "Have fun, you two." The door closed behind him, and the dead bolt groaned into its socket.

The stranger cocked his head, narrowed his eyes, and crossed the room, taking his time. His boots beat a sensuous rhythm on the plank floor, occasionally missing a beat as he hit a sticky spot. His damp black jeans clung, a greedy second skin. He swung his leg over a barstool in front of Simon, as if climbing on a Harley. He set his sunglasses down—a designer brand that had cost more than Simon's entire wardrobe, but the frame was cracked and bent. His fingers played the bar top, luring Simon under a spell. No rings. No bracelets. No watch. Nothing to detract from the natural grace of his white hands. His fingers never stopped moving, a waterfall of movement working an invisible piano. Occasional slabs of drop-dead beefcake saw the far side of Simon's bar, but this was no Chippendales cookie—something was off-kilter in his bolted eyes. A scratch nicked one cheek. Fine trembling ran through his body. The long fringe of his jacket danced.

"Suede in a downpour." Again, Simon popped the fuse that circled a crackling frisson between them. "Not too bright, I'd say." The expensive coat now looked like rotting seaweed, ensnaring the stranger in tangled tassels. A bluish cast hazed his anemic pallor. Probably an addict in need of a fix.

The stranger's gaze strayed between Simon and his own reflection in the backbar mirror, the crowning glory of Simon's joint. He'd spent months stripping and refinishing the arch of carved mermaids. But dust now caked their sunken eyes, caught in the ash of Simon's caldera. The barebreasted ladies would have sneezed if they were alive.

Simon blew cigarette smoke out of his nose. "You've got the wrong place, pal. Hooters is one street over."

Amusement flirted with the stranger's impassive expression, a fleeting glimmer in his glistening sealskin eyes, pupil blending into iris in the dim light of the bar. No. Just the headlights from a passing car playing tricks through the closed blinds. "Not a breast man, myself."

What a voice. Like the rain itself had come inside to converse. But flat. Emotionless. Out of tune. "Yeah? Well, I doubt you're in the market for what's on tap here."

"Don't be so sure." The stranger held Simon's eyes. His mouth twitched, as if the arched seabird wings of his upper lip might take flight into a smile, but settled back instead on glassy seas. "For starters, I'd settle for a beer. Make that half a beer since I missed last call?"

Simon leaned on the bar, hands splayed flat, beefy arms locked straight at the elbows. He couldn't judge the stranger's years with that unblemished complexion ike porcelain. "Got I.D.?"

"I haven't been carded in years."

"Yeah, so I hear if I didn't have my head stuck in the sand, I'd know who you are, but I stopped paying attention when the Bee Gees fucked up 'Sergeant Pepper's' with a remake. Figured it was all downhill from there. So excuse me if I treat you the same as everyone else—not like 'the Man' needs much reason to shut down a place like this."

"Doesn't look like you'd mind." He ran a finger along the bar edge and held his sooty pinkie up, smudged like he'd been marked for prison fingerprinting.

Simon leaned forward. The stranger's scent hit him—briny, like the sea, or tears, or sex. "Don't assume too much about me."

"Likewise. For knowing so little about me, you think you know an awful lot about me."

"I've seen enough to know that if you're swinging in my direction tonight, it's just a game. And I'm a man who's tired of games."

"I can see that. I like that."

"Slumming stars don't impress me."

"I like that too. But the truth is, I'm lost. Had to run or lose my scalp. You'd be amazed at the strength of hysterical girls. Saw the, ah, explicit signage out front and figured I'd be safe here—from them anyway. Glad your door was unlocked. Thanks for inviting me in." Another flicker rippled his bland expression.

So this striking human jetsam wanted some sport with nobody's prize. Fine. Now that he'd drifted in, Simon wasn't ready to throw him back out. This beached figurehead would steer Simon through the lonely predawn hours, when the city slept coupled together beneath clean cotton sheets while Simon habitually walked the beach alone, watching for the first glimpse of dolphins leaping to greet the sunrise. Simon would boot him out when he grew bored—but he didn't want the stranger choosing to leave. "So whyn't you call your friends to come save you? Have the president send Air Force One."

"Man like me has no friends, only people he pays."

"Man like me with a failing business has no friends either, only people he doesn't pay."

"Touché, then. How about that beer?"

Simon stripped off his apron and reached for a cup, flipping the switch on the water kettle. He turned back to find that the stranger had stolen Simon's cigarette out of the ashtray. A small lock of his hair glowed red. Simon reached out. "Watch it." The stranger didn't flinch with the forward thrust of Simon's burly paw, merely inhaled on the cigarette, his lips where Simon's had just been. "Your hair's on fire." A barbaric smell clawed the air.

The stranger exhaled. "So you care?"

"No. I'd hate to ruin something putting it out." Simon licked his finger and thumb and reached across the bar to extinguish the burning ember between his calluses. A coil of smoke rose in the shape of a question mark.

"What a relief. I was beginning to worry you were falling for me." Restless fingers played the cigarette.

Simon wound a lock of the stranger's hair around his finger. Lamplight played with the water droplets caught in its blue-black waves. Wet tangles curled past his shoulders, hung in his face, and fell in his eyes. The messy look lent him the vulnerability of a waking child, clashing with his haughty pose. The offer in those eerie eyes was no trick of the light. There he sat, provocative eyes on him, plain Simon. What a switch. Wray had liked to ignore Simon, making eyes at everyone, male and female, provoking Simon to jealous, violent lust so that Simon would love and punish him all in the same act—always fucking, never love-making.

And Simon was sure this stranger wanted the same thing— provoke the beast, leaving him no choice but to submit. Later he could kid himself that he hadn't wanted it. What else could this enchanting wanderer see in a crusty old barnacle like himself— brown hair, brown eyes, brown skin, brown life? A walking billboard for rough treatment, he had the physique of a teapot on steroids, a barrel chest mistaken for fat under his flannel shirts. Lovers tapped on it, asked if he was hollow, listened for his heart-beat—ha ha ha—when he used to have lovers, that is. Simon toyed with a silky curl, then gave it a tug.

The stranger hooked his hair behind his ear. Cigarette still between his fingers, he brushed Simon's lingering hand with the tip—a harmless singe, but a deliberate, slicing halt to the charged air that throbbed with the bare touch of callous to hair. "That drink?"

Simon stepped back, then set a steaming mug before the stranger.

The stranger flicked at the paper tag fluttering over the lip of the cup. "Tea? You're shitting me."

"Shut up and drink."

The stranger blew on the hot liquid, eyes lowered, dense lashes feathering pale cheeks. Despite the late hour, he lacked the midnight shadow that bristled Simon's face. He took a cautious sip, then another, then a gulp, tipping his head back, throat exposed and working.

He set the drained cup down, wiping the back of his hand against his mouth, running his knuckles back along the seam of his lips. The heat colored his waxen complexion. Something settled within him, like dying waves, and the trembling stopped. "I've done PCP. LSD. Ecstasy. But you give me tea." He half sang it, ending with a hum that ran off into nothing, his eyes drowsing.

"A poet." Simon leaned forward on his elbows.

"A hack. Future has-been."

Simon refilled his mug.

He cupped it with both hands, absorbing its warmth, staring into it. He drummed his fingertips on the side of the cup. "Thank you," he said. His wondrous gratefulness brought an unfathomable sorrow to his indifferent surface that just as quickly washed away. A tectonic plate heaved on the cold ocean floor of Simon's heart.

The stranger let out a breath. "So you've never heard of me."

"Sorry."

"Indigo. I'm called Indigo. My brand name, you could say."

"Oh, yeah, I've heard of that."

"Really?"

"Sure, in my crayon box. Good color for bruises."

Indigo pushed the tea away and slipped off his stool, moving about the room in slow unease, an off-course brook etching Simon's landscape. He touched the colored glass of a hanging lamp, wiping his dusty fingers on his wet pants, and drummed his fingers on the domed Plexiglas of the jukebox.

"You select the music?" He flipped through the cards.

"Some." Simon and Topher had quarreled over the music selection, and they ended up with Sinatra and *Madame Butterfly* as well as Topher's electronic noise. Customers raved over the eclectic mix that threatened to turn Simon's into a hip place, despite what Topher called Simon's best efforts to keep it in the red. Then the machine would quit, and Simon would neglect to call the repairman, though he had a nice ass. He savored the silence left by an ebbing clientele.

In a dull undertow of longing, Simon followed Indigo across the room. Simon couldn't catch his breath. Like the moon's limpid arms pulling the tide over his head, the stranger's draw left him no oxygen, only a transparent thread of light to reach for—and miss.

Indigo turned to him. "Play me your favorite." His cold touch left goose bumps on Simon's arm.

"Doubt it's up your alley."

He moved away, brushing Simon with his fringed sleeve. "Chalk up one more thing you could be wrong about tonight." He stood with his back to the end of the bar, elbows cocked and palms on the bar top, and hoisted himself onto it with ease. Feet dangling childlike, his heels struck the bar side with arrhythmic agitation.

Simon turned the key and pressed the button. Nothing happened. He gave an expert triple rap on the secret spot, fist slicing the air, the jukebox shuddering under his punch. The soprano's yearning aria churned into life, like a strangled sea creature coming up for air.

Indigo lay back on the bar top. He clasped his hands behind his neck and closed his eyes. His hair and fringes spread in a plume around him. Coat falling open, his dusk-smudged nipples cast twin stains beneath his white shirt. The ribbed T gripped his chest, sinking into the depression of his navel, a teasing nest for Simon's tongue. The image sent a jolt to Simon's groin, painful in its unfamiliarity. Since Wray's unexpected death a year ago—his absence such an unexpected relief that guilt tormented Simon— desire had turned to bile. He'd learned of the accident reading the *Times*. Of course the family—Wray's wife—wouldn't know to contact him, the monster in Wray's dark closet.

An odd echo chased the soprano as Indigo caught the tune and hummed along in a lower register with the foreign lyrics. His singing seemed unconscious, bubbling out of him without intent. Smooth as octopus ink. Inexplicable, carrying meaning beneath the untranslated words, like whale songs haunted with human emotion beyond language.

Sudden, choked agony cut off the soprano's yearning wail. Indigo opened his eyes. He rolled onto his side and leaned on one elbow, distracting Simon with his cocked, angular hip.

Simon swallowed. "Her name's Rusalka. You probably know her better as the Little Mermaid. She trades in her tail for human legs—it feels like daggers slicing into her when she walks. Disney rewrote the fairy tale's original tragic ending. She winds up in eternal purgatory because she dared to be what she wasn't sup- posed to be." Simon sensed that Indigo needed no explanation. Like the stranger's own voice, meaning trilled beneath her words, a hidden spring with an untraceable source. But Simon kept talking too fast, filling the silence. "She longs to be human so that she can love and thus be loved. She has the most beautiful voice in the sea. She sacrifices it to become a girl and loses her immortality."

Indigo sat up. He pulled off his boots and socks, tossing them away. A puddle of water and sand leaked out of the upturned leather. He stood up on the bar and glimpsed himself in the mir- ror. He danced a few steps to silence, watching his reflection. He moved with fluid ease, his body a flowing reed to his internal music. He tugged off his jacket and flung it aside. The wet leather clung to the mirror with a tentacle-sucking thwack. It hung over a corner of the frame, blinding the carved sea creatures. He pulled off his white tank top and dropped it. Hairless like a youth, he glowed with a disturbing bluish sheen to his pale skin, as if, like Rusalka, he had emerged from the frigid depths of underwater gloom to be warmed by his lover's consuming embrace. Dark nipples shadowed his ice surface.

He turned away from himself and paced, bare feet squeaking against the thick laminate of the bar top, and stood at the end of the bar. He perched there, toes over the edge, as if about to execute a dive. Simon moved to stand at his feet, gripping Indigo's ankles under the hem of his jeans. Indigo's fragile bones clenched in his fists flared his desire.

Indigo jumped. He snapped free of Simon's hold. Simon reached up to his waist, catching and setting him down. Indigo rested his palms over Simon's, pressing Simon's warm hands to his cold mannequin flesh. Simon leaned in to kiss him, but Indigo jerked away. Simon spat out a mouthful of hair.

Simon shoved him back against the walk-in refrigerator, knocking his head against the steel door. The dull thud of skull on metal reverberated through the sluggish channels of Simon's heart. The primitive sound stirred his blood like ancient drums. The familiar surge of sour pulsing in his veins saddened him. Was his own bitter ditch gouged so deep that he could not change course? He wanted to be aroused by the sun's gentle tickle of light through leaves, flirting with the surface of a lazy brook. Not this again. "That's right. Pretend you've changed your mind. Then lie to yourself later about who asked for it." Simon looked deep into those dull eyes, a stagnant pond. Simon shook him against the door, knee pressed to Indigo's crotch. Nothing stirred under Indigo's jeans, though Simon's own inseam threatened to pop. Understanding dawned. "You can't get it up."

Indigo blinked. "They call me a sex god."

"No pity party here. There's worse things to be called."

"You're wrong. Imagine living up to it. The humiliation of knowing you can't and having to hide it. At first it was brilliant, so many wanting me. There's nothing, no one, I wouldn't try. I tasted everything, everybody. But it was like staring into the sun. Too much, too long, you go blind. Can't feel a thing. Numb. Loved by millions, it's what I gave up—or what deserted me."

Simon grabbed a fistful of Indigo's hair and gripped his throat, rattling him against the cold metal. "So you think you can use me to help you feel again?" Simon turned him around. Shoved his face in the door, perfect features distorted in the reflection. He pressed himself against Indigo's back, an unmistakable and insistent arousal. "Who do you think you are?"

"I don't know." Indigo ran his hands, braille-like, over his wavering image. "I can't see myself."

"So you choose me to smash the mirror?"

Indigo touched the reflection of Simon's eyes. "You saw me as soon as I walked through the door. You looked right at me. At *me*. With you, I wouldn't have to pretend."

Simon caressed the slashed scar on the underside of Indigo's wrist.

"I tried again tonight," Indigo whispered. "I lied earlier. Nobody chased me. I walked into the ocean. Just kept walking. So easy. I drowned—everything went black, but then I wasn't alone. Something talked to me, carried me, saved me. I can't explain it. I woke up on the beach. No idea where I was. Nowhere near the place I went in. And I saw the lights from your place. That song, it called to me. You played it over and over."

"I'm not out to save anybody." Simon let him go, unable to comprehend such misery when nature had bestowed such rare gifts upon him. What right did this dark prince have to slash away a perfection that few were granted? Simon wanted to comfort him, nourish him, kiss his scars, bang his head against the wall.

Indigo turned to face him. "Neither was Prince Charming. He just wanted a little tail." A small smile at his own joke let Simon see what he could be, sun cracking through clouds.

"You're not my kind."

"The Little Mermaid didn't fall in love with her own kind either."

"I don't get it. Why me? You could have anybody."

"They treat me like glass. They worship me. You don't."

"So you want me to break you. A big dick to wake Sleeping Beauty and off you go with all the king's horses and all the king's men—except me you leave behind." Simon stared at his own reflection. Could nobody see *him*? Why not a lover instead of beast? "You've picked the wrong guy."

"I watched you through the window. You looked so sad."

"You mean mad."

"No, a sad seal face—whiskers and all. Putting the chairs up on the tables like the dead sat on each one. I must have stood outside for an hour, trying to get the sand out of my hair and find the balls to come in here. If you hadn't closed the blinds, I'd probably still be mooning around outside like a pathetic scene from a bad musical. But I had to see you." Indigo's skin seemed leached of all color, almost transparent. "Why chase everyone away?"

"Once upon a time a long time ago, I loved the wrong kind. And the ending wasn't happy." Simon recognized his own lie as soon as he spoke. He had never loved Wray. He had always held back, refusing to let himself feel anything but the urge to dominate because it was safe. Never risking his heart—maybe if he had, Wray would have chosen him. Maybe Indigo and he weren't so different after all; they numbed themselves against hurt.

"So let's do a remake, like Disney."

"Right, you give up fame and fortune for true love with me? Because I won't be quiet. Been there, done that."

A disturbance crossed the frozen marble of Indigo's face, a tossed stone warping his reflection in a glacial pool. Indigo's hesitation clunked in Simon's gullet.

"Didn't think so. Come on. You'd better get dressed." Simon picked up Indigo's T-shirt, finding it soaked with blood. He looked for a dent or blood smear on the refrigerator door. Had he knocked Indigo's head that hard? Had Indigo seen that capacity for violence? Is that all he wanted?

No, the shirt had lain in a pool of blood on the floor. "Hold still. You've cut yourself." He knelt and inspected Indigo's foot. A shard from Topher's broken glass had gashed the pad. How could he not have cried out? He hadn't even noticed. Simon picked Indigo up and set him on the bar top, like a dirty child set on a candy counter to get his scraped knee cleaned. Indigo clung to him, arms and legs wrapped around him, locked behind Simon's back. Simon stood rigid in the embrace, relaxed into it, hugged him back, buried his face in that mane of hair smelling of smoke and seaweed, and gripped harder.

"You could have done anything you wanted with me. Still could." Indigo's voice sounded far away, though right next to Simon's ear. "You wanted to. I felt it. But you didn't. Everybody else takes. They took until I was empty. You could sell me out or ask for money, but I know you won't. I was cold, and you gave me something hot to drink."

"I'm not nice."

"Or so you'd have everyone believe. But that's not what I see."

"What *do* you see?"

"When you looked at me, I saw myself again."

"But then who sees me?" Simon's voice cracked.

"You. When I look at you. When you decide to let me in."

Simon let him go. He pushed Indigo's hair off his forehead, tucked it behind his ears. He shredded the white undershirt and wrapped the wound. He pulled off his flannel shirt and stuffed Indigo's arms into the sleeves, as if dressing a doll.

Indigo lay his cold palm against the massive cavity of Simon's bare chest. "I hoped you had enough room in there to love someone like me. But I was afraid. You know how it hurts when your leg falls asleep and then wakes up?"

Indigo leaned in, his eyes closed, Simon's open. More breath than kiss, as if silk fluttered between their lips, their mouths lingered on the edge of touch. The change from not touching to touching was imperceptible…like the tide coming in, when only a long lapse in time reveals a bare rise in the water. Simon could not say when Indigo parted his lips, asking with his tongue for Simon to part his. He tasted of chamomile and salt. Simon felt no familiar urge to transfer power to himself, no desire to lunge forward, pin down, pound his breaching need into another body, swift relief that swiftly turned to despair after a union that left him drained rather than satiated. He stood pliant beneath Indigo's gentle kiss, a sea plant waving in the current. Indigo shifted into a pressing, longing insistence. Simon couldn't breathe, helpless in a whirlpool of neon colors darting behind his now-closed eyes. Simon's stubble rasped against Indigo's smooth skin. Indigo pulled away.

Simon steadied himself, his legs turned to jellyfish. Kisses with Wray were crushing, tongue-wrestling affairs, the first assault in a swift domination that Wray could provoke with the finesse of a jabbing welterweight—heady at first, a man drowning beneath your open mouth, and then suffocating in the monotony of absolute power. It's what all of his lovers seemed to want, to lay down beneath the stampede of his ramming bull, their bodies bruised beneath the pounding steam of his furious passion. It's all they seemed to think he was only capable of. "Who'd you practice that on? Some supermodel waif that'd turn to dust if you blew cake crumbs at her?"

"Just you. You're such a skittish rabbit. I didn't want to frighten you away."

"*You?* Scare *me?*" Simon moved to the jukebox and commanded Rusalka to sing. "Me a chickenshit bunny. *That's* a first."

"I've hung out all my dirty laundry. Now confess your secret. Admit it's true."

Simon rocked the jukebox, but Rusalka refused to sing. His fist elicited only silence. He jabbed at buttons, causing a manic flipping through the CD covers. A familiar blur caught his eye, and he flipped back. Indigo crouched on the cover of one, microphone in hand, eyes closed, mouth open as he sang. Bathed in a blue spotlight, fringes silhouetted, one arm stretched out to a frenzied audience. Thousands of them reached for a piece of him, but he hovered just beyond their possessive touch. Simon reached to stroke the cardboard face, but his hand bumped the Plexiglas, Indigo trapped like an exotic fish in an aquarium, gasping from the imprisoning depths of immortality. Simon knocked at the machine again, but Indigo too had fallen mute.

"I've always thought it was the saddest thing, her having to be silent to find love—she never found it. The man she loved had no idea who she really was." Simon turned to face Indigo. Maybe Wray would have leaped if he'd had faith that Simon would have caught him. Indigo, for whatever strange reason, trusted him and risked the fall. The stranger had much more to lose by admitting his shame than Simon. "It's true. Love at first sight, soon as I saw you. And I tried to kick it out." Just as Simon knew he lied when he professed love for Wray, he grasped the absolute truth of struggling against a terrifying eddy when the stranger stepped through the door. He'd seen the fragile glass behind the stranger's carved crystal exterior, wanted to cradle him, and wanted to crush him for the gash of yearning he slashed open.

Indigo hopped down from the bar, wincing on his sliced foot. His body swam in Simon's oversize shirt. He limped across the room. His wonder at the return of pain played across his face, like sunbeams skidding across water. He stopped close in front of Simon. "You almost did. But I knew I could love the man who built this place, who loved it once."

His jacket, slowly drying on the mirror's edge, let loose its sucking hold and dropped to the floor, leaving a swatch of dusted mermaids blinking into the light.

Indigo leaned into him. "So, what d'you say? Am I that sorry of a catch?"

"I'd say it's time to get you out of those wet jeans. Find out if you've got scales."

Stripping him of the damp denim was like peeling the mythical Selkie's skin. Simon tugged the stubborn, clinging jeans down. They sucked at Indigo's ankles. Simon pulled them free. Indigo's drowsy cock was not a humiliation but vulnerable—like a wet kitten Simon wished to cuddle and protect.

Indigo looked down at it. "Bit of a cursed frog at the moment."

"A few hundred kisses will lift it."

"You look that up in your fairy godmother manual?"

"Betty Crocker."

"I feel like I'm going under a spell, Simon, not coming out of one."

"But what happens now? I wake up to find you gone, and I'm

the pathetic pumpkin. Nothing left of you but broken glass."

"You've got it backward. We start as glass and a pumpkin. Then we wake up."

"So I'm a squash."

"Mm-hmm, one of those jack-o-lanterns left on the stoop too long, with a scowly face, all rotting and caving in. Until..." Indigo's fingers tiptoed up Simon's chest.

"I collapse."

"Unless..."

"A teenager smashes me in the street."

"You're hopeless." Indigo's laugh cut through Simon like light slicing through fog. "No, a confused boy in disguise walks up and fills you with candy. Until you're overflowing and brimming and stuffed."

"A stuffed squash. Thanks."

Indigo unzipped Simon's jeans and parted the fly. "A crook-neck squash, I'd say."

"Let's throw a ball. Here. Tomorrow. I'll clean the place up, fix the jukebox. Invite some fairies and fag hags. I want you to see what this place can be."

"It's complicated, Simon. I'm on tour. I'm supposed to be in Phoenix or Houston or some landlocked hellhole tomorrow. Hey, what's the matter? I'll come back. I promise."

"Right. Like in a hundred years." Simon collected Indigo's coat from behind the bar and held it out for him. He'd guessed right. Indigo would never be seen with him with the doors thrown open. And he'd rather wander his arid dunes alone than with masked lovers who demanded his silence.

Indigo padded behind him. He moved with ease despite his sore foot, his long and naked legs loose under the big shirt. "That pesky rabbit's in the squash patch again."

"Shoot it. Put it out of its misery."

Indigo scrounged a pen from behind the bar and scrawled on an order pad. "Look, tomorrow's headline: 'Indigo Bleuz Suffers Laryngitis, Cancels World Tour!'"

"You'd do that for me?"

"I don't need millions anymore, Simon. Just one. Just you."

"Kinda stinks being a mere mortal."

"It's all I've ever been."

"Come on. I want to show you something." Indigo, who had leaped like a dolphin through Simon's battered armor, would appreciate the sight of the aurora-worshiping porpoises. Simon carried Indigo through a misty half-light down the deserted street. Dark rain clouds scuttled toward the horizon, and they reached the sea beneath a swath of clear sky, as if a hand had wiped a fogged window silvering above them. Simon lay Indigo down in the shallow, incoming surf and watched the waves lick at his legs.

Indigo touched his shoulder. "What are you looking at?"

"To see if you turn into something else."

"Look. I am."

Indigo's cock yawned and stretched, rising toward the dawn. The ascending sun coroneted his blue-black hair, iridescent and alive in the waves that rushed around them. Morning's first blush tinted his cheeks. Simon kissed his nipples, shining like oil slicks in the foam. Simon whispered, "You go and sing. I'll wait for you. Just remember you promised to come back to me." He thought of the prince who cut through a murderous, spiked forest to reach his spellbound beloved. Indigo had hacked through Simon's thorns, and he believed that Indigo would return. Letting him go would be more difficult than withdrawing his claws, but the last thing Simon wanted was to silence the voice that had woken him, the most beautiful voice on earth.

"My squash blossom," Indigo hummed as their bodies joined, Simon as slow and gentle as Indigo's kiss. Emotions played across Indigo's once-remote face, a mirror's splintered pieces falling back into place. Looking down at his lover, Simon saw his own joy refracted back. And upon his broad back he felt eyes dancing across the waves.

LOVE AMONG THE HOLIDAYS

R.G. Thomas

The day I met Mark I fell down my sister's basement steps. Oh, it wasn't a bad fall, I didn't roll head over heels and land at the bottom in a pile of twisted limbs; I was much more subtle. And, unfortunately, it was the finale to a horrifyingly embarrassing day.

It was Thanksgiving Day, and as usual I spent it at my older sister Tracy's house. Our parents had moved to Florida five years before, so on holidays I had a standing dinner invitation with my sister and her family.

This Thanksgiving I arrived an hour before dinner as usual and removed my shoes in the garage before entering Tracy's immaculate house. I gave my sister a kiss, shook hands with her husband, Dave, a big friendly bear of a man, and hugged my nieces—Ellie, who is 11, and Patty, who is 9—as I fought off their golden lab, Rocky, who likes to stick his nose in my crotch. As the girls hauled the dog down to the basement, Tracy handed me a stack of plates with a cheery smile.

"Set the table?"

"Sure." I snagged a piece of turkey on my way to the dining room and started setting out the plates, returning to the kitchen a few minutes later with a spare.

"Here, you gave me one extra," I said.

"Huh? Oh, um, no, I didn't. I invited someone from work too." Tracy focused on mashing the potatoes, her eyes avoiding my face.

"Oh, OK." I headed for the dining room, then stopped and turned to look back. "Who'd you invite? Donna?"

"Donna? No, she's going to her parents' house." Tracy still wouldn't look at me, and I stepped closer, my senses now on full alert and a mild panic starting a slow boil in my gut.

"Who is it then?"

The front doorbell rang, and Tracy jerked her head up, eyes wide and face radiating guilt. I narrowed my eyes and whispered, "Oh, my God, what have you done?" just as I heard Dave open the door and greet the new arrival with a bellow of "Happy Thanksgiving!"

"Oh,stop it. I haven't done anything." Tracy smiled weakly as she wiped her hands on her apron and moved past me. "I just invited someone from work who was going to be alone for the holiday. That's all."

Clenching my jaw, I followed her to the front door and stood back, watching as Tracy hugged a tall, good-looking man who handed her a bottle of wine. Dave took the new arrival's coat, and Tracy introduced him to Ellie and Patty as Mark Radcliff. Mark crouched down to look in their eyes and shook each of their hands, saying, "Nice to meet you—what a pretty young lady you are," which sent my nieces into spurts of giggling. When he stood up again, Tracy reached back to put an arm around my shoulders and pulled me up alongside her.

"And this is my brother, Jeff." Tracy beamed at me. "Jeff, this is Mark. He's been working with me for about three months now—just moved up here from North Carolina."

"Hi, Jeff," Mark said with a gleaming smile that made my pulse race and calmed the mental curses I was slinging at Tracy.

I hate being set up. I find it completely embarrassing, as if my friends and family think I'm socially inept and can't find my own dates. But Mark, I must say, was handsome in a way that lanced my indignation and stoked the furnace of my nervousness and self-consciousness. His dark hair was styled with studied carelessness, his jaw was square with a perfectly centered dimple, and the corners of his brown eyes crinkled when he smiled.

"Nice to meet you," I said, reaching out to shake his hand and praying that my palm wasn't half as sweaty as it felt. "So, you work with Tracy. You must know about her addiction to stealing pads of Post-its and boxes of pens."

Mark glanced at Tracy, his smile slipping a little and his head pulling back in surprise. "Oh, really? I'll have to keep an eye on her, then."

Tracy let out a nervous laugh and pulled me back, hugging me tight against her side and digging her nails into my shoulder. "Oh, Jeff. You're so funny. Isn't he funny? And the really funny part, Jeff, is that Mark is our office manager and keeps track of things like that. See how funny it is when you look at it that way?"

I laughed a little too loud as a blush crawled up my neck. "Oh, sorry, sorry. Yeah, I was just joking. That's me—'Joking Jeff,' they call me—well, not to my face, just, you know, behind my back. Or so I've heard, since it's been said behind my back and not to my face." I took a breath and widened my eyes in what I hoped looked like intense interest but which Tracy later told me more resembled a psychotic episode. "So, North Carolina, huh?"

Tracy yanked me back into the kitchen, saving us both. She handed me the bottle of wine Mark had brought, and I opened it, pouring everyone a glass while she went to the basement for some serving bowls, muttering something about Post-its and younger brothers I couldn't quite make out. I took Dave and Mark each a glass of wine where they sat in the living room talking about their years playing high school football, then practically ran back into the kitchen. I stood by the steaming plate of turkey and started picking at the meat, my mind racing with images of a younger Mark in a jock strap and shoulder pads.

"What the hell is wrong with you?" Tracy hissed, walking up behind me and startling me out of my fantasy. She saw that I was eating the turkey and shoved me aside, snatching a piece of breast from my fingers. "Stop it!"

"Sorry, I don't know what I'm doing, I'm nervous," I whispered. "What were you thinking, trying to set me up with him?"

"I'm not trying to set you up with him," Tracy snapped back, arranging the pieces of turkey on the platter in an attempt to conceal the fact that I had been picking it apart. "He's a nice guy, he's all alone up here in Michigan, and I invited him to have dinner with us, end of story. Just because he happens to be gay and you happen to be gay doesn't mean I'm trying to set you up, OK? I mean, if you two were to get along and maybe start dating, that wouldn't be such a bad thing, would it? But just because you're both here for Thanksgiving and both single and both gay doesn't mean you have to worry about impressing him. Just be yourself and freakin' relax, would you?"

I stood with my arms crossed, eyes on the floor as I shook my head. "He's too attractive for me."

"Oh, for God's sake," Tracy sighed. "Knock it off. You're a handsome, outgoing guy with a great personality. Just try to shut your mouth five seconds before your brain runs out of words. And stop sweating so much. You look like you're having a heart attack."

She slapped my hand away as I reached for another piece of turkey, then she picked up the platter and carried it into the dining room, calling out in a singsong voice, "Dinner!"

Mark and I sat beside each other across from my nieces. The girls giggled and stared at us in turn, then leaned in to whisper to each other and giggle some more. I fidgeted and gulped down wine.

"Girls, stop it," Tracy said gently as she scooped stuffing onto their plates. "It's not polite to tell secrets."

Dave sat to Mark's left and kept up a running discourse on the fate of the National Hockey League as Tracy and I passed around dishes of food and tried not to look at one another too much. As Mark spoke to Dave, the timbre of his voice seeped into my ear and rattled down my spine to clench my stomach. I lost myself in the cadence of his voice as I layered food on my plate with reckless abandon. I felt an instant attraction to Mark; I had been reduced to a goofy high school kid. My head felt too big for my neck, my whole body was one big, active sweat gland, and my stomach churned. I was a mess.

After loading my plate with more carbohydrates than I usually eat in a week, I picked up the gravy boat and began to pour the thick, rich gravy over everything. At that moment Rocky stuck his nose between my legs and I jumped. My knees hit the bottom of the table and gravy sloshed out of the boat, across my sister's white linen tablecloth and into my lap. Wine and water splashed out of all the glasses from the impact and everyone else jumped as well, my nieces letting out loud, piercing screams. The smell of the gravy in my lap encouraged Rocky to force his nose deeper into my crotch, licking up the mess on my pants as I tried to push him away with my free hand.

"Here, give me that," Mark said, reaching for the gravy boat I was still clutching as it swung wildly back and forth. As he tried to take it from me, Rocky lunged harder into my lap, and I jumped again. The gravy boat wobbled, and hot, thick gravy splattered Mark's shirt and pants.

"Oh, God, I'm sorry!" I shouted. "It's the dog, I swear to God it's because of the dog. I'm sorry! Oh, God, I'm so, so sorry!"

Tracy grabbed the gravy boat and set it on the table, then got down on her hands and knees to crawl underneath and snag Rocky's collar. She dragged him out from beneath the table, his claws scrabbling to find purchase on the hardwood floor as he licked gravy from his muzzle. She pushed the dog into the laundry room and slammed the door, then came back to the table with a towel to mop up the spills.

After Mark and I changed into some of Dave's sweats, we took our seats once again, the extra-large pants hanging on each of us as our clothes tangled intimately together in Tracy's washer. Our first date and already we were washing our clothes together I thought but wisely decided not to say aloud. As Tracy took her seat, I turned and said, "I'm so sorry, Mark."

Mark didn't look at me as he scooped up mashed potatoes, but his voice sounded friendly enough as he replied, "It's all right. It was an accident."

The rest of dinner went off without any incident, and I kept quiet, listening as Mark answered Tracy's multitude of questions about his life in North Carolina and his family. My sister could be a government interrogator; I learned more about Mark during that first dinner than I know about some of my closest friends. By the end of the meal, I was glad to be wearing Dave's sweats as I sat back in my chair and let out a sigh. The girls cleared the table, and I helped Tracy wash the china as Ellie, Patty, Dave, and Mark all went down to the recently finished basement to play video games.

"Are you OK?" Tracy asked, handing me the cursed gravy boat to dry.

I shrugged. "Yeah, I'm all right. Your damn dog needs to go to obedience school, but I'm OK. I don't know why I get so nervous around guys I'm attracted to. It's like I become this bumbling caricature of myself. I'm going to die alone."

"Oh, stop it," Tracy said through a gentle laugh. "You weren't that bad. I think he kind of likes you."

"Really?" I asked, trying not to sound too hopeful and codependent.

She nodded. "Yeah, really."

After we had finished the dishes, I excused myself to the bathroom while Tracy joined everyone else in the basement. The door was closed, and I opened it, stepping in to find Mark sitting on the toilet, Dave's sweats puddled around his ankles. He bent forward, fists clenched in his lap and a blush erupting on his face.

"Oh, no!" I shouted and backed out quickly, slamming the door behind me. I stood leaning against it for a moment, eyes squeezed shut, as if I could wipe out the last minute just by wishing it gone. Finally catching my breath, I turned and knocked gently on the door.

"Yes?" Mark's irritated voice came back.

"I'm so sorry, Mark. I didn't know you were in there, honest. You must have snuck past us. I'm sorry."

There was no reply, and I retreated to the living room, sitting in a corner of the couch with my knees drawn up, just the Christmas tree and mantle lights illuminating my suffering. *What a spectacularly bad Thanksgiving dinner.*

Mark opened the door to the bathroom and walked past the living room without a glance in my direction, heading to the basement. I felt both relieved and disappointed at the same time. After a few more minutes of mental self-flagellation, I used the bathroom and started down the basement steps to say my goodbyes; I had had enough for one evening.

On the second step down, my sweaty, sock-covered foot slipped off the thick carpeting of the riser and I bounced on my heels down each subsequent step to the bottom landing where I ran face first into the paneled wall. I turned my head to look down the two final steps and found all five of them staring at me. Ellie and Patty burst into hysterical laughter and fell onto the floor. Dave turned away but not before I saw the flicker of a smile on his face as Tracy—dear, sweet Tracy—wore a look of concern and got up to approach me.

"You OK?"

I nodded, then looked over her shoulder and raised my hand. "'Night, everyone. I'm afraid if I stay here any longer I may burn the place down."

I shook Dave's hand, hugged Ellie and Patty and Tracy, then held out my hand to Mark.

"It's been interesting meeting you, Jeff," Mark said with a grin.

"Yeah, same here." I waved again and trudged up the steps to retrieve my folded clothes still warm from the dryer. Tracy pressed containers of leftovers into my hands and hugged me tight at the door.

"I love you," she said.

"I love you too. Thanks for trying." And I turned to walk carefully down the driveway to my car, my wing tips looking ridiculous beneath Dave's baggy sweats.

And so it became a tradition for Mark to join my sister's family and me for holiday meals and for me to do something to embarrass myself. At Christmas Eve dinner I put my hand down on the serving spoon in the green beans and showered everyone with butter-slicked beans. At Easter dinner I started to choke on a piece of ham and fled into the bathroom to cough it up, Tracy running after me with her fists clenched, ready to perform the Heimlich maneuver. Mark made a joke about chewing my food 32 times, but I didn't laugh. On Memorial Day I spilled an entire pitcher of lemonade on myself and my nieces as I attempted to serve them drinks. Mark smirked and turned away, apparently unable to come up with something witty enough. At the Fourth of July celebration, my Roman candle was the one that caught the garage roof on fire, which Dave quickly put out with the hose. Over the course of seven months, Mark Radcliff had infected me with his calm demeanor, quick smile, warm and friendly eyes, and infinite patience with my ridiculous antics, yet he still had not called me for a date. Imagine.

That Fourth of July evening, after the garage roof had stopped smoking, Tracy took the hose from Dave to continue watering down the roof while he cleaned up the grill. She held a large flashlight in one hand, shining it on the partially melted shingles to see where to aim the water. Now and then a few moths would flutter into the lens of the flashlight and I would wave them away. After several minutes of silence, she turned to me and said, "Maybe you should join a circus or something."

"Funny," I replied and sipped my beer. "Hey, this was your idea, remember? You said you weren't trying to set us up, but he's been at every holiday dinner and cookout so far. I'm not stupid, I know what you're trying to do, but it doesn't seem to be working."

She shrugged, eyeing the roof with a critical eye. "He likes you. He's told me so on more than one occasion."

"Really?" I stepped closer to her, intrigued. "What'd he say?"

She thought about it, then looked at me. "He said, 'Is Jeff going to be there?' when I asked him to the barbecue today."

My stomach fell. "That's it?"

"No, that's not it. Then he said, 'Your brother's a nice guy, clumsy as hell but nice.'" Tracy shrugged. "He thinks you're nice."

I sighed and finished my beer. "Yeah, great. 'Nice' is what guys call their great-aunts or best friends, but it's not what they call someone they want to date. And he's never called me, not once. You gave him my number, right?"

Tracy nodded and turned off the hose. "Yes, I gave him your number." She took a breath and looked at me so seriously I got a chill. "Look, he started seeing someone last year right around Christmas."

"What? Oh, for God's sake, why didn't you tell me?"

Tracy threw her hands in the air, "I didn't think it would last! Besides, you always looked forward to seeing him, I couldn't take that away from you."

I let out a breath and looked away to inspect the roof. "Doesn't look too bad. Dave should be able to reshingle it in no time, huh?"

Tracy took me by the shoulders and turned me back to face her. "He likes you, though, Jeff. And I don't think things are working out with this new guy. Just relax and be yourself, OK? You may have a chance with Mark yet."

I shrugged. "Yeah, OK."

We walked back into the house, and my nieces each grabbed a hand to lead me to the basement where we sat on the couch and played video games. We laughed and made fun of each other, and I rolled on top of each of them at critical points in the game. I was so involved with Ellie and Patty, I didn't notice that Mark had come in through the sliding door until he laughed at something I said and all three of us looked up at him in surprise.

"Oh, hi there," I said, grinning self-consciously. "I didn't hear you come in."

"Yeah, looks like you're pretty caught up in the game." He looked even more handsome than usual, dressed in a button-down short-sleeve shirt, khaki shorts, and sandals. He sat in the recliner and watched us play until Dave called the girls up to go to bed. I hugged each of my nieces tight, and they ran to hug Mark, then scampered up the stairs. I started to pack up the game controllers, but Mark moved to sit beside me, taking one of the controllers and pressing the restart button.

He cocked an eyebrow. "You can handle playing against little girls, but can you handle playing someone your own age?"

I grinned and grabbed a controller. "Well, let's find out."

We played for two hours, trash-talking and jostling each other at key moments to mess up a move. At one point Tracy and Dave came down to see what we were doing, but before Dave could sit in the recliner to watch, Tracy took his arm and hauled him back upstairs. Mark won the third and final game, besting me two out of three, and he leaned back into the couch, raising his arms over his head in a long, luxurious stretch.

"Well, I guess we know who the real video game master is," he said.

"Or we now know you have no social life and spend all your time playing video games," I shot back, and Mark laughed, then leaned up to clap a hand on my back. We had both been laughing, but it died in the sudden intensity of the moment as he sat close beside me, one arm around my shoulders, his other hand resting lightly on my knee. My skin burned beneath his touch, and all the spit evaporated from my mouth. I raised my eyes to his, and the expression on his face was so intense that I felt simultaneously frightened and thrilled.

Mark's cell phone chirped, loud and startling enough to shatter the mood, and he jumped back from me. He smiled apologetically as he got up from the couch, fishing in the pocket of his shorts for his phone.

"Sorry," he said and brought the phone up to his ear. "Hello? Oh, hi, how are you?" He turned and stepped through the patio door into the summer darkness.

I shook my head and packed up the video game system, shutting off the TV and lights as I ascended the steps to find Tracy unloading the dishwasher. She raised her eyebrows in a silent question, and I shrugged in reply.

"I don't know what's going on," I said. "But I'm bushed and have to get up for work tomorrow." I hugged and kissed her. "Thanks for having me over again."

"You're always welcome, you know that," she said. "I'm sorry about all this."

"Yeah, me too. Sorry about your garage roof." Tracy waved my apology away, and I glanced out into the backyard to see Mark standing by the trampoline, the blue glow from his cell phone illuminating the side of his face. I left the house, walking out through the garage without even waving good night to Mark. I was confused and intrigued and disappointed and excited all at the same time. But it was late, and I did have to be at work early in the morning. Besides, if he really wanted to, Mark had my number; he could call me.

The months went by and Mark never called. When Tracy and

I talked on the phone or over an occasional lunch or dinner, I would ask about him, and she would tell me he was fine, still dating someone, and we left it at that. Labor Day came and I went to Tracy's for a final summer barbecue, but Mark wasn't there.

"He went out of town for the weekend," she told me. "He asked me to tell you hello and he'll miss kicking your ass at video games."

I was somewhat mollified at the comment, even if it had been delivered secondhand. It felt personal and comforting: Mark and I had a private joke. I didn't ask if he had gone out of town with his boyfriend; I decided I didn't really want to know. And, as luck would have it, that day I didn't spill or break a single thing.

Halloween came and went without a call from or sighting of Mark. I dressed up as a pirate and helped Tracy pass out candy while Dave took Ellie and Patty trick-or-treating. We talked about Mark for a few minutes, in between the doorbell and shouts of, "Trick or treat!" then avoided the topic the rest of the night. At midnight, after a heroic evening of candy distribution and again no bizarrely embarrassing accidents, I pulled off my eye patch and got in my car to drive home, the fake parrot still perched on my shoulder.

The day before Thanksgiving my doctor delivered the diagnosis that I had bronchitis and strep throat. That's me, always the overachiever. My chest ached with each cough, and my throat simmered with infection. Tracy dropped off a big pot of home-made chicken soup, fussed over me for a little while as she did a few loads of my laundry, then headed home to start preparing for the next day's feast.

Thanksgiving morning I lay in a huddled mess on the couch, bleary-eyed and semiconscious as I watched the annual parade march down Woodward Avenue. At 3 o' clock, just as my sister's family and the newly single Mark—as she had happily reported the day before—were sitting down to dinner, I heated some left-over soup. I sat on the couch to slurp it up while the Detroit Lions game played out before me, the white noise of the announcers and crowd soon lulling me to sleep.

Hours later I awoke to a frantic pounding on my front door. I struggled to my feet, still half asleep, and shuffled to the door. Mark stood on the porch holding a plate heaped with food and covered with plastic wrap, flakes of winter's first snowfall dusting his shoulders and glistening in the dark tangles of his hair. I closed my eyes, cursing my appearance and the condition of my house, then took a breath and said through a wheeze, "Oh, hi."

"Happy Thanksgiving," Mark said. "I heard you were sick and thought I'd bring by a plate of food and check on you." He hesitated, then asked, "Can I come in?"

I blinked and shook the cobwebs from my head. "Sorry. Yeah, come on in. It's a mess, though." I moved back into the middle of the living room and watched as he stepped through my front door. He kicked off his shoes and looked around. "It's nice."

"Thanks," I replied and promptly fell into a fit of coughing that brought tears to my eyes. Mark set the plate of food on the coffee table, shrugged out of his coat, then grabbed my arm and led me to the couch.

"You need to rest. You sound awful," he said. "Bronchitis and strep throat?"

I nodded, tears running down my cheeks as I coughed into my fist, unable to speak and realizing somewhere in the back of my mind that maybe it was for the best.

"You poor thing." He sat beside me on the couch, his hand on my knee. "Anything I can do?"

I shook my head, unable to speak as my throat was now on fire and my lungs were threatening another bout of coughing. He put an arm around my shoulders and pulled me into him, kissing the top of my head between the corkscrews of my hair. "I missed you at dinner," he said. "I was really looking forward to seeing you today."

"Really?" I squeaked.

"Yeah." He looked down at me, his eyes filled with soft brown light. "I like spending time with you, dangerous as it may be."

I laughed and shook my head, croaking, "You're just saying that because I'm sick and you can tell me later I imagined all of this." Mark's hand touched the sweat-slick back of my neck before he got up to refill my water glass, and I sighed. I watched him move through the rooms of my house and was amazed at how natural his presence felt. I had imagined this moment for so long, it was difficult to believe he was actually here.

"Ellie and Patty wanted me to give you hugs for them," he said, sitting beside me once again and slipping his arm around my shoulders. He squeezed me a couple of times, then reached down to take my hand in his. He turned it palm up and frowned as he inspected it. Leaning forward, he dabbed a tissue in the water he had just brought me and wiped off my palm, then leaned down to place a kiss in its center. His lips were soft and warm on my skin, and my head spun from the sensations shooting up my arm. "And that's from me. A little safer than a kiss on the lips in your present condition."

"Wow," I sighed. "That was nice."

"You know," he said, "I've been wanting to call you for a while, at least since this summer, but the timing was bad. Besides, you seemed a little standoffish."

"Really? Well, I was nervous," I replied. "But I was interested. I mean, I still am." I shook my head and took a breath. "I just need to learn to relax with you. But why now?"

Mark shrugged. "I went to a bar after I left your sister's house last year and met Kyle. And, you know, dinner that evening was bad, you have to admit."

I nodded. "Yes, yes, it was."

Mark continued. "Anyway, Kyle and I started going out and we dated until just before Halloween this year, when I couldn't take his attitude anymore and broke up with him." He took a breath. "So this is me starting over. And I'd like to get to know you better. Preferably not around anything flammable or containing sharp edges. I've made a list I'll give you later."

I laughed and immediately fell into a coughing fit. Mark rubbed my back as I hunched forward, my face buried in a handful of tissues. When the coughing subsided, Mark pulled me into him and I lay with my head on his chest, his heart beating softly in my ear. I sighed before drifting off to sleep, thinking that I had one more thing to be thankful for this year and maybe now I'd have a standing date for the holidays.

ONE NIGHT

Nicholas Tomasetti

"OK, can we just discuss something for a minute?" I slurred, stumbling down the stairs to my basement, waving my unlit cigarette for effect.

"Of course," he replied with a laugh.

"What about Kathy Lahner's jeans?" I asked, followed by a bout of giggles.

"I fucking knew it!" he replied with a big grin. "You've talked about her outfit the whole walk home, which by the way was definitely more than 10 minutes."

"It totally was not. It was, like, maybe 10," I replied, grabbing an exposed wooden beam for support and dropping into the old kitchen chair left handily in the basement for when my father would sneak downstairs for a cigarette.

"Aw, you're so full of shit, it's comin' out your ears, buddy," he responded, tousling my too-long chestnut hair as he climbed up on the old wooden bench next to me. Needless to say, we'd danced that routine many times.

"No matter what's coming out of my ears, at least my thighs aren't pouring out the tacky holes in my jeans like—"

"Kathy Lahner?" he asked, raising an eyebrow in mock inquisition.

"How'd you guess?" I asked, also feigning amazement.

"Well," he said, leaning in so close to me that I suddenly forgot how to breathe, "I could tell just by lookin' in those baby-browns." He followed that up with his wry cock-boy's smile.

He might as well have punched me in the stomach.

I have confidence enough in my own appearance at this juncture in my life to say that he was way out of my league. At that point in our lives, we were so opposite; he possessed all of the traits of youthful manhood that caused the heads of women and men alike to turn well into their old age until they had finally arrived at the rueful destination where sex was too impractical to be contemplated. He was also like Narcissus in his vanity, but I never begrudged him the love he felt when he looked in the mirror because it was so well-deserved. When I remember how he looked to me then, he was more like a god than a mere man, with a beauty that literally made the breath harden inside my lungs so that try as I might to inhale when I first laid eyes upon him, I found that my entire chest had turned to granite. At 18 he possessed the kind of rare and effortless beauty that could make a person crumble; the type of flawlessness that I strived so hard to mimic but could never quite achieve for the simple fact that it was impossible to attain because it was the peculiar incident of his birth.

I was not ugly, bear in mind, for if I had been, I doubt he'd have taken the chance he did in outing himself to me that late night in the July that I was 17. I had a clear olive complexion and warm brown eyes, two oval almonds set nicely apart in a browned-honey face. My smile was charming and my laugh contagious. The beauty that I possessed then was more feminine in its quality; I was dark and shrouded in an air of Mediterranean mystery, a sort of effeminate mystique. But my body was childlike and soft, my dark face and features were still rounded, coated in a layer of baby fat that would expand exponentially in college until I finally burst forth from it around the age of 22, fully grown, the man I am today. On that summer night in my parents' basement, I was simply a child with a body that corresponded. He, however, was so much more than that.

Manhood had begun to touch Tyler around 15. When he chose me as his lover some three years later, he possessed none of the childlike qualities that clung so desperately to me for so many years past their welcome. I looked like a boy, and he looked like a young man, but a man nonetheless. His face was chiseled, with high, defined cheekbones that closed together in a small cleft of a chin, giving the overall appearance of a peach carved of marble. His skin was soft, ripe fruit; it was a pale cream color with flecks of pink and red at his cheeks and forehead. His lips were overstuffed plums, plump nectarine wedges. They were the type of playful lips that tell of soft kisses and whispered secrets, the pieces of honeysuckle so irresistible that one is willing to stick his hand in the hive for just a chance at one sweet taste. But most breathtaking of all were his eyes. They were almond-shaped as well, but they were crystal-clear pools of blue: small natural springs that caught and captured every single ray of sunshine and kept each one just below the surface so that when he looked at me, I would feel the strange disorientation of not knowing whether I was looking into his eyes or up from them—up from the water at some distant shoreline. When he fixed his gaze upon me I would dive into the stream, getting caught up in the green-flecked currents, and I would become paralyzed and powerless, always letting them take me wherever he wanted me to go.

"You've got really cool eyes. Has anyone ever told you that?" he asked, using what I would later discover to be one of the oldest lines in the book without a trace of irony.

"No, not really. Thank you," I replied with a small grin while inadvertently-on-purpose fluttering my thick lashes a little bit harder.

"I mean it. They're great," he responded with his little half-smile. That crooked grin would lure many men home with him in the future; however every single one of them would come after me. I was the first to shed my inhibitions at the sight of that full-lipped smirk, and nothing can strip me of that honor, not ever.

"As I said, thank you," I said, trying to be seductive. I didn't know much about being seductive then—and I'm pretty sure both of us knew that—but he played along by giving me a play-ful wink.

"So what did you think of that party tonight?" he asked, shifting gears from my painful attempts at seduction to casual guy-talk, much to my dismay.

"It was all right. I'm pretty sick of drinking in the woods with a bunch of losers who pretend to be drunk after two beers."

"Don't forget about the bugs," he said, raising a blond eyebrow.

"Oh, of course not, or the schwag weed Craig was blowing in everyone's face all night long," I said, shaking my head.

"Seriously, that kid thinks having a drug connection makes him cool, and it so doesn't. Especially since that shit looks and smells like oregano" he said, beginning a bout of soft laughter.

"I know, and the funniest part is that it still isn't enough to get his sorry ass laid," I spat, lighting a cigarette. I was amused with the conversation, and looking back I suppose it was because such conversations with Tyler were my first tastes of banter with another gay male; namely, they were usually catty and gossipy. Such discussions were most often reserved for my female friends; with my few other male friends, I was confined to topics such as girls and the Celtics. Even then, I longed for a place where I didn't have to care that another Boston sports team had lost again.

"But it wasn't a bad time overall," he said, pulling out his pack of cigarettes, then asking, "Could I split that one with you? I'm all out."

"Sure," I responded, trying to act nonchalant as excitement swelled from my chest and quickly shot downward. Cigarette sharing amounted to the touching of hands and a bit of saliva-swapping and sitting across from a man who'd appeared in so many of my teenage dreams, I couldn't think of anything more exciting.

"Thanks," he said softly, taking the cigarette from between my fingers with his. When our hands touched, I felt it, felt everything that was coming and everything it would do to me. The small shock of electricity that passed between us as my beautiful friend, Tyler, took my cigarette from me gave me a fleeting moment of both clarity and clairvoyance. I knew in that one moment that I was gay and that he was as well; I also knew that the thoughts and feelings I'd been having regarding members of my own sex were not in fact a fleeting phase but the reality, the future. I knew it would be a harder road than I'd planned on taking, but because of the chemistry that had ignited, because of the atoms that skyrocketed on invisible energy beams from me to him and back to me again, I knew it was right. This was the way love, or at least lust, was supposed to fee; this was what people lived for, died for, fell into disgrace for; not the forced, awkward intimacy I'd felt with all of my so-called girlfriends, but rather this crazy, unexplainable force that made me willing to forget the consequences of the actions I was about to take.

But not to be forgotten was the clairvoyance. I knew that it was July and that he would leave for college in August; I knew that he was an object desired by many and that he would have no difficulty bringing men more beautiful than me to their knees. I knew that he was a virgin by the awkward look on his face, the way his ever-cool countenance crinkled in nervousness as our hands touched and the spark ignited, but I also knew that unsure look would soon vanish because I was about to be his first. I knew that I had already started falling in love with him, and that he was potentially in love with me or perhaps on his way there, but that he would nonetheless fly out of my life and be gone without looking back, probably without giving me much of a second thought. He would take from me whatever I'd let him have, and he would move on to bigger and better things, more experienced things, more beautiful things. I believed that he was too good for me and so did he, and I knew when our hands met that whatever he felt for me was due in no small part to the fact that in our tiny, quiet town his options up until that very moment had been nonexistent. He was hungry to taste, and I was willing to be picked from the vine, so we would both let it happen. He would eat until he'd had his full and then he'd leave, forget, and never look back. On the other hand, I would be haunted by his memory forever, unable to ever find a man that lived up to the purity and beauty of innocence and first love. I saw all of this and could've turned back, could've let the moment pass and moved away, gone to bed, said goodbye. I could have done all of those things, but I didn't. Instead, I leaned in closer and embraced the less-traveled road, because after what felt like an eternity, I simply didn't have the strength to let this opportunity pass me by.

I loved the way he smelled, the natural scent that emanated from the slight frame that was crouched close to my slightly larger one as we passed a cigarette back and forth, all the while giggling like two little children. It wasn't his cologne; rather, it was the natural scent that pumped from his blood and through his pores that was the aphrodisiac, the slightly metallic smell of his excitement and his fear. It was animal attraction as we both sat facing one another, moving ever-so-much closer together with each moment that passed so that by the time the cigarette was nothing but a filter our legs were interlocked, our arms touching, our foreheads pressed together. I inhaled the breath that he exhaled and sent it back into him in a circular motion. Before our lips ever met, we had already started melting into one form, breathing in unison, hearts beating in rhythm. I was afraid at that moment but my desire overcame the fear, made it shrink and feel secondary, so I just let the dead cigarette fall to the basement floor and I closed my eyes. I felt him lick his lips in the small space between our mouths, and then he leaned in and was upon me, and our transformation into one solitary, interlocked puzzle-piece was complete.

In that second when our lips met, the entire world halted in place, simply stopped rotating altogether and stood perfectly still, leaning in on its axis the way I would lean in many times in years to come to allow a first date a good-night kiss. His lips were every single bit as pure and perfect as I'd dreamed they'd be, first meeting mine tentatively, as if a question mark were forming upon them. The answer was given quickly by my own, and I think perhaps I even whispered the word "yes" into his mouth. He grew bolder and so did his mouth, searching mine first in inquisition, then in exploration, and finally in passion. I'd never felt elation the way I did when I shared my first kiss with another man, and in that long moment when our lips first fumbled together, a bar was placed high above my head, an impossible benchmark was formed that men throughout my life would fail to reach forever after. I have never experienced such a feeling of sweet release as I did in the instant that Tyler's lips, in full bloom, pressed against mine.

Everything that I imagined would follow after we kissed did indeed follow, until finally we both lay exhausted and entangled atop our clothes on the cold concrete floor. We held each other close and both breathed shallowly, as if even the noise of our breathing could alert the outside world to what had just gone on. Millions of thoughts exploded through my head, humming and racing at the speed of light, with only one making its voice heard ever so slightly above the soft crackling noise that all the others produced, pushing upward in my brain in a shallow whisper, humming in my ear, *This is what love really feels like.* I don't know indefinitely if I loved him before it happened, if I fell in love with him during, or if it simply overcame me in the blissful moments immediately after, but whatever the timing may have been, it was the most amazing feeling I'd ever known.

He looked at me and kissed my mouth softly, finally saying, "I've wanted you like this for a long time."

I felt that he was lying but wanted to believe him, so I let myself. My response at first was only to smile and cuddle in closer to him. I wished that I could lie with him like that forever, that I could simply hit pause on the movie of my life and turn that one scene into an eternal tableau that I could live in forever.

Unfortunately, I was not able to keep silent and so finally asked, "So what does this mean?"

He looked at me and smiled, responding, "Dunno. What does it mean to you?"

"Hmm," I whispered into his neck, "I guess it means I won't ever get married."

"Yeah, I guess not. But who the hell wants to get married anyway? Marriage is for small-town losers," he said, flashing his trademark grin. He was the child of a divorce.

"Not always. Sometimes marriage can be a really beautiful thing," I responded. My parents were still happily married; in fact, they were probably lying in a position quite similar to ours a mere two floors above us.

"Eh, fuck it. So maybe no marriage. But think of all the great things you can have instead."

"Such as?" I asked seriously.

"Such as…amazing encounters like what we're having right now," he finally stammered.

I had a tendency to psychoanalyze long before I ever had the ability to define the word, and his statement immediately struck me as telling a big part of the story of Tyler. Amazing encounters. I looked at him and again felt a tad psychic. I could see Tyler in a year, wrapped in the arms of another man in a dorm somewhere, talking about life, rebuffing the convention that he believed had been his parents' downfall, all the while desperately trying to convince himself that being gay was in fact a more desirable alternative to the more traditional life he couldn't have. I saw his defense mechanisms churning away underneath his strong exterior; saw the doubts that floated up to the surface of his crystal eyes only to be quickly forced back down. Tyler would run from man to man, always in search of beauty and romance, of first kisses and amazing first-time sex. He would stay awhile but not too long, too petrified of waking up and being the gay-male version of his lonely and regretful mother. Eventually, every man who fell in love with Tyler would awaken one otherwise uneventful morning to find the other side of the bed unmade, never to be slept in again. As I thought of all of these things, I found myself praying that tomorrow wouldn't be my turn and that I'd get to hold him for a little bit longer before he slipped out of my grasp.

"I could live a life filled with amazing nights like this," was what I finally responded with, intuiting that my best chance of keeping him was to simply agree with his feelings, to adopt them as my own.

"I think I could handle it myself," he said, rolling on top of me and hanging his head close to mine so that his long sandy-blond hair hung in my eyes, giving me the sensation of looking up at him through sun-bleached reeds.

"You were my first…everything," I said, revealing more than I'd intended.

"You too," he said softly, moving his face closer to mine, so that his little button nose touched the tip of my slightly broader one.

"Did it mean anything to you?" I asked hopefully.

"Of course it did," he said, faltering slightly.

"That didn't sound very convincing," I said, trying to hide the wound I felt developing in my heart with a bit of humor.

He brought his hand up and touched my face, saying, "You believe what you want, but it really did mean a lot to me. I wanted it to be you…I wanted you to be the first."

"First of many," I said, finishing his thought.

"Possibly. But we're the only ones here right now," he said quietly. I brought my hand up and pushed his hair back, allowing myself to bask in his light without encumbrance. I saw that for all his beauty and his brave talk that he was in fact vulnerable. I saw it in his eyes, the pools that were just too clear to hide anything well. I saw that it really had meant something to him beyond the physical, that he too had sought me out because we were, at root, so much the same.

We were the ones who'd been discarded. For all of his beauty and all of my charm, we were still different from most of our peers, and unfortunately we were both too intelligent to not be painfully aware of it. As I grew up, I would learn to foster the things that made me unique, that made me stand out, those attributes that I believe make me special. But at 17, all either of us wanted was to be a part of it all, a part of the football games, the homecoming dances, the laughs and the parties and the teen normalcy that surrounded us. Try as we might, however, both Tyler and I were never much more than spectators, always relegated to watch somewhat sullenly from the side, wearing hardened, brave smiles. Before either of us had admitted our sexuality to ourselves, many of our schoolmates had identified it, or at least known that we were not like the majority of the guys at school.

The result was that both of us were forced to watch high school unfold rather than really experience it for ourselves because we were never granted full access. Each of us had friends, and on the whole we were well-liked by our peers, but the majority of them kept us at arm's length. Perhaps no creature that roams the earth is as cruel as the teenager faced with something he doesn't understand, something he perhaps even fears, and in our small New England town, nothing was feared more than the prospect of being gay. So I watched and so did Tyler, and I ached because of it and so did he. Finally, I reached out for something, and he was what I found, he who was himself stumbling around through the haze, trying desperately to connect with someone. So that was how it began for the two boys that lived their lives on the outskirts; they finally found each other and invited one another inside.

"You know, you didn't even have to buy me a drink. Isn't that how this type of thing usually works?" I asked with a smile, pushing myself off him with one arm while simultaneously fumbling around on the floor to find my lighter and my cigarettes.

"Why do I have to buy the drink? I think I should be the drink recipient," he said as he playfully pulled my arm out from under me, causing me to fall onto his chest.

"Because that's how it works and you know it," I said with mock reproach.

"How what works?" he asked playfully, cocking one brow.

"The one who's going to be…you know…sore in the morning earned the drink, and that's that. I have no more to say on the subject. It is elementary," I replied, letting out a long puff of silver smoke.

"All right, all right. You drive a hard bargain, buddy, but I think I can hang with it," he whispered, pulling my cigarette from my mouth and putting it to his lips.

"Hard being the operative word, mister," I said, unable to constrain my laughter.

"Tell ya what? Since we can't get into any bars yet, I could get you a beer at the next woods keg party. Is that cool?"

"Wow, Tyler!" I exclaimed, "I never took you for a romantic, but I'm happy to stand corrected."

"Well," he said, exhaling a trail of smoke and putting on his best James Dean face, "I like to be a little mysterious."

"You are nothing if not an enigma, Tyler," I said with playful sarcasm as I pressed my forehead against his and closed my eyes. I felt him jut his chin up and brush his lips lightly against mine, and I couldn't help but smile. Smiling soon turned into uncontrollable laughter.

"What's so funny?" he asked, looking slightly taken aback.

"I was just thinking, maybe instead of a beer at the next kegger you could get me some of Craig's oregano," I sputtered through laughs.

"You are nuts, you know that? And now you're gonna git it!" he said with a laugh, flipping me onto my back and rolling on top of me. "How'd you get so crazy?" he whispered into my neck.

"Just born that way, I guess. How'd you get so damn cute?" I replied, making an exaggerated kissing face at him.

"Just born that way, I guess," he said as he outlined my lips with his finger.

"Get your own material," I replied.

"Make me," he responded, whispering the words into my slightly opened mouth.

"Tyler," I whispered, suddenly very serious.

"Yes?"

"I won't ever forget this, not any of it. I couldn't have imagined it any better."

He looked at me, peering in the dim light until our eyes were locked. He didn't say a word, he simply leaned in and pressed his lips gently against mine and held them there for what felt like forever. There was nothing left that either one of us could have said without cheapening the entire experience, so neither one of us spoke. I didn't want him to lie to me nor did he want to, so we both said nothing. But when our eyes locked and our hands intertwined there in the dark, our bodies whispered to each other those words that our mouths would never get to say. I loved him so much that the feeling caused me to physically ache; it burned from the bottom up and made me light-headed. I don't think I could ever love a man again the way that I loved Tyler that night, and the way he made me believe that he loved me back. Wherever he may be now, a piece of him will always be down there with me, lying in my arms on a cold basement floor and helping the boy that I once was learn to accept the man that I was to become.

DEFUSED

Jordan M. Coffey

It's the latest in a string of long, hard days, and the fact that I got caught up in a hostage situation doesn't seem to be the worst of it. I'm just so fucking tired…a weariness I can't shake. It's not physical. I'm not one of those cops who lets himself go after so many years on the job. Even with knees that complain to me on rainy days, I still run at least five miles most mornings and try to get to the gym in my old neighborhood once a week for a few rounds with the heavy bag. These days, though, the best I hope for is that with every punch thrown I can beat back the urge to take a drink, and with every mile of pavement I pound I can out-distance my nagging sense of discontent.

Jerry Conway, this crazed bastard I arrested earlier, spent a lot of time babbling before he was taken into custody. Mostly the ranting of a troubled mind, but the gist of it got through to me…that he didn't want to hurt anyone; he just wanted his own pain to end and lacked the guts to do it himself. His answer was to create a situation where he thought the police would have no choice but to take him out. Unlucky for him, I'm damned good at my job. But I understood his morbid sentiment. Recently, there have been plenty of times when I seriously hoped I would go out in a blaze of gunfire—but I'm too chickenshit to actually sit at home and eat my gun.

Battling demons…I'm still doing it. Four years since my last drink, but sometimes it seems like only yesterday. Tonight is def-

DEFUSED

initely like that. The craving is unusually strong, and it doesn't
help that when I get home I'll be all alone. Once, Cruz would
have been there waiting for me. But about a month ago, after a
particularly difficult case and yet another of our increasingly fre-
quent arguments, I made him move out, told him I was tired of
him and he'd be better off without me anyway.

In truth, I'm surprised we were ever together at all. Unlike
the blond, muscled boys I used to hook up with, Cruz Severo is
dark-haired and brown-eyed like me. And he's much more serious, not quite as young as the other guys that I routinely let in
and out of my life. From the beginning, he made it clear that he
intended to stick around, that he believed in commitment, and
wasn't deterred by my past of a wife who had left me because of
my drinking, or how it had taken me so long to face what had me
drinking so much in the first place.

After my divorce, after I finally accepted that fucking men is
more to my liking, I tried once to have something more than just
sex. It was with a detective from another squad, who ended up
gunned down while off-duty by a kid fleeing a robbery. I was still
drinking at the time, and when he died, I got worse. Eventually, I
pulled out of it; it was either that or be canned, and the job was
the only thing I had left. It wasn't easy, but the department gave
me a choice: get help and stay on or stay drunk and get out.
Sober, I became a better cop, but I survived by thriving at work
while still skating through the rest. Then Cruz came along—an
electrician who gave a much-needed jolt to my worn-out exis-
tence—and everything changed. Three years we were together,
the last two living in the house I'd bought to signify the end of my
marriage. I can honestly say it was the best time of my life, but
then all of a sudden it seemed like we couldn't get through a day
without fighting. Sex itself took on an edge of anger and pain. But
nights like tonight I miss even that.

Common sense tells me I should go to Vinnie's and take it out
in the ring with a sparring partner, but temporary insanity has me
driving through the dark, rainy streets toward The Last Stop,
where I can get a drink and a fuck...lose myself in the welcome
heat of both a strong bourbon and a willing body.

At the bar, it's almost too easy to order my old favorite, but my hand is shaking when I try to take the first sip and I end up just staring into the glass, searching but finding no answers. With a deep breath, I turn my back on the alcohol and focus my attention instead on the men around me. My last birthday put me closer to 50 than 40, and everyone seems so much younger than they used to, but as I size up my options, I'm pleased to see that I still get my share of attention. A cute blond with spiky hair finally tires of the waiting game and tries the direct approach, but after some cursory attempts to connect, I find that I'm not into it as much as I want to be and leave both the blond and the bourbon, going home alone.

Thankfully, the rain has let up, because even without booze in my system, I'm somehow out of sorts, unsure if I should be behind the wheel. Yet I get home easily enough, struggling only when it comes to getting my key in the door. My brain is busy trying to formulate the perfect way to end this day, starting with a hot shower and hopefully sleeping as late as possible in the morning, but in spite of my preoccupation, when I open the door I immediately sense that something is wrong. My gun is already in my hand by the time I fully recognize the familiar figure lit by the dim light coming from my kitchen, about the same time that I register the smell of coffee in the air.

"What the fuck are you doing here, Cruz? Trying to get yourself killed?" I put down my weapon with shaky fingers and try not to be grateful that I don't smell like either alcohol or sex.

"Sorry, *Detective* Calabresi. I figured you'd notice my car outside."

I hadn't, which only emphasizes how bad off I am. I counter with, "You can't just show up like this. I might not have been alone, you know."

His shoulders slump a little, but his voice is strong enough. "Yeah, well, then I guess you should have these." He reaches into his pocket, pulls out his keys, separates two that are on a ring with a dangling little silver lightning bolt and throws them my way. "Just tell me where you put the things I left here."

"I don't remember seeing any of your stuff left," I lie, placing his keys next to my gun. After he moved out, I scoured the place for anything he might have left behind, gathered what I found, supposedly to pack it for him, but instead I hid the box high on a shelf in the den closet. More than once I had pulled it down, reminiscing. "I'll let you know if anything turns up," I add, lumbering over to the couch and dropping down on it. My eyes close almost instantly, the idea of sleeping in even more appealing. A strong hand grips the back of my neck, massaging a little, and my stomach goes into a slow roll.

I hear Cruz sigh, a weighty sound in the darkness. "Don't worry about it," he says. "The truth is I saw what happened on the news and I thought you might want some company." His voice is low and as dangerously soothing as his hand.

Why won't you just accept that I'm a mess and stay away from me? I think, biting back the urge to say that if I wanted company, I wouldn't have walked in the door alone. I pull away from his touch and stand up, putting on my "bad cop" face as he comes around the couch to join me. "I'm fine. I don't need a keeper. After all this time, you should know what my job can be like. And, no, I don't want to talk about it. It's bad enough living through it once without rehashing the whole thing."

"Damn it, Eddie, why the hell won't you just let me be here for you?" he argues, standing much too close.

"Let's not do this again, Cruz. We went through this shit a month ago."

"No, we yelled a lot, and I was stupid enough to let you push me out of here, but I love you and no matter what else is going on with you, I still believe you love me too."

Cruz sounds so sure, and my own convictions are wavering. I grab him, intent on shaking some sense into him or physically removing him from the premises or…something. But instead I kiss him. It's a rough kiss, almost violent, full of my fury and frustration and yes, true enough, the intensity of how much I do still love him. I savor it for a long, painfully sweet moment, before I find the strength to push him away, hands still on his shoulders with a white-knuckled grip. I'm much too wound up, desperately on edge, and I have the fleeting thought that maybe it would have been better if unlucky Jerry Conway had detonated his explosive vest and taken me along with him. "Cruz," I say, finally letting him go, "you should just leave."

But he does the opposite and gets even closer. Suddenly, he's touching me, and I close my eyes, trying to gather my defenses. His hands seem to be everywhere, underneath my shirt, undoing my pants, expertly caressing the flesh inside. "Cruz..." I start to warn, but he responds with lips in addition to fingertips, traveling leisurely down my body. I want to move, try to move, but can't, held in place by the rush of my emotions. He pushes down my underwear, licks my cock, and I moan.

"I want you to stop shutting me out." The words whisper over my balls. "I want to move back *home*."

He sucks me in down to the root, bruising my ass with his hold. There's a brief pause where I'm aware only of my heartbeat reverberating loudly in my ears, and then a wet finger probes between my cheeks before pushing painfully inside. My knees tremble at the burn and I grab Cruz's head when his mouth goes back to my dick. I haven't been fucked in years, and I'm sure not ever while sober. Cruz never expressed an interest in that direction, and the feeling of first one finger and then two plunging in and out of my body is only vaguely familiar, but increasingly pleasant.

"Everyone has to let go sometimes, Eddie," Cruz says, his other hand stroking the base of my cock while he mouths words around the leaking head. "You hold things in to keep from losing it on the job, to keep from drinking..." He slobbers over the tip of my dick, licks it with rough swipes, squeezing me tight. "But with me, it's OK to just"—his fingers move faster, thrust deeper, probing and finding—"explode."

I come so hard I can barely breathe, my eyes shut tight and my ass clenching around Cruz's fingers. I'm overwhelmed, unglued but not shattered. It's as if I've fallen apart but the strength of the experience is holding the pieces together. The feeling doesn't fade when Cruz pulls out and stands up in front of me, his lips wet with drops of come—lips that curve into a warm smile—and I realize that I still want the same things: to stay sober, to be a good cop and to share my life with Cruz Severo.

Wiping his lips with my thumb, I murmur, "Let's go take a

shower." I step out of my pants which had pooled around my ankles, pick them up and turn toward the stairs.

"Eddie."

I know that tone. "Please, Cruz, not tonight," I say, wanting to enjoy the feeling not analyze it.

"Just tell me. You do still love me, right? I mean, it wasn't really because you didn't want me anymore…wanted me out of your life?"

"No…I mean, yes, I love you, but you deserve better…easier."

"I'm moving back tomorrow."

I turn around; see him standing there still fully dressed, his arms crossed over his chest, a look of total determination on his face. Though half naked, I don't feel at a disadvantage, maybe a little afraid, but also extremely relieved. And lucky to find I truly have another chance. I give the only answer I can: "OK."

"Remember, from now on you have to open up and let me in more often." He grins a little, and I turn away, hiding the flush he might see even in the darkened room, thinking back to what just happened, though I'm almost sure that's not what he means.

Cruz joins me at the stairs, and I kiss him, tell him to wait right there. I go and get the things I left on the table by the door. The gun I lock in its usual place, and the keys I stuff back into Cruz's pocket. With that done, together the two of us go up to shower and wash each other clean.

TILES

Matthew Sterenchock

I used to be afraid of feeling old when I was younger. I was afraid of new lines on my face and Tempur-Pedic pillows, a different box to check when filling out a questionnaire. And I'm not even sure how I got here. I'm not even sure when I stopped being "younger" and became "older." Was it 30? Thirty-five? Or was it already happening when I was thinking about it at 26? Probably. But at that time 40 seemed another lifetime away.

I'm happy now. I'm happy with him. I'm in a committed relationship-we're living together—a concept I could barely grasp when I was 26. At that point in my life I'd had maybe one of note, but it was over quickly. It lasted a few minutes. I loved him, sure, and we were happy. But I couldn't commit, was afraid to think about the "forever" that he spoke of; I could barely plan what I was going to do the following week.

His name is Lane. He's in the shower right now, washing his old body. As I sit here lounging my old body. I am older now, but I always have the pleasure of saying that Lane is older still. He's got 10 years on me—not much now; in my 20s, it would have seemed a lot more. You know how, as we get older, years seem a lot shorter.

I love our shower. It's tiled, and we have one of those high-powered showerheads that blasts your old bones with therapeutic streams of water. It reminds me of hailstorms in late summer that I experienced while growing up. It hurts sometimes. It can be jarring in the early morning, but in a good way. I always wanted one of those showerheads. I especially wanted one when I was 26. The apartment I had the—my studio—had this old, drooling showerhead. No pressure. I could have had some friends line up and spit on me and would have been rinsed better. Still, I loved that apartment. It was such a great little space, with exposed brick walls and hardwood floors. I painted the walls different colors shortly after I moved in—one blue wall in the main room, one green in the bath, the kitchen entirely in red. I felt comfortable there, very inspired. It was my first apartment. I had lived on my own for four years before I moved in, but never completely by myself—never having the space that was all mine, to do with whatever I felt.

The tiles in our shower remind me of my neighbors' shower from when I was growing up. The Templetons. They lived across the street, and I think they're partly to blame for my always wanting more. I grew up poor. Not destitute—we never starved—but we never had much. I suppose we were lower middle class. My mother worked in a clothing factory, and my father did construction, both making just enough to get by. The Templetons had more. They owned a big house, twice the size or ours, and they had two nice cars. They both had good paying jobs: Janie worked as a nurse at a private clinic, and Al worked with computers at one of the hospitals in town. Every summer they went on vacation for two weeks to Virginia Beach with their equally well-off extended family, staying at fancy suite hotels right on the water. And they flew. We never flew. We actually never went on any vacations until I was 9; my father preferred to spend his days off around the house. Eventually when we did start going places, we drove. We stayed at very modest hotels. We did everything modestly. But I enjoyed it, getting away. Of course, once I'd caught a glimpse of the nicer oceanfront hotels and fancier restaurants, the details of our fabulous time relayed to friends were always a bit exaggerated.

The tiles in the Templetons' upstairs bathroom were so elegant. They were pale yellow and dark green. There was a row of lights just above the sink that gave off a soft amber glow and another light on the ceiling that was even softer. I spent a lot of time over at their house, and I inevitably spent a lot of time in their bathroom. I wanted to live in their house, to grow up there, to run down the staircase Christmas morning and find a lot of big gifts under the tree. I wanted their dining room with its long table and ornate chandelier; the large porch, high above the street, with the awning that covered the entire front. But the bathroom was really what I coveted.

Our bathroom was too bright. And it was small. It had a linoleum floor with this annoying pattern that I spent countless hours as a child trying to figure out. I could never understand what made it a "pattern" as opposed to just an ugly, strange design. The fixtures were a drab mauve-colored porcelain: the tub, the sink, the toilet. The light above the sink was fluorescent, covered by a ribbed plastic sheath. There was a big radiator next to the toilet that my father covered with a homemade wooden shelf, painted white. The countertop was also white. And on it was a permanent installation of disposable razors, a lumpy tube of toothpaste always being squeezed at different points throughout its body, four toothbrushes that could never seem to stay in the toothbrush holder fixed to the wall, my father's clippers, a bottle of Old Spice, cans of spray deodorant in varying sport scents, several different kinds of moisturizers my mother had leftover from when she sold Avon.

When I was 10 or 11, I decided that cleaning the bathroom was my job. I just saw other peoples' bathrooms and wanted in some way to emulate them—wanted there to be order, things to be put away where they belonged. I spent afternoons putting things away; if I didn't know where something went, I'd make a new home for it. Then I'd take the powdery stuff and clean the sink and tub, scrub them down. And then—and this was a big one—I'd fold the towels neatly and hang them on the racks and little hooks. I'd always try to find the ones in our linen closet that matched the best; to my knowledge a matching set never really existed. I just had to match similar shades. The Templetons' bathroom had sets of towels that matched the bathroom itself. The most I could hope for were two little hand towels that resembled each other. Once I was finished, it wasn't long before the bathroom fell into disarray again. My father and brother couldn't be bothered to keep things neat. Sometimes they didn't even flush the toilet after using it. I don't think they washed their hands much either, so I was always surprised to find the towels disheveled after they had finished. My mother made an effort, though. I think she appreciated what I was trying to do.

Now our towels all match in our bathroom. They match each other and they match the room. The bathroom was actually one of the few rooms in the house that didn't require much fixing up when Lane and I moved in, just a good cleaning. The tiles were already there. Maybe that's why I had a particular affection for this house as opposed to all the others we were looking at. This one was the closest to what I wanted, I suppose. Lane was indifferent. Not indifferent, really; he did care. He just saw how much I wanted it, and that's what mattered to him.

Lying on our bed now, I can see a crack above the bathroom door that I haven't noticed before. It's not big or threatening. I shouldn't mention it to Lane; he'll never be able to focus on anything else. That's the way he is, and I am too. I notice these little imperfections, but I don't let them get to me. It's really just a small crack. Sort of looks like it belongs. The Templetons had a crack in the ceiling above their stairs. I remember liking the look of it.

The air is nice tonight. I can feel it tenderly make its way into the room through the open window. It's one of those first nights of fall in Los Angeles, a time that always makes me strangely happy. It's still warm during the day, but once the sun goes down there's a sharp chill in the air that makes me think of leaves changing color and pumpkin pie, makes me want to sit in front of a fireplace. Lane will be cold when he gets out of the shower, but I can't bear the thought of closing it. After months of oppressive desert heat, I long for this time. The air is so crisp. I just want to lie in it. I could do nothing for days. I could lie here thinking about showers.

I should probably close the window. Lane gets prickly if he gets a chill.

We've been doing so well lately, I'd hate to give him a reason to ignore me. He does that; he can be so silly sometimes. Little things can push him over the edge, and he'll decide he can't speak to me for days, sometimes even a week. A couple of months ago, we hosted a birthday dinner party for one of his oldest friends, and Lane ended up throwing this terrific fit after everyone had left. Apparently, I had spent too much time commenting on how good his friend was looking or some such thing. I thought I was being polite. I knew they had a history, and I thought I might just show how comfortable I was with him and pay him some compliments on his birthday. I'd had a bit of the champagne. We always get Veuve Clicquot for our parties and I just adore it.

To be perfectly honest, I did feel a bit uncomfortable at the start because Lane didn't want me to invite too many of my friends, so I had Ananda, our live-in, refill my glass a bit faster than usual. He says my friends don't "behave well" with his friends. He calls them "the bohemians." It's funny, really. I think he's just jealous because they've known me longer than he has. Anyway, what followed was a weeklong silent treatment. He would relay messages to me through Ananda; that's what he always does, which only makes it more difficult on him, since she doesn't speak very good English. That's why these little squabbles generally last but a few days. It finally got to be too much for him. He came home early one day and said he had made reservations at L'Orangerie, one of our favorite restaurants. I appreciated that this was how he decided to break the silence.

When Lane and I first got together, he talked constantly. I did too. It was like we were both fighting for airtime; there was something so exciting about it. We couldn't say enough to one another. We don't really have conversations as we did then, but that's because we know each other so well. It just seems unnecessary. It can seem rather quiet here; he doesn't really like to have music on. I sometimes joke that we live in a library. That's another thing: Lane thinks all my friends are too loud.

Whenever we've had discussions about my friends, particularly about them being too loud, I find that that's when I'd like to see them most. I'll go ahead and make plans with them generally on a night I know Lane won't be able to join. He's always been really judgmental, and at first it was actually something I found quite attractive about him. He wore it well. I don't really see it like that anymore. It's just tiring now. So is his inability to say what's on his mind. Sometimes I want him just to attack, to really let me have i—not physically, of course, but really just to tell me that something I've done has pissed him off. Generally, I'm not one for confrontation, but there are times when I feel raised voices would do us both some good. We get enough "air," and we both have more than enough "time alone." He never seems to want to solve anything when it's actually happening. My friend Sydney, who in Lane's mind is the "leader" of the bohemians, thinks all the silence is doing a lot of damage to our relationship. I try to tell her that it's fine; that's just the way it is. We do get through it, just not in the way a lot of other people might—like Sydney, for example.

Sydney *is* loud, I suppose. She's always been someone to tell the truth, someone unafraid to deal with what's at hand. I admire that in her; that's why we've been friends for so long. I'd like to be a little more like her. It's not for want of trying. I have made attempts to fight with Lane, to get things out in the open. I've called him on things, told him he's being irrational or that he's just not listening. He usually just ignores me or thinks I'm joking. That tends to make me angrier, at which point I have to just shut up or leave the room. I'm afraid of what I might say.

He's been in the shower a long time. We used to take long showers together. It was nice. Sometimes we'd take long baths together too on cold afternoons in winter. That I loved. I could stay in there all day. He works a lot more than he used to, so we don't seem to have that kind of time. I don't take baths anymore, even though I don't work. It seems a waste of time. I usually prefer a quick shower.

There was another silence between us not too long ago, and I noticed Lane's showers taking a bit longer then. It seems to have become another one of his ways of dealing with his anger toward me. He just tries to wash it away. I was feeling particularly feisty the second or third night of it, and I took advantage of his inability to hear anything with the water running and said a few things. I stood outside the bathroom door and told him exactly what I was thinking. It felt great. I knew he couldn't hear me, knew he'd be in there for a while, so I had time. The fight was about a message I'd accidentally deleted or something of that sort. It felt silly at first, talking to the door. Then I started crying a little bit. I tend to be a bit more emotional than he is—a quality he callously uses against me sometimes. He knows when I'm upset and knows when turning away from me will hurt the most. So he does it, and it tears me apart, and I want nothing more than to throw whatever's available to me in his general direction.

I remember: It *had* to do with a phone message. It was from a friend of his about some meeting they were trying to set up. After I got caught up in a few other things later in the day, I lost track and didn't give the message to him until a few days later, when it was too late. For all I knew, his friend just wanted to catch up, to say hello. Lane didn't see it that way. To him, it was another careless mistake that was a direct result of my "laziness and irresponsibility." I saw the anger building in his face—his right eye starts to twitch, and he gets rather flushed—but then it went nowhere after that. He simply walked away.

I was so tired of being ignored that lashing out at the bathroom door gave me at least a bit of satisfaction, knowing I could say what I wanted to say and express what it was he was doing to me. I can't even remember particulars of what I said, but once I began, it was difficult to stop. There was a rush of words and I was afraid my mouth might not be able to keep up with my brain. Eventually, I slowed down when I realized that it really wouldn't change things because I wasn't speaking to him. It was enough just to say these things out loud. I went to our bed and lay there as though nothing had happened, as though it were any other night. After a few more minutes I heard him turn the water off. Soon he came out of the bathroom, and I went in. I needed to wash some things away myself.

It's interesting now to think back on a time when I was afraid of taking showers.

I don't remember what age I was when I made the transition from taking baths to showers, but I must have been young. It was difficult in the beginning. Suddenly, there were all these challenges. I was used to sitting in the water. One of the problems was deciding on what side to enter the shower once the water was flowing and the curtain was closed. I do remember my mom standing just outside the bathroom door, waiting to dispense advice if I needed it. I'm sure I called out to her to ask how I should negotiate the shower, not that I was necessarily afraid of doing it incorrectly necessarily. I just didn't want to find myself bombarded all of a sudden with bursts of water. She waited there for a few minutes, then called to me, "I'll be just down the hall if you need anything." She spent a lot time in her sewing room whenever I went upstairs for a shower. That was a comfort, knowing she was near. I was old enough that I didn't want her actually in the bathroom with me, but I definitely wanted her around. If she went too far, she would never hear me.

I got used to it after a while. But I still think about that. I still notice a particular routine that probably began with those first few showers. Even down to the way I towel off afterward. It's all very mechanical, as if I think about it too much—do I dry the left arm first or the right?—I might get completely disoriented and dry my face a second time. It all has to happen while I think of something else, like what I'm going to wear. Things like that.

The first time Lane and I took a shower together in our new house I was so in love. I was so happy and wanted never to be this intimate with anyone else but him. I felt that way when we started sharing a bed. I've watched him sleep sometimes, and it's amazing to witness. It's like he's been unplugged; no, it's like this stereo I used to have, how it shut off but was always in this sort of "standby" mode. It was never really off completely; a simple tap on any button on the remote and it would spring to life again. I suppose we don't all spring to life like that when we wake up: I don't think I would be ready to play a CD immediately upon waking, but it's similar.

I'm fascinated by our bodies—by *people*. It's something we take for granted. All of us need to do things like take showers or baths, sleep, eat, belch. We forget that that the person standing next to us in line at the post office may be digesting her lunch at that very moment, and it may not agree with her, and if she has a husband, he may inevitably experience that to some degree too. Lane doesn't eat a lot of dairy because it upsets his stomach. But every so often he'll enjoy a cheese plate with me somewhere and then suffer the consequences later. He tries to play it off, but I hear him. I know what's happening to him when he gets up in the middle of the night. That's fascinating too, that closeness. We learn to do all of these things on our own, and we get used to doing a lot of these things by ourselves. And then we meet someone, fall in love, move in together, and we don't have to be by ourselves. We experience our own lives on a daily basis—our own bowel movements, our own showers, our own breathing patterns, our own nightmares—but suddenly we also experience someone else's. Sometimes I'm a little messy when I eat; so is Lane. Sometimes I toss and turn in the night; so does Lane. Sometimes I have a large ball of wax just sitting on the inside my ear, and so does Lane.

A few days ago, we were sitting in kitchen having breakfast, and I noticed how tired his face seemed. I asked if he wanted more coffee, and I reached for his cup as he looked up at me. There was a pause—his eyes looked as though they hadn't closed in days—and then he nodded his thanks. It reminded me of how vulnerable he can be and how he seems to fight so hard in order not to show it now. But there was something peaceful about him; he looked content to have me sitting across from him. It made me fall in love with him all over again.

I poured the coffee and slid it toward him, then I topped mine off with the rest. He had the morning paper in front of him, and without looking, he slowly reached for the cup with his left hand. As he brought it to his lips, his mouth evenly letting out a bit of air to cool the first sip, he looked across again at me and winked. I smiled at him just as I had when we'd had everything to talk about.

THE BET

Gerald Libonati

The longshoreman felt out of place as he rushed among the throngs of young professionals, college students and theater patrons who frequented the trendy Himmarshee district. It was an area along the New River near downtown Fort Lauderdale jammed with cafés, shops, galleries, and anything else that drew people together when the sun went down.

There was no reason for Frank Domacci to feel awkward. He had abandoned his old jeans and T-shirt, the uniform he sported when unloading ships at Port Everglades. He looked presentable enough in his dark-blue pleated slacks and a striped long-sleeved shirt with the sleeves rolled up to his elbow.

He maneuvered along the broken sidewalk toward Trattoria Porto Fino, the restaurant owned by his father where he had been tending bar for the last two weeks following a temporary but unexpected layoff at the docks. He crossed the narrow avenue and turned into the first door on the right.

The interior was mostly wood and brass accented with gold-framed oil paintings. They were not images of Pompeii or other Italian landmarks but a more contemporary collection of pieces selected for their vibrant color content. A long bar was set up against the rear wall with the doors to the kitchen to the right and the restrooms to the left.

"Look who decided to show up," said his cousin Gina Bellazio as he passed her on the way to the kitchen.

"Hello to you too," he said as he pushed through the door, pulled an apron from the rack and checked himself in the mirror. He was a tall man with thick, black hair and an attractive but not handsome face. His deep-set eyes were as brown as the tile floors of his father's restaurant. The chin was sharply defined with a small cleft but he couldn't seem to get rid of the 5 o'clock shadow that had plagued him since puberty. He gave his hair a quick brush-through with his fingers, grunted, and pushed back through the doors to take his place behind the bar.

Wednesday evenings were slow, and the room was only partially filled with patrons enjoying the first half of a preplanned dinner packaged with a show at the massive theater down the street. The diners displayed their best qualities to each other as the voice of Andrea Bocelli filled the room. Some chattered, some were quiet but all of them seemed to be in good spirits as they clustered in couples. Except for table 9.

It was a booth along the west wall occupied by a young man who sat alone with a plate of Pasta Primavera. Next to his dish was a yellow pad on which he scribbled from time to time as if to compensate for the lack of conversation during the ample free time a freshly cooked meal could create.

He had come into the restaurant once before just a few days prior and Frank noticed him because he was alone then, too. And also because Gina, who waited tables, passed by him and sang, "Single on 9." But nothing was said that first night because the customer's privacy was to be respected. Although now, as Frank glanced at him from time to time, he thought it wouldn't hurt to do a little something extra, just to make a new customer feel welcome. It was the little things that built a good client base.

While writing on his pad the brown-haired man sensed someone at his side and turned with a startled look to see Frank standing there with a cup of cappuccino. "I didn't order any—"

"This is on the house," Frank said noticing the man's empty ring finger.

"Oh, thank you," he said looking up at the waiter.

"If you'd like dessert—"

"No, I'm fine," he said and complimented the meal.

Frank looked at the patron's hazel eyes and his thin frame before deciding to risk a personal question. "So, what are you writing?"

"Oh, this," he chuckled. "It's my attempt at a story."

"I'm impressed," Frank said. "You must be smart."

"No, it's just a way to stay sane."

"What's your name in case you get famous?"

"Jason," he paused and added. "Anderson."

"Well, Jason Anderson, I'm Frank and I hope we see you again." He said "we" even though he meant "I," and added, "If you need anything, just give me a wave."

"Thanks," Jason said and watched the tall man walk back toward the bar. Then he took a sip of his cappuccino. No more than 10 minutes passed before Jason collected his things, left a tip and paid the bill at the cashier near the door.

"Bye, Jason," Frank called from the bar.

Jason smiled and said goodbye.

Gina sided up to Frank, "And who was that?"

"A customer—who do you think?"

"Oh, a customer." Gina nodded and made a long face. "Now you say goodbye to customers you don't wait on?"

"Sometimes."

"A stranger across a crowded room?" she needled.

The vague musical reference was lost on the longshoreman. "Gina, you're my cousin, not my mother. And besides, I did wait on him. I brought him a cup of coffee."

"You never wait tables."

"Well…"

Gina was shorter than Frank with wavy black hair that she fastened in the back with a clip so that a portion of it hung straight down like a curtain gathered at the center. "You should let me introduce you."

He looked at his cousin. "You know him?"

"No, but when has that ever stopped me?"

Two nights later Frank was pouring a Scotch and water for a customer at the bar when he looked out over the restaurant and noticed Gina standing at a table taking an order from a single he couldn't see. A ripple of anxiety ran through his chest as he considered the possibility that it might be Jason. And worse, that Gina might say something about him, since they had briefly talked about the solitary customer that very afternoon. He pulled his apron off and went to where she was standing.

"Gina!" he said louder than he meant to, and when she turned around, he saw a 50-something man with glasses and a tattoo.

"Yes?" Gina said with a questioning tone.

He was about to say, "I'm sorry," but instead he said, "I'm taking a break."

"Fine," she responded and knitted her brow in confusion.

Frank was pissed at himself because now he had to go outside and wait in the alley as if he needed a break when he actually didn't. While he was standing where the alley met the side street, a red Camaro slowed in front of him and a blond man with a mustache said hi.

For the sake of business, Frank said, "How you doing?"

"You know where Himmarshee Street is?"

"Right there in front of you," Frank responded.

"Thanks," the driver said as his eyes dropped to the bartender's frontal bulge. "I like your pants."

"Yeah, well, try Macy's," Frank said and returned to the back door of the restaurant.

The voice of Sinatra crooning "I've Got You Under My Skin" was playing from a recording of songs Mrs. Domacci had put together for background music. As Frank stepped behind the bar, Gina was on the phone.

"Hold on a minute," she said into the receiver. "Would you check on the two at the end?"

"Sure," Frank said and walked over to a well-dressed couple sitting close together. She ordered a gin and tonic and he ordered a club soda.

The next hour went quickly as the staff got busier the way they usually did on a Friday night when the street in front of the restaurant was a mass of bodies moving up and down the sidewalks. Frank was washing glasses when he heard Gina say, "Don't look now, but I think the stranger from across a crowded room just walked in."

Frank's eyes snapped up to see Jason standing at the door being greeted by the hostess who took him to a small table next to an interior wood barrier with brass piping along the top.

"He's kind of cute," Gina said. "A little on the scrawny side but what the hell. I'm not the one who likes him."

"I never said I liked him."

"Then why do you keep talking about him?"

"Just curious, that's all."

"You gonna ask him out?"

He made an exasperated noise. "I don't even know the guy."

"So, what are you gonna do, give him another cup of coffee?"

"Maybe."

She struck a pose like a statue and looked at him. "Frank, you're never gonna meet anybody if you stay in your little shell. You've got to get out there and meet people."

"You mean like you?"

"Yes, like me. I'm not a slut, but I meet plenty of guys."

"I know. You're as pure as a motel sheet."

"Hey, every once in a while the sheets gotta get made—you know what I'm saying? You never go out."

"Yes, I do. I have meaningless sex with people I never see again."

"So try it with someone you like once in a while. You're a good-looking guy. I'm sure he'd be thrilled to go out with you."

"What are you talking about? I barely spoke to him."

"See, that's what I mean. I don't know how you got into this family. Me, your brother—we're all in everybody's business. But you, you're like one of those little Chihuahua dogs like Aunt Mary had. You remember how he used to shake all the time, he was so nervous? And I gotta tell you, shy is not attractive in a man."

"I'm not shy, and I don't shake."

"Not unless you see somebody you halfway like."

"Maybe I'm not interested. Did you ever think of that?"

"Yeah, like the fox ain't interested in the chicken."

"Are you calling me a fox?"

"Actually, I'm calling you a chicken."

"Don't you have a table to tend to?"

"Ah, they can't make up their minds," Gina said waving the air. "Listen, I will bet you my day off that you won't ask him to go out with you. I mean it; I'll work for you on my day off, if you do it."

"Oh, really?"

"And vice versa, really."

"We'll see," he said. He went back to the sink and pushed another glass down on the cleaning brush as Gina made subtle chicken noises.

She came up next to him and said, "I'll make it easy. He doesn't even have to agree. You just have to ask him. That's all."

"What, you think someone classy wouldn't go out with me?"

"I never said that."

"Like I said, we'll see."

"It's not a bet unless you agree."

Frank looked up at the sandy-haired man sitting alone at the table. "OK."

"OK, what?"

"I agree," he said with an irritated edge.

"Oh, this is gonna be the easiest money I ever made."

"Look, I thought you wanted me to do this."

"I do."

"Then why are you making it sound like it's impossible?"

"Oh, please, Frank. My girlfriend would kill to go out with you. But I know it's not your cup of tea." She looked him up and down. "He'll say yes."

Frank looked over at Jason again. Then, suddenly, he put the glass on the counter, pulled off his apron and picked up a pad. "Cover for me, would you?"

"Now you're talking," Gina said, giving him a pat on the back. "Go get him, tiger."

Frank went to Jason's table. "Good evening," he said to the young man.

Jason looked up. "Oh, hi."

"You came back," Frank said with a smile.

"Yes. I got hooked on that cappuccino you gave me."

"I know. We put extra caffeine in for the customers we like," Frank said and Jason laughed. "It's good to see you again."

"Boy you have good manners," Jason said.

"Dining alone tonight?"

"I'm always alone."

"Ahh," Frank said indicating disappointment but in truth he was glad. "I guess I should have brought you a menu. Hold on." *What an idiot,* he thought of himself as he went to the holder at the end of the partition and returned with a menu. "There you go. I'll give you a few minutes," he said and returned to the bar to recuperate from his embarrassment.

"Well?" Gina asked.

"Well, what?"

"Did you ask him?"

"Give me time. Jeez."

"That's what I thought," Gina said.

"You got to be subtle about these things."

"Yeah, subtle," she repeated sarcastically.

"Haven't you given that table enough time to make up their minds?"

"Oh, my God!" Gina blurted. "They probably lost 10 pounds waiting for me."

Frank shook his head and asked a customer at the bar if everything was all right. A few minutes later he returned to Jason's table, took his order ,and said, "No papers today?"

"Taking a break," Jason said.

"Are you a writer?" he asked, regretting the question immediately. *If he's writing a story, then he's a writer.* Even though Frank was attracted to the man, he felt oddly inept in his presence.

"Not really," Jason said. "But I do work at the library."

OK, the question might not have been that bad, Frank thought, feeling a sense of relief. "Right over here?" Frank absently made a gesture with his hand in the direction of the main library.

"Yes, I guess we're neighbors in a sense."

Jason spoke in an educated manner, and he worked for the library, while Frank had barely made it through community college and used to work in a warehouse. The gap between them seemed to widen. And to add to Frank's feeling of separation was the fact that he didn't even know the man's sexual orientation—a fact his pushy cousin never thought to consider. Sure, there was no wedding ring, but Jason could be a freethinker who had got married on a beach in the Bahamas in a ceremony with no jewelry.

"I thought you might be from out of town," Frank said, probing for more information.

"No, I live near 84. You know where the Metropolitan Community Church is?"

That was it, the clue Frank needed. Jason had just made a reference to a gay establishment: the Metropolitan Community Church. Guys don't make gay references to strangers unless they want them to know they are gay, and if he wanted Frank to know that, he must also be interested. Frank was highly encouraged and took it as permission to move forward.

"Yes, I do," Frank said as if to communicate his own orientation through the same code, even though he'd never been to the church. "Listen, I was just wondering—"

"Waiter," said a voice from the next table.

"Maybe you'd—"

"Waiter," the voice called more insistently, having noticed the order was already taken and the only thing separating her from good service was idle chitchat.

Frank let his breath out in frustration and said to Jason, "Excuse me, I'll go ahead and give your order to the waitress." He went to the next table and tried to be pleasant as he assured the woman in heavy makeup there was no soy in the cream sauce to trigger her allergies.

When Jason's order was ready, Frank asked a waitress named Barbara to take it over since it was her table he had stolen. Besides, he didn't want to seem overbearing. After all, the only reason the guy came into the restaurant was to eat his ravioli in peace. Frank had already decided he would bring another coffee when Jason had finished. But to do that he had to keep an eye on the table, which made him feel like a stalker.

Fortunately, Gina was tending to her own customers and didn't have time to harass him.

At the appropriate moment, Frank filled a short white cup with cappuccino and brought it to the table. Jason was about to speak but Frank leaned in and said, "My compliments."

"That's very kind of you," Jason said politely. "I'd ask you to sit, but I know you're busy."

"Just for a minute," Frank said, trying to keep his excitement from showing.

"Good. Now it doesn't look like I'm a total loser. They'll all think I came in to see you, but you were too busy until now." He laughed at his own whimsy.

"Believe me, you're not a loser," Frank said.

"Would you write that down so I can read it again later?"

Frank chuckled. This guy had a sense of humor too. He liked that. "I was gonna ask if maybe you'd like to get together for a drink sometime? I don't mean here—you know, out."

"Are you kidding?" Jason said. A flash of anxiety shot through Frank as he wondered if that was a yes or a no. "I'd like that very much," Jason said. He pulled a wallet from his pocket, searched for a card, and handed it to the tall man sitting across from him. "That's my cell so you can reach me anytime."

"Thanks. What time do you get off work?"

"I'm home by 6 usually, unless there's an emergency."

"At the library?"

"You never know. Some renegade teacher might go off the deep end and assign an unexpected book report. We have to be prepared for these things."

Frank laughed. "I'll call you tomorrow if that's all right."

"Fine."

"But right now I do need to get back to the bar."

"I understand."

"Enjoy your coffee."

"Thanks."

Frank returned to the bar feeling happier than he'd felt in a long time.

"So, how'd it go?" Gina asked.

"Looks like I'm getting an extra night off."

"No way!" she exclaimed. "You asked him?"

"Not only did I ask but he was really into it."

"You see?" she said, nodding. "Now if I hadn't twisted your arm, you'd still be bitching and moaning."

"I think that's your department."

"You know, there's nothing worse than a smart-ass. I hope you're not like that when you go out with this guy because that's not attractive in a man."

For their night out, Frank and Jason went to an outdoor café on the New River serving food that was *not* Italian. Jazz from the park could be heard wafting through the air and a parade of boats hummed their way over the placid water between an ancient railroad trestle and the Seventh Avenue bridge. When the wine arrived, they raised their glasses and both of them said "*santé*" at the same time.

"Isn't it strange how life works, sometimes?" Frank mused.

"What do you mean?"

"Like you and me for instance. What are the chances we'd ever meet? I mean, we're so different, you know?"

"Is that a bad thing?" Jason asked.

"No, no, not at all. It's like a dolphin who lives in the water and an eagle who lives in a tree. They're both beautiful creatures, but you wouldn't expect them to get together."

"But they do have one thing in common," Jason observed.

"What's that?"

"They both eat at the same place."

Frank looked at Jason and tilted his head slightly as his eyes beamed with recognition. "The restaurant."

Frank discovered he had more in common with Jason than he expected. And Jason discovered he liked their differences. As weeks passed and they continued to see each other, those differences became more obvious. Jason was a patron of the arts, literature, and theater; while Frank was the kind who regularly attended sports events and watched them on TV and loved bass fishing. But their differences were complimentary, and each man allowed the other his space, and occasionally they shared an activity just to be mutually supportive. In that way both of them expanded their participation in life.

One Monday night when the restaurant was closed, Frank and Jason invited Gina to Jason's apartment for dinner. It was located just north of the 17th Street causeway, which connected Fort Lauderdale to the beach. The living room looked out over a marina stuffed with yachts ranging in price from the very expensive to the unattainable.

Gina showed up with a plate of fresh zeppole, what Italians called fried dough with a sprinkling of finely powdered sugar. Frank and Gina were sitting in the living room chattering away about the crazy way people drive in Florida when Jason came in with a bottle of white wine and three glasses. He sat next to Frank on a love seat and poured.

"So, how you guys doing?" Gina asked, taking a sip from her glass.

"Great," Frank said.

"What's it been, a month since you met?" she asked.

"More than that," Frank said. "And I'm glad the two people I love most get along so well."

"What's not to get along?" Gina said. "I'm charming and he's got wine."

"Very good wine," Jason corrected and topped off her glass. "At least you both have the same night off."

"The downside is *you* had to work," Frank said, "and I'm missing my game."

"You can put it on," Jason said.

"What, so he can be unsociable?" Gina complained and looked at Frank. "You can watch a game anytime."

"I'm not watching it," Frank shrugged. "Give me a break."

"Every Monday night you're sitting in front of that damned TV," she said and took another sip from her glass. "Mm, this is so good."

"I told you," Jason said and followed her lead by picking up his glass and clinking it against Frank's.

"You guys make such a nice couple," Gina commented.

"I agree," Frank said. "And to think it almost didn't happen."

"What do you mean?" Jason asked.

"Well, you were a little standoffish when I met you."

"Was I?"

"I really had to work hard to get a date with you," Frank said and winked at Gina. "You have no idea."

Gina smiled at him knowingly, remembering the bet they'd made.

"But you're gonna have to excuse me," Frank added. "This wine is going right through me."

"We'll wait here," Gina said as Frank headed for the bathroom.

When she heard the door close she turned to Jason. "Isn't that cute? He thinks *he* got you together."

"I don't think it would sit too well with him if he knew I met you before I met him."

"No," Gina said. "What wouldn't sit well is if he knew I arranged the whole thing. So you gotta swear never to say anything."

"If he doesn't ask, I won't tell," Jason said. "But there's one thing I still don't understand."

"What's that?"

"I know why you told me to come in alone during his shift. But that one night, when you called and told me to drop everything and come over, you said this was the night, as if you knew something."

"Ah, yes," she said with a nod. "I knew he liked you, but that night I was talking to a customer and he thought it was you—but it wasn't, see? Anyway he comes rushing over like I might say something I shouldn't 'cause I'd been teasing him, you know? And when he sees he made a mistake, he gets all flustered. That's how I knew the man was ready for the next step. So when he went outside for a break, that's when I called."

"I had to trust your instincts on that one," Jason said.

"On what one?" Frank asked returning to the room. "Is she

talking about me again?"

"Only in a good way," Jason said.

Gina added. "I was just telling Jason my philosophy: All's well that ends well."

"What an odd thing to say," Frank mused.

"More wine?" Jason asked.

TROPICAL DAZE

Vincent Diamond

Fort Walton Beach, Florida. Early December

"I am *not* getting on that thing."

Steven smiled. "Come on, try new things in your life. I did and look where it got me. From cop to civilian in 60 days." He turned the horse in a circle, his long legs snug around her. Overhead, gulls cawed and laughed. The horse's hooves kicked up some sand, and she tossed her head, nostrils flaring. She snorted. "Conrad, meet Lady."

"Is this the big surprise?"

"Well, she's big, isn't she?"

"And this is not gonna work." I took a half step backward toward the safety of the motel room.

I smelled her, the rich horsey scent wafted over with the sea breeze. Her coat was a burnished gold, almost exactly the same color as Steven's hair. His sunscreen had a touch of coconut in it, and that made my stomach rumble from hunger. "I'm not sure about this. She's...she's huge."

"Yeah, she is. She's Belgian, and they're normally cart horses, but I needed a horse who could handle 400 pounds. Her trot is kinda bouncy but her other gaits are perfect."

I just shook my head.

"Look, she's really cool. Watch this." Steven dropped the reins and lay back on the horse's broad haunches. He put his arms out, and Lady stood still, calm. Steven's chest gleamed in the morning light, belly taut. He had a few freckles on his neck and shoulders. I wanted to lick down his torso in that second.

Eight months together and he still does it to me. Every time.

About the horse, though, I wasn't convinced. "I dunno."

I'd grown up in the city, running the streets of Jacksonville, playing the urban thug-lite card as a teen. I ran street raves once I got out of high school. I put together killer music for people who wanted to X their way through the night, and I DJ'd real parties and weddings for cash, upgrading my sound system every other week. Without being fully aware of it, I started to hang out with the wrong crowd, and it was Steven who had worked undercover to bust my friend, Marco, who *was* dealing.

But now Steven wasn't a cop anymore—because of me. Part of me felt guilty that Steven had taken the heat for letting me run the night of the bust; part of me was grateful that I hadn't gotten hauled in with the rest of ravers.

And part of me was falling in love.

"Tell you what. Let's eat breakfast here and you can get to know her. Then decide." Steven slipped off Lady's back and looped her reins over the brown railing.

She looked odd among the gleaming cars in the parking lot, two steps from our room.

Lady promptly put her nose down and began snuffling at the sparse grass in the sandy coating over the asphalt.

Steven had picked an inexpensive motel for our little vacation, and it had a rustic look—brown timber frames around a brick walkway, cedar shakes for siding. We left our room's door open, moved the table and chairs outside, and ate breakfast four feet from Lady: peaches over Cheerios, one of my favorites since childhood. I'd mentioned it one night in bed, just talking, and Steven came back from the grocery store the next day with both.

"Come on, give her a treat and say hello." Steven gave me a handful of Cheerios.

I stood an arm's length away from the horse. She was absolutely enormous, her back as high as my chest; her head looked to be three feet long and full of teeth. Lady's wide nostrils quivered as we stepped closer. Her hooves were as big as dinner plates. She stomped one on the sand, and I jerked back.

"Here's how to say hello to a horse." Steven leaned down and breathed into Lady's nose. She huffed back, her muzzle moving. "Come on, a little closer."

I stepped a little forward, fingers clenched on the dry cereal.

"Open your hand and have your palm flat when you feed her. That way she won't get a finger by accident," Steven said. His blue eyes were soft and understanding.

I put out my hand and felt Lady's quivering whiskers first, stiff as a broom, then her soft muzzle. It tickled as her delicate lips gathered in the cereal. I let my palm rest under her chin and stroked her—so soft, living velvet. She nuzzled up my arm, and her wet lips brushed my belly. "Wow."

"Yeah, she's 'wow.' Let's go for a ride."

"I'm not sure—"

"OK, then I'll just head down the beach and find some other hunky guy to wrap his arms around me and nibble on my neck all morning. How's that sound?" But Steven's voice was tender and joking.

"You'll go slow?" My belly quivered. Keeping 500 people dancing, drinking, high, and happy was a breeze; getting on this animal's back—and trusting her not to throw me and then stomp on me? An entirely different proposition.

Control. I always wanted to be in control.

Steven leaned over and planted a soft kiss on my neck. "I promise, we'll go as slow as you want."

"OK, then. Let's go."

"You gotta change. You can't wear those jeans." Steven was in swim trunks, neon-orange today. We'd both gotten some sun since arriving on Sunday, and Steven's skin was a warm golden tan; mine was now a deeper olivey brown. "Put on some trunks. You'll be more comfortable. Trust me—chafage, dude."

A minute later, I stepped back outside, shirt and jeans off, trunks on. I handed Steven the sunscreen; I'd long since given up arguing that I didn't need it with my Hispanic heritage and dark skin. It felt free and easy to be so open with Steven in this strange town. If people stared at us for sitting side by side in a restaurant booth, or for sharing a quick kiss in public, I didn't really care. I was vaguely aware that another room's door opened and closed as we stood there but didn't mind. Steven's hands were slippery with the lotion on my back, affection in every stroke.

God, I love this. He spoils me like Donalita never did.

"All right, pardner, let's git you up here." Steven's voice took on a jokey twang. He swung up onto the horse. Since he was 6 foot 2, his movement was fluid and easy. Lady wore a saddle pad, a thick cushion of cream fleece with a bright-pink girth. "Here, let's go over to the flowerbed. Stand on it."

I wavered on the brick side of the flowerbed—a foot off the ground and I'd still have to stretch up and over to get on Lady. I pressed my lips together, concentrating on not falling.

"You're doing fine. Ease over with your right leg and grab onto me. Come on." Steven's blue eyes held me, something beyond warmth in them. Love?

I stretched over, legs spread, felt the soft fleece along my thighs, and grabbed Steven's waist. Lady shifted once, and I gripped tighter.

"You're fine. Just sit there for a minute and get a feel for her."

I felt stretched; Lady was wide, wider than a normal-size horse, not that I would know. It was like straddling a barrel. I nestled my legs against Steven's long limbs, and our feet touched. I leaned closer and pressed against Steven's back, breathing on the bruises I'd left on his neck over the past four nights. "OK, cowboy, let's go for a ride," I said.

Steven clucked with his tongue, and Lady walked calmly out of the parking lot and onto the beach.

It wasn't even 9 o'clock yet, so the beach was empty, silent. Lady's walk was easy. I felt the shift of her hips with every step, felt her solid legs thunk beneath us. We rolled a little with her walk, our hips rocking. Her neck bobbed, and every once in a while she snorted; I couldn't figure out why. It made me smile, though.

"How'd you learn about horses, anyway?" I asked. I sighed

and pressed closer to Steven, a great place to be. The weather had been sunny and bright, cheerful for our little trip to get away from Tampa—"good bed weather," we called it. We'd spent the last four days playing Frisbee on the beach, sleeping late, eating like teenagers, and fucking—oh, yeah, a lot of fucking.

"Some of the families around Gainesville had horses; I learned hanging out in the barns when I was a kid. When I was a teenager, though…man, what a way to get horny. Better than dancing, even." Steven twisted back and planted a kiss on my nose. "Some of the best sex I *never* had was double bareback on a horse. I'd get home with blue balls and spend an hour in the shower jerking off."

I heard the smile in Steven's voice. "Double bareback— sounds romantic. You're always a sucker for romance, aren't you?"

"I'm trying to convince you it's OK. Is it working?"

"Yeah, I think it's working." I leaned forward and pulled my arms tighter around Steven.

"You were never around horses before?"

"In Jacksonville? Hell, no. I've seen them in parades. And I saw the cops use them at a concert once. The crowd started lighting fires in the street and the horses came in—there must have been about 12 of them—and that sure broke up the party."

"Yeah, the P.D. has a good equine unit; they train a lot." Steven's voice was quiet. Too quiet.

Shouldn't have brought up the department. Nice move, Conrad.

We were silent for a bit. The gulf's waves splished gently over the sand, and brown pelicans skimmed over the water, inches from its calm surface. I nuzzled along Steven's golden shoulders, then up his neck, and fastened my lips on one ear. "I didn't mean to talk about the cops."

"It's OK."

But it wasn't.

"Don't worry, you'll find a job," I offered.

"I keep telling myself that. Two months temping at an insurance company just isn't fucking cutting it." The bitterness was real, sharp and unpleasant on this cool morning.

"You've got to give yourself the time, the economy's tough, it's not just you."

"You got a job in three days."

"I know cars. Mechanics can find work on the moon. And I still spend half my day doing oil changes. Come on, don't be so hard on yourself. If things were reversed, would you really care if I was working or not?"

"I don't know. I just feel…useless."

"I like taking care of things right now. It's fine, really. And I like that you planned this trip and found this beach, and you got Lady taking us out for a ride."

Steven snickered and leaned backward, pressing his butt against me. "Say it."

"I'd rather show you." I palmed one hand down Steven's back then slipped it around to his belly. I rubbed his cock through the slick swim trunks. It grew in my grip, alive and warm.

"Say it."

I looked around. The beach ahead of us was empty, but I heard car doors slamming, and children's voice from the sand dunes on our left. I slipped my hand inside Steven's trunks, and marveled at the soft skin on his cock—softer than Lady's sweet lips. I growled and pressed closer, my own cock hardening.

I gripped his cock tighter. "I'm showing you."

"Say it."

Four kids bolted over the sound dunes on our left, screaming and waving kites.

Saved.

I exhaled against his warm neck. "I show you every day; I wake you with you in the morning, I sleep with you at night. We take care of each other. There, you happy?"

Steven stopped Lady and twisted around for a full mouth kiss. "Yes, I'm happy. Now, get your hands out of my shorts. We have an audience."

The sun shifted overhead; it felt warm as honey. We got to the lighthouse, its bright red stripes snappy as a flag in the morning. Steven brought Lady to a halt. "The stable master said this is the halfway point. We turn around here. Wanna trade places?"

"You mean me steer? Are you nuts?"

"If you want. I'm gonna hop down for a sec. Stay on her." Before I could protest, Steven swung his right leg over Lady's neck and slipped to the ground. He groaned and shook out his legs.

My heart fluttered. "Don't leave me up here with her. Jeezus."

I grabbed Lady's reins and gripped them tight. Her head snapped up. She snorted, then shifted sideways.

"Shit! Steven!"

"Relax, you're fine. Here, loosen her reins a little. Now scoot up." Steven held Lady's bridle from the ground and put a warm hand on my left leg. "Scoot up to here—good, there. Now just sit."

Lady was patient. She stood still, her mouth working the bit. I felt bad for jerking her reins like that. Steven walked forward, hand just beneath Lady's bridle, and we clopped along the damp sand. I sat still, legs tight against the horse, one hand gripping her mane. I felt it more in my seat and spine this time without Steven to buffer the movement; my hips rolled with each stride and my balls twinged a little.

Steven looked up. "See? Not so bad."

"Yeah, not bad at all. Kinda nice." It was pleasant and sensual and exhilarating all at once. I could feel her strength and power under me, so different than the motorcycles I'd ridden.

"Now just walk down a little ways and circle back to me. You'll do fine." Steven let go.

I swallowed. Lady's gait was soothing. I felt a little more relaxed but still had visions of her taking off at a gallop as I tumbled off her. We walked two dozen steps away, then I tugged on one rein, and Lady obediently turned and headed back to Steven.

Steven was grinning that huge golden smile that lit the morning. I grinned back. "Hey, it's like shifting gears."

We stopped in front of Steven, and his heated gaze made my belly grow warm.

"You look sexy as hell. I wanna nibble, let me up." With an oomph of effort, Steven swung up behind and snugged his hips up against my butt. "Oh, man, you're so beautiful, Conrad."

This time, I was in charge and I liked it. I held the reins in one hand and held Steven's hand in the other. We rocked together as Lady walked on. Steven clucked his tongue, dug in his heels, and before I knew it, we were trotting, awkward, lurching, too much bounce against my balls, Lady huffing as we jogged forward. Steven clucked again, and Lady pushed into an easy canter. I felt her stretch out and reach with each stride; it felt fast and slow at the same time. We rocked forward and back as she loped, water splashing up against our feet—one-two-three, one-two-three, the rhythm muffled by the sand. She huffed as she strode along, a chunky breath with each stride. Her legs bunched beneath us, and I felt her heavy body thrust forward.

Steven's hand slipped inside my trunks, unsteady, bouncing a little as Lady worked beneath us. Then he got a rhythmic grip—up, down, a little squeeze at the mushroom cap of my cock, his fingers cool as he stroked me. He kept at me, gripping and tugging. I was in a frenzy of sensation: the rocking movement beneath us, Steven thrusting against my butt, his hands working me. The fleece beneath my thighs rubbed against me as Steven nuzzled my neck. Icy fire, sharp as glass, pierced me.

"Come for me. Right here, right now. Let me feel it." Steven's voice was low and sultry.

I groaned and leaned back. I thrust with my hips, working now, the crest of pleasure between my legs, moving up into my cock. I ground hard against Steven's grip, held onto Lady's mane as we cantered, my legs tight against her, her rocking motion pushing us upward, my eyes closed now—*oh, there, right there, Steven, come for me, come for me*—oh, *Steven, there!*—and then the warm spurt of my semen, a gushing sweet ache, ears buzzing as my orgasm shook me.

The morning crystallized—the cool breeze, the smell of the gulf and Lady's scent, the wet on my belly, the feel of Steven's legs against me, arms around me, holding me, safe.

I'll never forget this moment.

"Lady, whoa, let's walk, Lady, walk." Steven leaned back and tugged on the reins. We bounced through her jolting trot again then she settled into her easy walk. "Good girl, Lady, good girl. Scratch her neck, Conrad."

I leaned forward; her neck was sweaty now, slick. It was hard work for her. "Thanks, Lady. That was a helluva ride."

Steven tugged on one rein, and Lady walked into deeper water. She went in until the water reached her chest, the water splashing around our ankles. It was kinda creepy; if Steven hadn't stopped her, I think she would have gone swimming, but he pulled her back to a stop. He splashed the cool Gulf water on my belly to wash away my come.

Steven pressed against me, cock hard again. "I'm gonna need another ride when we get back to the motel, I promise you that." There were people on the beach now, so Steven nibbled on my left ear.

"You can ride me anytime you want, cowboy. Let's run again—get back to the stables quicker."

"We can't. She has to cool off. Walk her from here on out."

"I don't think I can stand it. I wanna fuck you—now." Behind me, Steven was fully erect, his swim trunks made a slip-slidey noise against me. Lady's rocking motion made me want more than a canter on the beach.

"I could talk dirty to you. How 'bout that?" Steven's voice swooped down.

"You know I can't stand that either. Just shut up. Stop breathing on me and rubbing your cock against me, you big tease. Look at these girls on the beach. See that blond in the red bikini? Talk about her or something. Distract me."

"Maybe we should have a three-way some night—you, me, some hottie. Whaddya think?"

"I think you're trying to talk dirty to me again, Mr. Hardcock, and you need to stop it."

We laughed; the family on the beach stared at us. Steven raised one hand to them as Lady snorted.

Steven did ease off as we walked back to the stables. On our left, the Gulf water shone blue in the morning's sunny rays. To the right, the creamy sand dunes mounded between the beach and the road. When we got back to the stable, I was overwhelmed by the sight and smell of the animals—rich manure, fresh saw-dust shavings, clumps of hay all around. A half-dozen horses ate steadily from a hay bale, coats shiny, teeth grinding.

Steven slipped off Lady first and held her reins. "Be careful getting down; your legs'll probably be unsteady," he warned.

"Unsteady? This isn't boating, why should they be—" I carefully looped my right leg over Lady's rear, and dropped to the soft sand. My knees promptly gave way and I plopped straight down on my ass. "Jeezus!"

Steven grinned and held out a hand. "Your legs are unsteady. Told ya."

He pulled me up and I felt my knees go wonky again. "What the hell is this?"

"It's just muscles you've never used before. Give yourself some time. Hang here. I'm gonna get her turned in."

I walked carefully over to the paddock fence and was embarrassed to have to lean against it. My legs really *were* tired—just from sitting on a horse: It didn't make sense. The sun felt wonderful on my back and I stretched out my arms, keeping my knees loose. I heard some giggling, and turned oh, so casually back to the entrance. Three teenage girls, all dressed in some weird little tight pants and knee-high black boots, whispered to each other as they strode past. The blond made eye contact, then flushed and leaned into her friends.

Steven strode out of the barn, bare chest wet with sweat, hips lean in his swimsuit, and the girls giggled again. "Mornin', ladies," he offered.

The girls went still and watched him walk past, their mouths open.

"Guess we're a little underdressed, huh?" I smiled, enjoying the way the girls stared at us. It was silly but I liked it sometimes when women noticed me. More often than not, women noticed Steven first—tall, gorgeous surfer looks—but I didn't mind that.

Steven's gaze was direct, filled with yearning and lust. "Let's go, lover. No more flirting with the girls. It's my turn now."

"It's always your turn." I grabbed Steven's hand, and we walked to the car.

The girls watched us, and I waved at them as Steven steered away, slender fingers on the stick shift and my own fingers on top of them.

Back at the motel, Steven stopped the car, then just grinned at me for a few seconds. We sprinted for the door. Steven got there first. We had all four hands on the key, fumbling with the lock, then the door creaked open and we were inside. Finally, privacy. Our kisses were more like bites this morning, too much lust and fire for gentleness.

"I, you—wanna shower first?" Steven's voice was husky with that sensual timbre of arousal.

In answer I just licked down Steven's slick torso and pulled down his orange swim trunks. I loved to nuzzle at Steven's groin, loved to press my rough beard against Steven's soft belly skin and rub. Leave my mark. Steven smelled of pungent sweat and horse today, and beneath it was the visceral smell of Steven's cock. Nothing else was as real as this moment, nothing else mattered but Steven's panting gasps, the feel of his balls in my palm, and I swallowed him whole.

Beautiful.

After a few strokes, Steven whispered. "Oh, Conrad....I, uh, stop, you're gonna make me finish too fast. Stop." Steven pushed me away from his wine-dark cock; thrusting upward and full of blood, it glistened with my spit.

Steven led me to the newly made bed; housekeeping must have been inside while we were away. I tugged off my shorts, and snagged the lube from the nightstand, my fingers shaking.

We'd both been tested after a month together; we then retested in October and were still clear. I had made a little ceremony out of throwing away the condoms.

Steven pulled the lube from me, coated his fingers, and then wrapped them around my thick cock roughly. There was something new in Steven's eyes today, something wild and a little dark. It was so intense that I had to look away, nervous suddenly. Steven's grip was demanding. He worked the cool lube over me in seconds. Steven's kiss was fierce; I forgot sometimes that he was taller until moments like this when Steven grasped me tight, pushed my head back, and thrust his tongue in, demanding, pushing, controlling me.

My knees went wonky again.

Steven crawled on the bed and gripped the headboard. I knelt behind him, legs unsteady on the mattress. Steven grabbed a pillow from under the spread. I thought he would move it between his own legs, but instead, Steven stuffed it between the headboard and the wall. "Now, ride me, Conrad. Ride me."

I had never seen such a look on Steven's face. I couldn't tell if it was pain or lust or love, but it filled my belly and groin with a thick heat. My cock bobbed between us, then stilled as I pushed in between Steven's pale cheeks. The contrast of my own dusky skin with Steven's pale gold gave me another a jolt. "You done teasing me, pretty boy?"

Steven groaned and his head fell back. "Please."

I knew to wait—to wait for Steven to beg me, to grab at me and pull me closer, to grind his hips back and tremble. There was a distinctive tone in Steven's voice that I heard only in this moment, something boyish and husky and growly all at once. "Please, Conrad."

"You teased me all morning. Talking about sex and pretty girls and jerking off and now you expect me to just give you what you want? I don't think so." But I eased Steven's cheeks apart and slipped my cock up and down. Teasing. I ran my cock head up beneath his balls, stroking against his pink skin.

"Now! Give it to me now."

"I could make you wait." I eased my mouth over Steven's ear and neck, then nibbled on his shoulders. The nibbles turned to near-bites. I was marking him and wanted to do it. *Mine.*

Steven let go of the headboard and tugged me to him with both hands. "Do it now." He squirmed in my grip, hips thrusting, neck exposed as he panted.

And in that moment I didn't want to wait. I wanted to bury myself inside him, wanted to grip Steven's shoulders and fuck him and rock us both away.

I pressed the tip of my cock to Steven's opening and waited, just for a few seconds, just long enough to hear Steven's whimper—*oh, yeah, that's what I need to hear*—and then I thrust inside and went still. We stayed joined and quiet for seconds. Steven's hiss of pleasure grew into a groan as my hips moved, slowly at first, steadily up and down. Steven's legs thrust against me as we moved in time to the primal rhythm. Steven's warmth around me was maddening, soothing, and frightening all at once. I slowed for a bit, but Steven reached down and grabbed one cheek, and semipushed me deeper inside. I saw the pillow against the wall flatten and puff back with every rocking thrust. I pushed harder, deeper.

"Do you feel me, Connie?" Steven gasped out the words between each thrust. His words were part of the sex for us, real and deep, arousing in a way nothing else could be.

"Yeah." My body ached and in my chest, my heart ached with something else—something wet and warm, something just between us.

"Say it to me now. Tell me now."

"I love you, Steven." My eyes closed as the words slipped from me.

Steven's body lowered, and he eased his knees farther apart. He cried out, a throaty groan, inarticulate and demanding. He rocked back again, hard—once, twice, three times—and his back and shoulders tensed, his skin pink with effort. I knew it was time. I reached around and gripped Steven's hard cock, felt it pulsating in my grip, jerking, wet and—*now, oh, now, now, Steven, now, I'm coming now!*—and then I was lost. I couldn't hear Steven's cries, couldn't hear the mattress squeaking beneath us, couldn't keep my legs from trembling and shaking as I came, and my cock spilled into Steven, who was twitching and spent beneath me.

Steven's head dropped against the cheap painting over the bed. It wobbled on its hook but stayed in place. Our breath fogged the glass. We stayed joined together for a long time, my hands gentle now over Steven's shoulders and back, tongue licking our sweat off him, lips soft on Steven's neck. My thighs trembled. "Let's lie down, babe," I said.

I nearly stumbled when I got off the bed, knees wobbly. Steven pulled back the covers and snugged up the pillows, and we lay down together. I lay on Steven's chest and sighed. I wrapped one leg over his thigh, saw a glisten of semen on his belly. Beautiful.

"You OK?" Steven asked. His fingers stroked my scalp between soft kisses.

"More than OK."

"How're your legs?"

"Shaky, but I don't have to stand up anytime soon, do I?" I smiled up at him.

"Nah, we aren't going anywhere for a while."

I relaxed in his grip. My eyes closed. The sound of Steven's heartbeat soothed me, then turned into Lady's hoofbeats on the sand, and I slept, dreaming of a sunny beach and a horse beneath us.

And Steven in my arms.

Now We Shan't Never Be Parted

Paul G. McCurdy

Over the previous year I had seen him come into the store, sometimes alone, sometimes with a girl or two. I was friendly with most of the regulars and many a more occasional customer, but I had never really talked to him. His tastes were diverse, though, I noted when I looked up his family's customer history. They never came in, to my knowledge, so it was he who had rented *Labyrinth, Vertigo, The Music Lovers,* and some stranger: *L'homme Blessé* and *Turkish Delight.*

He was blond, his hair too long and with no purpose. Not wavy or curly or even straight, it just flopped there on his head, looking even a little dirty. It seemed somewhat thick and greasy where it sat heavy on top, but the hair hanging over his ears was fine and shiny and looked soft. His face was a bit unformed, the skin dry, raked, as if he had scoured it with snow, and his cheeks were even a touch red. His nose spread a little, and on its breadth I occasionally saw a few blackheads. The mouth was perhaps the most pleasant, though a bit exaggerated. Generally pink lips, the bottom full, would spread over broad white, rounded teeth when he smiled. His clothes seemed very much someone else's idea—someone else far away in distance and time. I only noticed when one of my coworkers pointed it out that he never wore jeans, and indeed he seemed to alternate between green and brown pants that probably came from Old Navy. His eyes, which I seldom had time enough to inspect, were green under strangely dark eyebrows.

212

And then one day he broke the distance between us. It was February, mild and bright outside, a few hours before sunset. Andrea had left to run some work errands, so the kid walked up to me and slid a videotape cover across the counter.

"Ah, *Maurice*," I said. "One of my favorites." I took the display box into the back to exchange it with the videocassette.

"Mine too," he said when I got back.

"Your what?" I asked.

"One of my favorites," he explained. I glanced in those green eyes, which looked right back at mine. Was he coming on to me, this kid who had never seemed the slightest bit interested? I typed in the bar code and brought up his family's account.

"So you've seen it before," I said, wondering now exactly how old he was. Fourteen? No. Between 15 and 17. Certainly he had never rented it here before, or I would have noticed it in the customer history.

"Yeah, lots. I actually owned it," he began. He looked down and bit his lip a little. "Loaned it to someone, never got it back."

I laughed. "Count on me to do that with all my favorite things," I said. He smiled and handed over the money for the rental. I gave him the tape.

He placed the fingertips of his right hand on the case. "Do you think," he began, "do you think Alec and Maurice make it?"

I laughed again, as much out of delight as out of shock. "I think—hey, what's your name, anyway? I mean your first name."

He picked up his hand and held it out to me. "It's P.G. McFadden," he said, shaking the hand I offered him.

"P.G.—?"

"Don't ask. I'll tell you sometime." He was still grasping my hand. I shuddered, then took a moment to reset myself.

"Well, P.G. McFadden," I began, slowly taking back my hand and fingers. "To answer your question, I think that they *made* it, despite and still, as they say, and they're lucky bastards for that."

"Ouch," he said, smiling and looking at me sideways. Then, suddenly: "Well, see you, Paul." I wasn't too surprised to hear that he knew my name; the regulars used it freely and loudly.

"See you, P.G. McFadden," I said, nervously reaching for the receipts beside the register and straightening them.

And I think I straightened them for the next 10 minutes until Andrea got back. I must have been shaking and giddy with the strangeness of it. Andrea asked if aliens had landed while she was gone, which was her usual way of checking if anything exciting had happened.

"Nearly," I told her. "You know that McFadden kid who rents weird movies?" She nodded. "Um, how old do you think he is?"

She shrugged her shoulders, then caught herself: "You sly fox—why do you want to know?"

"It's not—oh, it's not that, Andrea," I said. "I know I've dated my share of customers," I explained, at the same time aware that I sounded defensive. "It's just—I think he just came on to me, or at least came out to me."

"In that case," she said, "it's best if I tell you he's 10."

"Be serious," I laughed. "Seventeen? Sixteen? Fifteen?"

Suddenly Andrea's smile fell, and she turned rapidly toward the back. "Look sharp," she said, and then disappeared around the corner.

There in the doorway he stood: P.G. McFadden.

"Back for *Maurice 2: Clive's Revenge?*" I asked.

He laughed and walked up to the counter. "No," he began. "It's just… Well, tomorrow's my birthday—that's why I'm renting this. It's my favorite. I'm having a few friends over—some of the girls haven't seen it yet. And," here he looked away, and I saw the beginnings of a pimple on his cheek, glimpsed the overlong hair curling at the back of his neck, "and I was just wondering if you'd want to watch it again."

He paused, waiting for something, a yes or no from me, an encouragement, a rejection.

"It's, you know, like Tinker Bell," he explained. "It's like, Alec may get on that boat, leave for the Argentine, and never see Maurice again—unless—unless we're all rooting for him." He thought for a moment. "Unless we do believe in fairies." He smiled and laughed.

"Oh, I don't know," I said. "I've watched the movie a million times, and every time they end up together: 'Now we shan't never be parted' and all, and Clive lies to his wife, and all's well that ends well and all…" I trailed off. I fingered my receipts.

"So that's a no," he said, leaning on one foot.

"Oh, no, I don't mean that," I said. "I mean… Um, I don't even know you—P.G. McFadden," I tried.

He straightened up, planting himself on both feet again, and seemed tall. "Well," he began, "my name's P.G.—initials for Paul Gregory, one name from each grandfather, so it's like a compromise. *Maurice* is my favorite movie, tomorrow's my 16th birthday, and I'd like to have coffee with you sometime."

"Uh, whoa," I said, visibly backing away from the counter. I tried to say several other things, but my mouth just moved silently.

"It's OK," he said. "Think about it. I'll be back." And with that, he left.

I stood frozen for a few minutes, and then: "Did you hear that?" I squeaked. Andrea sauntered around the corner from the back. She leaned up against the doorway, her arms crossed sassily.

"You, Paul Sullivan, are in a heapa-heapa trouble."

Trouble I was in, though statutory rape was not foremost on my mind. Who was this kid? Why was he after me? And was I interested in him? He was intelligent, surely, and had interesting (if not good) taste in movies, but he wasn't particularly attractive—or was he? He was slightly shorter than myself, which was good, and definitely leaner, which was great. But he was blond, and his face was somehow—not distinctive. More like a clay mask than the marble bust I seemed to prefer. And he was—16! Sixteen! Older than Lolita but younger than legal. And certainly younger than tasteful.

That night I called my three close girlfriends and my one close ex-boyfriend. As usual, they all seemed to be of the same mind; and as usual, I suspected that they were merely reflecting what I had conveyed to them in my retelling of the story. Namely, this kid, P.G., was precocious and probably lonely. And probably—consider *Maurice*—an incredible romantic, maybe more so now, considering (God forbid!) the recent onset of adolescence. "I see it now," one girlfriend had said over the phone, "his pants down around his ankles, slow-motioning it through the full-frontal shot, his box of Kleenex at his side." I remembered the passionate kiss Alec gave Maurice, how I too had rewound it and rewound it, listened to the pop of their separating mouths, tasted that strand of saliva still connecting them, felt the heat of Alec's whisper on my own ear: "Now we shan't never be parted. It's finished."

"Oh, and if that little image excites you," she continued, "don't tell me!"

I fixed a pot of Earl Grey and sat in my armchair with the remote on my lap. There was nothing on. I tried to watch a movie but couldn't commit.

And so the consensus was to stay away. Which I accepted, at least that night. Though what I may have dreamed I cannot remember.

It was two days later, so the movie was due back. I had no doubt that he would be in, and I was even a little prepared.

Andrea brought him up first. "He's a nice kid, you know," she had said. "He used to come in with his mom when he was much younger. He was a lot quieter than all the other brats."

"And now?" I asked.

"Oh, he's still much younger," she winked.

I was organizing the new releases when he appeared in the open door, dressed in his green pants and a brown T-shirt too large for his shoulders. He nodded in my direction as he walked to the counter and handed the movie to Andrea, who smiled at him and seemed to know too much. I thought he was going to head back out, but he walked over toward me. I was caught standing there with no counter to protect me, and I was thankful that I had eight or so misfiled movies in my hands to make me look occupied.

I started my speech, "So did they—" but he interrupted me.

"You should have been there. Alec's in the Argentine now, and Maurice is back with the hypnotist," he said.

"No kidding!" I said, my prepared speech leaving me.

"And Clive was never forced to see his own inauthenticity,

and he and his wife had a baby and lived happily ever after," he continued. It seemed he was prepared.

I chewed my lip for a moment. "Good for them, I guess," I tried. "I never thought Clive deserved to be portrayed so negatively."

"No?" this little P.G. McFadden asked. "But being untrue to yourself"—he paused, searching for words—"deserves all the reproach the universe has to offer," he finished, raising his right hand to make some emphatic gesture lost in my peripheral vision.

"Well, that may be," I said, growing more and more uncomfortable. I wasn't even sure I was comprehending our conversation. I began to walk along the new releases, putting the misfiled DVDs into the correct places. "But it may not be that simple."

He followed me. "'I'm eager to hear more of your interesting ideas about words and deeds,'" he said with a sly smile, quoting the seductive Risley, who first introduced Maurice to the world of homosexuality at Cambridge.

"'It's only by talking that we shall caper upon the summit,'" I quoted, moving faster along the rack of new releases. He followed step for step, his head tilted slightly to the side, his eyes looking up at me.

"Then it's agreed," he said. "Surely you drink coffee?"

I stopped, hugged the remaining DVDs to my stomach.

"Are you asking me out?"

He laughed. "Yep," he said. "I guess I am."

At that moment the phone rang. I looked up to the counter and was relieved to see that Andrea must have been busy in back.

"Uh, hold on a sec," I said, then walked behind the counter, put my stack of movies down, and picked up the phone. It turned out to be a difficult call: someone looking for an early James Mason that may or may not have been released on video. I spent about 10 minutes looking for evidence of VHS or DVD copies on the Internet but could find nothing. I was writing an e-mail to one of our contacts for hard-to-find videos when P.G. walked up to the counter, took a Post-it note, and wrote something. He stuck the Post-it on my chest, winked, and walked out the door.

I stopped typing right then, told the man on the phone that I couldn't find the movie, hung up, and tore the note off of my shirt. "Meet me at the boathouse at Pendersleigh (Angelica's will have to do), 11:00—Alec (P.G.)."

I looked around bewildered. There was no one in the store. "Andrea," I called out. "Could you come to the front desk, please? Andrea to the front desk, please!"

She appeared immediately around the corner from the back. "I heard the whole thing!" she squealed. "Paul Sullivan, you are in trouble!"

Then she saw the note in my hand. "What does it say?" she exclaimed, tearing it from me. Then, once her eyes had moved rapidly up and down it, searching for meaning, she asked, "What is Pendersleigh? What boathouse?"

"It's from *Maurice*, dear," I said, taking the note back. "It seems we have a *Maurice* connection."

"What's that?" she asked.

"A period film, a costume drama. Well, a book first. By the guy who wrote *A Room With a View*, only this one's totally gay," I explained.

"A gay costume drama? Imagine that," she said.

"It's actually amazing, and it was even written in, like, the 1910s," I continued. "Very romantic. And very positive. For its time."

We bustled about putting some movies away then. It was just after 9, so the workday was coming to an end. We usually close the doors at 10 and then spend about an hour counting the drawers, cleaning up, restocking, and so on. And at 11…

Andrea and I finished what we could while the store was open and ended up back at the counter together. "So who are you in the movie?" she asked.

I had thought about it over the last couple hours but couldn't quite figure it out. "I'm not sure. I think Maurice, because he's just a lonely everyman who happens to be gay."

"Sounds like you," she smiled. "And who's P.G.?"

"That one I can't figure out. Maybe there's no relation," I tried. "I mean, if it had been *Death in Venice*…"

"Oh," she nodded. "Your little movie about the old man and the little boy." She laughed. "Well, at least that's not his favorite!"

"But he acts like it is," I said. "I mean, I may not look all that old, but I'm 28! Twenty-eight! Twenty-eight minus 16 is 12!"

"Let's see," Andrea began. "That means he was born in—"

"Don't tell me! I don't want to think about it."

We left it like that for a while. Then it was 10 o'clock, and I started vacuuming the store while she counted the drawers. Was I going to go to Angelica's? Would he actually be there? What would we talk about? I pushed the vacuum over the carpet as if in a trance. I couldn't see the dirt on the floor for the picture of Miss Edna May before me. When I got back to the counter, I asked Andrea what she thought I should do.

"If life throws you a UFO," she said, "run into the tractor beam."

"And if life throws you a piece of jailbait, go directly to jail without passing Go?"

"Honey," Andrea said, putting down the money she was counting, "weren't you ever 16?"

"Twelve years ago," I mumbled.

"Weren't you ever interested in an older man?"

"More than a few times," I nodded. "Teachers, waiters, nearly every sensitive stranger in my small hometown."

"And did you ever ask them out?" she asked.

I thought about it. Had I? Well, there might have been a few unsent letters. "Not like this little guy."

"So you never talked to one?"

"Nope. I didn't really meet anyone until I went to college, and then there were more than enough my own age."

"Well, sweetie, now's your chance to find out what you missed," she said. "Maybe it's not worth it. But it's not like he's just some dumb kid. He's got good taste in movies, anyway. Better than me. And he could pass for 18."

"And 28 minus 18 is…merely 10 years. You are so right," I said sarcastically.

She sighed, dropped her arms. "Just go, Paul. Just go so you at least have something to tell me tomorrow besides you went home and tried to watch another movie but you couldn't concentrate so you turned it off and went to bed."

At a quarter to 11, I was in the bathroom of the video store. It was a date, after all, even if I wasn't sure how I felt about it, and that meant a once-over of the eyes, a check of the hair. The lower eyelids were puffy with a day of work, the hairline and forehead shiny with sweat and oils. I washed my face and hands briskly, threw my fingers through my hair, and declared myself ready enough to go.

I was at the front door and Andrea was standing behind the counter to set the alarm. "Ready, Freddy?" she asked, borrowing one of my stock phrases. "Let's jet," I replied. She set the alarm, and we left and locked the door.

"Now are you really ready, Freddy?" she asked.

"I will be in about 10 minutes," I said, reaching into my backpack to pull out my Marlboro Reds. "Care to join me?" I asked, holding the open pack out to her.

"Can't do that stuff," Andrea said. "Got my own." She pulled a Camel Light out of a pack in her pocket, and I lit it for her, then lit mine.

"So we know my sordid story," I said. "What's going on in your romantic life, sweetie?"

"Just bitches," she replied. She blew smoke up and out.

"Your neighbor?" I asked.

"Wasn't even home," she answered. I started to commiserate. "Fuck it, she's not even gay."

"At least she's legal," I said, and then felt guilty for shifting the focus back on myself. Whether or not Andrea noticed, she exhaled one last puff of smoke and threw down her cigarette, stamping it out. She had a frown on her face but then clapped her hands together, spread her arms wide, and pulled me tight to her.

"Well, take care, Tiger," she said. She walked to her car and I walked along the other way, toward Angelica's. My cigarette had burned nearly to the filter, and I couldn't remember whether it had achieved the desired effect. Was I relaxed? Was I ready? Had I run through my mind a few greetings, tested out a few conversation topics? I threw the butt into the gutter and began to fiddle with my backpack to grab another cigarette when—

"Paul!"

I turned, and there he was, coming behind me through the light of a street lamp. He was dressed the same, but it was a bit cooler, so he was wearing a too-large blue jacket. But he looked somehow too bright for the street lamp, and I saw how his face continued to glow after he had left the circle of light. I looked up and saw the moon, full and bright, hanging close over the hills.

I put out my hand. "P.G. McFadden," I said, "hello."

He grabbed my hand with his right, and put his left around me—and in those few seconds I felt it: how the fingertips of his left hand hit my stomach, curved off to the side, how his palm moved against first my belly, then my side, the small of my back, the small indenture of my spine, and then took hold of my left side.

"I'm glad you came," he said into my ear, and then, just as I had melted from shock into comfort, his hand left my side the same way it had come. In that uncoiling, as I felt a lonely cold reassert itself around my waist, I remembered that morning six months ago when I had unwrapped myself from someone else, when I decided I was ready to face that cold aloneness and make some coffee, the last we would drink together.

"So how was work?" he asked, walking beside me now.

I glanced over at him. He was looking down at the sidewalk, his hands in his jacket pockets now.

"Same," I replied.

"I think I'd like to work there," he said. In his chitchat I noticed a hint of nervousness. "I mean, not forever or anything. Just for a little while. You must meet some pretty interesting people."

His striped sneakers landing in the light of Angelica's made me suddenly flirtatious.

"I did today," I said, kicking his shoe. "Go inside?"

He smiled and nodded. I held the door open for him and followed him to the counter. He asked me what I wanted; he insisted on paying since he, after all, had asked me out. "A double cappuccino," he told the lean and graceful Latino at the register, "and a regular coffee for my uncle here." He winked at me.

"Thanks," I said when the attendant handed me the coffee. His smile seemed to mock me.

While P.G. was waiting for his drink, I told him I'd try to find a place to sit down. As just about the only place in town open after 10, Angelica's was quite busy. The tables looked to be full and in disarray; parties of the wrong sizes had moved chairs from small tables to large, from large to small, so that it was now a maze. The benches that ran along the two side walls were also occupied, the tables pulled up to them this way or that to accommodate one, three, even five people.

"There!" I heard P.G. say, and then he bustled past me toward the corner. I watched with incredulity as he wedged himself past a large, regal woman and then between the table and bench. "Come on!" he said, gesturing. I excused myself as I squeezed past the large woman's party, then caught my foot on a table leg, tried to right myself, and fell heavily against P.G.'s side. I apologized and began to scoot away.

"No, stay," he said, and then he wrapped his arm around me, his hand cupping my side. I let it sit there a moment, found that I was holding my breath. Then I took his hand from my side, exhaled loudly, and dropped it in his lap.

"Look here," I said. "What planet are you from?"

He seemed to fold in on himself for a few seconds, and then replied, "This one, same as you."

"Are you with the police or something?" I asked, half joking but still anxious.

"No, but I'm glad you care," he said, smiling mischievously. If it was a joke, I didn't get it.

That or something else made me suddenly angry, and I remembered my friends' advice. "So you're just some lonely gay 16-year-old boy who dreams of love and has never found it?" I threw at him, taking a swig of coffee for emphasis. He likewise lifted his cup, drank, and then slid his arm along his lips to wipe off the foam.

"Yes," he said.

I put my coffee cup down.

"I'm sorry," I said, and I looked away, toward the large woman, past her, at the tables surrounded by people in animated discussions. "I'm sorry," I repeated. The loud talk around us became a stillness.

P.G. moved his coffee cup along the table. "And I know what you are too," he said. I looked him in the eye, raised my eyebrows. "A lonely gay 20-something-year-old man who's had lots of boyfriends and never love." My eyebrows fell.

"Touché," I said, took another swig of coffee, pushed the cup to the center of the table. "Well," I said, looking left and right to see how I might best escape, "it's been lovely. Really."

I started to squeeze out from under the table. P.G. made to follow me, and when I was half bent over the large woman, who at this point was laughing at something her companion was whispering to her, P.G. said, "If you go now, you'll never know."

I got free and stood up straight between two loud tables. I waited until he was standing next to me. "Never know what?" I asked.

I watched as he stood there, looking left and right, his mouth opening and closing. I tried to see what he was looking at. On the right wall was an abstract painting of blues and greens. On the left was a nude charcoal drawing of a girl. He was looking at me now, and his face seemed to be made of warm putty. It was falling. And then I saw the source of the mirage—his green eyes were wet, and as I tried to break his gaze a small tear rolled down the right side of his face.

He lifted his hand lightly, toward me, and I backed away.

"Never know what?" I rasped.

He sniffed, swabbed at his eye with the sleeve of his blue jacket.

"You'll never know—why I love you," he said.

And as I stood there trying to find meaning in the blues and greens on the wall, he brushed past me, his shoulder touching mine so gently, so gently, and then he disappeared. I turned, but the door had already swung shut, and I was alone.

REAL MAGICK

Raymond Yeo

When Daniel and I were old enough to drink, we stumbled onto Albuquerque's equivalent of the artsy café: Slackers Bar and Grill. It was an unassuming little place out in the middle of nowhere, frequented by old hippies and lost tourists. It was dark, dirty, and smelled of clove cigarettes. We'd spent countless late-night hours there, in a back corner booth talking about the movies we'd just seen, or how, if we had superpowers, we'd make the world a better place.

It was during one of those late night conversations that the topic of New Age *magick* had come up (the *k* is on purpose, to distinguish the "real thing" from sleight of hand). Daniel had been to Sedona, in Arizona, to visit family, and while he was there he'd discovered an expert on the topic of magick: a "channeled entity" called Zachariah.

"Think of him as a medium," Daniel said. "He's an ancient celestial being that speaks through John." John was John Moon Bear, a Native American and apparent radio transmitter of the supernatural. "Not only does he teach how to transform our lives through visualization," he went on, adjusting his wire glasses, "but he also revealed how we're all the descendants of aliens."

I nodded and tried to look open-minded. Our history together made me especially tolerant of his eccentric tendencies. We'd been friends since high school. I'd fished him out of a pile of locker-room bullies who were trying to make him eat somebody's jockstrap. I walked him home afterward—since his glasses were broken—and we naturally got to talking. As it turned out, we had read all the same comics and had seen all the same sci-fi movies. I guess we were just a couple of geeks, even though I wasn't so obvious about it.

"Evolution was true up to a point, but then they messed with our gene pool," Daniel went on. He pointed to the stained cork ceiling when he used the word "they."

I studied my near-empty bottle of beer, its label completely peeled off. I couldn't look him in the eye. I was half listening to the Doors' "Break on Through" coming from the jukebox.

But Daniel leaned in closer to make his point. He brushed a strand of red hair from his forehead, readjusted his glasses. "Well, we weren't totally human when it all started. Evolution is true, but only back to a specific point in time. Which I think explains the missing link."

Jim Jones flashed into my head. "You're not going to sell all your belongings and move to a desert commune, are you?"

Daniel smiled. "No, James," he said, "and I'm not going to shave my head and dance around with a tambourine. He paused for a moment and then added, "But I do have to be ready for when the mother ship comes."

I glanced up from the table just in time to catch the glint in his eyes. We both had an uncomfortable laugh.

Before I go on, you should know something about the company I worked for around the same time Daniel discovered magick. There weren't many mass-production video companies outside California, but I happened to work for one just east of Albuquerque. It was a big box-like building, covered in dust. It looked more like an airplane hangar than a business. The company's president and CEO, Jack Huff, preferred quantity over quality and had a piss-poor attitude toward his employees.

My supervisor gave me a heads-up before the particular incident, letting me know I was about to get reamed by Huff himself. "Jack is pretty mad," he said, "since you didn't ship Jesus on time." The Jesus project was a movie: *The Life of Jesus*. Our job was to copy it on VHS tape and ship it out to Third World countries. It was a televangelical proselytization subtitled in 47 languages.

To make a long story short, one shipment—to some backwater place in South Africa—went out a few days late. So less than a half hour after my supervisor's warning, I was sitting in Huff's office. I thought we'd have a normal discussion, like adults. "How are you today, sir?" I said starting out, feeling confident the mess would be cleared up.

But Huff was all business: "What happened, Jim?"

Nobody calls me Jim. My name is *James*. "OK. Well, sir, it was my understanding that—"

I didn't get to say another word. Huff was up out of his chair and leaning over his desk, pointing a sausage-like finger close enough for me to bite. "I don't give a *fuck* what you think *your understanding* is!" I remember he smelled like fried chicken. "You'll do what the *fuck* you're told! You listening to me?"

I guess I looked pretty stupid with my eyes all bugged out.

"It's because of you that we almost lost the Jesus project!"

I sank into the vinyl chair.

"When I let you take charge of *duplication,* you said you'd do a good job."

I did a good job.

"When you're told to do something, you better do it! Now get the fuck out of here and get to work!"

"Yes, sir." I mumbled the words and crept away like a dog caught stealing scraps from the kitchen table. The most I can remember afterward was standing in the men's room, in front of a urinal, and being so mad that I couldn't pee.

That night, Daniel and I camped out at our favorite haunt. Slackers' dim lights barely reached our secluded booth. The jukebox was unusually quiet and the waitress, who had become numb to our late-night ramblings, showed up only when I waved from across the room. Even so, we made it a point to leave a big tip.

"I guess I should quit," I said to Daniel. I took off my hat and ran my hands through my mop of blond hair. I was feeling pretty low. "But what else would I do?"

Daniel's eyes were sharp and attentive. "What do you want to do?"

"I think the issue is more what can I do."

"You can do anything you want." He fumbled with the bottle in his hands. He'd spend the whole night nursing it.

"Not without a college degree."

"Then go back to school."

"And do what? Get my BA in film and end up in California waiting tables with all the other unemployed screenwriters and Spielberg wannabes?"

Daniel stopped fumbling with the bottle and set it down on the vinyl tablecloth. "Zachariah shows us that we can create whatever we want through meditation and visualization."

It was New Age philosophy 101 again. And I wasn't up for hearing it.

"I don't know how to tell you this, Dan," I shot back, "but I think all this New Age stuff is right up there with Tammy Faye and the Moonies." My job had me fired up and I was just angry enough to speak my mind. "I need some real advice, not this pseudoreligious crap."

Daniel seemed unruffled. His face remained forever innocent. "I guess you're just not ready to accept it."

I hate when people talk to me like that—like they're on some superior nirvanic level, looking down on the rest of us. But I bit my tongue. I reminded myself of how much I cared about my friend. So I just said, "Yeah, maybe you're right."

Less than two weeks had passed before I was in Huff's office again, this time I was supposed to explain the drop in production that seemed to be connected to my department.

"You let me down again, Jim." Huff was behind his huge, cluttered desk.

"As my report explains, sir, the majority of the losses actually came from other departments."

Huff was silent for a few minutes. I wondered if he was considering what I'd said, or if he was just considering letting me go. "From now on," he said finally, getting up from behind his cluttered desk. "I want you to submit a weekly report, detailing every loss, and a clear explanation of what went wrong and how you're going to fix it."

My heart sank. It was hopeless.

"If production doesn't go up, you can bet you'll be in the unemployment line by the end of the month."

I should point out too that the work environment Huff had created over the years was a constant watch-your-back/every-man-for-himself attitude. And, seeing it more realistically now, I guess I was the easy target.

"It's the Kobayashi Maru."

Daniel and I had decided to get away from the city. Without aiming for any specific place, we ended up walking along a winding dirt road. It was an especially cool summer evening.

"If I report all of the losses, I'm dead," I went on, my hands shoved deep in my jean pockets. "And if I lie, then I'm no better than they are."

"You're right," Daniel picked up on my *Star Trek* reference (I mentioned we were geeks, right?). "It's Starfleet's no-win scenario." He took off his glasses and looked in the direction of the setting sun. The orange-gold light beamed off his red hair. "But Kirk didn't believe in the no-win scenario." He closed his eyes and smiled. He seemed to be enjoying the warmth on his face.

We stood for a moment, there on the road, with neither of us talking. I could tell what he was thinking: *James, take control of your life!* But there was something else too; something he couldn't say. It made me feel uncomfortable in a way. How can I describe it? It was like being caught sitting on the toilet, when you forgot to lock the bathroom door and someone walks in, and then when you come out and the person is standing there and you pretend it never happened. Know that feeling?

I also remember thinking during our walk that I felt thin, pale, and defeated. I was a ghost drifting through my life. It wasn't until we came full circle along the dirt road, back to Daniel's car, that he finally gave his honest opinion.

"You don't have to believe in Zachariah to change your life," he said. He opened the passenger-side door of his tiny red Geo. I dropped into the bucket seat as he came around the car and slipped in behind the steering wheel.

I didn't respond at first.

"Everyone creates their life," he began, making no qualifications or excuses. "We're all hardwired into a central power source that is responsible for creating everything." He didn't look at me as he spoke. He put the key in the ignition, started the engine, and pulled out onto the road. "It doesn't matter how you tap into it. You can worship Jesus, or you can listen and learn from Zachariah. In either case, *you can choose* to direct this power with deliberate, conscious effort, or you can deny it and let your negative subconscious run the show."

I looked out past the road, still in deep thought, and barely noticed the twisted rust-colored rock formations. The sun was just below the horizon. Overhead, a deep blue sky was turning purple, giving way to a million tiny stars.

"Call it psychology if you want," he went on, "but you have to admit that people who expect to fail *do* fail and people who expect to succeed *do* succeed." He took his eyes away from the road long enough to check my reaction. "You expect your current job to be your only option, *and so it is*."

There was another long moment of silence then as the Geo bounced along the dirt road. A thick cloud of dust went up behind us. The sun was all but faded against the southwestern hues of orange, purple, and red.

I was still off in my own thoughts when Daniel spoke again: "What's really so strange about it?" he asked. "We've had the Bible pounded into our heads the whole time we were growing up—is being the descendant of space aliens any more ridiculous than all of us being the children of Adam and Eve?"

I didn't say anything, still, but he knew I'd taken the bait. It made him smile all the more.

"And what does it matter what we believe *so long as it works*?"

Over the next several weeks, my job situation went from bad to worse. It seemed I couldn't make a move without reporting to

Huff. While the rest of the company was coming and going as they damn well pleased, I was stuck in a 9-to-6 grind, having to report my every move. Huff didn't check up on me directly, of course. He had his cronies to do it for him—all of those nameless, mid-level managers who continued to shovel their mistakes down the corporate flow chart. And it was now the end of the month and time for what was most likely my last meeting with Huff.

On the night before the scheduled showdown, I called Daniel. "I don't think there's anything that can get me out of this one—no visualizations or magic-*k*." I made it a point to draw out the *k*.

"Have you tried?"

"What? Magic-*k*?" I did it again. I wasn't trying to annoy him especially. I was just being a pessimist about my general situation.

"You can joke all you want," Daniel responded flatly. "But you're the one with the problem."

I stretched out on my bed. A well-worn groove in the center of the mattress fit my body like a mold. "You have a point." I switched the receiver to my left ear. I took a deep breath. "OK, so I'm not saying I totally believe in this Zachariah guy—"

"You don't have to."

"And I still think all of this magick stuff is just wishful thinking."

"But?"

"But I guess I don't have anything to lose."

"I'll be right over."

Daniel's Geo was in front of my apartment building within a half hour. I noticed it after he'd pulled up, just as the knock came from the front door. It was well into the evening and I'd already had a few beers.

When I answered the door, Daniel looked as he always did: tousled red hair, wire-rimmed glasses, T-shirt, and faded blue jeans.

"You want a drink?" I held up my own bottle, as if showing him a sample.

"No, I'm good." He stepped in, made himself at home—not

unlike the other hundred or so times he'd been to my place. This time, though, he had a cardboard box under his arm. I saw that it contained four candles, a thick bundle of sage (what looked to me, at the time, like dried oregano), and a small cast iron pot filled with glassy quartz crystals.

I watched him place the items ever so gently on my worn-out, ring-stained coffee table, in front of the equally dog-eared sofa (the furniture had come with the apartment—God only knows how far back it went before me).

"What's all this?"

"Tools," he said, not looking up. He placed the pot in the center of the table, with the crystals around it. The candles were lit and set on the four corners. "Kill the lights," he added while turning the whole setup 45 degrees, so each table point faced north, east, south, and west. It was as though he was setting a place for supper, as if all the stuff were as common as a fork and spoon.

I stepped over to the door and turned off the lights as he admired his mystical handwork. The room was lit with a dim yellow haze, effectively hiding all the years of unvacuumed grunge and yellowed paint. And when I turned back to face him, he said ever so casually (I'm not kidding), "OK, now take off your clothes."

I'm not a bashful guy. I can pee in front of other men, no problem. I've even skinny-dipped once or twice in mixed company. So it wasn't being asked to get naked that had thrown me. It was that *Daniel* was doing the asking.

I was frozen in place, holding the beer in my hand and grinning like an idiot. It took a second or two before the words got filtered through the denial center in my brain. "What?"

"It's called *skyclad*." Daniel took off his glasses and put them aside. He reached for the bottom of his T-shirt and, without missing a beat, pulled it up over his head.

"Wowowo!" I was backing up, my hands out in front of me. There was that feeling again—like getting caught sitting on the toilet in a public bathroom. Only this time the door stayed open.

Daniel had thrown his T-shirt aside and was going for his pants. "Relax, James. It's how ritual was practiced before Christianity came along, before people became ashamed of their bodies."

"I'm not ashamed," I said. "I just don't think we—*you and I*—should—well—"

He became annoyed then. "What are you afraid of?" He stopped, leaving the front of his pants hanging open. I remember thinking I hadn't pictured him as a white briefs kind of guy. I'd always assumed he'd worn boxers.

There was a pause. Daniel looked at me, waiting, his sharp eyes transfixed.

"You sure you don't need a drink?" I tried to smile naturally and ended up with a shit-faced grin.

"No." He shook his head. I couldn't tell if it was in response to my question or if he was just generally disappointed in me. "James, we've been best friends a long time. You can trust me."

Another pause. What could I do? If I didn't take my clothes off, he'd think I was being a macho jerk—that I was afraid of getting naked with him, or that maybe I had something to hide.

So I emptied the bottle I had in my hand, throwing it back in one gulp. I put it down on the table, right there with the candles, and started kicking off my boots. "'Skyclad,' huh?" I said. "I think you're making this up."

We avoided eye contact as we both stripped down to our birthday suits. My jeans and T-shirt joined the pile with Daniel's clothes, on the sofa, and we took up positions opposite each other around the coffee table. We sat down on the rust-orange shag, our legs crossed in front of us, and our willies hanging out for the world to see.

"I call upon the God, Goddess, All That Is," he began, speaking in a whisper. He took up the bundle of dried sage and held it over the candle flame. "I call upon the power from the east where the light comes from." He stood up then, holding the sage away from his body, walked in a circle around the table, around me. "I call upon the power from the south where the light comes from." The smell of the smoldering leaves filled the room. It made me think of camp—a heavy, burning wood smell.

"I call upon the power from the west…" Daniel stepped around in front of me, coming full circle. I looked up at him and tried not to stare at his slender body. It was, well, amazingly tight and well proportioned.

It wasn't like I'd never seen him naked before. But this was different. The candlelight, the hushed tones of his voice, our rhythmic breathing...

"And from the north, where the cold comes from." He placed the sage in the cast iron pot and offered me his open hand. "Stand up."

I did. I took his hand and pushed up from the floor. I have to admit I wasn't totally ignorant of what might happen. But still, I felt a little embarrassed, maybe even a little terrified to reveal my hard-on to him. But again, what could I do? Run from the room with my hands over my crotch?

If Daniel noticed my erection then, he casually ignored it. He took my hands in his, over the table, and said, "Repeat after me." He cleared his throat and recited: *"There is one power that is an infinite spirit—One power that is a divine source of creation."*

I repeated the words, feeling a little stupid, but willing to go along. Maybe I just felt embarrassed. Maybe I didn't like to lie to my friend. And pretending to go along with the New Age stuff felt like a lie to me. It was like all those times I'd said prayers in church and didn't believe in anything I was saying.

He continued: *"And I, James Malcolm Mitchell, am a complete manifestation of this power."*

"I, James Malcolm Mitchell, am a complete manifestation of this power." I couldn't help but smile. I thought I might even laugh out loud. Not because of the words, but from the strangeness of the whole situation. Of all the things I thought I'd be doing that night, holding hands with Daniel, naked, with a hard-on wasn't one of them.

"I use this power here and now to manifest a perfect solution, a perfect separation, between me and my job." Daniel squeezed my hands. "Be serious." He looked me in the eye and shook my arms in an attempt to stop my stupid grinning.

I cleared my throat and tried to shake off the smile. But it just made me want to laugh even more. I still made an honest attempt, though, to repeat Daniel's words: "I use this power here to manifest a solution for my job—" I started to shake my head. "I'm sorry, but I can't do this."

I broke Daniel's hold and stepped back from the table. "I'm sorry, Dan." I kept shaking my head as if to say no.

"OK, let me do it." Daniel took a deep breath. He lowered his head as if to gather his thoughts.

"What are we doing here?" I motioned to him, to his naked body, to my (still) full-blown erection.

"Let's just stay focused." His words were calm, carefully measured. *"We use this power here and now with harm to none and good will to all."*

My heart was thumping in my chest like a drum.

"Just say the words," Daniel ordered, his eyes closed, his head still bowed.

"Fine! *We use this power with harm to none!*" I said the words in a singsong, mocking voice. "Now can I have my pants?"

I didn't wait for Daniel to oblige. I stepped over to him, reaching around his body, to the sofa, fumbling for my clothes. My bare hip pressed against his as I bent over. But he didn't move. He stood his ground. I felt his hand on my arm then, pulling me to face him. We were suddenly nose to nose. His eagle-sharp eyes were looking into mine. He looked pained, maybe heartbroken. And I understood what he'd been holding back during that walk several weeks ago.

So I kissed him.

Maybe it had something to do with the all the beer I'd had before Daniel even got to my door. Maybe it was the candlelight and the whole strangeness of the moment. Or maybe it was that I really did (and still do) love him. Maybe I'm gay. I guess, technically, I'm at least *bi*—I'd have to be, wouldn't I?

We crumpled to the floor, our lips locked in an embrace, right there in front of the candles and the burning sage. At first we were just a mass of tangled limbs, grabbing and pulling at each other. It was strange to feel such firm, hard legs and arms pressing against mine. Daniel was smaller in stature but just as strong. The realization of what we were doing was erotic. It was like teenage sex—that taboo feeling—the thrill of knowing you might get caught. It was backseat, lover's lookout kind of sex. We were 17, feeling the same clumsy fumbling.

We ended up in a tired, sticky heap—both of us on our backs, our chests rising and falling with each heavy breath. I was holding Daniel's hand, looking up at the cracked plaster ceiling. Neither of us wanted to say the first words.

But of course it was Daniel who spoke up. "Are you OK?"

I didn't turn to look at him. "Yeah. Sure. I'm fine."

"But you're not gay, right?"

"I don't think that's a fair question to ask right now."

Daniel sat up, took away his hand. He reached over and picked up his glasses from the table and then turned back to face me. "I love you," he said.

Then I did turn to look at him. His eyes were fixed on me. "Daniel—"

"It's OK. I know you love me too. Just maybe not that way."

I shook my head, rubbing my head against the carpet. "I don't know."

Daniel got up from the floor. He put on his clothes and went out. I stayed on my back until the candles had melted over the side of the table.

The next day I was fired from my job. My supervisor was waiting at the time clock when I came in. He didn't need to say anything. I could tell by his expression. He had the resigned look of a humorless doctor about to report a dark spot on my chest x-ray. "Don't sweat it," I said, "It's not like I didn't see it coming." He shook my hand and that was that.

I had mixed feelings at first. Mostly relief. I walked away from the giant aluminum box and found myself thinking, *Why did I hang in there so long in the first place?* I can't say I'd enjoyed working in such an oppressive place. It was the "known devil," I guess. Looking back, I was just sorry it had to end like it did—mostly because I didn't get the last word. I also think it didn't faze me because in that moment I was more worried about my friendship with Daniel.

Of course I didn't think that having sex one time with another man automatically made me gay. But who makes the rules? Is it like vampires? Three bites and you're turned forever?

I just couldn't see myself living with another guy, listening to show tunes, collecting fancy antiques, and paying more than 10 bucks for a haircut. It just wasn't me.

I tried calling him a few times. But whenever I'd pick up the phone I'd realize I still didn't know what to say. I finally made up my mind to go to Slackers and try to run into him sort of by accident.

He was there on my first try.

"I'm not as pathetic as I seem," he said, looking up at me from our dark, secluded booth. "I haven't been hanging out here alone, just waiting around for you to show up." He shrugged, looked down at the table.

"Mind if I sit down?" It felt stupid to ask but I also felt like we were meeting for the first time.

He just shook his head as if to say, *Don't be an idiot.*

Our favorite waitress brought me a beer without having to wave from a distance. We were silent for a moment as she dropped a napkin on the table and deposited the bottle. When she was gone I said, "It worked."

Daniel didn't seem to hear me.

"Your magick—it worked, I guess. I don't have to deal with my job anymore, since I got canned."

He took a breath, adjusted his glasses with a finger to the bridge of his nose, and then jumped right into an apology as if he'd been rehearsing it for the past week or so. "It was my fault. I led you on. You don't have to say anything. I understand why you haven't called—"

"You didn't lead me on."

"I should have just been honest with you and told you how I felt. I feel like such a jerk."

"Daniel."

"It isn't like I thought you were gay. I mean, I know you're *not* gay. Right?"

"Dan—"

236

"It's just that I've been carrying around these feelings and I assumed you felt the same way since, well, since we seemed so close."

"Will you listen to me?"

He stopped and took another breath, waiting for me to have a turn.

I took a long drink, put the bottle down squarely between us. "We *are* close."

Daniel looked at me. The words had grabbed his attention.

"But I'm not gay."

His eyes dropped. He looked at the label on the beer bottle without really seeing it.

"I'm sorry. I think maybe I was the one who led you on. I was searching for the right words and feeling like a traitor. "I think I was confusing sex with love. You know?"

He was still staring at nothing. I could see his heart sink to his stomach.

"I guess I can't call myself straight, exactly, but I know *that* isn't what I want."

Daniel leaned back in the booth, still staring at the bottle he held in his hands. "Kobayashi Maru."

"No," I said. I waited for him to look up at me and then added, "I don't believe in the no-win scenario."

Someone had put a few quarters in the jukebox then, and Jim Morrison started crooning "The End of Night." Daniel looked back over his shoulder, toward the main part of the bar. He winced. "You want to go somewhere else?"

I looked around at the bar, as if seeing it for the first time. It was especially dark, somber, and lifeless. "Yeah. Let's get the hell out of this place."

THE DUKE OF WELLINGTON

Matti Jackson

The walls of the Duke of Wellington's front bar were faux timber paneling hung with newspaper cartoons in bargain-store frames, and the windows were tinted darkly. Even with the ceiling downlights on, it was the little light that entered through the windows that lit the room. It was because the bar at the Duke was dark at any hour of the day that it was popular with lawyers, police, and the clients of both. The room was entered through one or other of two west-facing doors opening directly onto Williams Street.

James had told Eddy he would be in the Duke by 6 at the latest. Eddy was, as usual, early. James, not for the first time, was late. Eddy had switched to wine after his second glass of water. As he had each time for the previous hour, he looked up to the sound of the street door on the other side of the room. It was unlikely anyone else in the room even heard it. Glare framed the silhouette of a man entering alone. Eddy took in the look of him—straight trousered legs, narrow hip, square shoulders, short hair. Their suit was too good for a detective or most businessmen. The door swung closed against the setting sun and the room turned to black. Eddy lost him and the whole room but even before his eyes adjusted he knew it wasn't James.

He ordered another drink, the same. He left it two-thirds full as a marker before making his way along the corridor behind the servery. The toilet was the only place one was allowed to smoke anymore. Standing at the urinal, he looked through the window louvers into the back lane and his cigarette's rising vapor trail until someone came in and stood beside him. Eddy pretended to wash his hands before flicking his butt past the man's leg into the trough. It sizzled as it landed in the froth of the man's urine.

There was a touch he recognized on his elbow as he walked back into the bar. He would have preferred it have landed on his tush, but James would never do that with the people of his work world around. Rising from nowhere, anger flushed through Eddy's neck. Why should he be treated as something on the side? A public tiff would be cathartic, but Eddy kept himself from responding.

"What have I done?" James was right on Eddy's heels. He put his glass on the table between them and slid another next to Eddy's—red for himself, white for Eddy. Eddy shook his head. After a second he started to lean toward James, then caught himself. He lifted his glass to his lips. As he lowered it he allowed himself the hint of a blown kiss.

James cracked a smile and straightened his back. James talked. He always talked—in the dark at night, while he chewed his breakfast, as Eddy soaped him down in the shower, whenever. The only way Eddy knew to shut him up was to plant a wet tonguey kiss hard upon his lips. As they sat James talked about his day in court—the way the prosecutor and he worked together to unfold their story, how the defense attempted to trip him up then twist his meaning, the way the beak sided with the perpetrator, the way James sweated like a pig to carry the day.

It had been a long while since Eddy was much interested in any of James's stories. He wasn't expected to add to them or have an opinion himself. He pressed a knee between James's legs. It kindled no response. If they were some other place or there was a tablecloth, he'd have been rewarded with a squeeze or a hand. "Ready to eat?" he hinted, but James's story wasn't finished. He ordered another round. Fourth for him, second for James. He kept count, James would be too.

Eddy made affirmation noises at the conclusion of James's tale. James, he thought, looked good in blue. Eddy had never been inside a courtroom. He imagined James standing in a movie version of one with everyone's eyes upon him. He imagined James naked—shoulders, chest, buttocks, calves, thighs, cock, balls, the bald patch on his crown. They would want to lick and kiss James all over just as Eddy, at that very moment, did.

Eddy became aware that James was silent and looking at him. He blushed and turned his eyes down. His glass was almost empty. James's was barely touched. James's hand was on the tabletop close to his glass. Between his fingers was a jeweler's box. James flicked it open, and inside was a single ear stud. Eddy looked up. James lifted his other hand to his own ear and a stud like the one in the box. When he'd left the house that morning James's ear had been unpierced. Eddy's eyes watered. He bent forward. James ducked his kiss.

Eddy was on his feet. The drinks made him unsteady, his tears blinded him. He stumbled down the corridor and into the men's. Alone, he took deep breaths. After, he rinsed his face. He bundled a wad of tissue and dabbed his face dry. He got more tissue and blew his nose. He was in the stall tossing the soggy mess of tissue into the bowl when James came into the room. Eddy gave a wan smile.

"Wrong?" James was without his usual swagger.

"Very right." Eddy kissed him. Their noses collided and then their teeth. Eddy's arms were around his lover. James's hands landed against Eddy's buttocks. Eddy pulled him into the stall. Still kissing, he pushed the door closed, latched it then found James's zipper. He undid James's fly.

"We can't do this here."

"Then arrest me, Detective Sergeant." Eddy's chin and nose bumped down James's chest as he slid to his knees and extracted his lover's cock.

SOMETHING SLOUCHES TOWARD BETHLEHEM

Rick R. Reed

Johnny would be dead before the night was through.

Alan knew that, and yet it didn't stop him from squeezing his lover's hand and dreaming about miracles. When he looked at Johnny, lying there in the mahogany sleigh bed the two had purchased together more than 15 years ago, he saw someone he didn't know. He remembered Johnny as if he were already gone: the olive skin his Italian heritage had given him, the wavy black hair and green eyes, the vanity-inspired shifting facial hair (goatee, full beard, mustaches in different lengths and thicknesses) and the body he had always worked so hard on, made lean from years of running, muscular from years of free weights, defined by black curly hair. But now the person lying before him couldn't be Johnny, could it? This man, this shriveled, hollow-eyed, shrunken-faced *thing* couldn't possibly be the man he had loved. How could one man change so fast? He had been diagnosed as HIV-positive only a year and a half ago, Alan pondered, maybe even less than that.

AIDS didn't work that fast, not anymore, not here, at the beginning of the 21st century, when Alan thought the disease had become not a death sentence but a treatable illness like diabetes. Johnny had tested negative—Alan paused to calculate, aligning the date of Johnny's last test with his birthday, remembering how the two were nearly on the same day—about two years ago. So that would make his positive test result—at the most—less than a year and a half ago. Even accounting for a "window period" false negative two years ago, he couldn't possibly have been positive for more than two years.

That's what they had thought. Johnny had gone to the Wilson Aimes Health Center faithfully every six months, to have blood drawn and later to steel himself for the results. The day would come and Johnny would invariably be irritable, worried what the outcome might be, but he always came out of the office smiling, relief glowing like neon. Except for the last time. Alan would never forget waiting outside the caseworker's office while Johnny was inside getting his results. Why would this time be different from any other? Alan had skimmed a *People* magazine, wondered if they should have chicken piccata for dinner or maybe just broiled orange roughy. And then the door opened and he looked up into a stricken face, eyes bright with tears. Alan's first thought was that Johnny was putting him on, that this was some sort of macabre joke. He was desperate for it to be a joke. After the tears and the hours of silent holding each other, Alan had told Johnny he had nothing to worry about. What with catching it so early and all the promising new drug cocktails, he didn't have to worry about dying any more than the next person.

"Look at me," Alan had said, forcing himself to smile. "Fit as a fiddle and poz for 10 years."

And that's how he had allayed his lover's fears. Until the night sweats and the diarrhea had begun, a week after the positive test results. He noticed his first Kaposi's sarcoma lesion three days after that. His weight began dropping and Alan would get mad, trying to force Johnny to eat when he could only stare at whatever he had made him, the soups and the milkshakes, with nausea, finally turning away with a whispered "I'm sorry."

It wasn't even a month before they needed help: a black man from a local nurses' service that provided home health care. Johnny refused to go to the hospital, certain until these last few days that he would beat this thing, that the protease inhibitors he was taking would kick in, that he would begin to feel better, like Alan, like so many of their friends whom the drug cocktails had helped.

But nothing worked. Whatever the drug, whatever the combination, no matter how many pills he tried to keep down each day, the drugs had no more effect than sugar pills. He got pneumocystis and Alan had pleaded with him to go to the hospital, but Johnny held fast, letting Dwight, the big, kind man who came to their house each day, give him his doses of Bactrim, bathe his fevered forehead with a cool cloth, and read to him when he was cooled down enough to concentrate.

And now Johnny lay before him: a wraith, unrecognizable. A humidifier spat out steam in the corner. Outside the bedroom window, the leaves were turning. Autumn. The season when things begin to die. Alan put a fist to his mouth, fast, to choke back a sob. He rose and looked out the window: Damen Avenue, on Chicago's northwest side, in a neighborhood called Ravenswood, bustled with traffic below. How long had they lived here? Seven years? Or was it eight?

It didn't matter. They were "growing old together" much faster than Alan had ever dreamed.

The cars below swarmed by. The afternoon rush hour was in full swing, and for just one moment Alan wished he could be among the commuters, hurrying home to normal lives: dinners and TV shows, phone calls to friends, working out at the gym. It seemed those below should have some respect, or at least recognition, for his plight. They should dim their headlights as they passed the red brick courtyard building.

"Are they here yet?" Johnny asked, his voice thin and watery as a kitten's: an embarrassment. It made Alan so mad. He wanted to turn to Johnny, grab him up off the bed and shake him, until he ended this nonsense and came back to being the man he loved.

Alan had begun getting mad a lot lately. The rages overtook suddenly, unexpectedly, over the smallest thing: like yesterday, when they were out of mustard for his ham sandwich, he had torn almost everything out of the refrigerator, breaking bottles of salad dressing on the floor, flinging the plastic milk carton against the kitchen wall. Not thinking, just doing, just destroying, until he stopped, panting, and laughed at himself until the laughter dissolved to tears.

And then he cleaned it all up.

"Are they here yet?"

Alan took a deep breath and sat down next to Alan on the bed, ran his fingers through his coarse hair, what remained of it anyway, scalp hot beneath his fingers. "They're on their way. I told you that a half hour ago." Alan looked into his eyes. "They'll get here. They said they would, didn't they?"

Johnny's family, his mother and two sisters, in New Jersey, had promised to be there by early that afternoon when Alan had called them the night before, telling them if they wanted to say goodbye they should get to Chicago as soon as they could. Johnny's mother had been cold, but he couldn't blame her. People had different ways of showing their grief.

But if they didn't get here soon, Johnny would die, and Alan supposed they would never forgive themselves for denying themselves, and Johnny, a farewell. Louise, his mother, had said they would catch the first plane they could get out of Newark and be there, she thought, by the next morning.

It was 3 o'clock. Three o'clock...dusk in just a few hours, then darkness. What would Johnny think? That his death wasn't important enough to warrant a visit from his family? Alan felt the rage boil up in him again, longing to pace the room, riling out at the DeSarro family, their heartlessness, their hypocrisy about family mattering above all else.

But he couldn't do that. Johnny had dozed off and Alan ran a trembling hand through his fine blond hair. He looked down at the face of his sleeping lover. Lately, Johnny could doze off in the middle of a sentence, Alan's or even his own.

Alan stood, walked to the maple framed Shaker mirror that hung on the bedroom wall. He looked at his reflection: the pale, watery blue eyes, the straight nose and thin lips that some said made him look cruel, shifty. He turned his head, feeling his neck for swollen lymph glands, as he had done a million times for the past 11 or so years, when he had first started hearing about the symptoms.

But there was nothing but smooth skin, no swelling, no lesions. How could he have carried the virus in him for so many years and still be healthy when his lover had probably had the hateful thing in him for only a short time? Johnny's life was about to blink out, a flame that had hardly flared. It wasn't fair.

"Are they here yet?"

Alan stiffened at the question, wanted to whirl on Johnny, scream at him, but he bit his lip hard enough to taste the copper of his own blood, and let the wave of anger subside.

"Soon," he whispered. "They'll be here soon."

Darkness claimed the room. Alan had lit scented votive candles and set them around their bedroom, placing the little candles on saucers, in holders, in shot glasses, in whatever he could find. There was a faint spice and pear aroma in the room that almost masked the sour smell of Johnny.

Every few seconds, the light from a pair of headlights would crawl across the opposite walls, and it made Alan feel like a prisoner, trapped inside here while others remained free.

What had he done to deserve it? To be locked inside with death and despair? Was it just because he was queer? Whose fault was that anyway?

He stroked Johnny's hair. "It's been good, honey," he whispered, wishing he could think of something profound to say. Alan wanted to deny it, but Johnny's imminent death had invaded the room, like a stranger standing in the deeper shadows of the corner. Death waited patiently, silently for his inevitable time when he would cross the hardwood floor and carry Johnny away, leaving nothing but a husk. Leaving nothing for Alan but the ache of memory and the trauma of life ahead.

Johnny looked up at him. Even in the dark, Alan could just make out the moss green of his eyes. "It has," he croaked. A lone tear ran down his face and Alan leaned over, licked it away, tasting the salt, wishing he could lick the virus away, suck it out of his system.

"Shhh, don't try to talk now." Alan stroked the hair away from Johnny's forehead, feeling the crisp hardness of one of the KS lesions.

Johnny's hand gripped Alan's, moving it away from his forehead and bringing it to his lips. He kissed the hand and pulled Alan's thumb into his mouth, sucking on it, staring up at him. After a moment, he let the thumb go.

"They're not coming, are they?"

Alan shook his head.

"I really thought they would."

"I'm so sorry, sweetheart."

"Not your fault." Johnny squeezed his hand. "You're here. You're my family. No one but you."

Alan reached out with his free hand to stroke Johnny's face: withered skin, stubble. Even now, the most beautiful man in the world. "I know I am. And you're mine. You have been since that first night. Remember?" Alan tried to smile, but it came out as more of a grimace. "You cruised me on Hubbard Street." And he saw Johnny, how he had looked back then, in the early '80s, wondering how someone so fine could have been drawn to him. He didn't care. All that had ever mattered was that Johnny was there. No matter what, he was always there.

Slight pressure on his hand. He returned his focus to Johnny.

"I have to go now." Johnny looked away from him, as if embarrassed by the admission. "Maybe I'll see you sometime."

"What are you…" Alan paused in mid sentence and realized he was talking to a dead man.

He gripped his hand and a choked sob escaped him just as the buzzer rang from downstairs. "They're here now," he leaned over and whispered.

He pulled the sheet up over Johnny's face and went to answer the door.

THE REUNION

Eumenides

It was odd, Henry thought, looking over the valley seeing the rows of tents neatly aligned, the embers of campfires spitting sparks into the summer sky of this Pennsylvania night. Familiar songs drifted on the air with the haze of the campfires, and it took only the slightest bit of imagination to take him from this Great Reunion back 50 years to 1863, where young Henry Barrett, scarce 19, waited on the cusp of his first battle.

The songs had been less mournful then. There had been a sense of excitement, a feeling that the long nightmare that had begun with triumphant rebel yells and "We'll whip the Yankees and be home by Christmas" and had dragged on through two years of mud and misery might be coming to an end. They'd pushed into Pennsylvania, had finally taken the battle to the enemy, and nothing could stop Lee's glorious army now.

So that first night there'd been hope, and the songs and talk around the fire had been of the girls left behind, of mothers' gentle and loving hands, of groaning boards laden with hams and chickens and potatoes and rice. But Henry, who'd joined the 24th Virginia Infantry only a few months before the quick march north through Pennsylvania's green fields and rolling hills, had sat just beyond the edge of the fire's circle, listening and watching.

He'd done a lot of watching from the outside in those days, never truly feeling that he belonged. His own three-room home was nothing to brag on, a hardscrabble farm barely able to sustain his small family. His mother, though he loved her dearly, was no gentle lady, but a hardworking farm woman with rough and calloused hands. And girls, well, he'd never thought much of girls, really. His brother, Stephen, had always said he just hadn't found the right girl yet, but then Stephen always was sparking one local miss or another.

Stephen. His beloved brother, who'd enlisted the very day that Virginia seceded. Stephen should have been here, welcoming his brother to his regiment, teaching him army ways. But Stephen was dead, blown to pieces at a place called Manassas. Henry had been fixing the south fence when he'd seen the lone rider coming up the dirt path to the house, holding a tattered letter. Henry had held the missive with trembling hands, reading aloud. The carefully crafted phrases penned by Colonel Terry were so obviously meant to be a comfort to them, but the words had dropped like icy stones into the cabin, turning spring to winter.

Henry had known immediately what he had to do. He folded the letter neatly and placed it in his breast pocket, kissed his mother goodbye, took the long rifle that hung over the door and started walking. Though he was not the man Stephen had been and could never replace his brother, not at home nor in the regiment, he'd come to finish Stephen's work.

And now, 50 years later, standing on a low hill that had about killed him to climb, he could remember how very hard it had been at first. Sleeping on the cold ground, picking weevils from his bread, drinking watery soup and foul water that led to endless bouts of illness. And the loneliness. Mostly the veterans had been kind, but they were tired of war, tired of making friends only to lose them, and nobody had much time for Stephen Barrett's kid brother.

Nobody except Alec. Stephen had written him about Alec; the letters described the other young man so completely that Henry had no trouble picking him out the minute he'd seen him. Dark hair tousled over a handsome countenance, flashing, mischievous eyes, and a smile that lit up his face, making you forget the stabbing pain in your feet and the eternal ache in your neck

from carrying your pack. He'd been strong and slender and ath-
letic, well-read with a proper education, everything Henry wanted to be and was not. And yet he'd never once made Henry feel
like the ignorant farm boy he knew he was.

"You're buried treasure, Henry," Alec had said once when
Henry had asked why he bothered with him. "A man has to look
beyond the surface with you."

"Mostly they don't bother," Henry admitted, thinking of how
people's eyes tended to slide right over him as though he weren't
even there.

"Their loss and my gain." Alec's strong hand had clapped him
on the shoulder.

He'd taken the young Henry under his wing, protecting him
from the older men, some of whom were no better than they
should be. Too many of the gallant cavaliers had feet of clay, and
Alec taught him to guard his pack even while sleeping. Once,
when a grizzled veteran from another company approached him
with an odd gleam in his eye that Henry hadn't understood at all,
Alec had been there to pull him away to safety. The old man had
laughed at them, using words Henry had never heard before but
which made Alec's face flush with fury.

And then they'd come north. The night before the battle, he'd
come to the top of this tree-covered rise with Alec, slipping away
from the camaraderie of the campfires against Captain Hammet's
express orders. He remembered clear as crystal how the tall grass-
es slapped against their legs as they ran pell-mell through the
fields, making for higher ground and the privacy of a small grove
of trees. It was truly amazing how little the scene had changed.
Trees aged so much more slowly than men.

There, right there was the oak they'd sunk down under, laughing breathlessly at their daring escape. The piles of dead leaves
seemed just the same, as though 50 years was as nothing in the
life of the forest. He could almost reach out and touch the past;
the sounds and scents recalling to his mind how Alec had collapsed into the bed of leaves, pulling him down. He'd tickled
Henry till he squealed with laughter, unconcerned by the possibility that the Yankees or their own officers might discover them.

He was young; the next day would bring his opportunity to prove himself a man and a soldier, but that evening all that mattered was the peace of the night and Alec so young and strong beside him.

Alec had flexed his muscles, rolling them over so he was atop Henry, and they'd both suddenly stopped as though the world had frozen on its axis and all nature held its breath. Henry held his breath, looking up into the welcoming eyes of his friend, and had seen wonderment and pleasure and a hint of fear there; then Alec had smiled, and his hands had come up to tangle in Henry's red hair.

Their lips met, briefly at first, then Alec had kissed him again, tongue flicking out to test the barrier of Henry's virgin mouth. Henry had yielded, opening to the marvelous sensation of Alec, his body all sinew and bone hard against him, and their tongues and lips and teeth had clashed again and again as Henry had grown hard with longing for something he could not even name.

Then Alec had broken off the kiss and rolled off to his side, smiling indulgently at Henry. Henry could remember that he'd asked him if he'd minded, and he'd been too shaken to talk, had just shaken his head. He shouldn't have liked it; he knew that from the preacher and the way the older men back home had talked when they'd thought he wasn't listening. He knew kisses were for girls with big doe eyes and blond curls, but once Alec's lips had met his own, there'd been no thought of girls. There could never be a girl who would be to him what Alec was becoming.

Henry had relaxed into Alec's arms as they lay side by side, feeling utterly and completely safe despite the forthcoming battle, the masses of blue uniforms that were just beyond their sight, the knowledge that what they had done, what he was feeling and thinking was surely mortal sin; none of that mattered a tinker's damn. Taking the initiative, he leaned forward and brushed his lips against Alec's and in the process brought his lanky body to fit close against his friend's. Their bodies seemed made for each other, he remembered thinking, and when their groins had come together it had been like a spark tossed onto dry grass.

Alec moaned deep in his throat, and the sound of it lodged in Henry's stomach, turning his bones to liquid. When Alec's hand had slowly begun working the buttons of Henry's trousers and then closed on his straining organ, he'd thought his heart was going to pound out of his chest.

"Do you like it?" Alec whispered, and Henry had nodded shyly, wanting desperately to thrust into Alec's hand, but afraid, uncertain of how to proceed.

"That's only the beginning. There's so much more I want to teach you." But the sounds from the campfires had begun to die away as soldiers found their bedrolls, and they both knew they needed their sleep before the rigors of the next day. So Alec withdrew his hand, carefully closing the trouser placket, stroking Henry's cheek with one war-roughened finger. "After this is over, when we've sent the Yankees packing and are marching on Washington, you'll see. It's marvelous, there's a wonderful world of pleasure waiting for you, Henry, and I promise I'll show it all to you."

A promise that should not have been made. A promise threatened by the merciless guns of the Federals as they stepped from the woods to engage the enemy. Even now, so many years later, he had only to close his eyes, and he was there, amid the crush and confusion as their company had been given their duties; as Alec, a corporal, had taken a few chosen men to spy out the enemy position. And Henry, of course, had been one of the chosen.

Alec scrambled to his feet and beckoned to Henry and the two men with him. "That's the signal, let's move." He turned to survey the field from their vantage point on the hill. The smell of smoke lingered on the morning haze, and the heat was rapidly burning off fog and dew. Henry was about to comment that he wished he was swimming in Hodge's Run back home when the sharp retort of a rifle resounded above the growing din and the gray of Alec's jacket bloomed dark with blood.

He fell into Henry's arms as the calls of the Yankees moving toward them sent the other two fleeing back down the hill to the safety of their regiment.

"Ah, sweet Jesus, Alec!" Shaking his head, what should he do, there was so much blood, his hands had pressed against the wound, trying to stanch the pulsing flow, but it was no use. Smoke and iron and sweat and fear clogged his nostrils.

Alec's eyes were still open, but the sparkle that had always been there, the encouraging glint that Henry had come to know so well was fading rapidly, and his aquiline face, pale and sweating, contorted with pain.

"Fuck, Henry, it hurts, oh, God, it hurts!" Alec was crying; the world was ending.

"I'll get you to a doctor—it's going to be all right." Henry looked frantically around him. The battle had begun in earnest and was raging around them—lines of men were advancing across the killing fields and everywhere was a sea of blue. He'd never get Alec back to their lines in time.

And Alec knew it. "Too late. So sorry, Henry...can't stay...would have...I wanted...will wait, love..."

Tears, hot and salty, streamed down his face as his throat constricted. "I love you, Alec," he choked out, taking the other man's hand, which tightened convulsively, then went slack as death, the eternal guardian of the battlefield, took yet another victim.

Henry cradled the lifeless body in his arms, closing the unseeing dark eyes as the angry whirlwind of battle had swirled around him. There was neither glory nor honor to be found in these red valleys.

But there had been Federals aplenty, and they'd found Henry there, taking Alec away to be buried in an unmarked grave and Henry to Andersonville Prison, where he'd rotted and mourned till the war ended.

So the promise had remained unfulfilled as Henry had made the long trek back to Montgomery County when the war was done. He'd closed off the memories of Alec to marry the daughter of a neighboring farmer, raising sons and daughters who had grown in their turn married and given him grandchildren. The eager young man had become a tired old man, Springfield rifle replaced by a cane, and his bowdlerized war memories were now fodder for his grandsons, who took up sticks and ran through the woods and fields of their farms playing Johnny Reb.

And today, July 3, 1913, he'd come back to Gettysburg for what he knew would be the last time. Exhausted by the climb, Henry sank down under the tree, in the exact spot where Alec had pulled him into his rough embrace. His eyes seemed heavy and he closed them gratefully, picturing clearly in his mind the face of his fallen friend. The Pennsylvania night was colder than he'd expected after the suffocating heat of the day, but he no longer felt it; and the noises of the former soldiers, Yankee and Confederate mixed now, their differences forgotten in the face of their shared past, faded into silence.

Something unknown, beyond his senses, prompted Henry to open his eyes, and he was immediately aware of a dark shape standing in front of him. Surely this could not be real—Alec, tall and strong and handsome in his uniform, and though at first he seemed translucent like a shade, as Henry blinked, the shape solidified, and when Alec reached his hand down to pull Henry to his feet, the rough hand was warm and welcoming and *real.*

At first, dazed and filled with wonderment, no words were exchanged as they came together in gentle exploration; a flurry of touches and kisses, and somehow Henry's legs no longer ached and he felt younger, lighter, as Alec's hands slid inside his shirt and he felt the blessed feel of skin against skin, of nimble fingers teasing across his chest, flickering over his nipples.

Never in nearly 50 years of sexual congress with his wife had Henry felt such a sensation. His prick was huge and swollen, and as he stood leaning against the old oak, Alec slid down his gray uniform trousers (he was dreaming, he had to be dreaming) and knelt before him, stroking his length lovingly, then, oh, God, reaching out with his tongue to lap at the tip; the sensation of warm breath against his prick sent shivers running through Henry's body.

Then dazzling dark eyes smiled up at him as Alec took his organ into his mouth, engulfing it in warm cavernous wetness that was unlike anything he'd ever known. Tongue and lips and teeth, oh, sweet Jesus, his teeth, just gently grazing the ridge and Alec's hands on his shaft and balls; it was cool water on a hot day, it was the gentlest of breezes wafting over his bare body, and so much more. It was more intense and beautiful than anything he'd ever known, and he felt the pressure building, mounting in waves till his entire body seemed to explode from his toes upward, and he pulsed his release into Alec's mouth as his fingers tangled in his friend's coarse hair.

Then Alec rose and kissed him, and he could taste himself on the other man's tongue—how could he dream the taste of a thing he'd never known before? He stepped back, wanting to give the same pleasure to Alec, but the other man gestured back to the tree where Henry saw himself, old and wrinkled, lying as though in deep sleep under the tree. Not dreaming then.

"Am I..." he could not bring himself to say the word. This wasn't what he'd expected from death. Nor from life either.

Alec nodded solemnly. "I knew you'd come back. I wanted to keep my promise."

"Is this heaven?" He'd known both heaven and hell wearing this uniform, had found and lost his greatest dream in this place - it seemed fitting that his life should end here. Or was it a beginning? "I never thought...that a ghost could *feel*."

"If you want it bad enough," Alec answered. "You'll see. We have all eternity to figure it out." He took Henry by the hand, and led him away from Gettysburg's killing fields into the wonderful world promised on a July night 50 years before.

THEIR TOWN

Simon Sheppard

The drama coach was mowing his lawn dressed only in his bathing suit. Again.

But then, Mr. Knippel never seems to care what people think. I guess when you're born with a name like "Richard Knippel"— which he says is Pennsylvania Dutch—then you build up calluses. Dick Knippel. A lot of the guys in his English class think it's hysterical. Actually, I think it's pretty funny myself.

I was on my way over to Jody's when I saw Knippel mowing away. Now, I can understand why mowing on an unseasonably hot May afternoon can be sweaty work, why a guy might not want to do it fully dressed. But a skimpy red bathing suit? One you could basically see the outline of his dick through? That would be asking for trouble. In Mr. Knippel's case, it was. As if there weren't enough rumors about him, in his late 30s and never married. But Knippel didn't seem to care what anyone thought.

I wish I could not care what people think about me.

Not that I'd ever mow the lawn dressed like *that*.

"Hey, Jody."

"Hey, Tom."

Blumenkrantz gestured broadly, like a butler in some old black and white film. "Walk this way, sir."

I tried for Groucho Marx. "If I could walk that way…"

We headed up to Tom's bedroom.

"I saw Knippel on the way over here."

"Yeah?"

"He was mowing the lawn."

"Uh-huh."

"In his bathing suit."

"*Again?*" Jody was putting an album on his turntable. His family was better off than mine, and he had a brand-new KLH stereo. An achingly pure soprano voice came from the speakers, one of those folksingers Blumenkrantz liked. I'd always been more into show tunes, and Ellyn Miles sounded nothing like Barbra Streisand. Still, there was something appealing about the clunky earnestness of the song.

My love for you is wide as the ocean is wide...

"So what do you want to do today?" I asked. "It's a really nice afternoon..."

"Let's just stick around here and talk, OK?"

As dark as the road ahead of us is dark...

Jody flopped back on the bed, next to where I was sitting, and stretched his hands above his head. His CLASS OF 1972 T-shirt rode up enough for me to see a trail of dark hair on his belly.

Our love is full of danger, unbounded as the sea...

The song—though Jody had played it for me several times before—was getting me kind of bummed. It wasn't the sort of thing for a sunny spring afternoon. But *Funny Girl* wouldn't have been right either.

And then Jody smiled, showing the braces he was usually so self-conscious about, and it didn't matter what kind of music was playing. It didn't matter at all.

We were doing *Our Town* for the senior play. I know, I know. *Every*body does *Our Town*. But Mr. Knippel was updating it. Not really changing the lines, which were kind of holy writ to high school drama clubs, but just doing some audiovisual stuff. Beatles music, posters about the Vietnam War, that kind of thing. It sounded a little silly to me—hey, if he'd wanted to do a contemporary play, he should have picked one. But I figured good ol' Thornton Wilder could withstand Knippel's pretensions.

Jody and I had both auditioned for the plum role of the Stage Manager, but I'd gotten it. Jody had gotten the small role of Professor Willard, which meant he'd be understudying for me and for Ronnie Fell, who played Mr. Webb. So he'd also ended up on the tech crew, which meant that he'd be at rehearsals, but he really wouldn't be doing all that much till the tech work started in earnest a couple of weeks before opening night. It's true that Jody is sort of a geek—he used to be in the AV club—and it's also true that I'm probably the better actor. So he took his assignment well, though he and I both knew he would like to have beaten me out for Stage Manager.

We were nearing the end of rehearsals—dress rehearsals were just three weeks off—when Ronnie Fell, who hadn't shown up at school for over a week, sent word that he was withdrawing from the cast. Ronnie had always been a bit—well, "high-strung" is a nice way of putting it. He was kind of an overachiever: 3.8 average, debating team, swim team, senior play. But lately he'd been seeming especially unhappy, or at least withdrawn, so it hadn't been a total surprise when he dropped out of *Our Town*. But that did leave Jody on the spot, having to take over the role of Mr. Webb on short notice as well as keep up with his tech work. And with the rest of school, of course. And with me.

"Hi, Mrs. Blumenkrantz." Lately, since her divorce became final, Jody's mom had been dressing…younger. This time she was wearing a bulky blue sweater, stretch pants, powder-blue leg warmers.

"Oh, Tom. Come on in. Jody's upstairs."

"Thanks."

"I'd offer you a Coke or something, but I'm just on my way to yoga class."

"That's fine, Mrs. Blumenkrantz." I was already heading up the stairs.

Jody was lying on his bed, reading the *Our Town* script. He looked up at me and smiled. "Jesus, now I wish I hadn't agreed to understudy. There's a lot to memorize."

"Yeah, well, you're lucky you didn't play Stage Manager, then,"

I said. "I have half the lines in the play." *Don't worry about it*, Mr. Knippel had said to me. *If worse comes to worst, you can just read parts of it from the script. It's not a realistic play anyway.*

Jody threw the script aside. "Poor baby," he said.

"So why did you ask me over?" I assumed the New England tones of the Stage Manager. "Aya, what in tarnation was so all-fired important, eh?"

"I heard from Reed," Jody said. Reed College was Jody's number 1 choice. It was prestigious and experimental. It was also in Oregon, a continent away. I, on the other hand, would be living at home and going to State, which was pretty much all my family could afford.

"What did they say?"

"Accepted!" He gave a little yelp.

"Jody, that's great." And that's when it sunk in: After September, he would be thousands of miles away. I might see him again after that, but it wouldn't be the same. There was a long moment of silence. I was wishing Ellyn Miles was singing in the background, anything.

"Tom?" Jody said at last. I'd never seen look so cute. Why did he have to be so goddamn cute?

"Yeah?"

"I know."

"What?"

"Shh," Jody said. And then he leaned over and put his mouth on mine.

I'd never kissed a boy before. Hell, I'd only kissed a few girls, and that from a sense of duty. And now my tongue was hitting his braces, finding his tongue in turn. He grabbed my arms and drew me close. My dick had immediately gotten so hard it almost hurt.

"I'll miss you," Jody said, when the kiss finally ended. "I'll miss you too."

I was, well, "dumbfounded," I guess is the word the Stage Manager would use. "Now what?" I asked, feeling both hot and stupid.

Jody smiled, revealing the shiny metal my tongue had just

tangled with. "Well, my mom won't be back from yoga class for hours."

"What's going on?" my father asked over dinner a week later. "You seem different."

"It's nothing, Dad. Not really. Just nervous about the play, I guess."

My little sister looked up from her tuna casserole. "Tommy's got a girlfriend," she singsonged.

"Shut up, Beth. I do not." Which was, strictly speaking, the truth.

"Now, now," my mother said. "Go easy on him. He's just got a lot to deal with, finishing up high school and whatnot. Right, Tom?"

"Yeah," I said, grateful. Sometimes, though, I wondered just what my mom was thinking. Like whether she knew more than she was letting on.

My mother, as she often did when things were getting tense, changed the subject. "Anybody ready for pudding-in-a-cloud?"

The opening night of *Our Town* didn't go quite as expected. I'd managed by that time to memorize all my lines, and though I always got lost in the middle of the long metaphysical speech at the start of act 3, that night I managed to muddle through. And it was a little strange having to say, "Almost everybody in the world gets married—you know what I mean? In our town there aren't hardly any exceptions." At the end of that speech, Mr. Webb—Jody—was due to make his entrance, and I couldn't help thinking about what we'd done over the last few weeks and how that meant that I would probably be one of the "exceptions."

But the *really* weird stuff happened because of Knippel's "updating." He hadn't really changed the lines, though instead of the choir singing "Blessed Be the Tie That Binds," he substituted "Bridge Over Troubled Water." That kind of thing. The real problems started with the audiovisual stuff. Some of it I didn't even know about beforehand. It started in the first act. When Mrs. Webb and Mrs. Gibbs were talking about Gibbs being a Civil War buff, I heard some gasps from the audience and maybe a boo. I turned to see what the matter was. On the big screen in back, where the plan was to project some Matthew Brady photographs of Union soldiers, there was an image from Vietnam instead, that photo of the napalmed girl running down the road, screaming. That changed to the famous picture of the South Vietnamese soldier shooting the guy in the head, and this time there was an audible "boo." I managed to recover, though, and when my next line came, I introduced Professor Willard—who was being played by fat Marty Dillaplane, since Jody had been moved up to playing Mr. Webb—and he proceeded with his intentionally dull lecture on the geology and anthropology of Grover's Corners.

Things calmed down then, until I started talking about what was going in the cornerstone of the new bank. I was supposed to look at the upstage screen as I spoke, and there, interspersed with pictures of the Bible and the Constitution, were shots of an anti-war poster and Mao's Little Red Book. This time there was hissing.

"How could you *do* that to us?" asked Janet Wallace, livid beneath her painted Mrs. Gibbs wrinkles.

Mr. Knippel seemed genuinely puzzled. "I told you I was going to update the play, didn't I?"

"But this Communist stuff? My parents are going to be *furious.*" Janet seemed on the brink of tears.

I caught Jody's eye. He must have been aware of the changes in the slide projection. I figured he might feel at least a little guilty, but there was a twinkle in his eye.

"OK, everyone," Knippel called out. "Relax for the rest of intermission. Second act's in 10 minutes."

I walked over to Jody. "I hope you're proud of yourself, young man," I said, trying to remain in my Stage Manager character.

"Yeah, I am, actually." He was so funny-cute all dressed up in an antique suit. He looked around backstage. "Come with me and I'll explain things."

I followed him to a dark corner behind a hanging drape.

"Yeah? Explanation?"

And Jody just leaned over and kissed me on the lips.

"Hey! Don't muss my makeup!"

He stroked my face, greasepaint and all, and kissed me again.

With only five more minutes till I was due back onstage, I gave him a pat on the ass and walked away to compose myself. It just wouldn't do for the Stage Manager of *Our Town* to appear onstage with a roaring hard-on.

The start of act 2 went fairly smoothly, though Janet flubbed her lines a couple of times, making Mrs. Gibbs seem more than a bit distracted. But then came the wedding. Up on the screen, among the photos of happy brides and grooms, came a slide of two men kissing—just like Jody and I kissed—and there were scattered giggles, boos, and a shouted "Fags!" And then after Emily and George kissed, when there was supposed to be the Wedding March, the Rolling Stones came over the sound system, singing "Let's Spend the Night Together." I couldn't help myself; I started to laugh. Luckily, it was very near the end of the act.

That was Friday night. There were just two more performances scheduled, but by Sunday night there had been an angry letter published in the town newspaper, and several members of the American Legion were picketing outside the school, demanding Knippel's resignation.

I'd kind of figured that the controversial slides would have been gone by the second performance. No such luck, but Knippel did make a speech before the curtain went up—well, this being *Our Town*, there *wasn't* a curtain, but you know what I mean. He kind of apologized to the audience and the cast, in case anyone was made really uncomfortable. But then he started in on free speech, and how art meant that drama had to reflect the times, and by the end of it, I doubt anyone concerned was really satisfied, one way or the other.

After the performance, some of the cast members suggested we talk it over without Mr. Knippel there. He agreed, and we all sat around backstage and decided whether we'd ask him to revise the production for the final performance. Janet demanded that the "offending material" be removed, and other students agreed. Stan Keeler, who'd been a precinct walker for Youth for Nixon, even demanded that the school board investigate.

But then Jody spoke up.

"I know that some of you disagree with what Mr. Knippel did. You may even think that it reflects badly on you, personally. But this is *art*, folks. Actors don't necessarily agree with what their director wants, or what a playwright says. But they do their jobs. And at this point, the damage is done. By giving in to the pro-testers, Knippel would be admitting they were right. And after all, there is a war going on, and Mao Tse-tung is an important part of our time. We don't live in Grover's Corners, folks, and we never did. So let's just go up there tomorrow night, ignore the boos, give the best performances we can, and get the hell on with our lives."

I'd never heard him quite so impassioned before. And though I didn't necessarily agree with what he'd said—I thought he and Knippel springing that stuff on the rest of us was pretty unfair—I had to admire his guts. Apparently most of the rest of the cast did too. Despite some grumbling from Janet and Martin, the meeting broke up pretty quickly. The Rolling Stones would sing on Sunday night.

The next day, Mr. Knippel asked me to stay after class.

"Tom," he said, "since you had so much of the play on your shoulders, I wanted to tell you in particular that I hoped I didn't cause any problems for you." Tall and angular, he looked down at me with the droopy expression of an oversincere basset hound.

"Well, my dad's a right-wing Republican, so things were a little edgy around our house on Saturday morning. But he got over it."

"And you? How did you feel about it?" Knippel seemed like he really cared, wanted to know.

"I kept wondering why you did it. Were you just trying to make trouble?"

"Tom, I didn't start out with that intention. I just wanted to do a production of *Our Town* because, well, that's what high schools do, isn't it? Stage *Our Town*?"

"I guess, but…"

"It's just when rehearsals started that I really began to hate the play, its smugness, its shallow celebration of unexamined, conformist lives. You understand?"

"I guess."

"Yes, I think you do." He gave me a piercing look. Did he know about me and Jody? Or at least suspect? "Tom, I..."

I looked away. The afternoon sun was streaming through the blinds. Millions of dust motes hovered over the worn leather briefcase and stacks of books on Knippel's desk. I could see every one. "Mr. Knippel, I have to get going to the next class."

The intense moment passed. As I headed through the hallways, I saw that Ronnie Fell was back in school. As I passed him by, I heard some guy mutter "fag." I figured it was aimed at Ronnie, maybe. But it should have been aimed at me.

That night, Jody borrowed his mother's Dodge, and he took me for a drive.

"So how does it feel to be part of the most controversial production since the premiere of *The Rite of Spring*?" Jody grinned, his braces gleaming in the oncoming headlights.

"How could you do that to us, you and Knippel?"

"You're not serious, are you?" Jody laid his hand on my knee. We were heading out of town, past McDonald's and Dairy Queen and J.C. Penney, over the river and, as they say, into the woods.

"Well..."

His hand crept upward on my leg.

"Face it, we *don't* live in some goddamn perfect little Grover's Corners, and we never did. Especially not you and I." He switched on the tape player. Bob Dylan.

"Jody?"

"Yeah?"

"You really *don't* feel bad, do you? About us?"

"No. Why should I?" He seemed genuinely untroubled, like the thought that what we were doing might be wrong had never entered his mind.

"I don't know, sometimes I just..."

"I love you, Mr. Stage Manager with the big dick."

"I'm going to miss you so damn much." There was so much else I wanted to say to him, too, but that's what I came up with.

"Then let's go away somewhere this summer, just you and

me." He stopped the car at the end of a dirt road. We got out and walked a little way from the car, hand in hand.

"My, isn't the moonlight *terrible?*" Jody said. It was a line of Emily's, one that, thanks to Sarah Fosbergh's overwrought line reading, had sent me and Jody into gales of laughter at more than one rehearsal. Even during the Sunday night performance, I'd had to stifle a giggle.

"Terrible," I agreed. "Terrible moonlight."

Jody stopped, turned toward me, and threw his arms around my waist. At that moment, the beautiful eternity that Wilder prattled on about during act 3 seemed very close at hand.

"And just wait till I get these damn braces off," Jody said. "I'll be able to give much better head." And he dropped to his knees there in the woods, there beneath the terrible moonlight.

And, aya, that's how life in the town went, the town that wasn't really our town, Jody's and mine. If I'd really been the Stage Manager, exempt from the rules of time, that night I could have looked into the future. I would have known that Mr. Knippel would survive the controversy and then, just a few months later, in his early 40s, get married for the first time. I would have seen Jody going off to Reed, promising to come back, swearing he'd love me forever, then going off and settling down on the West Coast, where I wouldn't see him for years to come. There would be the months I felt his absence, sure that my heart would break. And then my getting over it, moving on, though still remembering the great times we'd had that summer after graduation. And that moment when Jody Blumenkrantz came back to visit his hometown, found me still living there, and—in a moment of cheap-drama wish fulfillment I doubt even Thornton Wilder at his most sentimental could have stomached—realized that, yes, he still was in love with me, a moment that led to my moving west with him, leaving Their Town far behind.

I would even have been able to look ahead just a few days of that long-ago spring, to that moment over dinner when my dad insisted that I'd have to work all summer in order to pay for college, despite my willingness to take out a student loan, and I realized that if I did, I would never be able to go off with Jody and go camping or swimming or just have sex in cheap motels. That moment when I said, as soon as Beth had left the table, "Mom, Dad, I've got something to tell you..."

Contributors

R.D. Cochrane lived in Tuscaloosa, Alabama, before moving to Texas to work as a technical writer and editor. Cochrane developed a system of healing energy-work based on more than a decade of experience with AIDS caregiving and corporate stress management, and would like to thank Timothy and Tom for their energy and inspiration.

After 20 years of working with numbers, **Jordan M. Coffey** rediscovered the joy of working with words. Since taking the plunge into professional publishing, Jordan has had several stories accepted by anthologies and is damn excited to still be above water.

Curtis Comer grew up in the Midwest and moved to San Francisco in 1987. His stories have been included in the Alyson anthologies *Starf*cker, Best Gay Love Stories 2005,* and *Ultimate Gay Erotica 2005.* In 2003 he relocated to St. Louis, where he writes and lives with his partner, Tim.

Lou Dellaguzzo's stories have appeared in *Best Gay Love Stories 2005, Lodestar Quarterly, Harrington Gay Men's Fiction Quarterly,*

Velvet Mafia, Blithe House Quarterly, and the anthology *Bi Guys: Firsthand Fiction for Bisexual Men.* Lou has a short story collection called "All of a Suddenly." He is at work on a novel.

Vincent Diamond is a Tampa, Florida–area writer whose first novel is with an agent and being marketed to publishers. Work on its sequel is underway in addition to more short stories. Diamond's work has also appeared in *Best Gay Love Stories 2005* (Alyson), *Chance Encounters* (Torquere Press), and *Men of Mystery: Tales of Erotica and Suspense* (forthcoming from Haworth Press). Time away from the keyboard is spent riding horses, gardening, and pondering the inestimable beauty of tigers.

Eumenides is a librarian who lives on the East Coast of the United States, where she enjoys writing, historical reenactment, and spending far too much time online. More information and excerpts from her published and unpublished works of erotica and genre fiction can be found at www.rwday.net.

Much to everyone's amazement, **Richard S. Ferri** has three graduate degrees: two masters degrees and a doctorate. He has learned that no one needs three graduate degrees. He lives in Provincetown, Massachusetts, and drinks martinis. He was managing editor of NUMEDX from 2001 to 2005. His work has appeared in *The Boston Globe, Pox, The Advocate,* and the *Provincetown Banner,* to cite a few. His first novel, *Confessions of a Male Nurse,* will be published in the spring of 2005. You can also hear him occasionally rant commentary on National Public Radio.

David R. Gillespie, a former Presbyterian minister, is the editor of *Out in Asheville,* a monthly newspaper serving the LGBT community of western North Carolina, upstate South Carolina, and northeast Georgia. His work has also appeared in *My First Time vol. 3, ByLine,* and *Open Hands.*

Michael Graves is 26 years old. He lives in Massachusetts with his partner, Scott. Michael's fiction has appeared in several literary journals, including *Lodestar Quarterly, Velvet Mafia,* and *Cherry Bleeds.* His work is also featured in the print anthology *Eclectica Magazine: Best Fiction* (volume one) as well as the forthcoming collection, *Boysex.* Additionally, his book reviews can be found in *Lambda Book Report.* He is an MFA candidate at Lesley University. Contact him at MBoyBlunder@aol.com.

Matti Jackson lives and writes fiction in Tasmania, the bushy triangle at the bottom of Australia. His short stories have been published on many Internet sites and in the print anthologies *Hot Summer Sizzlers* and *Best S/M Erotica 2.* He can visited at http://www.mattijackson.com.

Timothy J. Lambert coauthored *Three Fortunes in One Cookie* and *The Deal* with Becky Cochrane and is one fourth of the Timothy James Beck writing team. His short story "The End of the Show" was in *Best Gay Love Stories 2005.* Timothy currently lives and dances in Houston. www.timothyjlambert.com

Gerald Libonati is an award-winning journalist who writes for the *South Florida Sun-Sentinel.* He has also written for *The Miami Herald* and *The Advocate.* His novels include *The Adjuster, The Artist's Life, Blue Nights in Atlantis,* and the historical novel *Season of Thunder.*

Originally from Peachtree City, Georgia, **Paul G. McCurdy** now lives with his boyfriend in San Francisco. His poetry has appeared in *Lynx Eye* and in various online magazines. This is his first published short story.

Tom Mendicino is making his second appearance in *Best Gay Love Stories* with this story from his collection *More Fun in the New World.* Again, he thanks Casey Fuetsch for her wisdom and insight.

Sean Meriwether's work has been published in *Lodestar Quarterly, Skin & Ink,* and the second installment of *Best of Best Gay*

Erotica. He is also the editor of *Outsider Ink* (OutsiderInk.com) and *Velvet Mafia: Dangerous Queer Fiction* (VelvetMafia.com). Sean lives in New York with his partner, photographer Jack Slomovits. Stalk him online at SeanMeriwether.com.

Scott D. Pomfret is coauthor of *Hot Sauce,* the first-ever same-sex marriage novel (Warner Books 2005). *Hot Sauce* is one of the Romentics brand romance novels for gay men (www.romentics.com). Pomfret also writes short stories that have been published in *Post Road, Genre* magazine, *Fresh Men: New Gay Voices, Best Gay Love Stories 2005, Best Gay Erotica 2005,* and many other magazines and anthologies. For more information visit www.scottpomfret.com.

Rick R. Reed's fiction embraces the demimonde of Chicago, where serial killers, pedophiles, and those who've bargained with the devil seek life's simple pleasures, including torture, pain, sexual degradation, addiction, and murder. His published novels include *A Face Without a Heart,* nominated as best novel of 2000 by the Spectrum Awards. His books *Penance* and *Obsessed,* published by Dell, together sold more than 80,000 copies. His short fiction has appeared in more than a dozen anthologies.

J.D. Roman's work has appeared in *Best Gay Love Stories 2005, Friction 7: Best Gay Erotic Fiction, Velvet Mafia,* and *Wet Nightmares, Wet Dreams.* Contact J. D. at ginproductions@hotmail.com.

Rob Rosen lives his own Best Gay Love Story every day with his wonderful husband, Ken. Rob is the author of the critically acclaimed novel *Sparkle: The Queerest Book You'll Ever Love,* and his short stories have appeared in numerous anthologies, magazines, and literary sites. Visit him at www.therobrosen.com.

Simon Sheppard is the author of *Sex Parties 101, In Deep: Erotic Stories,* and *Kinkorama: Dispatches From the Front Lines of Perversion.* His work has appeared in over 125 anthologies, including many editions of *The Best American Erotica* and *Best Gay Erotica,* and he writes the columns Sex Talk and Perv. He's at work on a historically based anthology of gay porn—those with vintage smut are encouraged to get in touch. He's at www.simonsheppard.com.

Matthew Sterenchock writes plays and fiction. He graduated in 2000 from Bennington College and is program associate at the Alpert Award in the Arts. He lives in Los Angeles, where he likes to play around with his camera, cross things off lists, discuss big ideas, sing in his car, and smoke cigarettes after 5 P.M.

R.G. Thomas has several unpublished manuscripts in his desk drawers and cluttering up his mind. He lives in a suburb of Detroit with his partner of many years and their orange tabby cat who believes he is a dog. To feed and clothe himself, he organizes software testing.

Nicholas Tomasetti is a 26-year-old man who doesn't look a day over 21 and currently lives in New York City. He is mildly sarcastic, largely irreverent, and remains begrudgingly hopeful that love exists. "One Night" is taken from his first novel, *Still I Falter,* not yet in publication.

Raymond Yeo resides in Penn Hills, Pennsylvania, with his partner of 17 years and their 3-year-old son. He is currently a scholar at the University of Pittsburgh, where he studies creative nonfiction, art, and religion. He hopes "Real Magick" is the beginning of a long, abundant career in writing.